M. J. McGRATH

The Bone Seeker

MANTLE

First published 2014 by Mantle
an imprint of Pan Macmillan, a division of Macmillan Publishers Limited
Pan Macmillan, 20 New Wharf Road, London N1 9RR
Basingstoke and Oxford
Associated companies throughout the world
www.panmacmillan.com

ISBN 978-0-230-76903-8

1 3 5 7 9 8 6 4 2

A CIP catalogue record for this book is available from the British Library.

Map artwork by ML Design
Typeset by Palimpsest Book Production Ltd, Falkirk, Stirlingshire
Printed and bound by CPI Group (UK) Ltd, Croydon, CR0 4YY

Visit www.panmacmillan.com to read more about all our books
and to buy them. You will also find features, author interviews and
news of any author events, and you can sign up for e-newsletters
so that you're always first to hear about our new releases.

For Ian Jackman

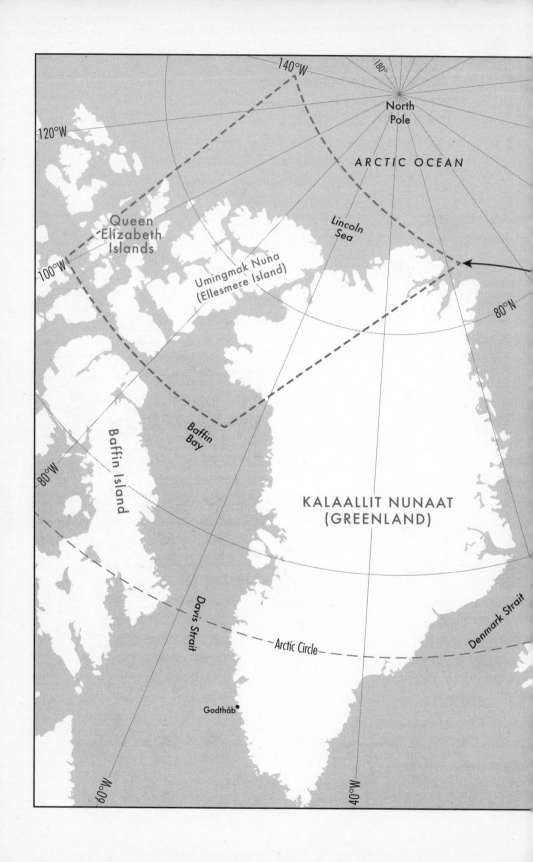

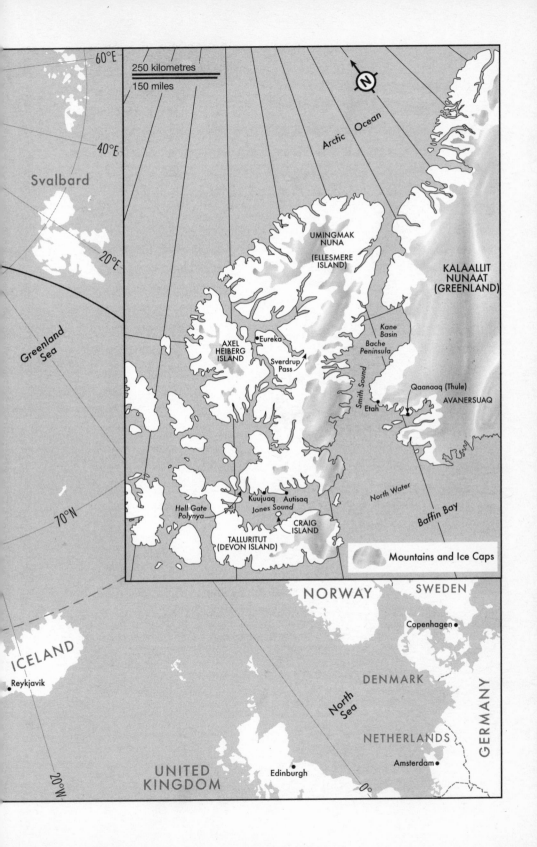

1

That Friday afternoon in late July was the last time Edie Kiglatuk saw Martha Salliaq alive. As the school bell signalled the end of a long, sultry day and students tumbled out into the corridor, eager to get to their summer fishing camps, Martha spilled the contents of her purse on the floor. Pens, crayons, an eyeliner pencil and a stick of lipstick went skittering across the hot linoleum. As a rule, Inuit girls didn't wear make-up. Her curiosity aroused, Edie went over.

'Going somewhere special?' she asked, holding up the lipstick.

Martha took the stick and dropped it back inside her bag. She flashed her teacher an embarrassed smile.

'Just curious.' Edie palmed her hands in surrender.

'No offence, Ms Kiglatuk.'

Edie laughed. 'None taken.' All the same, in a small, remote corner of her heart Edie was a little stung. She'd been teaching Martha three weeks and in that time she'd grown fond enough of the girl to have to hide her favouritism. The old teacher's pet syndrome.

They finished picking things up. Martha zipped her purse into her backpack and slung it over her shoulder.

'Well,' said Martha, 'thanks for helping.'

Edie watched the back of Martha's head as she made her way to the door, and for the first time since she'd moved from Autisaq a month ago, she was struck by a sudden burst of longing for female company.

The girl wore dark braids in traditional Inuit style, tied together at the back. A week or so ago she'd added a subtle blue tint to the colour. Unusual.

'Hey, I like what you've done with your hair,' she shouted after her student.

Martha turned, touched her head and smiled, pleased. 'My parents hate it.'

As the two women stood facing one another, some connection passed between them. Edie found herself thinking she wished they knew one another better. Then the girl looked away and the moment was gone.

'*Saimu*, Ms Kiglatuk.' Bye. It was the last thing Edie Kiglatuk would ever hear Martha Salliaq say.

That evening Edie spent reorganizing her tent. Her police friend Derek Palliser had recommended her for the summer job at the school then found her a cabin to rent on the outskirts of the settlement. They'd both agreed that, after the last summer, she'd be better off spending July and August away from her hometown of Autisaq, 70 kilometres to the east. Here in Kuujuaq it would be easier to escape daily reminders of the death of her beloved stepson, Joe. She'd arrived in the settlement fully anticipating hunkering down in the little rental cabin but it turned out that Kuujuaq was more sheltered than Autisaq and the ambient temperature occasionally topped 10C, turning the interior into a furnace and driving her back outside under canvas. Her tent was now pinned in the front yard of the police detachment where Derek had obligingly given her use of the bathroom.

An hour or two into her reorganization, and for no good reason she could discern, the conversation with Martha came back to her. *Going somewhere special?* What a dumb question to ask a teenager! She laughed and shook her head and thought, a little wistfully, that her own evening was turning out to be nothing special at all. The last couple of weeks she'd taken to spending a good deal of her off-time with Chip Muloon. Probably too much. Chip was the first white guy she'd ever been with and since they both agreed there was no future in it, she had to wonder if she wasn't playing out some kind of father thing, her own daddy being a *qalunaat* like Chip, who'd abandoned her and her mother when she was six. Sometimes even casual relationships were so hard to decipher you had to take time out or risk going crazy. Picking up her hair oil, she climbed the wooden steps to the detachment and looked forward to a long, cold shower and an early night alone.

The following day she got up early, packed some dried fish, her Remy 303 and her fishing rod and lure and drove her ATV out past the military camp onto the harsh, rocky landscape of the polar desert. The joint demands of work and Chip had left too little time for exploring the terrain and she was feeling the familiar pull of open ground. A swollen, rushing river meandered through the rubbled plain that opened into a broad bay. The land was dotted with sedge meadow and hummock tundra and was unlike her home terrain in subtle ways that only someone who had made their living on the land on Ellesmere Island would notice. The tundra here was, if anything, more beautiful than at Autisaq, a jewel box of saxifrage and Arctic poppies set off against soft limestone gravel, fields of black basalt splashed with map and blood-spot lichen, and for hours she meandered happily along thin trails, stopping every so often to collect goose eggs or fish for char by the river, navigating only by the man-shaped cairns, or *inuksuit*, silhouetted against the summer sky, whose granite arms pointed the way back to the settlement.

On her return in late afternoon there was a note waiting for her in the tent. She put down the fish she'd caught, wiped her hands on her summer parka and picked it up. A Ranger friend of her ex-stepson had swung by to say that he was hoping to come into town that evening and would drop in on her. Willa Inukpuk was stationed at a rappel training camp a few kilometres from Camp Nanook, the summer military encampment established by Canadian Joint Forces North as part of their regular SOVPAT sovereignty patrol exercises.

Her heart quickened at the thought of Willa's visit. She and the kid had history together. Mostly bad. Mostly her fault. She'd always loved his brother Joe a little too much and Willa never quite enough. Her drinking, his drug habit and the break-up with Willa's father, Sammy Inukpuk, hadn't helped. It was only after she'd lost Joe that she realized how much she missed his brother. In the year since Joe's death, Willa had stopped drinking and smoking weed and got himself together. Joining the Rangers was one of the few good decisions he'd made in adult life. Another, even more recent, had been to set aside his resentments and try to rebuild a relationship with his ex-stepmother. Until now she had always been the one seeking forgiveness and Willa had always rebuffed her. Now it seemed that things between them might finally be thawing.

Setting aside the plumpest Arctic char and a handful of goose eggs for their supper, she gutted the remainder of the fish – pegging them on the line to dry in the sun – laid the fire with heather and peat to light on Willa's arrival, then went to the store and bought a packet of his favourite choc chip cookies for ten dollars, and returned to the tent to tidy up. The note hadn't given a specific time. Inuit never planned things that way. She was happy to bide her time. While she waited she reminded herself of the good times she'd shared with the boy before her drinking took hold and he stopped wanting to be around her. Like the first time they watched Laurel and Hardy together and he asked if everything in the south was black and white. Or the summer he and Joe had caught their first harp seal and Willa stuffed his pillow with the blubber and said it was because it was soft even though they both knew it was because he was so proud of becoming a hunter.

Eventually, when hunger began to overtake her, she went outside and checked the sky. The sun was behind cloud now and the air had taken on the dumb stare of midnight. There were no birds about. She went back inside the tent and reread the note and saw that it said that Willa only *hoped* to come and reminded herself that Inuit never committed themselves to these things in the way *qalunaat* seemed to. Flexibility was a necessary tool for survival up here.

It was too late to eat now. Trying not to feel unreasonably disappointed, she peeled off her summer parka and her shirt and clambered between her sleeping skins. It was only as sleep was stealing over her that she remembered she'd said she would go round to Chip Muloon's house for supper and sex. It was also too late for that now. Her appetites had clocked off for the night. Within seconds of the thought, she was asleep.

*

4

Sunday came and went. Sometime in the mid-morning she went around to Chip's cabin and, finding him out, left a message to apologize for not showing. In her – admittedly limited – experience of *qalunaat* she'd sensed that they could be picky about form. Most assumed that Inuit would play by *qalunaat* rules. Very few ever thought to accommodate themselves to the Inuit way of doing things.

Outside the wind was soft and the air was nasty with mosquitoes. She spent most of the rest of the day in the tent avoiding them, catching up on marking school papers and mending the soles of her favourite sealskin kamiks.

At some point in the afternoon Derek looked in on her. He scanned her few belongings, now neatly arranged.

'My, you been remodelling in here? Next time you got a couple free hours, my apartment could use a woman's touch.'

'I'll touch it all you like, but you can get someone else to clear it up, if that's what you're getting at,' Edie said.

'We a little ornery today? Need to eat maybe?' She saw him eyeing the remaining goose eggs and realized two things: first, he had an agenda and second, dammit, he was right.

'You like 'em raw or soft-boiled? I got some fish in here somewhere too.'

His face erupted into a grin.

She shot him a salty look. 'Just as well for you I could use some company.'

Early evening, she took herself back to Chip's place and found him sitting at his kitchen table surrounded by papers. His lips were stiff when she went to kiss him.

'Don't be like that,' she said.

Chip had arrived in Kuujuaq a few weeks before and taken over an office from the school counsellor, whose job had gone in the latest round of cuts. That was how they'd met. He was working on something dry and technical to do with long-term health outcomes among High Arctic populations and seemed pretty dedicated to it. They'd never discussed his work in detail. Neither was under the illusion that they'd got together to exchange ideas. It was a sex thing mostly, and that was fine. There were unexpected but welcome differences. The hard angles of his body. Inuit men were generally superbly fit but theirs was a kind of lean, compact and wiry muscularity. By contrast, Chip was tall and bony, with large hands and venous, rocky feet. His eyes were the colour of icebergs with depths she couldn't read. She liked the hairiness of him, and the odd, milky-brown colour of the hairs, like a ptarmigan in summer plumage.

They were both outsiders in a town that didn't exactly open its arms to strangers. In September, when his contract came to an end, he'd be heading back to his office in the Health Sciences Building at the University of Calgary and she'd return to Autisaq. For now, though, they could do a fine job of keeping one another company.

'I left you a note,' she said.

'I got it.' They operated in separate universes. His, a world of clocks, written reports and predictability. Hers, well, not.

She went in for an Eskimo kiss, an exchange of breaths, and sensed him soften.

'God, I wish southern women knew how sexy those are,' he said.

'You can teach them.'

He pulled her in close. 'First, some more practice.'

Part way through the night, it was hard to tell when exactly because it never got dark at this time of year, Edie woke in the middle of a dream and from it managed to hold on to Martha's face as she turned at the door; then the picture faded and was lost, leaving behind a drift of emotion too fragmented to put a name to. For a while she lay awake, listening to the soft purr of Chip snoring beside her, then, restless suddenly, she crept out of the cabin and down the little track to her tent, where she fell into a profound and dreamless sleep.

When Martha Salliaq failed to show up for class that Monday morning, Edie was surprised, but it was only when the dream resurfaced a little later that morning that she felt a prickle of disquiet. Traditionally minded Inuit thought dreams were visits from the spirits. She wasn't one of them, least not as a rule, but the coincidence of the dream with Martha's no-show was enough to unsettle her.

At morning recess she caught up with Lisa Tuliq by the door to the classroom. Lisa was small and plump, with the pinched, repressed air of a kid who'd grown up watching her parents slowly dismantling themselves with alcohol. She and Martha sat next to one another in class and Edie had sometimes seen them leaving together. But Lisa had nothing to offer on Martha's whereabouts. She'd been out at her family's summer camp all weekend, and hadn't seen her friend.

'My uncle gave me a ride in this morning.'

'Did Martha say anything on Friday about where she might be?'

'Not to me,' Lisa said simply. She looked longingly down the corridor for a means of escape. 'Can I go now?'

Edie followed the girl out into the corridor, passed through a fire door and knocked on Chip Muloon's door. The knock was a little too hard and hurt her knuckles. She'd picked up frostbite in Alaska in the spring trying to track down a bunch of people traffickers and still tended to forget how supersensitive her fingers were. A hard rap and it was as though a wire in her body had shorted.

Chip was at his desk flipping through some paperwork. He shot her a low, withering look.

'I guess you know it's rude to sneak out in the middle of the night without so much as a "See ya", right?'

'No,' she said. In her culture it wasn't.

'Well it is,' he said, as though that settled the matter. It was one of the things she found most difficult about him, not that he lived in another world, but his refusal to meet her somewhere on the bridge between them.

'Martha Salliaq didn't show this morning. It's not like her. I was wondering if she said anything to you?' It was this she really wanted to talk about. There was no point in wasting time trying to resolve the rest. Come September it would resolve itself anyway.

'Why would you think that?'

'Because you two talked.' It was an odd question. She'd seen them chatting in the corridor a few times and once bumped into the girl coming out of his office. She had no idea what they'd talked about. She'd never asked him about it.

'Not really.' His eyes fell back on his paperwork. 'She's probably still at summer camp.'

'In this dream I had . . .'

'Oh, OK, you had a *dream*,' he said.

She forgot about Martha for a while in the afternoon. The effort of trying to teach a class of kids who didn't want to learn a bunch of stuff the government insisted they must took up all the space in her head. And if that wasn't enough the heat in the classroom made her hands worse. Whoever had designed the building hadn't understood how things worked up on Ellesmere and failed to make any allowance for the continual summer sunshine blazing through the picture windows, which barely opened. There was no air conditioning and either no one had thought to order blinds or they'd not had the money.

At 3.30, Edie thought the hell with the geography of British Columbia, set some homework and let the class out early. She was rubbing the whiteboard clean when Martha's father, Charlie Salliaq, appeared.

'Martha here?' The old man swung about, scoping out the class as if his daughter might be found among the empty desks and vacant chairs.

'No, and she hasn't been in all day,' Edie said. The faint, distant shimmer of unease which had accompanied her most of the day suddenly condensed into a dark, forbidding cloud.

Charlie leaned back and pinched his chin between his fingers. 'We were expecting her over at the camp on Saturday afternoon. I figured maybe she'd got tied up with schoolwork. I had to come into town anyway. Ran into that friend of hers at lunchtime, Lisa. She told me Martha hadn't shown up for the morning session.'

Derek had warned Edie about Charlie the moment she stepped off the plane. As one of the oldest men in town he felt entitled to respect and, for the most part, got it. Unlike most Inuit, Charlie could be as blunt as a duck's beak. Most folks respected his achievements. For more than a decade he'd lobbied the Defence Department to cede land at a Cold War era Distant Early Warning radar station back to the people of Kuujuaq. When the department had finally given in to his demands five years ago, he'd begun another campaign to force them to pay for a full decontamination and clean-up of the site, known as Glacier Ridge, a battle he'd won only last year. All that fighting had made him uncompromising and ill-tempered and most people preferred to keep him at arm's length.

'You checked the house?' Edie asked.

'Do I look senile to you?' Salliaq's brow knitted. 'I don't know what could have gotten into her,' he went on. 'She hangs out with her uncle Markoosie when we're out of town and he hasn't seen her since Saturday morning. She picked up a schoolbook she'd left at his house. Her ATV's still parked outside.'

'I'm sure she'll turn up,' Edie said, to reassure herself as much as anything. The dream came to mind again but she decided not to mention it. She realized that Martha hadn't talked much about her life out of school. 'Is there anywhere else she'd be likely to visit?'

'The bird cliffs up by Glacier Ridge, but I went by there on my way here.' Salliq's face locked into a series of frowns and lines like some glacier-scoured rock. 'I'll go over to the town hall and put out a message on the red radio.' The local CB network was always the first port of call for any urgent requests or news. 'But I don't like it,' Salliaq went on. He was leaning against the desk now, as though having to steady himself. 'Not with all those *unataqti* just outside of town.'

The thought had already occurred to Edie. For the past week, several hundred soldiers, Marines and Rangers, had stationed themselves at Camp Nanook, a temporary encampment a few kilometres from the settlement. This year the Sovereignty Patrol, or SOVPAT, forces were headquartered in Resolute, a few hundred kilometres to the south of

Kuujuaq, on Cornwallis Island. It was the first year they'd deployed on Ellesmere. Camp Nanook was their farthest flung satellite and something of an experiment.

The sudden influx of *qalunaat* into an otherwise quiet and remote Inuit settlement had, unsurprisingly, created a few problems. In the week since they'd arrived, several dozen *unataqti* had made their way into town in the evenings, looking to drink and gamble and meet young women. There had been a few insignificant cases of harassment, a couple of minor brawls. Many local families had decided to take no chances and moved off to their summer camps on the coast earlier than usual. Others were happily profiting from the new arrivals, setting up impromptu bars to cater to their desire to drink and even, rumour had it, establishing a brothel, though none of the locals seemed to know where it was or who was working there.

'Listen, *avasirngulik*,' Edie said – she was careful to use the respectful 'elder' with him – 'you want help looking for your daughter, I'll come along. I've hunted this way a few times, though I don't know the land around here real well. Either way, I think it's best if we go see Sergeant Palliser at the police detachment. Maybe he'll organize a search plane.'

Sergeant Derek Palliser was the more senior of the two members of the Ellesmere Island Native Police, who between them were responsible for policing five hamlets and a couple of weather stations scattered across a frigid desert of mountains, fjords and rocky scree the size of Wyoming. Right now, Derek's deputy, Constable Stevie Killik, was on a computer course in the south, so Palliser was on his own, but he knew the land, he knew the people and, more to the point, he was Edie's friend. They'd solved a couple of tough cases and she trusted him to know what to do.

'The Lemming Police got nothing to say that I want to hear,' Salliaq said. The local people found Derek's scientific interest in lemming population dynamics quirky at best. Salliaq had nothing but contempt for it. For Palliser himself too. Edie wondered if it was because Derek was half Inuit and half Cree. Charlie made no secret of the fact that he didn't trust Indians or *qalunaat*. There were exceptions, of whom

Edie was one. He'd heard about her going after her stepson Joe's killer and seemed impressed.

'They tell me you're half *qalunaat*, but you don't play by *qalunaat* rules,' he'd said when he'd first met her.

'Only set of rules I know is mine,' she'd said. 'And I don't have any.' That tickled him.

Now, though, his mood was more sombre.

Edie picked up her bag and made a move towards the door.

'Well, I don't suppose you have any objections to my talking to him?' She'd already decided she was going to do just that whether the old bigot liked it or not.

'You can try. Won't do anyone no good, though.' Salliaq shrugged. For a moment their eyes locked.

'You do what you like,' the old man grumbled, finally. 'What I heard, that's what you always do.'

'I'll take that as permission granted,' Edie said. As she followed him out into the corridor, Martha's face reappeared as it had in her dream and a rush of foreboding rolled towards her like a low, dark wave.

2

Derek Palliser lit his seventh cigarette of the day, put down his empty coffee mug and returned to plugging the hole in the window frame of his lemming shed. He was making slow progress, though, on account of the stiffness in his fingers, which had continued to plague him long after his hands had healed from the frostbite he'd suffered last spring. He'd planned to spend the morning working out a route for the summer patrol, but the weekend rain had swollen the window frame and busted out the glass. Once Constable Stevie Killik returned from his combined computer course and summer leave, Derek intended to start a programme of exterior renovations in preparation for the winter, but the window on the lemming shed was one chore that wouldn't wait. If there was one thing the rodents couldn't stand it was draughts.

The cigarettes and coffee were keeping him just the right side of alert. Truth was, he could have done with a few more hours in bed and would have taken them if he'd thought that there was a chance in hell he'd sleep. He had to remind himself that he'd felt this exhausted every summer since he'd first arrived on Ellesmere nearly thirteen years ago. The constant light – and absence of anything approaching a normal 'night' – from March through to September always left him wired and ornery. White noise cascaded through his brain, as if a permanent avalanche had set up inside his head. He knew from bitter experience there was nothing for it except to keep himself pepped on nicotine and coffee, but this year, somehow, everything seemed even more of an effort than usual.

Hearing something behind him, he turned to see Edie Kiglatuk, waving and trying to get his attention. He stubbed out his cigarette and went over. Her face was strained.

'Trouble?' he said, swatting away an eddy of mosquitoes. He'd allowed himself to get bitten while he was working. Thin, braided rivers of sweat and blood made their way down his forearms.

'Maybe,' she said. 'I'll tell you inside.'

If Derek had been honest with himself, he'd have seen a long time ago that the interior of the detachment was no better than the outside. The old wooden floor was warped and the boards needed replacing and the blinds at the windows were cracked from sun and frost. He'd lived quite happily in a state of bachelor-style semi-squalor until Edie had arrived. Now he was a little embarrassed by it. Something about her presence made him want to fix the place up, make it look nice. He scouted around for a spare chair.

'Now, that trouble . . .'

The instant she mentioned the Salliaq family, his spirits sank. Years back, when they'd been having a really bad problem with loose dogs, he'd impounded several huskies belonging to Charlie Salliaq and made the old man pay a fine to retrieve them. Ever since, Salliaq had taken gleeful pleasure in bad-mouthing him. In Derek's mind the animosity between them had nothing to do with stray dogs and everything to do with the fact that Derek was half Cree. Inuit and Cree had never been the best of friends. The word Eskimo derived from the Cree for 'head louse'. Just one reason why Eskimo in the eastern Arctic preferred to go by the name Inuit. These days, though, most folk had got over the old hostility and learned to rub along, conscious that both their futures depended on presenting a united front. But Charlie Salliaq was old school; he held on to grudges the way others held on to their hats in a blizzard.

As Edie's story unfolded, he felt a growing sense of relief. Everyone went a little crazy in the summer and it sounded very much as though Martha had just gone AWOL for a while. Ten to one she was visiting friends in some distant summer camp and, either through thoughtlessness or teenage defiance, hadn't told her parents she was going. Maybe she'd picked herself a boyfriend from among the soldiers. The military camp had only been up and running a week but already there were plenty of lean young *unataqti* hanging around town in the hope of meeting local girls. And succeeding. He'd seen them, half cut, clinging on to their conquests like they were life-vests. Broke his heart a little, tell the truth.

'Who saw her last?' he said.

'So far as we know, her uncle, on Saturday morning. She went round there to pick up a schoolbook. Charlie said he's gonna put out a message on the red radio, hope someone will call in to say they've seen her.'

'They won't if she's with a soldier.' No one was going to volunteer to be the person who broke *that* news to old Charlie Salliaq. 'But, look, even if she's on her own somewhere she won't have gone far.' It would have been different in winter. But the polar bears had left for the north with the ice and the wolves were too busy feasting on lemmings to bother humans and he thought it was unlikely she'd come to any harm. In this weather she wouldn't freeze.

'I wouldn't be too worried,' he said. 'Even if she's twisted an ankle or something, there'll be someone passing who'll pick her up. The place is swarming with soldiers out on exercise.'

'It's the soldiers Charlie's worried about.'

Derek took out a cigarette, lit it and hungrily sucked in the smoke.

'I wouldn't be surprised if Charlie Salliaq isn't using this as an excuse to make trouble. He's made his views on the military clear. Doesn't like them and doesn't want them up here. The old man wields a lot of power round these parts. He's managed to keep control of the Council of Elders for years and he likes to remind everyone of the fact. People don't necessarily like him but they don't feel they can oppose him. There's not many old folk around here with the authority.'

'I noticed that. Assumed they were all at summer camp.'

Derek stubbed out his cigarette. 'Some of 'em are, but a lot of Charlie's generation died young. Problems with game numbers back in the seventies and eighties I believe.' The name of the place meant

Big River, but for years even the fish had stayed away, he said. No one knew the reason and there didn't have to be one. The Arctic was unpredictable that way.

Edie sat back and thought about what Derek had said and decided it didn't add up. So what if Charlie Salliaq was troublemaking. Nothing she knew about Martha suggested that she was the kind of girl who went off on flights of fancy. One thing she sensed above everything else was that Martha was hungry for an education. She wanted to have options in life.

'I guess it just doesn't make sense to me that she would skip class unless something serious had happened,' she said.

Derek smiled. 'The girl's eighteen. What you think is serious and what she thinks is, are probably two totally different things right now.'

Edie frowned. 'I had this weird dream about her on Saturday night.' The stirred feelings from the dream hadn't gone away.

Derek pulled his chin towards his neck and gave her a long-suffering look. 'Oh, you should have said.' He went on, his voice laced with the banal sarcasm of the sceptic.

Edie stopped listening. She'd heard it all before, most recently from Chip. Instead, she gazed out of the window to the muddy road and further, to the rotting snow banks piled up against the fishing shacks, and thought about the girl.

Derek was pulling on his jacket now.

'I need to get back to that shed. Martha'll be fine, you'll see. Let's wait this one out a bit.'

'You're probably right,' she murmured.

He smiled to himself. 'It has been known.'

She made for the pile of sleeping skins at the back of her tent. For a while she lay down and stared at the soft light filtering through the canvas. She was beginning to realize that neither her head nor her heart had yet fully recovered from the ordeal of the spring, when she'd first stumbled on the dead child in Alaska. She was conscious of feeling raw and oversensitive, like some nocturnal creature suddenly brought out into the midday sun. The midnight sun too, come to that. Sometimes it felt exhilarating to be around so much light, other times only painfully exposing. Maybe Derek was right about Martha. Maybe a dream was just a dream. She pictured the girl's face, the black hair tinted raven-blue, the eyes wide with life, and she thought of herself at the same age, heard her voice saying, *Going somewhere special?* The words repeating themselves over and over in her mind.

No, she thought, she wasn't prepared to let this one slide. She got up, walked back out into the white, crystalline light towards the lemming shed and called Derek's name. His head appeared from around the roof of the shed.

'Remember last spring?'

He turned, squinting at her. 'I've been trying to forget.' They'd been dumped out on the sea ice and left to die and Derek would have done just that if Edie hadn't built a shelter and kept him alive until help came. He owed her one.

'Look,' he sighed. 'I know why you've come.' He stepped down from the ladder and rested his hands on his hips. The sun shining on his face lent him a ghostly air. 'You had some dream and now you want me to send out an SAR. Do have any idea how expensive a search and rescue is? Or how hard it is to bring this detachment in on budget?'

He wiped his hands on a rag and picked up a can of wood preserver. 'This can, that ladder, the brush I'm about to use. All that comes straight out of my own pocket.'

It was a lot to ask, she knew. Budgets, reports, justifying spending decisions to HQ, but none of that meant anything when someone's child was missing.

'I just want to find her.'

He pressed his lips together. She could see he was softening. 'Look, it's not that I don't trust your instincts or respect your concern. It's your motivation I worry about,' Derek went on. She could see impatience in his eyes. 'You can't turn back time. You can't mend people, Edie.'

He'd seen what she was only just beginning to realize was there.

This wasn't only about Martha. It was about her stepson, Joe. About the knots she'd tied herself in wondering if Joe would still be alive today if she'd acted more decisively after he had gone missing. About living with the guilt, the endless nagging doubt. She didn't want anyone else to have to go through that. Not ever.

'What if we don't look and it turns out that something bad has happened to her?' she said. She tried to put herself inside his head. 'What about your credibility in the community?'

'Ha!' His laugh was as bitter as old coffee. 'I represent *qalunaat* law, remember? In the eyes of the Kuujuamiut I have no credibility. I'm irredeemable. A scumbag.' He met her gaze for a moment then rolled his eyes. 'OK, OK. If the girl doesn't show up in the next hour we'll fly.' He held up a hand. 'But you're not coming. I don't want the compliance folk on my back.'

She stood her ground. He pulled off his work gloves

'Holy walrus, Edie.' He was half exasperated, half amused. 'All right, you can come in the plane, but not in any official capacity. Now, if you wanna make yourself useful, go ask Markoosie to put a message out on this evening's radio show. He's the nearest we've got to a proper shaman in this town. The way that show works, it's kind of like the old shamanic drums and song duels. Come back here after. We'll ride to the airstrip together.' He leaned in and trained a steady eye on her. 'And listen, this makes us evens. In fact, if anything, you owe me one.'

'I'll try and remember that,' she said.

Derek spoke briefly to Pol, his pilot, to tell him to prep the plane, then courtesy-called Colonel Al Klinsman, the officer in charge at Camp Nanook, to inform him about the SAR and let him have Martha Salliaq's description just in case someone at the camp was hiding her. After that he fixed some tea in a vacuum flask so they'd have something to keep them warm when they were in the air. As he was walking back into the office, the door opened and Edie's face appeared, those black eyes of hers almost frighteningly intense.

'Everything sorted with Markoosie?'

She nodded.

'OK, then, let's go.'

Pol took the Twin Otter up over the hills just west of the settlement and turned east along the shoreline, coming inland over the bird cliffs. The plane rose over blustering clouds of thick-billed murres. Then they followed the white rush of the great Kuujuaq River, heavy with melt-water. A series of tracks criss-crossed the slump fields, cutting through the sporadic vegetation northeast to the lake on the boundary of the old Glacier Ridge Distant Early Warning radar station and on to Camp Nanook. For a while they kept to a course parallel to the shoreline overlooking Jones Sound. Near Jakeman Glacier they flew over a silvery cord of narwhal making their way west towards Hell Gate. Further ahead a group of walrus hauled out on the beach began scattering for open water, but there was no evidence of any human agency. At Derek's suggestion, Pol switched back and began to head in an arc across the Sound inland towards the bleak, bevelled table rock at Glacier Ridge and down past the abandoned buildings of the old radar station. The plane dropped altitude once again, then rose as the ridge gave out onto low, flat tundra.

Beside him, Derek noticed Edie turn her head, craning out of the rear window at something he could not see.

She was gazing down at a dip in the land that locals called Lake Turngaluk, the Lake of Bad Spirits, though it was mostly dry now, pitted here and there with bowls of pewter-coloured pools and ponds, separated by windings of briny marsh. Locals said the area was a portal to the underworld and that birds wouldn't fly over it for fear of being sucked under but Derek didn't hold with that kind of nonsense, prefer-ring to believe that the birds didn't bother to visit because what was left of the water was devoid of fish, a fact that had nothing to do with spirits or the underworld and everything to do with contamination from the radar station. So far as Derek understood it, the site should have been cleaned up years ago but it had got mired in political horse-trading until, about a decade ago, Charlie Salliaq had dismissed the old legal team and called on the services of Sonia Gutierrez, a prominent human rights lawyer specializing in aboriginal land claims. They'd finally won their case against the Department of Defence last year. One of Colonel Klinsman's jobs was to organize a working party to begin the necessary decontamination at the station and on the surrounding land, including the lake.

'How odd,' Edie said. She pointed out of the side window but all he could see were a few thin strings of cirrus.

'What?' Derek undid his belt and twisted his neck around, though it made his head swim to do it.

'A bear. They're usually on their way north to the floe edge by now.'

'You want me to swing back?' Pol asked Derek.

The policeman nodded and prepared himself for the stomach lurch. Ahead, the rows of tents and prefab units of Camp Nanook stood on the tundra in incongruous straight lines, as though on parade. The plane rose higher then banked sharply and wheeled round, retracing their route through a patch of cloud. Coming through into clear air they caught sight of the bear. Spooked by the sound of the aircraft engine, it was running for the safety of the sea.

The surface of the pool where the bear had been appeared to be bubbling and seething. Derek first supposed it was a trick of the light, but as the slipstream from the plane passed across it, the western bank seemed to expand, as though it had suddenly turned to gas. He realized that he never seen anything like this before. He turned back, leaning over Edie to get a better view.

'What the hell is that?'

She curled around and caught his gaze. There was something wild about the way she was looking at him now, the muscles in her face taut, her black eyes blazing.

'Mosquitoes.'

He began to speak but she cut him off. 'They're feeding on whatever attracted the bear.'

3

On the flight back to Kuujuaq Edie tried desperately to stop herself from imagining the worst. As they descended, a memory surfaced in the odd way they sometimes do when you least expect it, or perhaps when you need it most. This one was from when she was seven or eight, a year or two after her father had left. Every year the annual supply ship brought up two or three films in cans. People sat in the church and watched them projected onto a roll-up screen. One year they showed *The Red Balloon*. The dazzling, crimson purity of the balloon against the stark black and white of the film. How often she'd seen its equivalent. The dark winter sky, blood sitting on snow. Nature red in tooth and claw. Years later, she read that a newborn baby recognizes red before any other colour. This came as no surprise. Somewhere inside her the child was still reaching for that red balloon.

After Pol dropped them at the landing strip, they drove their ATVs to the nursing station and picked up Luc Fabienne, the nurse, and the gurney trailer and headed out along the muddy track towards Lake Turngaluk. For long stretches on either side of them the rock was bare, or loosely laced with brilliant red and yellow lichens, but as they moved further from the coast and the ground dipped, the slick rock was replaced by pucks of muskeg tufted with cotton grass and mountain sorrel and eventually they found themselves on a desert pavement which stretched all the way to the mountains. In the past week, the summer heat had alchemized the tundra, transforming the cold, dark, peaty substrate into a bright, living carpet. The high sun, shining from the south in the day, from the north during the bright night, had exposed the carcasses of half-eaten animals entombed by the ice through the long winter and brought them to the attention of foxes and ravens. All around them there were freeze-dried body parts, racks of antlers, remnants of fur and hoof. Before the summer was out, whatever remained of the flesh would be picked clean and new plants would spring up: snow buttercup, polar chickweed and moss campion, blooming around the bleached bones like grave flowers.

For all that, though, the tundra smelled sweet and freshly vegetal and from time to time the scent of Arctic heather blew up on the prevailing northwesterly breeze. It was only as they moved out of a hollow and up a slight incline that the unmistakably abrasive, sour tang of decomposition hit her and Edie felt herself slowing, a feeling of hollow dread holding her back. Derek came up alongside, pointing to his nose.

'What's up?' This from Luc.

Edie swallowed. 'Blood.' A scent as individual as the grooves in a fingerprint.

There was nothing for it but to press on. Bumping across rocky scree, they descended into a soggy hollow then up another low incline. The smell grew stronger and they found themselves on a patch of slick rock overlooking the pool where the bear had been. They keyed off their engines and sat for a moment looking out. In her mind's eye Edie could see Martha Salliaq, sunny-faced and smiling, chatting in the breaks between classes, the flash in her eyes suggesting that there was more to know. She thought back to that Friday afternoon, to the girl she'd half hoped to recruit as a friend. Then she heard herself whisper, *If it has to be someone, don't let it be Martha.*

She was right about the mosquitoes. They were dancing and dipping, trying to work their way further in towards the water. Derek and Edie exchanged glances. Mosquitoes didn't usually bother cadavers, which meant that the blood must be in the water, along with whatever had supplied it. They walked on, more carefully this time, their progress slowed by the curtains of mosquitoes which flared up from the muskeg beside them and by a heaviness of heart that made each step drag.

They descended to the water's edge in silence. The liquid lapping at their feet was greasy and terracotta-coloured, a bloody soup. Edie glanced at Derek who blinked grimly in return.

A body was floating in dark water not far from the bank, naked, face down with the arms spread on either side like a cross. The swelling, the shadowy patches on the skin suggested that it had lain in the water some time. The hair was short, exposing the neck, and for a moment Edie felt a rush of relief. She moved forward, her legs propelling her towards the lake, and before she really knew what she was doing she was stumbling through the mud in the shallows, the mosquitoes whirling up around her like black hailstones in a thick wind, yelling, 'It's not her, it's not her!'

Then there were splashes behind her and a shrill voice. A pair of hands landed on her shoulders, pulling her back towards the waterline. She felt herself being whirled around, caught up in Derek's arms and unable to move.

'Stop!'

She froze. For an instant nothing happened then she felt Derek begin to drag her from the water, his arms squeezed so tightly around her that there was nothing she could do to resist him. They stood at the water's edge, panting a little, the policeman's face etched with anger.

'If you behave like that again, Edie Kiglatuk, so help me I will arrest you for interfering with an investigation.' He let go of her and stepped back, leaving his frustration draped between them.

Luc was standing at the water's edge staring at the body. 'If it's not Martha, who the hell is it?'

Derek stood with his arms hugging his chest. 'Whoever it is, we're gonna have to bring them in. I hate to do it. Procedurally, we should leave the body at the scene until the medical examiner and the forensics team get here but it's a three-hour flight from Iqaluit, and that's assuming they can leave immediately. If we don't get the body out of the water that bear'll be back before you can blink. Then I'll have to shoot it and the damned Wildlife Service'll be all over me. Not to mention the elders for depriving them of one of their hunting tags.' He ran a hand across his face but the anguish in his expression remained. 'But let's not jump to conclusions. We don't yet know a crime has been committed here.' His lips tightened into a thin line. To Edie he said, 'Luc and I will get the body. I need you to check around this pool here then the boundary of the lake.' He reached into his pack and took out a camera. 'Look for prints, tracks, objects, anything that might be useful.'

Edie hesitated. She felt sidelined, and she didn't like it. 'But . . .'

Derek shot her a dark look, his brow furrowed, hands on hips. 'Please, Edie, just do as I ask and try not to be such a pain in the ass.'

The lake consisted of a series of pools linked by slow-running channels. To walk around them all took some time. By the time she returned, empty-handed, the men had already removed the body. It was lying on the gurney zipped inside a bag. They were now fixing wooden stakes around the immediate area. Derek passed her a roll of crime tape and motioned to her to help him string it around the stakes. Before she had the chance to ask whose body it was, Derek said,

'What'd you find?'

'Not much. Some newly broken willow twigs. Looks like a vehicle came this way, but nothing you can follow.' The weather had been rough over the weekend, with squally rain. Any tracks had long since disappeared back into the willow and the mud.

'Any drag lines? A blood trail?'

'Uh nuh.' She knew he trusted her hunter's eye to have picked up anything like that.

They finished with the tape. She jerked her head in the direction of the body.

'You know who it is?'

Derek nodded. Something on his face made her heart quicken and a dull dread fill her belly.

'I want to see the body.'

Derek shook his head. His voice cracked a little. 'I don't think that's a good idea. It's been in the water a while.' He scraped a hand across his forehead. 'In this heat.'

But he was too late. Edie was already striding towards Luc's ATV. Luc glanced across at the policeman, who shrugged.

At the gurney she stood for a moment to gather herself. Then she took hold of the zip on the body bag and pulled. In an instant, Martha Salliaq's face appeared from under the plastic, as if in some terrible hallucination, puffy, the skin mottled, a greenish-purple web already creeping across its surface. Edie heard herself give an involuntary cry, more animal than human, like the moan of a gull. Her hand was shaking, her whole body electrified. Something fluttered uncontrollably in her chest but she barely recognized it as her heart.

The girl's eyes were still part open, the mouth slack and watery, the lips blue-tinted now to match the hair, which had been cut crudely into a short bob. But there was nothing on the face to suggest anything other than a kind of calm and remote unreality, as though the skin had only ever contained an impression of life, a reflection perhaps. As she stood an implacable sadness came over her, as though she'd reached a vast wall at the end of a dark track.

She reached for the zip again and the nightmare disappeared under the plastic.

Derek came towards her with his hand outstretched, a pained look on his face. She pulled her arms tight around her body. Last thing she needed right now was sympathy. She thought about the girl's firebrand father, Charlie, then about her fragile mother, Alice; how this news might crush the life from them both.

'When?'

Luc gave a little shrug. 'Hard to tell. The condition of the body suggests a while ago, maybe a couple days, but I'm no expert. I'm guessing from all the blood that she was alive when she went in.'

Edie suddenly felt numb and useless. 'Her hair. Someone cut it. Why would they do that?'

'A trophy maybe? I don't know, Edie.'

She heard herself give a low moan. 'You're sure she was murdered then.'

'It looks that way,' Luc said.

'Do you know how?'

For a moment no one answered. She saw Luc cut a sideways look at Derek, seeking permission to speak, then bite his lip and avert his eyes.

'It looks like a stab wound. We can't confirm anything yet. There will be tests, an autopsy,' Derek said.

There were no signs of injury on the girl's face or neck. None on the body, at least what she had seen of it.

'A stab wound where?'

Derek threw a glance at Luc and braced himself.

'*Utsuk*.' The vagina. 'It looks like the knife went a long way inside her, most likely severed the uterine artery, Luc thinks, which led to the blood loss. But it's not inside her now.'

Edie felt something inside her melt. An ill vapour spread through her body.

'At this stage it's hard to say whether or not she was raped, other than with the knife of course,' Luc added hastily.

A steadying hand landed on her arm but she didn't need it. Part of her felt strangely energized. She guessed it was the shock, or the adrenalin, or both.

'We should tell the Salliaqs,' she said.

'I think that might be best coming from you,' Derek agreed. 'Before the gossip starts. You know how it is up here.'

She did. Her own home settlement of Autisaq was exactly the same. There were only two kinds of secrets in the High Arctic: the open ones and the ones you took to your grave.

'Don't say anything specific about where the body was found if you can help it. It'll be hard for them to hear that she was in Lake Turngaluk. The Kuujuamiut go out of their way to avoid coming here. They say it's evil.' He arced a finger in the air. 'You'll notice all the *inuksuit* point away. If they ask how she died just say she was stabbed. Right now, it's important to keep the information to a minimum. For the investigation as well as for their sanity.'

Turning to Luc, Derek said, 'You and I need to get the body back to the nursing station. I'll call the forensics unit and make sure the folks at Camp Nanook are kept informed.'

Edie felt Derek's eyes searching her out. 'Can you do this?'

It was a question that didn't deserve an answer.

An hour later, she was making her way on foot in the direction of the Salliaqs' house. At the shoreline track, just south of the store, a voice called to her. In her daze she found it hard to place. She swung round and saw it belonged to Chip.

'Hey,' he said, throwing her a quizzical look. 'You OK?'

She blinked away the film in her eyes, pressed her lips hard and shook her head.

'Martha?'

At her nod his shoulders fell and he reached out an arm.

'I'm sorry.'

She nodded but didn't touch him. 'The family don't know yet. I'm just on my way to tell them.'

'Don't worry, I won't say anything.' He crossed his arms. 'No one round here speaks to me anyway. You wanna come see me afterwards, you know where I am.'

She met his eye. 'Thank you.'

'It's the least I can do.'

The Salliaqs lived in one of the identikit boxes that had been hastily erected parallel to the shore in the seventies and eighties to replace a row of canvas tents and rudimentary cabins constructed from bits of old packing cases insulated with caribou hair and heather. The houses represented a victory for the Kuujuamiut. The Canadian government, who had removed them from their homeland on east Hudson Bay and brought them to Ellesmere, had been promising to provide housing for twenty years. Ellesmere was so dry there was rarely enough snow for snowhouses. A whole generation had grown up surviving in tents lined with caribou skins in winter temperatures that frequently dipped to −50C. They'd begged the government to return them home. To make the journey on their own, two thousand kilometres on dogsleds across the harshest terrain on the planet, was impossible. But the Canadian government refused to take them. It needed Canadians on Ellesmere to strengthen its claim on the territory. So they had no choice but to accept that they were on Ellesmere to stay. They'd done what Inuit are uniquely gifted at doing: they'd made the best of it.

The houses were drab and overcrowded but functional and, most importantly, warm. Over the years those who could afford to had added on little personal flourishes. In Charlie's case, a small outhouse, heated with overhead pipes diverted from the main house. Martha had once told Edie that her father went there to escape from the women of the family. Ironic that seemed now.

She let herself into the snow porch without knocking, as was the custom, and slid off her shoes. There were voices in the room next door, seemingly oblivious. She took a breath and walked in.

The family had gathered to wait for news. All except Charlie were sitting in the front room. Alice Salliaq was on the couch. Edie had got to know her well enough to pass the time of day with. She was a soft-spoken, self-effacing and delicate woman in her mid-forties, the perfect foil to her gruff, firebrand older husband, and it would be easy to imagine she lived in his shadow were you to miss the quietly determined cast of her eyes. Beside her sat Lizzie, Martha's elder sister. Edie had seen her at the store with her mother. The siblings were physically alike, taller and plumper than their mother, with high cheekbones and generous, uneven mouths, but the difference in their characters made them seem less so. Though she had never really spoken with the girl, Lizzie had struck Edie as a kind of pale imitation of her younger sister, a moon to Martha's sun, more conventional, less ambitious, the kind who would marry early, have babies and lead a life that was essentially the same as her mother's. Alice's elder brother, Markoosie Pitoq, sat in a chair beside the sofa. He was leaning forward, his hand on a mug on the coffee table, but his head shot up when he heard her come in.

She greeted them.

'Take a seat,' Alice said. Edie moved towards a chair but in that instant the inner door swung open and a *qalunaat* woman with an immaculately groomed head of chestnut hair swept into the room. She glanced about without seeming to notice Edie.

'Where's Charlie?' the woman said. Her English was heavily accented but she spoke with the kind of unquestioning confidence Edie more usually associated with missionaries, though from her clothing and air of glamour it was clear that she wasn't one of these. Edie had seen her around the community, often heading towards the town hall building, once or twice in an oddly customized ATV on the track to Camp Nanook, then again coming out of the hotel. For a moment she thought that the *qalunaat* woman might already have heard the terrible news and was about to blurt it, but a glance at her face reassured her. A relief. The Salliaqs should hear about the death of their daughter in Inuktitut.

With the thin authority of a man who had unilaterally declared himself in charge, Markoosie reported that his brother was still checking out the area around the bird cliffs.

Finally clocking Edie, the woman held out a hand and introduced herself as Sonia Gutierrez, the lawyer working with Charlie Salliaq on the decontamination of the old radar station at Glacier Ridge 'and family friend'. Edie noticed Alice frown slightly when she said this. If Gutierrez *was* a family friend, she was no pal of Alice's.

'You have news?' Gutierrez asked.

Silence fell, everyone waiting for Edie to speak. She looked between the faces gazing expectantly at her. A little crack opened up in her heart, knowing that what she was about to say would break theirs.

4

It was now a couple of hours since Derek and Luc had carried Martha Salliaq's body up the steps of the nursing station and into Kuujuaq's tiny morgue, and news of the discovery was spreading fast. Someone had seen the body bag being unloaded from the gurney and before long the settlement was alive with gossip. Already people were saying crazy things, speculating that Martha had been taken by evil spirits or that she had been sacrificed or that the *unataqti* had used her in some kind of hazing ritual then dumped her body when they were done.

Sonia Gutierrez had gone directly to the nursing station to speak to Derek while Edie stayed behind in the Salliaqs' house, locking the doors and closing the blinds in a bid at damage control. The family didn't need to hear that stuff. A handful of friends and neighbours had made their way over to commiserate or offer help but Edie had sent them away with promises to keep what they thought they knew to themselves. Charlie Salliaq was still making a tour of outlying camps and didn't yet know his daughter had been found. One of his cousins had been dispatched to break the dismal news and escort him back to Kuujuaq. Until then the less that was said, the better.

Once Gutierrez rang with news that Charlie had been located and was making his way back to the settlement, it was felt best to bring Alice and Lizzie to the nursing station to await his arrival there. Since neither woman was in any fit state to formally identify Martha's remains that task would fall to Charlie as soon as he arrived. Derek was with Markoosie at the radio studio, launching an appeal for information, but he'd be along too as soon as he could.

Edie thought about Charlie Salliaq hurrying back across the tundra to identify the body of his murdered daughter and of the medical examiner down in Iqaluit gathering her things for the flight north. She'd seen enough of murder now to know that each act of killing was unique, an unrepeatable encounter between victim and killer. The only resemblance one murder had to another was the cascade of process and procedure each inevitably initiated: the grim rubric of morgues prepared, medical examiners and pathologists alerted, forensics teams dispatched, investigators and attorneys briefed, forms filled. But however much you reduced each event to a series of knowable processes, nothing could ever make sense of it. The boundaries of murder were unlimited. Like some far distant universe, every individual act of killing was dark and vast and unknowable.

In the station office Luc was preparing some of the initial paper-work. Edie stepped inside the room and closed the door to protect the Salliaqs from overhearing. She wanted to know whether Gutierrez had said anything to him about who she thought might be responsible, but he said not.

'What about Alice and Lizzie?' He'd been on his own with them, briefly.

Luc shook his head. 'Not to me. I think they're still in shock.'

'There are some wild theories going around.' Gutierrez had outlined a few of them on the phone.

'You can't be surprised by that. You know how murder usually goes up here. Two people who've lived side by side all their lives get into a fight about sex or money. Usually sex. Nine times out of ten there's alcohol involved and the perpetrator fesses up within an hour or two,' Luc said. 'This is something new. Premeditated, the body dumped, the positioning of the knife, the way the hair was cut. Stuff like this just doesn't happen here.'

'Except it just did,' Edie said. They let this sit. 'I guess everything in the Arctic's changing. Why should murder be any different?'

Luc gave his neck a stretch and rolled his shoulders. 'I think I liked it better the old way.'

When Edie went back into the waiting area she found Alice Salliaq where she'd left her, rubbing her fingers together in an unconscious and almost certainly futile bid for comfort. Beside her, Lizzie stared into the middle distance, her face blank, then, without warning, she let out a strangled sob.

At the same time, in the radio station, Markoosie was wishing his audience a peaceful night. He flicked a few switches and took the show off air. He looked drawn and tired.

Derek, who had been leaning against a shelving unit trying to stay silent, gave a little cough.

'Anything to report?'

Markoosie took off his headphones and hung them on a hook on the desk. 'You heard the last quarter hour. The rest of it was pretty much the same. A ton of calls, but no one who'd seen Martha since she left my house Saturday lunchtime,' he said, pressing a finger into the corner of an eye to wipe a tear. 'A *lot* of bad feeling against Camp Nanook. You get that?'

'The timing sure looks bad,' Derek said. He thought about the local girls he'd seen hanging around with soldiers. How glamorous those young men must seem to them, with their cash, their well-travelled sophistication, their stories from the front line.

'Looks pretty perfect to me. One week the *unataqti* move in, the next my niece is dead.'

'That's kind of what I meant,' Derek said.

Markoosie reached beneath him and switched off a power socket. 'Folk seem pretty clear in their own minds that this is the work of some *unataqti*.'

Derek shook his head. 'It's too soon to say.' He rubbed his jawline with his hand. 'Take me through the last time you saw her again.'

'Like I said, she came over Saturday morning to pick up some schoolbook she'd left.'

'You remember the title?'

Markoosie began to tidy the papers on his desk. 'I'm not a big reader. She wanted to know if me and Toolik – that's my father, Martha's grandfather – were all fixed for lunch. She often cooked for us when Alice and Charlie were out of town. She was brought up good that way.'

'Were you? Fixed for lunch?'

'We weren't hungry.' He popped the papers into a plastic bag at his feet. 'After that she left.'

'She didn't say where she was going?'

'Only that she was expected at the family summer camp.'

'If anyone does call in with any information, no matter how small, you'll let me know, won't you?'

Markoosie nodded. 'She was my *hanaji*, you know, little Martha. It was me who named her.' He signalled to Derek to turn off a couple of power switches on his left. 'When she was little I made her an amulet from walrus ivory and green stone and my own hair. It was supposed to keep her safe.'

No jewellery had been found on the body, though it was possible that it had fallen into the mud at the bottom of the pool.

'Could you sketch it for me?'

Markoosie reached over the desk for a scrap of paper and drew a sketch of a bangle with two small round beads and three larger elaborately carved pieces of ivory.

'She wear that all the time?'

'Pretty much. For all the good it did her.'

Back at the police detachment Derek punched in Todd Ransom's home number in Iqaluit. Ransom had come over from Yellowknife to head up a new forensics unit based out of the Nunavut capital. The growing problem of northern crime had been met by an uncoordinated, piecemeal response from central government. As much as Derek welcomed the new forensics unit it was frustrating that there remained only one investigative officer whose job it was to coordinate cases across the whole of the Canadian Arctic, a region not much smaller than India. The new unit was supposed to be a joint facility, shared between the Royal Canadian

Mounted Police Arctic division and the various native police forces in the region. In practice, Derek wondered whether the Mounties would always get priority over smaller, native forces like the Ellesmere Island Police.

Derek had met Ransom once on a trip to Iqaluit, and found him energetic, if a little too cocksure. He'd been impressed by the man's efforts to learn Inuktitut, which most *qalunaat* living and working in the north didn't bother to do, but until now they'd had no reason to work together. It was late to call, but Ransom would be used to antisocial hours.

A woman picked up the phone. Derek apologized for the lateness of the call and asked to speak with Todd. There was a pause, then a man's voice on the line.

'*Ainngai, qanuitpin?*' Hi, how are you? Todd's accent was almost impenetrable, but Derek appreciated the effort.

'*Qaniunngittnga.*' I'm fine. 'Listen, Todd,' Derek continued in English, a relief to them both. 'We got a situation up here.' He outlined what had happened. 'I've already had to bypass procedures . . .'

'We all have to do what we can with the resources we got,' Ransom said blandly.

'Still, I'm gonna need Anna right away.' Anna Mackie was the new medical examiner, a Ransom appointee. 'Plus a forensic unit to run the usual print, fluids and fibre checks at the crime scene, the victim's room, her ATV.' The lab work would have to be completed in Iqaluit or maybe Ottawa.

'Listen, Todd,' Derek went on, his voice sounding more defensive than he'd intended. 'We got five hundred soldiers up here. I have no idea how the military is gonna see this, but you can guess the local view.'

'Sounds like a powder keg,' Ransom responded. 'But you got a nurse out there, right?'

'Right. Luc Fabienne. We've had to move the body to the morgue and we're awaiting a formal ID from next of kin. Luc's taking care of the preliminary paperwork, but . . .' He tailed off, conscious, suddenly, of the elephant in the room. 'Is there a problem?'

There was a pause.

'Fact is, we're gonna need a little patience here, Derek. Anna's on summer leave until Wednesday. We were supposed to get cover but the guy phoned in sick. They're trying to find someone at short notice but getting anyone to travel north of Winnipeg, well, you know how that is. Ask the nurse to take hair, blood, skin, you know, the usual, label 'em up and stick 'em in the freezer. I'll send someone along soon as I can.'

Derek pulled the phone from his ear and stared at the handset, wondering if Ransom had actually heard anything he'd said. He also didn't like the use of the word 'we', as in *we*'re gonna need a little patience'. In Derek's book it was usually the sound of responsibility shifting.

'Todd, I'm not sure what I'm hearing here. You want me to go back to the parents and tell them we can't investigate the murder of their daughter because the medical examiner's working on her tan and the cover's got a headache? Help me out here. At least send the forensics guy.'

'It's a long way, Derek. It's not gonna be possible to justify two trips just now. Budget issues.' Ransom's tone of voice suggested reasonableness in the face of impossible demands.

'How's about I send Pol down in the detachment plane?' He was trying to be accommodating. Making it easy for Ransom to say yes. But Ransom didn't say yes. What he did say was,

'Listen, bud, I'm doing my best here. We had a contractor got messed up in a brawl over the weekend and forensics is all tied up with that just now. Anyway, you know as well as I do how native slayings go. Someone got drunk and let rip. The boyfriend or the father. Why don't you make a start and the team can fill in when they get there?'

'Boyfriend, father.' Derek blew the air out of his nose in frustration. 'Are you even listening to yourself?'

There was a long exhale and an edgy little cough. 'Believe me, bud, if I could change this situation, I would. In a heartbeat. But I can't. It's like you guys are always saying, *ajurnamat*.' Too bad. Ransom produced the word as though it was some kind of trophy. It was the first time Derek heard a *qalunaat* say it. Didn't make it sound any better. He screwed up his face, trying to contain his irritation.

Common sense told him to hold back but the rest of him overruled it. 'Listen here, *bud*.'

'All ears, Derek.'

'Since you're so keen on native expressions, I'm gonna teach you a new one. *Qitiqthlimaqtisi arit*. Repeat it enough and you'll pick it up. It means go fuck yourself.'

The conversation left him shaky with anger and needing a cigarette. He fetched a mug of coffee, pulled out his pack of Lucky Strikes. A year or two ago Ransom would have been right. Whenever there was a murder the killer would almost always turn out to be someone from the same community as the victim, the motive simple and often alcohol-fuelled. Most killings involved a hunting rifle, the remainder a knife. These days, not only was murder becoming more common but the Native Police Association bulletin was full of reports of stabbings, knee-cappings, burns, beheadings and the kind of sexual assault that made your blood freeze. And that wasn't all. Victims and perpetrators were becoming more international and the motives for killing less transparent. The focus of law enforcement had shifted from apprehension to detection. The death of Edie Kiglatuk's stepson, Joe Inukpuk, last year proved the point. What started as an investigation into a suicide turned into a terrifically tangled manhunt. On the surface of things, the body of a young woman found dumped in a lake a few kilometres from a military encampment bore all the hallmarks of a garden variety sex murder, but who was to say that the knifing of Martha Salliaq would turn out to be any less complex?

So far as he knew no one in any of the native police forces had received any extra training or resources to help them cope. He sat back and tried to focus on his next moves. In the absence of any immediate assistance from a forensics team he'd have to work that much harder and smarter. These first hours after the discovery of the body were vital. First, he'd need to tell Colonel Klinsman at Camp

Nanook that he was designating the area around Glacier Ridge a crime scene – at least until the forensics team had been and probably for a good while longer. The scheduled clean-up works would have to be postponed and he guessed he'd have to find some way to fence off the whole area. He'd need to arrange for someone to drain the pool where Martha's body had been discovered in case the murder weapon was lying in the mud at the bottom. While that was being done, he'd focus his efforts on discovering as much as he could about Martha's movements over the weekend, then try to come up with a list of suspects.

In all likelihood the gossip would prove correct and the killer would be found among the incomers into the area. But he'd need to cover all bases. A couple of teams of scientists were working on research projects in the region. Those who intended to leave the settlement were required to register at the detachment. He'd never known anyone not respect this rule. So far as Derek could recall, there were a couple of zoologists studying the wolf population in the Bourne Peninsula and a party of glaciologists based out at Jakeman Glacier, but both teams were a couple of days' travel away. If they'd been in the settlement over the weekend, they would have stayed at the hotel, and Derek had already confirmed that the only guest over the past week had been Sonia Gutierrez, the lawyer. More likely the killer or killers would be found among one or more of the five hundred soldiers stationed at Camp Nanook. The movement of individual soldiers shouldn't be too hard to track. Each man was presumably required to clock in and out of the camp.

Tracing the activities of local people would be a lot trickier. At this time of year the population of Kuujuaq was as fluid as meltwater. Most of the local men were at summer camps spread out across hundreds of square kilometres. Every once in a while they would reappear to collect supplies, but there was no order to it. Sometimes they stayed over, other times they came and went in the same day. You never knew who was going to be in town, when and for how long.

All in all it added up to a lot of work. He guessed he could recall

Stevie Killik from summer leave, though his constable was even less experienced in this kind of thing than he was. One possibility was to ask for help from Camp Nanook. Would Klinsman be willing to cooperate if his own men were implicated? It would constitute some kind of conflict of interest. The locals certainly wouldn't like it. They gave him a hard enough time about the camp as it was. As though he'd had any say in it. To run to the military for assistance would also undermine his own authority. No, he'd just have to manage on his own. Step one: call Klinsman about the crime scene. He checked his watch: 9.30 p.m. The colonel was unlikely to be at his desk, but he dialled the satphone number he had for him all the same. To his surprise a voice answered.

'Colonel Klinsman there?'

'This is he.' It was the voice of a man a young woman might want to take back to meet her parents: solid, masculine, reassuringly modulated.

The colonel listened to Derek's explanation of events without interruption. In a sincere and only slightly guarded tone he thanked Derek for the notification and assured him of his full cooperation. If Derek could give him a specific time period he'd be happy to come up with a list of all personnel who were out of the camp at that time. Postponing the clean-up would be a little more complicated, since the military were officially acting on Defence Department instructions, but he agreed to call his contact in Ottawa in the morning. In principle, he didn't see that there would be a problem.

The two men finished the call cordially. Derek put down the phone, pushed his chair back and lit a cigarette. Klinsman had been more helpful than he'd anticipated. He had to hope the man would stay that way. He scrolled through his to-do list again and realized he'd been overambitious; even with Klinsman's cooperation this was too much to do for one person. He was thinking about Killik when a more immediate and practical solution came to him. The phone rang. He picked up and barked his name and instead of the colonel's voice, as he'd imagined, he got Luc Fabienne's.

'Charlie Salliaq's just got back,' the nurse said. 'You need to come.'

'Is Edie Kiglatuk with you?'

Luc said she was.

'Good. I'll be right over.'

Edie saw Charlie enter before anyone else. It was clear from his face that his cousin had broken the news. The trembling jawline, the drooped despair in the eyes. He scoped the room then immediately came over to where the remainder of his family were sitting; he kissed his daughter on the forehead and sat down beside his wife. Then he drew both women in with his arms and for a while the three of them sat with their hands clasped together, heads touching, keeping out the world. After a time he tore himself away and, ignoring Edie, went over to speak with Luc. The two men stood huddled together, talking in low voices before moving across the room and through the door at the side that led down to the morgue. Not long after, they reappeared, Charlie in the lead, rubbing his hand across his face. Alice looked up, eyes wide and questioning, as though it was still possible that there had been a mistake and that her daughter was alive, but on Charlie's shake of the head she slumped forward.

Just then the outer door opened and Derek walked in, nodded to Edie and took a chair beside the Salliaqs. He spoke to them for several minutes, his forearms resting on his thighs, lifting a hand every so often to make a rolling gesture as though he was running through procedure. Edie watched a scowl gradually darkening the elder's face. Evidently Charlie Salliaq didn't like what he was hearing. Moments later he jumped up, and cutting the air with his right hand, said, 'All I want to know is when you're gonna get down to Camp Nanook and arrest whichever one of those damned sonofabitch *unataqti* killed my daughter.'

Derek raised his palms in a steadying gesture. 'I understand this probably isn't what you want to hear right now, but we need to know a lot more about Martha's movements, the people she hung around with. At this stage we're not making any assumptions about who did this.'

Salliaq closed his eyes for a moment then took a deep breath and began mumbling something in a threatening tone. Beside him, Derek bristled, then collected himself, his mouth tightening. He eye-rolled Edie, came over and took the seat beside her, a grim expression on his face.

'The forensics team won't be here till Thursday.' He spoke quietly but in an urgent tone, one eye on the Salliaqs. 'They've given some *qalunaat* business down in Iqaluit first priority. Short of flying down there myself and kidnapping them, there's nothing I can do about it. It means we're gonna have to do some of the preliminaries ourselves.'

Edie sat up and swung around to face him. *'We?'*

'Sure. I've checked the books and I can squeeze some money out of the budget for a Village Public Safety Officer.'

'I'm not the sharpest icicle on the roof, but I have no clue what you're talking about,' Edie replied.

'It's an idea I'm borrowing from Alaska. A temporary post.'

She swung back and held up a hand. 'Wait up there. I've got kids to teach. In any case, what about Stevie?'

Derek gave her a look to say he'd already thought this through. If Stevie didn't complete the course he was likely to get overlooked for promotion.

'Besides, he hasn't had the experience. Please, Edie, I could really use your help. I can ask the school head to sort out another supply teacher for a while. We can make this work. Look, I got a forensics unit that won't play ball, a population who've already decided who killed Martha Salliaq and five hundred soldiers who may or may not be cooperative. Plus Charlie Salliaq hates my guts.' His voice had taken on a pleading tone she didn't like. It sounded too much like desperation.

'I don't know, D. I don't want to let those kids down. And, really, I'm a stranger here.'

He grabbed her hands in his and leaned in. 'That's what makes you perfect for the job. No axe to grind. No enemies.'

An image of Martha came to mind. The hand touching her hair. The sweet, sly smile of adolescence. *Going somewhere special?* She felt her resistance crumbling.

'You sure you can square it with the school?'

'Hand on heart. I'll match whatever the school are paying you so long as it isn't much. I'd like to say the role comes with regulation uniform but my spare won't fit.' He winked then grew sombre. His eyes cut to Charlie Salliaq.

'Your first job is to halt that particular stampede. In fact, he's yours for as long as the investigation lasts. Break it to him that we're gonna need them to stay somewhere else until forensics has been over their house. Anyone requires any personal items, you can fetch them, but you'll have to wear shoe protectors and overalls. I got spares at the detachment. It's late now. Tomorrow morning we'll interview the family again.'

He got up and went over to the door, leaving Edie alone with the family. She stood and approached Charlie.

'*Avasirngulik,*' elder, using the polite form. She explained the situation. The old man's face was covered with tiny reticulations, as though it had been colonized by a red rock lichen. There was something wrong with him beside grief, she thought. A kind of sickness.

When she was finished, Salliaq reached out a bony hand.

'We want justice. Not southern justice. Inuit justice. Do you understand?' For a moment he locked eyes with her.

'Yes,' she said. 'Yes I do.'

5

The Salliaqs' house seemed eerily untouched by the cataclysm which had just befallen the family. In the front yard sat the usual mess of outdoor gear, old snowbie parts, dog chains. While Derek hitched Martha's ATV up to his own and towed it back to the detachment, Edie went in, noting the family's boots and parkas hanging in the snow porch, the knick-knacks, laundry basket still full of unwashed clothes, the crockery carefully stacked in the kitchen, all nothing more than remnants now, mere shadows of another life forever lost.

She pulled on a pair of vinyl gloves and, following Charlie Salliaq's directions, went along a corridor at the back of the house to the second door on the right. A plastic sign, flowery, announced Martha's room, in fancy script. It was more of a cubbyhole than a room, four almost bare walls, simply furnished with a bed, a nightstand, a cheap lamp, and a plywood dresser. On one side was a small, built-in closet opposite a window which looked out over the yard behind.

Derek had told her to check for anything unusual in the girl's bedroom. As a woman, she'd know better than he what that meant, he said. She scoped about and, seeing nothing untoward, began to search more thoroughly, going through drawers in the dresser, feeling beneath the mattress. Under the bed she found a tattered world atlas bearing the school library stamp. Unusual? A little, she guessed, at least for an Inuk kid. But nothing you'd think odd, not if you knew Martha. The top drawer of the dresser contained the usual paraphernalia of Inuit girlhood: hair oil, a few fishing lures, some shower gel the girl didn't want to leave in the bathroom, nothing to arouse any suspicion.

In the next drawer down, under a pile of underwear, she found a photograph of the girl sitting below the cliffs near Glacier Ridge holding a basket of dovekie eggs, a big smile on her face, her hair not yet tinted blue. Nothing written on the back to indicate who had taken it and when, but this past late spring had been freakishly warm and the dovekies had started breeding early. That fact and the vegetation around Martha dated it to early July this year. A couple of weeks back. Nothing special about the picture, except that it had been hidden. Edie slid it into her bag and made a mental note to ask the family.

She sealed off the room with crime tape, did a quick check of the rest of the house, pressed a length of tape across the front door and went back along the track towards the nursing station.

The sun had painted the rubble of ice and seawater on the horizon a deep pewter. A week or so ago you could still hear ice music in the breeze but the rot had set in for the summer and even the shore-fast ice here at the margin was too soft be played by the wind and currents. Far out on the Sound patches of dark light reflected from the open water. More distant still, a band of clouds dazzled with ice blink, sunlight reflecting back from some faraway ice floe. She went down to the shingle beach, feet crunching over patches of sea lungwort and scurvy grass, and looked out for a moment. A berg floated across her field of vision, moving west on the current, and she was reminded of the old Inuit saying, that water was just melted ice. *Qalunaat* thought the opposite of course. One of the many ways Inuit were profoundly different from those living to the south. Murder was another, she realized now. For *qalunaat* it was the taking of a life, but for Inuit it was something else, the removal of a body from its rightful owner. Not an offence against life, which went on regardless, but something more elemental: an outrage against the spirit.

When she got back to the nursing station Luc and Derek were in the office in deep discussion. Luc had swivelled his monitor around so that Derek could read the screen. As she walked in, he was saying,

'A lot of what I'm saying here is educated guesswork. I'm a nurse not a pathologist. When people die, that's usually where I leave off.'

He stopped. Both men looked at Edie. Luc hastily returned the monitor back to face his side of the desk.

'You find anything in the house?' Derek said.

'Maybe.' She took out the photo. Derek studied it for a moment or two, flipped it over to check the back, then turned it face side up again.

'Any idea who took this?'

'Must have been taken between two weeks and a month ago.'

She detailed her earlier observations about the image.

Derek pointed to the amulet on the girl's wrist. Edie and Luc both craned over to look.

'Was this in Martha's room?'

Edie shook her head. She was certain she would have seen it if it had been there, but that was unlikely. Those Inuit who wore amulets rarely took them off.

'She looks happy,' Luc said.

There was a pause while they took this in. Martha's face rose up in Edie's mind, like something gradually surfacing from the bottom of the sea. She found herself smiling at the wry grin, the sense of something illicit and delicious just behind the eyes. Then, once more, it was gone.

'What's on that screen you don't want me to see?' she said.

Luc shifted in his chair. His left knee began knocking on the underside of the table.

Edie eye-rolled Derek.

'Just tell her what you told me, Luc. I could do with hearing it one more time myself.'

Luc sat back and began to scan the screen. 'It's been a long day. But, like I said before, if I had to guess – which, by the way, I have – I'd say the knife pierced the uterine artery and caused significant exsanguination. There seems to be some water in the lungs but whether Martha Salliaq died of blood loss or from drowning I don't know. The amount of blood in the water and the absence of any traces of it around the lake suggests that she was alive but probably unconscious or only semi-conscious when she went in the water.' He looked up, an expression of distaste on his face.

'You got a time of death?'

'Sometime on Saturday night. I can't be more specific than that.'

'Anna, the medical examiner, should be able to give us a death window,' Derek said, adding bitterly, 'If she ever shows up.' He gestured for Luc to continue.

'It's almost like someone held her there until she bled out,' Luc said. 'She wasn't in deep water. There's a small knife wound on the wrist which looks like it was made sometime prior to the final assault. It's very superficial. It may or may not have been the same knife that caused both injuries, but if it was, the intention was different. Whoever nicked her wrist wasn't intending to hurt her. That amulet you pointed out in the photo, it's my guess someone cut it off her and broke the skin in the process. It definitely happened before she died but I see no signs that she resisted. I couldn't find any restraint marks or other defence wounds, either on her arms or upper body or on her thighs. If there had been a struggle I imagine we'd see more evidence of it. Skin or maybe blood and hairs under the fingernails. Certainly more scratches or knife cuts. A lot more bruising.

'The internal injury is of another kind altogether of course.' The nurse rubbed a hand across his hair. He wasn't finding this any easier the second time around. 'The knife went right up into her body. In my opinion, whoever did it intended to bleed the body out. That's kind of interesting because the killer could have achieved the same thing more easily by cutting Martha's throat or wrists.'

'So why go into her vagina? Some kind of sexual thrill?' Edie said.

Luc frowned. 'It's possible, but I doubt it. I've seen plenty of sexual violence and there's almost always some other kind of injury, often to the breasts or genitals, sometimes to the face. Bruising, bite or punch marks, that kind of thing. This . . . it's more like as if the killer was trying to reach Martha's core . . .' He tailed off and gestured at Derek for a cigarette. Derek sparked up his Zippo and lit one for him. 'Of course, we're talking as though there's some kind of answer to this. But there never is to any murder, is there? Not one that makes any sense.'

'It's our job to try and find one,' Derek said.

'I wouldn't mind betting that she was either taken completely by surprise,' Luc went on. 'Or that she knew and trusted the guy who killed her or that she was drugged.' He looked up. 'You were right about the hair, Edie. There were little pieces of it stuck to her clothes. She wore it in traditional braids, didn't she?'

'Tinted blue.' Edie smiled to herself at the remembrance of their last conversation. 'Her little act of rebellion.'

'If I had Charlie Salliaq for a father, I'd want to rebel some,' Derek said.

Edie's eyes narrowed. 'But why would anyone cut it?'

'I don't know any more than you do, but my sense is that it was a memento of some kind.' He shifted his weight. 'Ask me, this whole thing's a puzzle. This guy chooses the most intimate way of taking Martha's life, but he doesn't seem to have wanted to cause her pain or humiliation. He cuts her braids – assuming it *was* him – but he leaves her pubic hair untouched; and, apart from that knife wound, he doesn't mutilate her.'

'Any evidence of penetrative sex, consensual or otherwise?' This from Derek. He'd taken a notebook out of his pocket and was writing in it.

'I would say no. There's no bruising around the inner thighs, but you're not gonna find any semen, not the way she was cut or how long the body was in the water. Another oddity – there's no damage done by fish, larvae, waterworms, anything like that.'

'That's an easy one at least,' Derek said. 'Lake Turngaluk is dead water. No life in there at all. I guess that's one of the reasons it holds such a powerful taboo with the locals.' He looked at the clock on the wall. 'About those samples?'

'I'll do them before I leave tonight.' Luc glanced at his watch. 'I could run a preliminary toxicology test if you want,' he added helpfully. 'But you'll need to bear in mind that it would only be preliminary and the results might even be misleading.'

'Thank you, Luc. Whatever you can do would be great. We're running a paper and string operation here. Everyone understands that.' Derek gave the nurse a reassuring pat on the shoulder. 'Are we any good to you here?'

On Luc's head shake, Derek pushed back his chair and stood. He spun his pack of Lucky Strikes across the desk towards the nurse, then turning to Edie he said, 'Let's go get a couple hours' sleep, then talk to the Salliaqs first thing in the morning.'

6

Edie woke just before 6 a.m. and forced herself to rise. She'd only managed a couple of hours' sleep and her head felt like an old, abandoned ball. She brewed some tea on her Coleman stove and stirred in a small nugget of seal fat. The tea sharpened her up. She drained it, threw on her summer-weight parka and her outdoor boots and went out to face the day.

The Pitoqs' house, where the Salliaq family had spent the night, wore the slightly forlorn, unloved air of a typical bachelor set-up. The front yard was full of engine parts and antlers and someone had hung assorted skulls on the steps up to the shabby front door. The windows were crusted with salt on the outside and the blinds, old-fashioned metal venetians, looked like they hadn't been opened in years.

On the steps up was a *tupilaq*, a curse object, fashioned from a piece of walrus tusk wrapped in the face fur of a fox. Edie picked the thing up, turning it over in her hands. Whoever had constructed it hoped to bring harm to a family member. Charlie, most likely. You couldn't be as abrasive as he was without picking up a few enemies. Small towns had long memories. She walked down to the sea and, tucking a pebble inside as ballast, threw the rotten thing as hard as she could into the water.

Back at the house she removed her boots in the snow porch and walked through the inner door. Lizzie and Alice were already up and sitting on the couch, staring into the middle distance, their eyes deep, dark pools of anguish. Beside them Alice's father, Toolik Pitoq, stared blankly ahead. The old man had memory problems and it was hard to know what he might be thinking, or even if he had been able fully to absorb the news. Charlie was at the table with Sonia Gutierrez. The lawyer glanced over at Edie, then, reaching out and placing a hand briefly on Charlie Salliaq's arm, got up and came over.

'Markoosie has gone to the town hall to check for messages. The radio station phone line has an answer machine.' Gutierrez pursed her lips. 'I hope I don't have to tell you this is going to be very difficult for the family.' She met Edie's gaze and held it a little too long. 'They are worried about *tirigusukut*.' Taboo.

A stab of irritation worked its way up into Edie's brain. So now she was being lectured by an outsider on how to be an Inuk. Like most Inuit, she'd been brought up to think of the newly dead as *tariaksuit*, or shadow people. The tradition had it that if you tried to speak with them or even about them, the *tariaksuit* could find themselves torn between the spirit world and the world of the living, not knowing where to belong. If this went on for long enough the *tariaksuit* would be cut adrift. That was when they became disruptive and angry. *Tuurngaaaluit,* Inuit called them, evil spirits. It was *tuurgnaaaluit* who supposedly inhabited Lake Turngaluk. If you believed in such things – Edie swung between belief and scepticism – it would be easy to imagine that Martha might have encountered *tuurgnaaaluit* as she lay dying in the waters of the lake. For Inuit, to be dead was at least to belong to the spirit world. To be *tuurgnaaaluit* was to belong nowhere at all.

'We can interview you here if you prefer,' Edie said, addressing herself to Charlie now. She had already decided not to mention the *tupilaq*. Nothing to be gained by it.

Charlie glanced at Alice and Lizzie then shook his head. 'This is a home. If we have to talk about things that are *tirigusukut* it is better to do it in a *qalunaat* place.'

Back at the detachment Derek was busy laying out chairs. Edie left everyone to settle and fetched a tray of tea and coffee. When she returned, the three Salliaqs were seated in a row with Gutierrez off to one side, fiddling with a notebook and a digital recorder. Derek had asked Edie to take the lead in questioning. He was keen not to antagonize Charlie. He'd only butt in, he said, if he thought she was heading in a wrong direction.

'We need to know as much as possible about Martha in general and specifically her movements from Friday afternoon onwards,' Edie began.

Charlie's brow knitted. 'We shouldn't be talking about these things now. My daughter is *tariaksuit*.' He glanced at Gutierrez. There was a look of terrible sadness on his face.

'I know this goes against our customs, but we have to do it all the same,' Edie said.

Charlie turned momentarily to Gutierrez, who gave him a tiny nod of encouragement.

'Perhaps you could start from when you moved to summer camp?' Right now, so far as Edie and Derek understood it, the Salliaqs knew only that Martha had been stabbed, her body found outside the settlement.

Charlie took a breath and sighed. He saw he had no choice but to cooperate. 'It must have been about week or so ago. Martha stayed behind so she could go to summer school. She's smart, but I guess you know that.'

'The smartest,' Edie agreed.

'She was supposed to come out and join us on Saturday for the weekend. Her mother wanted her to come earlier, on Friday.' Charlie glanced not at Alice but at Gutierrez. 'Martha is very serious about her studies.'

'Did you have a disagreement?'

'About that? No!' Charlie rose a little in his seat then looked away. 'No. We don't disagree about anything.'

Implausible, but also typical. Inuit families found it more difficult than most to admit to trouble.

'When did you begin to get worried about her?' Edie said.

'Not till Monday. We figured she'd forgotten. But I told you all this when I came to the school.'

Edie pressed him. 'Did Martha often forget things?'

'She's eighteen.' There was a pause. Beside him, Alice began to sigh and tremble. He went on, 'This time of year, she sometimes likes to go collecting eggs, so that's what we thought.'

Edie pulled the photo from her pocket. 'We found this in her room. Do you know who took it?' Charlie peered at the image. Alice blinked. 'No,' he said, catching Alice's eye. His wife shook her head.

'Was there someone she went out on the land with regularly? Fishing or egg collecting, say.'

A light sheen had appeared on the elder's face. 'Only family and friends.'

'Who *were* her friends?' Derek cut in. 'Any misfits among them? Someone unstable, with a record maybe?'

The family looked at each other. Lizzie spoke first. 'Lisa Tuliq?'

They waited for the young woman to elaborate, but when she didn't Edie took a breath and went on, conscious that she was about to say something Charlie wouldn't like. 'Did Martha have a boyfriend?'

Charlie's eyes sharpened. 'We don't allow the girls to date.' He glanced at his wife, who looked away. Something there, she thought. She repeated her question, directing herself this time to Lizzie. At the young woman's shrug Edie made a mental note to speak to her alone sometime after the main interview had finished.

'Could Martha have been seeing someone in secret?' Derek asked. Edie saw Charlie Salliaq bristle.

'You don't know my daughter. She wouldn't do anything like that.'

'We need to find out if anyone might have wanted to hurt Martha. Some boy she rejected, maybe?' Edie said.

Charlie shifted on his seat. 'My daughter is *tariaksuit*. It's dangerous to talk about her like this.'

'We appreciate this is hard,' Derek said. 'I'm Inuk myself.'

'Half Inuk,' Charlie added drily.

Derek's mouth tightened. Edie threw him a warning look. Whatever he and Charlie thought about each other, there was no sense in provoking the old Inuk now. She waited for her boss to rearrange his features then went on.

'Was there anything in Martha's behaviour over the last week that seemed uncharacteristic? Anything at all?'

'All these questions,' Charlie Salliaq said. 'I've already told you the answers. Martha was focused on her studies. She didn't have many friends. There was no boyfriend, nothing like that.'

No one said anything. The atmosphere in the room thickened. Then, all of a sudden, Charlie seemed to fold inwards, as though he'd finally absorbed something of the horror of what had happened to his daughter, and when he looked up again his face was drained of any life. Edie saw Sonia Gutierrez gently reach out a hand but he shrugged her off, unwilling to be comforted. For a while he simply stared ahead, his eyes ablaze, then, when he could no longer keep the horror in, he curled and grasped his head and tears began rolling down his face. Picking up on his distress, Lizzie began to sob too. Alice turned to look at her, a dazed expression on her face. Shock, Edie thought. It could do that to you.

'We'll need you all to give us DNA and fingerprint samples. For elimination purposes,' Derek said. Addressing himself to Gutierrez, he added, 'Markoosie too.'

The lawyer jotted something in her notebook. 'Do you have any suspects?'

'Not at this stage, no. Right now we're not ruling anything out,' he added firmly.

Charlie Salliaq had gathered himself now and wiped away his tears. Turning back to him, Edie said, 'If you could go on with what you were saying, *avasirngulik*.'

Gutierrez gave Salliaq another of her little nods.

'No Inuk would ever leave a body in Lake Turngaluk. Not ever. That place is *tirigusukut*.' So he *had* heard, Edie thought. It was impossible to keep anything under wraps for long. She felt for him. The terrible details could only have added to his pain.

'We were at summer camp,' he went on. 'We always move out of the settlement when the cotton grass starts blooming.'

'Three weeks, then,' Edie said. He'd previously said a week or so. Most Inuit didn't own a watch and didn't compute clock time in their heads but rather sensed it from the position of the sun, from shadows and the condition of the ice. This only added to the complexity of the investigation.

'Martha stayed alone in the house during the week,' Salliaq added, ignoring the correction.

Next Alice spoke up. 'We wanted her to move in with my brother but she said she preferred to have time on her own to study—'

'Look, I don't understand why we're wasting time talking,' Charlie interrupted her. 'Everyone knows Martha was killed by one of the *unataqti* from Camp Nanook.' Directing himself at Derek, he added in an accusatory tone, 'You were any good at your job, you'd be up there now.'

The room fell silent. Edie looked over at Alice and saw alarm in her eyes. Was she afraid of her husband? Or only of his temper?

Gutierrez cleared her throat. 'My client is understandably upset. But the family are determined to cooperate with this investigation any way we can. Whether with you or with the military police at the camp.'

Now it was Derek's turn to prickle. That was the trouble with men, Edie thought. They were so territorial. He reminded the lawyer that Martha's body was found on civilian land, within Ellesmere Island Police jurisdiction.

'I see,' Gutierrez said, writing something in her notebook.

The front door opened and Markoosie came in. Derek stood up and pulled over a chair. Markoosie nodded a greeting to each of the Salliaqs in turn then sat.

'Anyone call in?' Edie said.

He shook his head miserably. 'Not with anything useful. You know how it is with us. We don't like to stick our necks out when there are *qalunaat* involved.'

Gutierrez blew air from her mouth in a gesture of impatience. Outsiders always wondered how it could be that people who thought nothing of scaling glaciers or hunting polar bears could become overwhelmed by feelings of *ilira*, awed fear, and *kappia*, a fear of unpredictable violence, in their interactions with southerners. Even outsiders as generally sympathetic as Gutierrez.

'Do you remember what time Martha came to your house on Saturday?' Derek said.

Markoosie looked pained. A thought crossed his face. He was about to speak, when his attention was drawn to the actions of his brother-in-law, who was wiping furiously at his nose, the back of his hand bloody. Gutierrez began to fluster in her bag for a handkerchief but the elder waved her away, saying he was OK, that it was just a nosebleed and that he was used to them. Still dabbing at his nose he stood up. He had no intention of staying and, in this state, there was no point in requiring it of him.

They'd reached the door when Edie called Markoosie's name. The man looked back.

'You were about to say something?'

He closed his eyes. 'Oh yeah. After she came round, Martha said she was going to the store.'

'Is that all? She say why?'

Markoosie shook his head and turned away.

Only Sonia stayed behind.

'I know this won't be at the top of your mind right now,' she said to Derek. 'But I think it's important that the decontamination work scheduled to start at Glacier Ridge this summer goes ahead. Charlie Salliaq's been petitioning the Defence Department for years to get that green-lit, well, we both have.'

'You're right. That's not at the top of my mind. Glacier Ridge is an active crime scene.'

But Gutierrez wasn't about to give up.

'The pool where the body was found, of course, but the entire site? That's a pretty large area. The clean-up is important work, sergeant.' Gutierrez sounded a little more defensive than she had probably intended. 'The Defence Department's under tremendous financial pressure. They're quite capable of using this as an excuse to pull out.'

'My job is finding Martha Salliaq's killer, Ms Gutierrez, and I'd like to get on with it.'

Gutierrez nodded, tight-lipped, and was about to rise from her chair to leave when Edie stayed her with a hand.

'A moment?' She lowered her voice. 'Between us, do you know of anyone who'd want to hurt the Salliaq family?' she said.

Gutierrez looked puzzled.

'I found a *tupilaq* on the steps to the Pitoqs' house this morning. A curse object.'

Gutierrez grimaced. 'Charlie Salliaq can be abrasive but he's very respected.' She paused, as though recognizing the importance of the question. 'I guess there *was* some opposition to the plan to clean up Lake Turngaluk. Something about stirring up bad spirits. Superstition.'

'From?'

The lawyer gave an exasperated sigh. 'You know how it is. No one actually said anything openly. It was just kind of in the air.'

'If it comes down to earth, you'll let us know,' Derek said.

Gutierrez grunted a yes, then stood and, brushing herself down, made for the door. Derek waited until she was gone before wheeling about to face Edie, his face blush with anger.

'Why didn't you tell me about the *tupilaq* beforehand? Dealing with team Salliaq is enough like wrangling a pair of wounded walruses without my VPSO withholding information from me.'

'I'm sorry, D. It won't happen again.' There was a pause. 'How's about I make myself useful and go see Sam Oolik at the store?'

Derek swung around on his chair so that his back was to her.

'That *is* the general idea,' he said, irritably.

A blast of lukewarm, damp-smelling air hit Sonia Gutierrez face on. In all the years she'd been flying up to Kuujuaq to work on the land-rights claim she'd never noticed just how awful the hotel was, more like some kind of overpriced homeless shelter than guest accommodation. A cleaner was supposed to come in daily whenever there were guests but it was rare that anyone showed up. On one occasion she left an empty bottle of shampoo in the bathroom and it was still there on her next visit four months later. There were no permanent staff. You checked in at the mayor's office, where they gave you a room key and, if you were lucky, a towel and a roll of bathroom tissue. At the end of each visit you'd take the phone log to the mayor's office, they'd tot up what you owed for calls, add on some insane sum to cover non-existent 'administration' and charmlessly send you on your way. The whole experience was less pleasant sojourn, more organized extortion.

Palliser's indifference to the clean-up programme was frustrating but hardly surprising. She, however, had put more than a decade of her life into pursuing first the land claim then the decontamination programme and she wasn't about to see her efforts stymied, even by something as terrible as a murder. Her fee was dependent on the works being completed and, though she was fond of Charlie Salliaq and sympathized with the Salliaq family, she had family too, back in Guatemala, and they depended on the money she sent them every month to get by.

She moved out of the hallway to the communal area where the phone sat, perched on a shabby plastic chair, and picked up the handset, flipping through her notebook for the number. Then, abandoning the call and marching back outside to her ATV, she keyed the engine and buzzed along the track that led out to the river and across the sedge meadows to Camp Nanook. Some things were better tackled face to face.

The security detail at the camp kept her waiting while they called through to Colonel Klinsman, then escorted her along the boardwalks past the lines of prefab units and tents to the administrative block, where Klinsman smiled her into his office. The camp commander's name and physique both suggested Germanic origins. He was a tall, angular man with watery-brown hair running to grey, and remote, disciplined eyes; mid- to late-fifties but fit and with no discernible paunch. She'd seen him once at the Defence Department's offices in Ottawa and a couple of times since he'd arrived on Ellesmere Island, and had found him polite but professionally formal.

Klinsman's office was a perfect reflection of the man: ordered, authoritative, if a little bland. Or perhaps elusive. It was hard to tell which. She'd known men like Klinsman back in Guatemala with offices more or less like this. Men who, despite the lawless and outrageous violence of their natures, operated on a day-to-day level every bit as though they were calmly invincible rationalists. You saw them on golf courses all the time, she'd noticed, pretending to relax in their $300 shoes.

Sonia guessed that Klinsman, like Palliser, wouldn't care too much if the clean-up job got done or not. His primary responsibility was to direct the SOVPAT exercises up on Ellesmere. The decontamination programme was a side show funded not by the military but by the Defence Department. A man like Klinsman might even resent having to play second fiddle to the bureaucrats. She didn't expect the colonel to take sides – he was too clever for that – but she did hope to be able to persuade him to put pressure on Derek Palliser to reopen the Glacier Ridge site for the clean-up crew.

She took a seat and declined his offer of coffee.

'I'm sorry we've both got caught up in this,' she said.

'It's unfortunate,' he replied carefully.

'My concern is that the case could drag on. And get pretty sticky. The local feeling is very anti-police. To be frank, they're not particularly keen on Camp Nanook either. An in-built suspicion of southerners.' She gave a brittle laugh. 'I should know. Took me a decade before I got my party invite.'

Klinsman glanced at his clock. 'I'm not sure where you're taking this, Ms Gutierrez.'

A thin needle of anxiety pricked her. She couldn't let him lose interest until she'd got what she came for.

'What I'm saying, colonel, is that the clean-up works mean a lot to these folks. It would really improve community relations to get going on them. Take people's minds off this terrible killing. Show them who the good guys are.'

'I see,' Klinsman said impeccably.

Sonia leaned in. 'I'm not sure that Sergeant Palliser shares our priorities. He's a small town man, has trouble seeing further than his own nose. A call from you, colonel . . .'

'Perhaps you're right,' Klinsman said enigmatically, checking the time again. Something inside her fell away. She'd lost his interest. Whatever she said from now on, he'd only be going through the motions. It would just be humiliating to continue. She stood and, thanking him for his time, swept out of the door.

On the drive back to Kuujuaq she allowed herself to feel discouraged. The sun had poked through some early morning cloud, sending motes of creamy sunlight onto the huddle of decommissioned buildings at Glacier Ridge. From a distance they looked like an abandoned movie set.

At the split in the track she peeled off left towards the waters of the lake. At one of the muddy banks, far from the pool in which Martha's body had been found, she dipped in a hand and splashed at the greasy water. Turngaluk, the Lake of Evil Spirits. *Tirigusukut*, taboo. How odd, she thought suddenly, that in all these years she'd never thought to ask why.

On her way to the Kuujuaq Northern Store to question the manager, Sam Oolik, Edie passed a handful of soldiers working off their hangovers on the beach. A young Inuit woman sprawled beside them, half clothed, mouth open, snoring lightly. Edie was reminded of what Luc had said last night, that Martha Salliaq had probably gone willingly with her killer. But the girl Edie knew was nothing like that luckless, discarded creature on the beach. It pained her to think of Martha following some strange white man from the south for the money in his pocket and a mouth full of promises. Martha had wanted more than Kuujuaq could offer her. Edie supposed the question was: what lengths had she been prepared to go to, what risks had she been prepared to take, in order to get it?

The store wasn't officially open yet but Sam Oolik was standing at the back with a bottle of syrup in his hand, organizing the stock.

'Hey,' he said enquiringly.

'Edie Kiglatuk.'

'I know who you are.' He was tall, strongly built, with the kind of eyes that tell two stories at once. 'You're working with the police.'

She confirmed this with a blink. 'I have a couple questions.' She carried on without waiting for him to say OK. 'Martha Salliaq came into your store on Saturday.'

Sam Oolik put a hand on his back and rubbed at some stiffness there.

'Yeah, around lunchtime,' he said warily.

'Was she with anyone? Did she seem any different? Upset?'

He shook his head then corrected himself. 'Hung-over, maybe.' He began rearranging the syrup bottles.

'Hung-over?' The word sat between them. Edie wondered whether she'd got Martha wrong after all.

'Yeah,' Oolik said. 'You know, quiet, rough, a bit spaced out.' He carried on stacking bottles. Edie got the strong sense that there was more to say but he had decided to make it tough for her. She guessed this was how it was going to be. From now on, every move she and Derek made would be scrutinized, chewed over and likely found wanting.

'You remember what she bought?'

'Aspirin. A soda.' Sam continued to fix up the shelves.

'Did you guys talk about anything?'

'Not much, just the weather,' Oolik said, finally. It had begun raining on Saturday morning. By Saturday afternoon, a thick summer mist had settled over the tundra which hadn't lifted till late Sunday.

'She say where she was heading next?'

Oolik considered this for a moment. 'She told me she was thinkin' about going egg collecting, only the wet made the cliffs slick.' He stood up. That back again.

'Alone?'

Oolik shrugged. 'Maybe, or maybe she was fixing to show that fella.' A sly almost-smile played around his lips. He'd been biding his time for this moment. Relishing his little game of hide and seek.

'A fella?' She knew enough to sound grateful for the tip-off without coming over as desperate.

'Yeah, fella she was talking with outside the store.'

'You get a look at him?' The coolness in her tone disguised the banging in her heart.

'*Unataqti.* Tall, built like a bear. First Nations. Cree if I had to take a guess. I couldn't hear them talking but from what I saw, it didn't end too well.'

She ran all the way back to the detachment. Derek listened with growing interest. When she was done, he said, 'This might turn out to be a whole lot easier than we'd imagined.'

Then he reached for the phone and dialled Colonel Klinsman's number.

7

While Derek and the colonel were speaking, Edie went into the kitchen to get something to eat. The run back from the store had brought home to her how depleted she was. She hadn't eaten properly since Monday morning and her body was starting to flag. There was tea in the kitchen cupboard and a pile of raw fish heads in the fridge. She threw the heads into a pan to fry and brewed up some tea. By the time the food was done, Derek had finished his call and was in the communications room talking to someone on the radio. She left a mug of tea and a plate of fish on his desk and went over to Stevie Killik's spot. Derek reappeared, took a sniff at the food and made an appreciative humming sound.

'That was Larsen on the radio.' He picked up a head in his fingers and sucked. 'Supplies coming in on Thursday. Timing couldn't be worse.'

It was Derek's job to oversee the docking and de-cargoing of the annual supply ship. The ship's arrival was usually a celebratory time, with families coming in from summer camp to pick up the piece of hunting or fishing equipment they'd ordered last year or to collect new supplies of medicines and food. There were barbecues and races and movie screenings. In the circumstances, it was hard to see the celebrations going ahead this year, but there was bound to be a frantic day or two when even a murder investigation was liable to get lost in the general chaos.

Edie wrinkled her nose. 'Can't you put it off?'

'Let me see. Oh yeah. Why don't I just launch an iceberg or drum up a quick blizzard?' Derek wiped his hands on his shirt. 'I may seem like a god to you, Edie, but the truth is I'm just a police.'

'Stop, you're breaking my heart.'

He fought back a smile. 'You have one?' They could go on like this for hours. A version of the old Inuit song duels, without the singing.

Derek finished his food and lit a cigarette.

'Klinsman said he'd get a camp personnel list together in the next hour or two. They got some wargame thing going on over there today. If the guy Sam Oolik saw turns out to be our man then we might be able to get this thing sewn up pretty quick.'

'Klinsman not worried about the bad publicity?'

'Seems not. I think he's been told to play nicely with the locals.'

'It might have helped if he'd passed on that message to his men.'

Derek frowned. 'We don't know for sure that the killer is *unataqti*. Though it does seem like one hell of a coincidence.' He reached out for the pen on his desk and began spinning it between his fingers. 'By the way, Klinsman told me that Gutierrez went over there first thing. She's worried I won't release the crime scene till it's too late to begin the clean-up works, apparently.'

'And?'

'And nothing. I'm not having some southern lawyer playing politics with my case.'

He put his pen down and flipped on the old radio he kept on the windowsill behind his desk. A singer was halfway through 'Amazing Grace'. Afterwards, Markoosie Pitoq's voice appealed for anyone with information as to Martha Salliaq's whereabouts over the weekend to call in on the phone line, or if they weren't near a phone, on the red radio, saying he'd patch them through.

Derek drained his tea. 'You taught the girl. Notice anything different about her?'

'She seemed pretty keen to get out of class on Friday, I guess. That was unusual for her. I asked her if she had plans, but she sidestepped me. There was some lipstick in her purse. Not many Inuit girls wear make-up.'

'Not many Inuit guys like it.'

'That might suggest she was seeing someone outside the community. She was more outward-facing than most Inuit girls her age,' Edie said.

'My guess is, we find whoever took that picture of Martha down at the bird cliffs, we'll have our killer.'

'What can we usefully do while we're waiting to hear back from Klinsman?'

Derek picked a speck of fish from his teeth. 'Why don't you go visit Martha's friend, the one in class? See if she knows anything. If Martha *was* involved with someone, my guess is she would have kept it from the family.'

Edie knocked on the door of her old school classroom. Her role had been taken over by Les Ferguson, the lean, bustle-faced *qalunaat* head teacher. Only the boys were in attendance now. Kuujuaq had emptied of all the young women with family who gave a damn. Including Lisa Tuliq. A cousin of Lisa's told Edie where she'd be likely to find the girl.

On her way out, she knocked on Chip Muloon's door.

'Hey,' he said, flashing her a sorrowful smile. 'Les told me you're gonna be helping Palliser out.'

'For a while,' she said. Could she detect jealousy, or just curiosity, in his voice? One thing about Chip, she'd noticed, he was good at making all the right noises while keeping his real feelings to himself. Like most Inuit that way.

'Any suspects?'

'I can't really talk about it.'

Chip pressed his lips together. 'No, of course not.'

She offered him a smile of gratitude, then went on. 'Did Martha ever say anything to you about a boyfriend?'

Chip steepled his hands. 'Not that I recall, but she did come to see me a couple of times, wanting to know stuff about life in the south.'

'Stuff?'

'Yeah, you know, whether it was as hot and crowded as everybody said. Whether Inuit living down there had a hard time. That kind of thing.'

'What'd you tell her?'

'I told her she was better off up here.' His eyes reached for Edie's face and rested there a moment. Then, looking away, he said, 'I was wrong about that.'

The journey to the Tuliqs' summer camp took Edie along a thin part-willow-covered track, then out across the desert pavement towards Jakeman Glacier. It was a route Edie knew from guiding hunters, though she'd never used it in the summer. Break-up coming early now, summer hunting parties usually relied on boats. For good reason. The ground was boggy and hard going, the wheels of the ATV sliding across mud slicks and throwing up sprays of meltwater. A group of snow geese flew over, cackling.

The camp itself consisted of three duck canvas tents surrounded by the usual midden of fire rings, ATVs, equipment boxes and fishing gear. A man in his forties with hair cut in a spiked flat top came out and stood, squinting, waiting for her to key off her engine.

'You the summer teacher?'

Edie clambered down from her vehicle, took off her goggles and put on her friendly face. The man introduced himself as Mattie Tuliq, Lisa's father. He didn't want Lisa in Kuujuaq right now, he said, least-wise not until Martha Salliaq's killer had been found.

'I'm not trying to get her to come back to school,' Edie said, 'I'd just like to talk to her for a few minutes.'

The man tipped his head in the direction of one of the tents.

'She's sleeping.'

'I'll wait then.'

The tent cracked open and Lisa's face appeared, looking washed out, eyelids red and swollen. It looked as though she'd had a bad night. She registered Edie, then transferred her gaze to her father, waiting for his permission to come out.

'You heard the news,' Edie began.

Lisa nodded grimly.

'I'm sorry. I know you and Martha were good pals.'

The girl pulled her T-shirt tight around her body like armour. 'Not so much. Only really at school.'

'Is that why you didn't see her over the weekend?' Edie asked.

Lisa pursed her lips. Her eyes flicked across to her father. 'I guess maybe Saturday morning I went around to her house to visit, but she said she was hung-over.'

Edie left a pause in the air. This tallied with what Sam Oolik had said.

'Any reason you didn't tell me this when we spoke yesterday?'

Lisa frowned. She crossed her arms, balling each fist under the opposite armpit. 'I didn't know someone had killed her.'

'Ever see her with a tall *unataqti*, First Nations maybe?'

Lisa shrugged. Edie couldn't work out whether she was just teenage sullen or actively holding back. 'Was it a regular thing? The drinking I mean.'

'I have no idea. Martha was kind of secretive about what she did outside school.' The girl began shifting on her feet, anxious to be gone.

Pulling out the picture of Martha at the bird cliffs, Edie said, 'You know who took this?'

Lisa shook her head. For some reason the question appeared to irritate her. For a moment she turned away, until Edie reached out and touched her elbow.

'She have any boyfriends? Drugs problems, anything like that? Any other friends you can tell me about?'

'Not really. Look, I don't know, OK? I mean she had friends but she sort of stopped really hanging out with them much.'

The girl pressed on the corners of her eyes and began to move towards her father. 'I really, really don't know anything, OK?'

On the way back to the settlement, the wind came up, bringing some temporary relief from the mosquitoes. Across Jones Sound, at the tender selvedge where the shore-fast ice met with the yearly pack, a commotion of sorts was going on in an area of clear water where the current came through. A pod of orca it looked like, thrashing about in the water. The animals had only started coming up this far north in the last year or two, one more manifestation of climate change, and they hadn't yet established a migration route. She watched them for a while. Behind her the tundra yawned wide and seemingly still, but to think of it that way was a mistake. The Arctic was all about movement, the transformation of ice into water then back again, the arrival and disappearance of vegetation, the vast annual migrations of birds and marine mammals, the ceaseless wandering of bears and caribou and wolves. Up here, the longer you stood still, the less likely you were to survive. She wondered if Martha Salliaq had understood this and it was why she had wanted to get away.

At the town hall building, she made her way down a corridor by an empty vending machine towards the radio station studio. Ellesmere Island Community Radio occupied a small room near the administrative offices. Outside, the red on-air button winked a warning. Markoosie spotted her and held up a finger. He'd extended the morning show to allow anyone who wanted to call in to get themselves to a radio or a phone. It was just winding up. A few moments later he flicked a switch then waved her in.

'Anyone call in?'

His mouth twitched. 'Not with any information. There's a bad feeling about Camp Nanook though. Folk already talking about a cover-up. People say the *unataqti* won't give up the killer in a hurry.'

'We don't yet know who the killer is.' Markoosie raised his brows and cocked his head. 'We're still trying to work out Martha's movements. Are you sure you didn't notice anything unusual when she came by Saturday?' she asked.

He rested his chin in his hand and gazed into the middle distance as though reimagining the scene. He was looking at her now, his eyes bright with tears. 'She was my *hanaji*. You know that? We were connected in here . . .' He went on, tapping his head. 'And in here . . .' A finger on his heart.

She blinked sympathy, then backtracked to the subject in hand. Right now, what Martha meant to them could wait. They had a killer to catch.

'After Martha left, what did you do?'

'I watched the game with Toolik then I came here, did my Saturday evening show. After that, I went back home and got some sleep.' He shot her a look she couldn't make out and swivelled his chair back to face his mixing desk. 'You wanna check, ask Toolik. Now, I'm sorry,' he went on in a businesslike manner, the tearful softness of a moment ago quite gone, 'but I got to finish up an insert for tonight's show.'

Markoosie's father, Toolik Pitoq, sat by himself on an old La-Z-Boy staring at an NFL game between the Maple Leafs and the Jets. It was hard to say how old he was exactly, but he had the look of someone who had survived many High Arctic winters. A querying expression weakened by the blare of the sun on ice, unsure whether the visitor was someone he should recognize. The skin on his face was brown and hardened, stretched over bones sharpened by the winter wind; his hands as calloused as an old bull walrus. She introduced herself as Sergeant Palliser's deputy.

Toolik grunted and went back to the game. 'They're with the *qalunaat* woman, the one with lotsa hair.'

'I've come to see you.'

The old man looked up in mild surprise.

'I was hoping you could tell me when you last saw Martha?'

'I don't keep track of the days too well,' the old man said, inspecting the rough terrain of his hands. 'Saturday, was it? Yeah, maybe then.' When he looked up again his expression had changed. 'This is *iktuariik*, young lady.' Taboo. He began wagging his index finger. 'We don't talk about this.' He seemed a little bewildered. She wondered how much he'd really been able to take in.

'I respect the old ways, *avasirngulik*, but we need to find whoever took Martha away before he does it to someone else's granddaughter,' she said.

'Them men at the base took her. The way those *qalunaat* are. Think they have a right to anything they like the look of.' His eyes, clouded over with cataracts, became suddenly beamy and intense. 'It was up to me, I'd take the culprit to those cliffs at the back and push him off. But that won't happen. Nothing will happen.' He shrugged, defeated, his eyes moving back to the screen. 'I don't know, I don't like to talk about *tariaksuit*.'

Edie went into the kitchenette and put some water on to boil for tea, using the break to begin on a different tack.

'Martha seem any different on Saturday? As though she'd been drinking, maybe?'

Toolik chuckled. 'Oh, so that's what it was. Markoosie won't have booze in the house, even though he knows I like a drop. Calls it *qalunaat* water. He says that's how they control us. He's my son and I love him, but he's got some funny ideas.'

'Do you remember what you and Markoosie did the rest of the day?'

His head swivelled round and there was a quizzical expression on his face, as though he found the question oddly amusing.

'We watched the game, then I listened to my son's radio show. It was a good show on Saturday. Lots of music, not too much chat. I can't stand listening to people grousing and moaning about one another.' He took the tea and for a while seemed to drift off in the steam. When he lifted his head, his eyes had gone back in time. He was looking at the floor now, as though the past was a ledge on a cliff, from where he could watch the waves battering against the rocks below and still feel the bittersweet sting of their spray on his face. He opened his mouth to speak but the words were gone. Then, with a look of puzzlement on his face, he said,

'What are you doing here, young lady, and where's Martha?'

8

Edie walked back to the detachment and retrieved the remains of the fish heads from the kitchenette. Through the back window she could see Derek returning from feeding his lemmings.

'Any luck?' he asked.

She told him it looked as though Martha had been drinking on Friday night.

'Any idea who with?'

'No, not yet.' Edie downed the last of her tea and went on. 'But I'm beginning to get the feeling something happened in Martha's life to make her stop talking to the people she loved. Chip told me she was asking him about the south. Maybe she was thinking of moving down there? Perhaps that's why she started drinking. Couldn't face breaking the news to her folks.' She picked up the last fish head and sucked out the eyes. 'Klinsman get back with that list yet?'

'Not yet. But one of us should go tell Gutierrez that running to Klinsman behind our backs could be construed as interfering with an investigation. I'm not opening up the site because she says so. We don't yet know where Martha was first attacked but my guess is that it was likely to have been somewhere in those old buildings.' The old radar station consisted of half-a-dozen units in various states of disrepair scattered across a rocky plateau which sloped down to Lake Turngaluk. 'We're gonna need to drain that pool, see if we can't find the murder weapon. I've called Joseph Oolik and told him to stand by.' Sam Oolik's cousin drove the settlement honey truck and emptied the sewage tanks twice weekly.

Edie stood and picked up her empty plate. 'I'll go have a chat with Gutierrez. Woman to woman.'

'Or should that be woman to wolf bitch? While you're at it, you might mention the drainage thing to Gutierrez, check there's nothing in that water that's likely to be dangerous. She'll have the list for the decontamination works, I'm guessing. But, Edie . . .' He lowered his voice, though there was no one else about. 'That water has a lot of Martha's blood in it. I want to keep that part from the family as far as I can. You know how Inuit can be about blood. Source of spirit, all that stuff. If Charlie Salliaq finds out, it's bound to cause trouble. I don't want the locals all over us saying we've disrespected the culture.'

'Leave it to me, boss.'

Edie pulled on her outerwear and headed for the hotel. After she called out, a door upstairs opened and the lawyer appeared on the landing. They sat on a couple of unloved chairs in the bleak TV area.

'How's the family bearing up?'

Gutierrez sighed and rubbed her hands lightly along her thighs. 'Do you have a sister?'

Edie shook her head.

'I do, back in Guatemala. Her name is Carlita,' Gutierrez went on.

Edie was struck by how unusual the lawyer was. Most of the *qalunaat* in the High Arctic were escapees, adventurers, desperadoes, drunkards, criminals and misfits. If they had families they didn't talk about them.

'Carlita and her family mean everything to me, but there was a time when I hated her.' She shot a sideways glance at Edie. 'Do you see my point?'

'I can be quite stupid when I want to be and sometimes even when I don't. Like now,' Edie said. She hoped Gutierrez didn't always talk in puzzles.

'You asked me about the family. My answer is that it's terrible for everyone, but it's worse for Lizzie. Even in death Martha outshines her. And soon, even in memory.' The lawyer pressed her hands together and, changing gear, said, 'But you came for something? Maybe Sergeant Palliser has reconsidered his position?'

'Once Derek's made up his mind, he rarely changes it,' Edie said.

Gutierrez's face immediately darkened. For a moment she struggled to collect herself.

'You know, I have a lot of experience of the military. Where I grew up, in Guatemala, there was a succession of military governments.' She leaned forward in her chair. 'The military have their own rules, Ms Kiglatuk. They justify their actions by claiming to be working for us, the people. But they are generally working only for themselves.' She pulled back and crossed her legs. 'So, why *are* you here?'

Edie outlined the plan to drain the pool at Lake Turngaluk and asked Gutierrez about possible contaminants.

'So far as I'm aware the water contains heavy metal deposits, PCBs, petroleum and creosote, that kind of thing. It's noxious but not life-threatening. Make sure whoever is doing it is well covered and wears a face mask.'

Eddie nodded. 'We'd rather keep the details from the Salliaqs. It might be distressing for them.'

Gutierrez took this in without comment. 'And what about the site?' she said.

'Ellesmere Island Police are going to need to keep the whole area cordoned off for the foreseeable future. No access.'

Edie returned to the detachment with the impression that, in spite of the appearance of cooperation, Sonia Gutierrez was not a woman to take no for an answer. Derek was in the front yard packing the trailer of his ATV. She noticed his service rifle there, then remembered the bear. There had been no sighting of it since the search and rescue flight but July was a hungry month for bears. The earlier the ice broke up, the more desperate they got.

'She doesn't have to like it. She has to respect it,' Derek said when Edie filled him in. 'I told Joe Oolik we'd meet him down by the lake.

He said he'd bring his coveralls and face mask. Sounds like that should be OK.'

They headed inland, following the track through the sedge meadows to Lake Turngaluk. In the far distance, Camp Nanook glittered in the sun and a halo of heat haze shimmered above it. The entry gate was busy with vehicles and men heading off to exercises. A whole different world.

Joe Oolik had already parked on the mud beside the pool and was working the controls of the pumping mechanism on his truck. A loud rattle obscured the sound of their engines but he caught sight of them as they drew nearer and stood waiting for them, his hands on his hips.

They parked up, keyed off their ATVs and walked over to where Oolik was standing.

The man flipped up his face mask. His mouth was turned down. 'You said contaminants. You didn't say nothing about blood.' The mosquitoes had mostly dissipated, discouraged by the vibrations from the pump, but the smell was if anything worse than before.

'It's a crime scene. Blood comes with the territory,' Derek said.

Oolik didn't move. His jaw started working. Not happy. 'This stuff I'm sucking up, where do I take it? I can't just dump it.'

Derek took off his police cap and scratched his head. He hadn't thought it through. Neither of them had.

'How's about you wait for the outgoing tide and let it run out into the sea?' Edie offered. 'We'll say a prayer.'

Oolik looked from one to the other and blinked agreement. 'OK, if that's how you want it,' he said.

'There's no need to tell anyone exactly what you found here, Joe,' Derek said. 'The condition of the water, the mosquitoes, the bad smell. Hard for the family to hear that stuff. Better not to mention you were here at all, but if anyone asks, the official line is we drained the pool in the hope of finding the murder weapon. Oh, and, you find an amulet in that water, we need to hear about that too. In fact, whatever you find, you come tell us.'

Oolik raised his head. 'What if I don't find anything? You want me to start somewhere else?'

Derek and Edie exchanged glances. The lake bed was dotted with dozens of watery concavities. The killer could easily have thrown the murder weapon into any or none of them.

Back at the Kuujuaq Hotel, Sonia Gutierrez was scanning the decontamination contract on her laptop. She'd considered raising the issue at her morning meeting with the Salliaqs but Charlie was clearly in no mood to focus on anything but the murder investigation. She was looking for anything time sensitive in the programme of works, hoping to find some loophole that might force Palliser's hand. Having helped draft it, she was pretty familiar with the contract, and couldn't think of anything that might help her case. Her reading now only confirmed that. Beside her laptop, the pages yellowing, the print on them slightly fading, was the environmental impact report, which had been drawn up just before she'd taken on the case and with which she wasn't so familiar. Checking through it now, it appeared that the contamination was all old, historical stuff from Glacier Ridge's life as an active Cold War radar station. The station had been officially closed for twenty years and non-operational for thirty. It would be hard to go back to the courts and argue that any of the work was urgent from an environmental point of view. She considered it unlikely that a case on grounds of physical safety would be successful either. The site was three kilometres from the settlement and no one really went up there, so it would be hard to argue that the condition of the buildings on the site rendered them so unstable and dangerous as to make their immediate demolition a priority.

All in all, it was disappointing and she was about to close the report when she noticed the sign-off. When she'd seen it before nothing had stood out. Then again, she hadn't been looking. But now, she could see, there was definitely an anomaly. The report's author, Dr Richard Price, had added 'Environmental Impact Division, Department of National Defence' under his signature. Yet, from her strong recollection, the environmental impact survey was supposed to have been carried out by an independent body. In all the years she'd been working with the department she'd never heard of an Environmental Impact Division and she was pretty damned sure no such division existed.

Edie and Derek decided to make a check of the area around the lake again. It was always possible that Edie had missed something the first time around. They moved slowly in circles, covering the ground in the Inuit way, looking for evidence as they went. The patches of broken willow Edie had first spotted were still there and they saw a dark stain that might have been oil from an engine and which she hadn't noticed before. Nothing else stood out except a circular area of rubble over on the far side of the pool, on the outer boundary of the lake itself. On closer inspection, though, they decided it must have lain undisturbed for a long time because there were cotton grasses and sedges scrambling over the surface. After an hour or so, and without finding anything else, they drove along the track around the lake which led to the old, abandoned buildings of the Glacier Ridge Distant Early Warning radar station. For a while they wandered around here too, but the site was littered with half-demolished buildings, rusted metal and dead equipment and it soon became clear that, with only the two of them looking, it would be a miracle if they found anything. The sun was winding around the horizon towards the north. Before too long the heat would begin to leak from it, leaving only the blank light of late afternoon.

Derek suggested they take a look around the spot where Martha had her picture taken and so they made their way along the edge of the cliffs and down the winding, rocky track towards the sea. Above them, hundreds of thousands of murres and their chicks stirred and flustered, and from a distance it looked almost as though the rock itself was alive. They parked their vehicles and walked for a while along the shoreline, their legs shin-deep in the luxuriant, guano-fed cottonheads growing there. The stink and the roar were mind-blowing and as Edie and Derek made their way they had to shout above the cacophony to make themselves heard. Not that there was much to say. Soon they'd reached the end of the bluff without seeing anything.

Martha Salliaq wasn't yet three days dead and already the natural world had entirely erased her from the place she loved best.

Derek decided to check in on Joe Oolik once more then head back to the detachment. They rattled back towards the lake. He and Joe exchanged a few words then the policeman came striding back.

'Joe says some woman showed up just after we'd gone. From the description, I'd say it was Sonia Gutierrez.' He turned and pointed up towards the rocky incline leading to Glacier Ridge. 'She headed up there. I think we should go check it out.'

They drove around the lake and up the steep path onto the ridge, from where they could see a covered ATV making its way back towards Kuujuaq along the coastal road. Putting on some speed, they caught up with Gutierrez just outside the settlement. The lawyer brought her vehicle to a stop.

'What the hell do you think you were doing tramping around an active crime scene?' Derek said.

Gutierrez raised her eyebrows. She seemed put out. 'Trying to make sense of things, sergeant, same as you.' She offered a half-hearted apology, but any fool could see she was completely unrepentant.

'Next time you'll ask my permission,' Derek said.

As she bumped off along the track, he reached up under his hat, scratched his head and wiped the sweat from his brow.

'We need to watch that one,' he said.

The personnel list Klinsman had promised them was waiting in Derek's email inbox when they got back. He pulled it up, hit a key, then another. On a table beside his desk, the printer began to tick. He removed a print-out a few pages long. Dividing the list up, Derek sat at his desk and began to run his eyes along the names. Edie went over to Stevie Killik's desk and did the same.

'Jacob Namagoose sound like an Indian name to you?' she said.

Derek's head shot up. 'Cree. My mother counted Namagooses among her relations.'

'Royal Canadian Infantry Corps. He's a private.' She marked the name with a cross. They continued on, but when nothing else sprang out Derek reached for the phone and pressed speaker.

A young-sounding voice patched him through to Klinsman.

Derek listed the name and regiment and asked if Private Jacob Namagoose was a big fellow.

'We got five hundred personnel here, sergeant. Army, navy, air force and Rangers.' The colonel sounded distracted. 'We don't list them by size, but if you'll hold a couple minutes, I'll get someone to check his profile.'

They heard him relay the information then he came back on the line.

'According to his file Jacob Namagoose is one hundred ninety centimetres. One oh five kilos. Does that answer your question?'

'We'd like to interview him,' Derek said.

A pause, then Klinsman again. 'Can I ask on what basis?'

'At this stage? Person of interest.'

There was a pause, then the sound of a keyboard. 'He's on a local exercise, but nothing I can't pull him off. An hour be OK? I'll have someone leave your name down on the list at camp security.'

9

In the early evening light two ATVs bumped along the track towards Camp Nanook. The last of the day's heat was rising from the tundra, the horizon shimmering silver-grey. To the north the great icy peak of Mount Aqiatushuk lay silhouetted in the sun. Beyond it lay the central cordillera, bound together by the great icecaps and glaciers of the remote interior.

At the sentry gate Klinsman acknowledged them both with a weak smile.

'I can't imagine you see many murders around here.' His face was solemn now, with a distant expression, as though he was going through the motions.

'More than you'd think,' Derek said.

'I sincerely hope that none of our men is in any way involved in this tragedy, but I want you to know that whatever the outcome we'll do everything we can to assist you in the investigation,' Klinsman said. 'Now, you haven't been here before.' It was a statement rather than a question. He'd obviously checked the logs.

'No,' Derek confirmed.

'It's unfortunate that your first visit has to be in these circumstances. I would have invited you for an official tour once we were properly up and running but I hope you don't mind my giving you an introduction now. It's quite a show.' The colonel's eyes softened with pride. Faintly distasteful, Edie thought, but then you never knew with *qalunaat*. Odd bunch.

Klinsman launched in with a few facts and figures, finishing up reminding Derek and Edie, as though they needed it, that this was the first time that Joint Forces North had established a major operation as far north as Ellesmere. He was particularly looking forward to joint exercises with the local Rangers, he said.

'My ex-stepson, Ranger Willa Inukpuk, is helping run the rappel training programme up at that spur camp you got a few kilometres northwest of here,' Edie offered.

Klinsman smiled blankly. He finished his introductory speech and then led them along a boardwalk towards some tents and prefabricated buildings. Men in uniform strode purposefully along the walks, alone or in groups, sometimes talking as they went, otherwise silent. They stopped what they were doing as he passed, to salute. At the end of the path Klinsman turned and directed them towards a row of tents and module buildings.

'Have you been up to this part of the Arctic before?' Derek asked, by way of conversation.

Klinsman smiled politely. 'No,' he said. 'It's a pity we're so busy, and now with this . . . I would have liked more time to explore.'

He waved them into a large domed building and showed them where to put their outerwear. He took them down a corridor and waved them to a seat in his office while he took the larger chair on the other side of the desk.

'Before we go in to see Private Namagoose, I thought I should explain a couple of things. There are currently no military police on the site, but we are working within the framework of Joint Forces North protocols. You'll understand that we will be taping any preliminary interviews conducted with military personnel whether on or off site. If this goes any further, we might require a legal presence. Just a formality. We'll appreciate being kept up to speed, so far as is possible, with the progress of any investigation, whether or not it involves our personnel.' He paused. 'Obviously, we understand that this case is your jurisdiction.'

'Of course,' Derek said. 'We appreciate that.' From the look on

Derek's face Edie deduced he was as wary of this kind of talk as she was. *Qalunatter*, they called it. Abstract, formal, designed to dazzle.

'I gave the victim's family lawyer the same message,' Klinsman added.

Derek rocked back on his chair. His face twitched. 'Ellesmere Island Police doesn't share Ms Gutierrez's priorities right now.'

Klinsman looked unruffled. 'The contract for the works at Glacier Ridge is between the hamlet of Kuujuaq and the Defence Department. We're just the clean-up detail. I've made the department aware of the situation, but strictly speaking, this is between you and them.'

'Thank you for making that clear,' Derek said. He seemed a little dazed and it struck Edie – not for the first time – that she and Derek were both more at home with sled dogs and bear migration than with the language and formality of military protocol. 'Maybe you could give us some background on Private Namagoose before we go in?'

Klinsman looked away. 'Perhaps it's best you just meet him. Then maybe you can ask any supplementary questions later?' He stood. 'Now, shall we?'

They followed him along a cramped corridor to a door marked with the number 3. Klinsman reached for the handle and they went in. The room was windowless and dominated by a large foldaway table behind which sat a thickset man in fatigues and khaki T-shirt, with his arms out in front of him and the fingers interlocked, nervously stretching himself. A video camera stood on a tripod in one corner.

Klinsman made the introductions. Jacob Namagoose blinked at his name but was otherwise expressionless.

They sat. Derek removed his hat and placed it down on the table. Namagoose stole a glance at it but did not look up.

'We are investigating the death of Martha Salliaq. At this stage we just need you to clarify a few things.'

Namagoose nodded and folded his arms around the back of his chair so that his biceps flexed and you could see the hard fist of muscle rising up on each shoulder. On his right arm there were tattooed patterns Edie recognized as aboriginal totems and a motto, *Facta non*

Verba, which she guessed meant Deeds not Words. His left arm was largely bare of decoration except for a tattoo at the top, only part of which was visible. From where Edie sat, it looked like a killer whale.

'Namagoose. That's a Cree name, isn't it?' Derek asked. Namagoose grunted. He had those deep hazel eyes through which you could see right down past generations. 'Out of?'

'James Bay.'

'My mother came from down that way,' Derek said. 'Cree also.'

Namagoose blinked, an implacable expression on his face.

'You been in the army long, Private Namagoose?'

Namagoose rocked in his chair. 'Five years. Since just after I left high school.'

'Private Namagoose has an impressive record,' Klinsman interjected. 'One tour in Iraq, two in Afghanistan.'

Namagoose spotted Edie looking at the orca tattoo. He flexed his shoulders and it temporarily disappeared. He seemed nervous, Edie thought, but was playing it cool. Relied on his size a lot, she figured.

'Do you have a camera, Private Namagoose?' Derek said.

The soldier frowned, puzzled. 'No.' He corrected himself. 'There's one on my cell phone. But there's no signal up here, so . . .' He tailed off.

'So you haven't taken any pictures.'

'No.'

Derek took out a notebook. 'Can you tell us what you did at the weekend?'

Namagoose removed his arms from the chair and leaned forward. 'Like I already told Colonel Klinsman, Friday night I got a ride into Kuujuaq and had a couple of beers there in the bar with the guys.'

'Anyone who can corroborate that?'

Klinsman confirmed that Private Namagoose had checked in with the sentry gate at 10.34 p.m.

Edie scribbled this down in her notebook. Namagoose went on. 'Saturday was a free day so I went into town again. If you can call it a town.'

'You seem to have left out the part about Martha Salliaq, Private Namagoose,' Derek said. The man stared straight ahead, working his jaw.

'I met her on my way to the store, that's all. I asked her about the mosquitoes.'

Derek raised an inquisitive brow. 'Did she look like an entomologist?'

Namagoose unlaced his fingers, rubbed the back of his head with his right hand and glared straight ahead.

'I thought she was cute. It was just something to say.'

'But you parted on bad terms,' Edie said.

Namagoose glanced sideways at her.

'I wouldn't say bad terms. I was a little pushy and she got cranky with me, so I backed off. Big deal.' Both hands were back on the desk now and he was using one to pick at the fingernails of the other.

'What happened after you left her outside the store?'

'I went to the bar. Sax was there so we shot some pool, had a beer. Then we went out on the land. Did some hiking, birding.'

'This Sax, he a friend of yours?' Derek asked.

Namagoose stretched his legs so that his left foot made contact with Edie's. He met her eye, doing his best to unsettle her.

'We hang together sometimes so I guess that makes us friends.'

'He got a real name?'

'Private Skeeter Saxby.'

'So,' Derek said, 'you and Private Saxby went out bird hunting.' Klinsman leaned forward and held up a hand, interjecting, 'We don't allow unauthorized hunting expeditions.'

'I like birds,' Namagoose said simply.

Edie shot Derek a look. He didn't believe it either.

Edie's chin flicked to the man's left arm. 'Facta non Verba. Deeds not words.'

'Special forces,' Namagoose said. He scratched at the tat with his fingernail. 'They RTU'd me.'

'Which is?'

'Returned to unit,' Klinsman cut in. 'It's a highly competitive entry process.'

'But what Private Namagoose is saying is that he didn't make it,' Derek said. His eyebrows lifted. 'Must have been a heartbreaker.'

Namagoose reddened and the cords in his neck stiffened. 'I got over it.'

'Have trouble keeping a cool head, Private Namagoose? Is that why you were RTU'd?'

Namagoose didn't answer. The sudden anger seemed to have subsided into resentment.

'Either you or Private Saxby see Martha after Saturday lunchtime?'

'Nope. Leastwise, I know I didn't. Don't figure how Sax could neither, seeing he was with me the whole time.'

'Privates Namagoose and Saxby checked into the gatehouse at nine forty-six on Saturday night,' Klinsman said.

The interview went on, but Namagoose was either telling the truth or playing close enough to his chest not to give anything away. After an hour or so when they hadn't got anything more out of him, they let him go. Klinsman escorted them in the direction of the sentry gate. A rainbow had appeared in the sky but it wasn't raining.

'We'd like to check in with Private Saxby,' Derek said.

'He's out on exercises, but I can have him recalled. Won't be tonight though.'

'Tomorrow then?'

'That's fine.' As they made to go, Klinsman held out a hand.

'My personal opinion, Sergeant Palliser, is that neither Namagoose or Saxby had anything to do with the death of Martha Salliaq.'

'Oh?' Derek enquired, in a tone of polite interest.

'If I were you, I'd be looking closer to home.'

Back at the detachment, Edie and Derek debriefed over hot sweet tea and seal blubber.

'Well, now at least we understand Klinsman's position,' Derek said. 'He'll cooperate but he thinks it's all bullshit.'

'Namagoose was lying about the birds,' Edie said.

'Sure he was. But that doesn't prove anything.'

'The guy doesn't have his own transport. Martha's ATV was at home when she disappeared. If it *was* him, they must have walked out to the lake. Would she be likely to do that with someone she'd only just met?'

'Maybe he ran into her there.'

'And happened to have a knife?'

'If he and Saxby were out hunting, sure. You wanna hunt birds, the cliffs are a pretty good place to do it. Charlie Salliaq said Martha walked out to the cliffs all the time. The lake's not far from there.'

'But Charlie didn't think she'd been to the cliffs,' Edie said.

'He didn't think she'd collected any *eggs*,' Derek corrected her. 'Maybe she went up there for other reasons.'

'To meet someone?' Edie thought about this for a moment. 'In that case, I doubt it was Namagoose. Sam Oolik said Namagoose and Martha parted on bad terms. Namagoose admitted as much himself.'

'More of a reason to want to hurt Martha.' Derek stubbed out his cigarette. 'I'm gonna call Ransom at home again, see if I can get him to move.'

While he was on the phone, Edie went over to the school building, hoping to catch Chip before he went home, but she found his door locked, and it wasn't until she was leaving the building and her eye settled for a moment on the clock in the entrance foyer that she understood why. It was already 10.30 p.m. though the sky, sunny now, with a smear of high cirrus, gave no hint of night. In a few weeks from now there would come an evening when just after midnight the sky would shift, just a little, and then it would be fall and the darkness would come down.

On her way out, she spotted Markoosie leaving the town hall building across the way and went over to meet him.

'How's the family?'

'Holding up.' His voice grew solemn. 'We're disappointed that you haven't kept us in the loop.'

So they'd heard about Namagoose. Derek had already warned her not to go into any details of the investigation but gossip moved as fast as a spooked seal here. How they were going to keep any of it to themselves, she had no idea.

'Sounds like the Cree did it,' Markoosie said.

'We're talking to a lot of folk, right now.'

Derek was still on the phone when she got back. The conversation didn't seem to be going well. She went into the kitchenette and put on hot water for tea, remembering that, except for a little blubber, she hadn't eaten since the fish heads this morning. It was too late now though. Derek's face appeared around the door.

'Any improvement on Thursday?' She passed Derek a mug of tea and added six spoons of sugar to her own.

'Apparently I'm supposed to be grateful that the lousy nose bot is willing to send anyone at all.' He took a sip of his drink. 'Any day now there'll be yet another article in the *Arctic Circular* about the failure of the law enforcement agencies to tackle the rise in violent crime across the region and someone will put the blame on the native police forces. How are we supposed to investigate crime when the resources always go to *qalunaat*?'

Edie scoffed. 'You really want me to answer that question?'

They said goodnight and Edie took her tea out to her tent. At the sleeping platform end she'd sewn a series of hooks into the canvas and from these she had hung sealskins which acted like curtains, shutting out most of the light and preventing the air from heating too much once the temperatures began to rise after what passed for the dawn. She lit her *qulliq* and burned enough seal oil to ward off the mosquitoes, then undressed. She was tired, but her mind whirred like a clockwork toy. For a while she lay staring up at the canvas. When she was a kid, after her father left, her mother would take her out into the night to look at the stars in the sky. She always said the lights were the spirits of the dead and it gave her comfort to be among them. They would sometimes stay for hours, taking it in turns to pick out the stars of their ancestors, before retreating into the warmth of the snowhouse where her mother would tell her about the old times, when people became wolves and wolves became people.

Things had changed since those days. Relations between wolves and people were clearer cut now, shapeshifting no longer held the same kind of magic as it did, and somewhere along the line she realized she had stopped believing that the stars were the ancestor spirits. For an instant she was filled with a bitter regret at how the world had altered and was changing still. But she was too exhausted for any feeling to last long and gradually, as her eyelids began to grow heavy, she felt herself moving to some deep place inside herself, and in the still spaciousness of sleep she imagined her father, Peter, smiling and stroking her hair; and opening her eyes she saw a face that did not belong to her father at all. It took a moment for Chip Muloon's features to come into focus.

'Hey,' she said.

'Hey. You were going to come over, remember?'

The softness of his mouth was on hers, a welcome heat spreading across her groin, and she reached out and began to unbutton his shirt, her hands cradling his chest, the fingers exploring the still surprising carpet of hair. There was a rush of cool air as he opened the sleeping bag and then the soft, spicy smell of his skin as he lowered himself in beside her. Her body turned automatically, one arm reaching up around his shoulders, fingers feeling for the tuft of hair at the base of his neck, while the other reached down. There was a brief, fleeting moment, when he looked at her and the blue of his eyes reminded her of the blank summer sky, but she brushed the thought away and allowed herself to drift into pleasure.

Afterwards, when their bodies were slick with sweat, they wrapped themselves in blankets, and went down to the shoreline, splashing about in the icy water, then returning to run their fingers along their goosebumped skin until they were shivering not with the cold but with pleasure once more.

And then they lay in silence on top of the sleeping skins, their bodies touching, wilfully lost to the world. Time passed. Eventually, Chip opened his mouth as if to speak. She raised a hand to stop him, unwilling to lose the closeness of the silence between them, but it was too late.

'You went to Camp Nanook.' His tone was matter of fact, as though he'd started a sentence and was expecting her to finish it.

She propped herself up on an elbow and caught those blue, expressionless eyes again. 'You know I can't talk about that,' she said.

For some reason the answer seemed to unsettle him. He removed his gaze from her and sat up a little.

'Do you think it's this guy everyone's talking about, the Cree?'

'I don't know,' she said. 'And I won't be able to think at all unless I get some sleep.'

He shifted into a sitting position. 'You know, you Inuit folks are always very eager to blame your problems on outsiders.'

She looked at him and saw that he was being perfectly serious.

'I mean, it's pretty messed up here, Edie.'

'It's pretty messed up everywhere,' she said.

He laughed. It wasn't a wholly kind laugh. 'How would you know? You've never been anywhere.'

She turned to him, her eyes fierce now.

'And you assume that you can see what northern life is like with those watery, southern eyes of yours?' She saw him start, as though stung. 'Maybe you've never been *here*, Chip, not really.'

His face grew dark. 'You want me to go?'

She settled back into the sleeping skins and turned away.

'Whatever,' she said. Sleep was cresting over her like a wave. 'I'm going to get some rest.'

Whether he left then or later, she did not know, but when she woke in the morning he wasn't there.

10

Edie went to the detachment to take a shower. Derek was out feeding his lemmings, which she was glad about, not wanting to expose him to her bad mood before she'd had a chance to wash it away. She was just finishing up when he came in and offered her some tea. Feeling better, she told him she'd go back to the tent to dress then return in five minutes.

She was crossing the little front yard and trying not to think about what Chip had said last night when she heard a pair of wings and a screech and from the corner of her eye she saw something dark and hectic bombing through the air towards her. Instinctively her arms rose to protect her face. There was a rush and whirr of wings, then the attack was over and the aggressor was sitting on the overhead cable eyeing her. A jaeger. This particular individual was either inexperienced or disorientated, because it had made its nest, a chaotic agglomeration of willow twigs and settlement trash, under the frost pilings in the back yard. She and Derek had been observing it over the past couple of weeks, assuming that sooner or later it would realize its mistake and leave, but the bird had remained, steadfastly brooding its eggs, and now there were four tiny, blind chicks to feed and protect. Only one or two would grow to adulthood, fed on the bodies of their weaker siblings. Nature threw away life with casual indifference, but flesh was precious. Nature never wasted flesh.

Walking back to the tent she wondered whether Chip had a point. Maybe she'd been a little too defensive. It was just that *qalunaat* seemed so often to label Inuit either as victims of the south or of each other. Inuit could be insular and suspicious of outsiders, but in that regard weren't they just like any other group of human beings? She reached for the tent flap, wondering if she shouldn't make Chip some peace offering without conceding her point that he really had no right to judge.

To her surprise, Willa Inukpuk was waiting for her inside the tent. Her ex-stepson was in his Rangers uniform but he looked as though he hadn't slept much. After he hadn't showed on Saturday night she'd got a message that his ATV had broken down. Since then she hadn't heard from him and wasn't expecting to either.

She went towards him, hoping to get an exchange of breaths, but his body stiffened.

'I figured you wouldn't be able to resist playing detective again,' he said pointedly. 'Everybody's talking about it at Camp Nanook. That soldier you interviewed.'

She decided to ignore the bitter tone. 'You know him?'

Willa shook his head. 'But the guys at the camp don't think he had anything to do with it and they're pretty pissed to hear that the police are just *assuming* the killer's a soldier.'

'That might be what folk in the settlement are saying, but we're not assuming anything.'

Willa sucked on his teeth as though he found this hard to believe.

'Is that why you came to see me?' Edie unwound the towel around her head and threw it on the sleeping platform. 'To tell me to back off the investigation because you're getting some heat?'

Willa shook his head and eye-rolled. He leaned his elbows on his thighs and put his head between his hands, so he didn't have to look at her.

'Maybe I should just leave.'

'I'm sorry,' she said. Their relationship had only just started to improve. She didn't want to sabotage it now. 'Don't do that.'

Willa took a deep breath. 'Listen, you should probably know, Lizzie Salliaq and I have been seeing one another these last few weeks.'

This was another surprise.

'We've been keeping things under wraps,' Willa went on. 'Be glad if you kept it that way too. You know how Charlie Salliaq is.' He inspected his fingers. 'I just thought with what's happened . . .'

She stood looking at him for a moment, struck by the sense that he was telling her this in order to avoid telling her something else.

'Did Lizzie mention something? Is that why you've come?' Edie began combing her hair with her fingers, remembering the odd little lecture she'd had from Gutierrez on the subject of sisterly relations. Wouldn't sisters share confidences? She suddenly felt on unfamiliar terrain.

'Nothing about Martha, if that's what you're getting at. She didn't tell Martha about us, either. I'm just saying, if my name comes up.'

'Why would it?'

Willa frowned. 'It wouldn't, OK? But if it did. I'm just saying.' His legs began to bounce up and down.

'So you don't think it was anyone at Camp Nanook?'

'Did I say that?' He was making no effort to hide his irritation. How often it started out OK between them and ended up like this.

'If I understood right, you seemed to be saying we should be looking closer to home.' She recalled what Klinsman had said about that. 'What about the old man, Charlie? He's pretty possessive, isn't he?'

'I don't know the fella. I fixed his ATV for him is all.' When he wasn't doing Ranger work, Willa took on mechanic jobs for cash. His father always said there wasn't an engine Willa couldn't fix. 'That's how I met Lizzie.'

'But do you think Charlie would have been capable of hurting Martha? Say, if he found out she'd been seeing someone?'

Willa narrowed his eyes, considered this a moment then shook his head. 'Might have made her life miserable for a while, but, nah, he wouldn't have hurt her. He's ornery but underneath – from what Lizzie says about him – he's OK. Martha was his favourite. Martha was everyone's favourite.'

He stood, anxious to get going. 'Listen, don't mention to anyone I came, not even Lizzie. I don't want to get her into trouble.'

*

Edie dressed in a hurry and walked over to the Pitoqs' house, intending to speak to Lizzie about her sister, see if she could detect some sense that Lizzie thought Charlie might be responsible, but the whole family were sitting in the living room with Sonia Gutierrez, evidently discussing their approach to the case, and it was clear they didn't want her around.

Back at the detachment, Derek was sitting at his desk staring at his computer screen.

'Your tea went cold,' he said without looking up.

She told him where she'd been, leaving out the part about Willa.

'I was hoping the lawyer would make things easier for us. Now I'm not so sure.' Derek lifted his arm from the table and began rubbing his temple. 'I don't like the way she's been prowling around this investigation.' He reached for the pack of Lucky Strikes sitting on his desk and slid out a cigarette.

'You think she knows something we don't?' Edie volunteered.

'About what?'

'Camp Nanook? She gave me this whole speech about dealing with the military.'

'I think she's used to keeping things close to her chest. Like I said, I think we should keep an eye on her.'

The conversation ended. Edie went into the kitchenette, opened the fridge and felt a tiny thud of disappointment. Three fried caribou ears which, by the look of them, had been in there some time.

Derek's face appeared around the door.

'If you're looking for that soup, I got peckish in the night,' he said. 'Microwaved the shit out of it. Have to get you to show me how to work that thing sometime. By the time I got it out all that was left was a little brown rock stuck to the bottom of the bowl.'

The phone rang and Derek went to answer it. Edie absent-mindedly crunched on a fried ear, thinking about how much she'd love to wash it down with a cold beer right now. It was like they said. Alcohol was the one relationship you never got over.

Back in the office, Derek was still deep in conversation. He signalled to her then, turning his attention back to whoever was on the other end of the line, said, 'No, we'll come to you. We got a lot of folk making their way in from their summer camps today to meet tomorrow's supply ship. I'd rather keep this contained.' He finished the call and hung up. His eyes were bright.

'Klinsman searched Namagoose's quarters. Seems he might have found something. A woman's amulet. Namagoose claimed it was his mother's, but they got some kind of expert there who says it's Inuit.' He bit his lip and curled his mouth. 'Dammit, though, I can't be running around after him on this. We need to be seen to be more proactive.'

Edie thought back to her conversation with Luc. Maybe the nurse was right. Murder *was* changing. And just now it looked like the Ellesmere Island Police was having a hard time keeping up.

Colonel Klinsman walked them along the by now familiar route towards the doorway of the administrative unit on the east side of the compound. His face wore an expression of practised sincerity and there was no sign that he felt rattled by this latest development.

'There may be a perfectly innocent explanation for this, but I want you to be confident that we at the camp are doing everything to cooperate with your investigation. I had Namagoose's clothing bagged up. You asked him about a camera. We didn't find one, only his cell phone, as he said. The battery was down so we recharged it. I'm happy to hand it over to you, but the only pictures you'll find are of the private's family, I'm afraid.'

'I appreciate that, colonel, but in future if I need some help I'll ask for it. We have police procedures to follow.'

Klinsman smiled graciously and in a pleasant voice said, 'Got it, sergeant. We're bringing Private Saxby in from exercises this afternoon. As you requested, I believe? You should be able to speak to him as soon as he arrives. We can search his locker too.' He hesitated, adding carefully, 'If you think it necessary, of course, but if it's all the same to you I'd rather do that after he gets here.'

He held open the door into the corridor. As they walked through, he said, 'I see you've made a start on draining the lake area. If there's anything we can help with, pumps, plant, anything like that, you'll let us know?'

'We've got it covered,' Derek said carefully.

They were at the door to room number 3 when Klinsman stopped and turned. 'We're as eager as you are to put this whole thing to bed with as little publicity as possible.' He said this very deliberately, as though the form of words had been chosen beforehand and rehearsed.

'We can all agree on that, colonel.'

Klinsman nodded, and swung the door open. The room was set up as before, with the video camera in one corner. Jacob Namagoose sat behind the table, this time with his legs spread, eyes fixed on the middle distance; determined, it seemed, not to take any notice of the newcomers.

Klinsman punched in a number on the desk phone.

'Marty? We're ready for you.' He put the phone down and explained that the camp counsel, Marty Fielding, would be joining them.

'Procedures,' Klinsman said pointedly.

It struck Edie as a little jumpy for a camp with no military police to retain the services of a lawyer. Suggested they'd been expecting trouble with the locals from the start.

A plump, dark-haired man in uniform knocked and came in carrying a folder of papers and a ziplock bag. He seemed nervous and out of sorts, a dark half-moon of insomnia slicked beneath each eye. Edie recalled what Chip had told her, that thirty per cent of Arctic postings returned to the south with some kind of mental disorder. Looked as though Marty Fielding might be among them.

He handed over the ziplock bag to Derek, who peered at it before passing it to Edie. Inside was a small, delicate bracelet exactly matching Markoosie's drawing.

'Our expert said you guys don't give these things away. Don't sell them either,' Fielding said.

All eyes turned to Namagoose, who sat in silence, a look of boredom on his face. The orca on his tricep twitched its tail.

'Tell Sergeant Palliser what you told me,' Klinsman said.

Namagoose leaned back in his chair, looking as relaxed as a sunning seal.

'I didn't do nothing,' he began.

'How's about we talk about what you *did* do, soldier,' Derek said.

Namagoose sighed, as though what was being asked of him was unreasonable. 'Friday night I took the shuttle into Kuujuaq to have a drink.'

'Meet the local women?' Derek cut in.

'That ain't illegal, is it?' Namagoose had spent an hour or so in the Anchor then taken himself off to the Shoreline Bar. 'There was this girl standing there.'

'Martha Salliaq,' Derek confirmed.

Namagoose didn't answer. 'She asked me for a drink. She said the guy behind the bar would only give her a soda. She was upset so I got her a beer.'

'She say why?' Edie asked.

Namagoose shrugged. 'Why all women get upset. Gotten into a fight with her boyfriend. That's what she said, anyhow.'

From the corner of her eye, Edie saw Derek and Klinsman exchange glances, something between men she couldn't pick up on.

'We had a few drinks, she said she was hungry so we went to get some hot food from that dump around the back,' Namagoose went on.

'What time was that?'

'Around seven forty-five, maybe eight.'

'Were you drunk?'

Namagoose's jaw pulsed. 'A little, maybe. There's nothing says a man and a woman can't have a drink together.'

Derek nodded. It was a fair point. 'Did you go on anywhere else?'

Namagoose closed his eyes and groaned, a cornered man waiting for the first punch to hit. 'Look, OK, I'm gonna tell you the truth here. The girl asked me back to her house. She was up for it, man. I didn't force her or nothing. She was all over me.'

'So you had sex?' Derek asked.

'You Inuit men don't think much of us Cree, I know that.' A smirk slid across Namagoose's face. 'But seems your women got different ideas.'

Derek let this pass. 'What did you do afterwards?'

'I came back here. Didn't want to get listed AWOL.'

Klinsman interrupted. 'You and Saxby clocked in together.'

Namagoose looked shifty but he said nothing.

'Did Saxby come back to Martha's house too?' Derek asked.

'Uh nuh.'

'You sure about that?'

'Yup.'

Edie found Derek's gaze. He blinked to signal that he'd sensed Namagoose's lie and went on,

'Tell us about the amulet.'

Namagoose leaned forward, his forearms resting on the solid muscle of his thighs. 'She gave it to me. Said she didn't need it no more. Got out this little pocket knife and sliced it right off her wrist.' Namagoose's eyes flashed about then landed on the ziplock bag. He began gesticulating with his hand. 'Take it out of that plastic, you'll see. She just cut the thing clean off.'

'She said she didn't need it any more,' Derek repeated. 'What did she mean by that?'

'I don't know, man.' There was a tone of righteous indignation in Namagoose's voice, as though there was something ridiculous or maybe demeaning in the question. 'People say all kinds of shit when they're wasted.'

'Can you describe the knife she used?' Edie said. She recalled seeing a small pocket knife in one of Martha's drawers and thinking nothing of it. Everyone on Ellesmere kept a blade of some sort.

Namagoose made a space about ten centimetres long between the forefinger and thumb of his right hand to indicate the length. 'Mother-of-pearl handle, maybe.'

The description fitted. Edie tried to catch Derek's eye but he was staring intently at the Cree.

'You took it, didn't you? What else did you take from Martha Salliaq?' The counsel raised his eyebrows but Namagoose answered anyway.

'Say *what*? Some shitty Inuit thing don't mean nothing to me. Look, we were both pretty drunk. Maybe I made her a few promises I didn't intend to keep,' he added, trying to sound reasonable, 'but I didn't have nothing to do with what happened. Nothing, zero. She was unhappy so I cheered her up. That's all.' Edie looked up. Namagoose was staring straight at her, that tree-like stillness in him; maybe trying to unsettle her.

'What did you two fight about on Saturday morning in front of the store?' Edie said.

Namagoose's nostrils flared with irritation at the question, but he kept his cool. From his side of the room Marty Fielding signalled to him to continue.

'I told you, she thought I was being pushy, she told me to back off. Wasn't anything else in it. I tried it on – that's what men do.' He looked at the men in the room for confirmation. 'But I didn't really care whether she said yes or no.' Namagoose sat back in his seat, brow furrowed. 'She seemed OK or I wouldna gone after her. She wasn't some skank type.'

'But you still expected sex from her again and got mad at her when she wouldn't give it to you.'

Namagoose's eyes rolled. 'I was fine about that. So she didn't want to see me again? Big deal. You win some, you lose some. It was *her* who got mad at *me*.'

'And you didn't think to mention any of this to us before?' Edie said.

An expression of alarm moved momentarily across Namagoose's face. Under the table the private's left leg was jiggling about like a fish on a hook, all traces of his earlier calm gone.

'You people and my people don't get along,' he said simply.

'Which people you talking about, private?' Derek sounded riled, maybe at his own failure to draw Namagoose out the first time.

'Inuit people.' He looked up and there was a sly cast to his eyes. 'Eskimos.'

Derek's face went red. Using the E word was provocative and

Namagoose knew it. 'That didn't seem to worry you when you had sex with Martha Salliaq,' he said.

'Martha and me, we pretty much had the same opinion of this dump. She didn't wanna be up here either. Couldn't wait to get away,' Namagoose said. 'Sex was her idea.' He added, petulantly, 'We were all drunk.'

'All?' Edie interjected.

'I mean me and the girl.'

Namagoose folded his enormous arms. 'You can't just pin this on me because I'm Cree. It's discrimination, I have rights, man, I have rights.'

Derek took a breath and leaning forward said in a calm voice, 'No one's taking anyone's rights away. We'll follow up your story with Private Saxby. If it doesn't check out, then it doesn't matter who your people are or whether or not I like them or they like me, you're in deep shit, brother.'

Namagoose looked up from under his eyelids, a thunderous expression on his face. 'I ain't your brother,' he said.

On the return trip Edie and Derek stopped off at Lake Turngaluk. Joseph Oolik reported that he'd gone home around ten o'clock yesterday evening and only got back an hour or so ago. He'd filled the tank several times and, as Derek had asked, driven the truck over to the coastal track and discharged its contents out into the Sound. One time a pod of orca had come in close to shore, no doubt smelling the blood, but he'd squared what he was doing with his conscience and said a prayer like they'd suggested. Now there was virtually nothing left except mud.

'I'm fixing to finish up sometime today,' Joseph Oolik said. He wiped his hands together as if he was trying to rid them of something. 'This place gets to a fellow. Aside from, well, you know, the thing that happened.' He seemed profoundly uncomfortable. 'If I didn't have so much respect for the Salliaqs as a family I'd have left long before now,' Oolik said. He stretched his neck to take in the *inuksuit* all around. 'You see that, every last one of 'em pointing away.'

Derek smiled. 'That's nothing but how folk built them, Joseph.'

Oolik tutted and shook his head. 'Well, that's as you say, sergeant, that's as you say.'

They left him to finish up and on their way into the settlement took a detour by the run-down clapboard outhouse currently serving as the Shoreline Bar. The building was closed and there was no one about.

'No point wasting time waiting,' Derek said. 'We'll go back later.'

Next stop the nursing station. The place was always busy around resupply as patients showed up early in the hope of being first in line for a script for some of the new medicine that would be coming in with the ship. Luc was in his office looking tired, his hair rumpled into strange crests where he'd been pulling at it. He'd finished taking the preliminary samples from Martha Salliaq's body late last night. They were now labelled up in the freezer, waiting for the arrival of the forensics team. He had yet to take the elimination samples from the family but was intending to do that too once his morning clinic was finished.

'You seen any of them since last night?' Derek asked.

'I went by Markoosie's house late to ask if anyone needed something to help them sleep but they said they were OK,' Luc said.

'How they seem to be holding up? Anyone behaving oddly, maybe, a little out of character?'

'I'm not sure they've really taken it in yet. One thing. Confidentially, I think Charlie Salliaq's sick. You see how pale he's looking? I noticed his gums are swollen and he looks exhausted. He's been having nose-bleeds for some time and I did suggest he come see me about it a couple weeks back but he gave me a spiel about *qalunaat* medicine. One more way white men control Inuit, blah blah blah. It was quite something.'

'Charlie's an equal opportunity bigot, I wouldn't take it personally,' Derek said drily. 'But thanks for letting us know.'

Luc responded with a nervous smile.

At that moment the front door swung open and Chip Muloon strode through the waiting room. He nodded a greeting.

'What's he doing in here?' Derek said.

Luc followed Derek's gaze. 'He's interested in the annual ship's medical records for the research he's working on. I keep the files in a cupboard, historical stuff . . .' Luc faltered, suddenly remembering Edie's connection to Chip, and added, 'But I guess you'll already know that, Edie.'

'We don't talk about each other's work,' Edie said. She wanted Derek to know she had boundaries.

Luc checked his watch and threw his hands in the air. 'I'm sorry, guys, but I really have to start clinic.'

As they were going out the door he called them back.

'Oh, I almost forgot. It's just been crazy this morning. Those two fellas from the Defence Department?'

Derek and Edie exchanged alarmed looks. Luc picked up on them. 'The ones who came over to look at Martha?'

Derek's eyes widened. 'Military?'

'Uh, I think they said Defence Department. No uniforms. Any case, they told me you and Colonel Klinsman had both authorized it.'

Derek moved back inside the door. 'What did they want?'

'To see the body. Take a few photos.'

'That all they took?'

'I didn't see them take anything else, and I was with them the whole time.' Luc swung his head. 'Sorry, folks, I should have checked.'

Derek gave him a reassuring smile. 'Don't worry about it. I'm sure it was just routine.'

Edie waited until they were outside. 'What was that about?'

Derek pursed his lips in the way he always did when he was thinking something through. 'Maybe they're looking for an excuse to cancel the clean-up, like Gutierrez said. Or maybe it's just that the body was found on ex-Defence Department land. I'll bring it up next time I speak to Klinsman.'

They separated, Derek returning to the detachment while Edie went back to the Shoreline Bar. The front door was un-padlocked now and the owner, Tom Silliq, was making his way around a ragged assortment of cracked plastic tables and chairs with a greasy mop. The Shoreline didn't have a licence like the Anchor, so it was officially illegal. She remembered reading a piece in the *Arctic Circular* a while back which talked about the Kuujuaq Council of Elders voting in personal limits on alcohol orders. The limits were wildly over-generous and those who didn't drink often sold their allowances to those who did, so she supposed it hadn't been hard for Tom to get the place stocked and running. Locals avoided it, saying there were too many *unataqti* and Tom's prices were too high, none of which bothered Tom any.

When he saw her Tom stopped what he was doing and leaned on his mop. There was a roll-up in his mouth. When he removed it, Edie could see one side of his lip was broken and cankerous.

'You're the teacher.' He poked at her with the stub. His fingernails were yellowed and heavily ridged. 'Out of Autisaq, Maggie Kiglatuk's people.'

'That's right.'

'Why you working for the Lemming Police?'

Derek had told her he and Silliq had had words a couple of times over graffiti and loose dogs, then once more recently over his bartending activities; and Derek had heard the rumours that Silliq was effectively pimping local girls to the soldiers at Camp Nanook, though no one had yet produced any evidence of this.

'Fella ain't one of us. His people don't come from around here.'

'Nor do our people, you remember your history,' Edie said. 'In any case, I've come about Martha Salliaq.'

The bar owner wiped his nose on the back of his hand. 'Take a seat,' he said. 'You want a beer?'

'Yup, but I'm not gonna have one,' she said. 'Gone that way too many times in the past.'

Silliq let out a knowing chuckle. 'I had a loonie for every time someone said that to me. Doesn't stop 'em though.'

'It stopped me. I was a lousy drunk,' Edie said, humouring Silliq now. 'You wouldn't have liked me.'

'Don't know if I like you now, working for that Lemming Police.'

'How's about I'm working for Martha Salliaq. For the family.'

Tom raised an eyebrow and considered this. 'I guess that makes it different,' he said.

'You remember Martha coming in here on Friday, Tom?'

'Sure I do.' He had a disconcerting habit of picking at his ulcerated lip as he spoke. It made him hard to understand and harder still to look at. 'I went outside to fetch some more beer from the store, she was sitting on the little wall I got out there. Face was all puffy like she'd been crying. But I told her to come in, sat her down, gave her a soda. It was early, hardly anyone in the bar.'

'Know what she was upset about?'

He sucked his teeth. 'Oh you know how girls are. I didn't ask her about it.'

'Did she go home?'

'I guess so, eventually.'

Edie frowned and Tom Silliq went on.

'A while after I left her, some fellas come in, *unataqti*, I'm setting them up a few beers and the next thing she's joined them. They were talking and laughing. It was getting busy and she seemed OK, so I forgot about her.' When his eyes blinked, his nostrils flared.

Edie pulled out the mugshot of Namagoose that Klinsman had given them.

'Fella she was with look anything like this?'

'Oh yeah.' He stabbed at the image with a yellow fingernail. 'The tall one.' He turned and began rearranging the coasters on the bar. With his back to her, said, 'The other one was smaller, hair the colour of piss, skin like piss, looked like one big piss you ask me.'

'They all leave together?' Edie had returned from Camp Nanook convinced that Namagoose had lied about Saxby's involvement. Here was a chance to catch him in the lie.

Silliq closed his eyes, reluctant to say more. 'Look,' he grumbled, 'I can't afford to have the *unataqti* decide not to drink here any more. Any case, I told you everything I know. I got busy. I didn't see the girl leave.' He pushed himself up from his chair and reached for the mop. 'Busy now, come to that.'

Seeing she wasn't going to get anything more out of him right then, Edie made her way back to the detachment, making a mental note to go back later, stand old Silliq a drink or two.

Derek was already by the door, pulling on his outerwear. He reached for his hat and pointing to her boots he said, 'No need to take those off. We're going back to Camp Nanook. Klinsman's got Saxby. They've searched his locker. Man's knife is missing.'

11

Sonia Gutierrez had been sitting in the communal area of the hotel, leafing through copies of the documents in the decontamination agreement between the settlement of Kuujuaq and the Defence Department until they'd given her a headache. Remembering the Tylenol in the hotel kitchen, she now made herself some coffee, got the pills and went up to her room.

She tried to work out why it was that the agreement seemed to mean so much to her. A young woman – her client's beloved daughter – had been horribly killed. You'd think that might be her primary concern, but something in her just wouldn't let the clean-up go. All her life she'd been fighting power, first in Guatemala, then in Ottawa and now here in the High Arctic, and she was intimately acquainted with the way power covered up after itself, the tiny gaps and small inconsistencies it left behind. The timing of the girl's death, just before the start of the clean-up, and Klinsman's eagerness to cooperate with the police investigation had set alarm bells ringing in her mind. The anomaly in the environmental impact report increased their pitch. There was nothing she could put her finger on right now, but long years of experience had taught her to trust her instincts. And her instincts told her that something wasn't right.

What she really needed was someone to talk all this through with, a fellow lawyer or maybe just a good and trusted pal, but after the embezzlement scandal, lawyers she had once counted as her friends no longer wanted anything to do with her in case her near-disgrace rubbed off on them. There were one or two people in Ottawa who remained on her side but she couldn't in all honesty call them confidants. The obvious candidate was her sister in Guatemala but she'd tried calling her a couple of times and not got through.

And there was Chris Tetlow. Calling Chris would mean swallowing a little pride, but the way she was feeling now she figured it was probably worth it. Picking up her phone card, she went downstairs and tapped in the various codes until she reached Tetlow's cell. The journalist picked up. From the slur in his speech and the time it took him to register her name, she guessed he was in a bar and that he'd been there some time.

'Hey, Son, wassup?' There had been a moment, a few years back, when Tetlow had been one of her loudest cheerleaders. He was a freelancer then, one of the few in the north, with a particular interest in native affairs. They'd scratched each other's backs and more. Tetlow hadn't behaved well, dumping her by text, and she'd subsequently discovered he'd been seeing someone else almost the whole time they'd been together. For a while relations between them had soured but, mostly through her efforts, they'd now managed to build a cordial if slightly awkward professional relationship. These days Tetlow worked for the *Arctic Circular* based out of Yellowknife and Iqaluit. Since so much of Gutierrez's work involved native land claims it was useful to her to have Tetlow onside.

'You hear about the murder of that girl in Kuujuaq, near the SOVPAT camp earlier in the week? Martha Salliaq?'

She could almost hear the cogs in his mind turning over. 'Rings a bell.' He sounded remote, as if he was too drunk to take this in or maybe just didn't care, but she felt so in need of an ally right now that it almost didn't matter.

'You up there now, Son, or what?' He'd gone somewhere quieter so that she no longer had to strain to hear him.

'Yeah. I've been negotiating a clean-up of the old DEW station at Glacier Ridge. You remember?' They'd talked about it a few times over the years. 'Thing is, Chris, I can't put my finger on it but I think there's something going on. Apart from the murder, I mean, but maybe connected to it.'

'Go on.' Tetlow's journalistic instincts had kicked in and he sounded almost sober now.

Sonia outlined the events of the past few days, including the anomaly she'd found in the documents.

'Isn't Derek Palliser in charge up there? The lemming fella? There's more to that man than meets the eye. He comes over as some small town loser, obsessed with rodents, then last year he pulls off this amazing investigation into a big-time Russian oil developer. Made international waves.'

Sonia hadn't been up on Ellesmere last year but she remembered reading about the case in the papers.

'Well, I'm beginning to think he's either amazingly naive or he's working with the Defence Department.'

There was noise in the background at Tetlow's end.

'Maybe he just wants to get the investigation out of the way as quickly as possible so they can get on with the clean-up? You think of that?' Tetlow's voice flared in and out, as though he was focused on something else in the room.

'No, Chris, that never occurred to me . . . Of *course* I thought of that.' She paused. *Dios mío*.

There was a pause.

'I met that girl's mother one time by the way,' Tetlow said suddenly. 'Alice. A story I was working on a while ago about a bunch of babies that died at birth in the seventies and eighties.' He hesitated. 'Uh, I guess that would have been before your time. Any case, it didn't stand up.' She heard a woman's voice, then Chris say, 'Two minutes,' and he was back on the line again.

'But listen, you got anything more concrete?'

'I told you all I got.'

He sounded disappointed.

'Maybe you should come up here, help me get some more.'

The woman's voice again, louder this time.

'Uh, look, Son, I gotta go. Call me if you get any closer to something . . .'

'Concrete?' she offered, but he'd already put down the phone.

Back in her bedroom she flicked through the documents once more. It made sense to go back to the beginning and take a look at the site plans. There were two sets, as it turned out, the ones she'd worked from and a much earlier version from before she'd taken on the case. The early drawings dated from 1960, not long after the site had been built. She'd never had cause to look at this set before, partly because the clean-up negotiations had always worked from drawings dating from 1974, and partly because the earlier documents were hidden away in an obscure addendum which had been drawn up before she'd taken on the case. These days the site no longer much resembled either set of plans. The Defence Department had torn down some of the structures after they'd abandoned the place in the mid-1990s. A few of the remaining buildings had got frost damage and crumbled and a few more had succumbed to the 180-kilometre-per-hour winds that regularly swept down from the Arctic Ocean.

Nonetheless, the plans showed that during the fourteen years between 1960 and 1974 there had been considerable additions to the permanent structures on the site. In itself this was no big deal. Many of the radar stations on the Distant Early Warning line had been remodelled over their thirty-five-year lives, as monitoring technology became more sophisticated and strategic needs changed. What seemed peculiar about Glacier Ridge was the extent and type of enlargement. The 1960 plans showed the classic radar main station format, buildings arranged in an H and built into the prevailing northwesterlies. By 1974 the site had more than doubled in size. The basic H shape remained, but the area had been filled in by a more random-looking cluster of buildings, none of which were facing northwest. This kind of expansion could only have resulted from a change in function. In which case, what had the station become – and why, in the decade she'd been involved in negotiations, had no one ever mentioned the change?

Sonia stared into the middle distance for a moment, trying to recalibrate her thoughts. Her head told her she was on to something.

But what?

12

For the third time in thirty-six hours Derek and Edie found themselves at the sentry gate at Camp Nanook. This time Klinsman kept them waiting for a few minutes, and apologized with his usual formality, but he seemed if anything more distracted and for the first time, Edie thought, wary.

'Private Saxby was on exercise in Alert. We flew him down as soon as it was practical.' The joint military and weather station lay seven hundred kilometres to the north, not far from the Pole. It was a desolate spot, a death zone, and Edie had to wonder what soldiers would do up there. 'You should know that we allow the men here to carry their own knives to use in training. Each soldier begins exercise with a kit inventory. Private Saxby flew out here with a SOG Seal Team brand hunting blade. That knife is currently missing from his locker. He's not yet aware that we know.'

'We appreciate your cooperation,' Derek said, 'though it seems that message didn't get through to your men who went down to the nursing station. I had to find out about them from the nurse.'

They had reached the iron-grey dome of the command office. Klinsman hesitated at the door. 'I apologize. I asked them to call ahead.'

'I'm assuming they were plain-clothes investigators? But perhaps you could tell us exactly why they were taking photographs of the victim's body?'

Klinsman's hand hovered over the door handle.

'I'm afraid you'll have to take that up directly with the Defence Department.' There was a squeal of metal as the door swung open. He directed them along the corridor. 'As I understand it, the visit was routine protocol. The department can be protective of their sites, even the abandoned ones.'

'The site belongs to the people of Kuujuaq,' Derek said firmly. 'And as I've said before, I'd be glad in future if you'd leave procedural matters to me.'

Klinsman nodded. His body gave off a relaxed vibe but his voice was rattled. 'Of course. An oversight. But unfortunately the men have already left. If they'd had any problems, I'm sure they would have let you know.'

They were standing outside door number 3 now.

'Shall we focus our attentions on Private Saxby?' Klinsman said.

The missing knife's owner was in the same chair that Jacob Namagoose had occupied only hours before, but there any similarity between the two men ended. Skeeter Saxby was a wan-faced man-boy, slim-built with freckled skin and dirty-blond hair. One long piss to look at, just as Tom Silliq had said. He was cracking his knuckles and seemed edgy and ill at ease.

Klinsman showed the two visitors to the same plastic seats, called in Marty Fielding, repeated the terms on which the interview would take place and asked Saxby if he understood. Without lifting his eyes, Saxby said he did, and returned to his knuckles.

Derek leaned forward and placed a hand on the table.

'Nervous?'

Saxby stilled his hands. His right leg began to jiggle. He pushed it down and returned his arms to the table, and as he did so his sleeve travelled up his arm and a killer whale tattoo appeared. Edie glanced at Derek and saw that he had spotted it too.

'Got no reason to be,' Saxby said.

Derek scrutinized his face for a moment. 'That so?' He leaned back and folded his arms across his chest. 'Then why do you think you're here?'

Saxby reddened, a tic appeared under his right eye, but he said nothing.

'I see you and Private Namagoose got matching ink,' Derek went on.

Saxby blinked and glanced at the spot on his arm. Edie saw him fight back a grin. Dumb ass had no idea how much trouble he was in. 'What you do, nail a few Taliban?' Derek said.

Saxby was smirking now. 'Something like that.'

'That why killing Martha came so easy?'

Saxby's face fell. He turned to look at Klinsman but neither the colonel nor the counsel appeared to be willing to come to his rescue.

'We didn't touch that girl.' Saxby's eyes glistened. His voice was trembly. Easy to break, Edie thought. Give up his friend too, most like.

Evidently, Derek had the same thought. He went on.

'You owe Namagoose something? Is that why you're covering for him? You should know he's not returning the favour. Your buddy already told us that you had sex with Martha Salliaq at her house.' A stretch, but not an unreasonable one. Neither Derek nor Edie believed Namagoose's story that he and Martha were alone in her house. Edie figured he was trying to keep Saxby out of it to protect him, or more likely because he knew the kid was plenty stupid enough to blow it for both of them.

Saxby's eyes widened. His breath quickened. 'I didn't touch that girl.'

'You're lying. When the forensic team comes and checks Martha's room they're gonna find your DNA, aren't they, Private Saxby?'

Saxby sat up indignant, then he sighed and fell back. His forehead folded like dough. 'I was sorry that girl died, sir; she was a nice girl and all. But me and the Goose didn't have nothing to do with killing her. We only went back with her on Friday night because she asked us to. I didn't even . . .' He fell silent.

Edie caught Derek's eye. They were seconds from the truth.

'You didn't even what?' Edie said.

Saxby reddened. 'I just looked on.' Clearly he thought that this excused him. Even dumber than she thought.

'Is that why you went back on Saturday and killed her, because she wouldn't have sex with you?' Edie went on.

Marty Fielding took a deep breath but made no attempt to intervene.

'You explain why your knife is missing, Private Saxby?' Derek's tone was mild.

Saxby's face drained of colour. He leaned his elbows on his legs and put his head in his hands. For the first time he realized what a mess he was in.

'I can explain the knife.' His voice was quiet and there were beads of sweat on his forehead.

'Saturday I met the Goose in that place.'

'The Anchor Bar?' Derek cut in, to throw him.

Saxby hesitated then frowned. 'No, the other one.'

'We coming to the knife?'

Saxby took a sidelong glance at Klinsman. 'The Goose said he'd set a snare near where he'd seen some jack rabbits, wanted us to go back up there, see if there was anything in it.'

'We don't allow weapons off-base unless they've been authorized,' Klinsman interjected.

'Seemed like a long way to go for jack rabbits to me. We took a couple half-sacks to pass the journey. There was this big old buck in the snare, so we killed it and I skinned it with my knife while the Goose made up a fire.' Saxby explained that the two men left when the rain began to come down and walked directly back to camp. 'We was soaked so bad, you can ask anyone in barrack,' Saxby said. He didn't notice that his knife wasn't on him till Sunday, when he was due out on exercises.

A silence fell. Klinsman glanced first at Derek, then at Edie.

'You'd be able to show us this place?' Derek said.

'I reckon so.'

13

Klinsman, Fielding and Saxby rode in a jeep while Edie and Derek brought up the rear on their ATVs. At Lake Turngaluk they waved briefly to Joe Oolik then turned off towards Glacier Ridge and up onto the bird cliffs. To the south, the waters of Jones Sound shimmered silver in the summer sun and in the far, far distance, where the earth curved, heat trembled the craggy coastline of Devon Island. The journey, which Saxby said had taken him and Namagoose an hour and a half to complete on foot, lasted less than fifteen minutes.

Saxby led them towards a sheltered area, surrounded by low rock, where there was a fire ring and a number of beer cans. Burnt remains of a small animal lay scattered over the site, but there was no sign of Saxby's knife.

'Maybe someone took it?' Saxby offered, scoping about.

'You say you left here and went back directly to camp?' Derek said. A raven wheeled overhead and landed on a bank of rotting snow a short distance away. Saxby nodded a yes.

'Show us the route.'

Saxby pointed out a path in the willow with his hand.

Derek eyeballed the soldier. 'We're going to walk that route, soldier, and you better hope we find that knife.'

Anxious to get on, Klinsman asked if the interview was done and moments later Edie and Derek watched the three men disappear down the track back towards the camp.

After they had gone Derek and Edie walked the route. They did not find the knife.

*

By the time they got back they were both hungry. Edie made tea and nibbled on a caribou ear while Derek chowed down on a bowl of ramen noodles.

'You think they did it together?' she said.

'Could be. Saxby didn't ship out to Alert till Monday so they had Sunday to work up a consistent story.'

'You seem real sure Namagoose is the one,' Edie said. She hadn't yet been able to ditch the version of events in her head that had Martha with a secret boyfriend or that something had happened to her on Friday afternoon between leaving school and the time Silliq saw her crying on the wall.

'You got any better ideas?' Derek said. 'You saw how Namagoose is. A blowhard. He admitted to having sex with Martha the evening before her death and he was seen arguing with her the day she died. He said himself he was trying to fix up another date with her. When she refused he got mad and killed her. Man has a violent temper. What cost him a place in the special forces. Oh, and by the way, I checked out that special forces training. Turns out it includes an intensive course in Eskrima, Filipino martial art. Hand-to-hand knife combat. Namagoose knows his blades.

'You saw the view from their fire ring. Right over the bird cliffs. They could have spotted Martha collecting eggs and invited her to come cook them, share a beer maybe. Kind of kiss-and-make-up for Namagoose's shitty behaviour outside the store. They even had the knife on them. Maybe Saxby participated, maybe he just watched. We lean on him a little more, I think we'll get to the truth.'

This all made sense. So why, in Edie's reckoning, didn't it tell the whole story?

'What about the photograph?' she asked.

'One of them is obviously lying about the camera.'

Edie's throat tightened. 'The picture was taken before the *unataqti* even arrived.'

'Forget the photograph, Edie. It doesn't prove anything either way.' He raised his bowl to his lips and finished off his noodles.

Edie watched him with a growing sense of alarm. Was the pressure on him to close the case getting too much, she wondered? Wasn't the first rule of a police investigation to keep an open mind?

'Her purse was full of make-up. She was meeting someone. Then Silliq sees her a couple of hours later crying on a wall. And Namagoose mentioned a boyfriend.'

'Well, he would, wouldn't he? Look, it's been a long day. I've still got prep for the arrival of the supply ship to do, plus I'll need to check with Luc that we're all set for Anna and the forensics guy tomorrow.' He went over to his desk and started shuffling some papers. 'You could check with that takeout place next to the Shoreline Bar, see if anyone remembers Namagoose and Saxby coming in with Martha on Friday night? After that, why don't you take the evening off? There's not much else we can do till tomorrow. I'll come find you if anything happens.'

The sky was now a matt-grey sheet. On the corner by the store and the school building, Edie stopped to think. Derek's haste to close the investigation bothered her. She'd seen that he was a brilliant investigator when he wanted to be but she'd also noticed that he sometimes had to be reminded not to take the easy road. It hadn't helped that Klinsman seemed to be encouraging him to tie the case up quickly. The colonel was obviously eager to resolve the investigation as quietly and painlessly as possible so that he could get back to the main event. Maybe Namagoose and Saxby *were* the killers but, in the absence of conclusive evidence, the Ellesmere Island Police owed it to Martha to investigate every possible scenario with equal vigour. You didn't fix on a hunting ground until you'd explored all the terrain.

The eatery Derek liked to refer to as the 'takeout place' – and most locals knew as the Shack – was a summer business Tom Silliq's wife Susie had set up in an old fishing shed behind the Shoreline Bar. Edie had been there a couple of times when she'd first arrived and was living in the cabin. She and Susie had got chatting once or twice. Susie was a straight talker, unusual among Inuit, and Edie guessed she'd seen a thing or two, being married to Tom. Susie explained that in past summers the Shack had catered mostly to the scientific expeditions passing through the settlement and to men coming into town to pick up supplies, but this year she'd expanded the operation in the hope of attracting *unataqti* from Camp Nanook. Mostly, Susie managed the Shack on her own, with the help of her and Tom's grown-up daughter, Louisa. This summer she'd taken on another pair of hands for the weekend evening shift, a young southerner by the name of Rashid Alfasi, who worked a day job taking weather readings at the meteorological station.

'Some folk are a bit sniffy I gave the job to an outsider,' she said to Edie one time. 'Say he can't be trusted.' Then she'd roared with laughter and added, 'They say the same about you too.'

Straightening herself up now, she said, 'You need to ask Rashid about last Friday. I was too busy in the kitchen.' She slapped her thighs, keen to get on with her work. 'He's renting the doctor's old cabin, you wanna find him.'

Rashid Alfasi's house was an announcement that he hadn't lived long in the north. None of the usual mess of dog kennels, hunting equipment, drying fish or sealskins stretched on racks, no old and rusted equipment, homebuilt storm shutters, vehicles cannibalized for their parts. She walked up the steps and knocked on the door, figuring that Rashid, being *qalunaat*, wouldn't appreciate her just walking in. When there was no answer, she let herself into the snow porch, opened the inner door and stood on the doormat.

The living room was more homely and colourful than she'd anticipated. On the floor there were richly woven rugs of a kind Edie had never seen before. The surfaces were covered with tiles and ornate glasses, reminders, she supposed, of home. There was a powerful smell, part floral, part spicy.

A door at the back opened and Rashid emerged, looking dishevelled and still half asleep. He wrapped himself more tightly in his robe, embarrassed to have been caught napping.

'Migraine,' he said, by way of explanation. He was a slight, thin young man, in his mid-twenties, the fuzzy down of youth still on him. From the yellow tan of his face and hands and his dark, straight hair you might at first mistake him for an Inuk, but the bony angularity of his form and his slender, beaked nose marked him out as an outsider. A pair of searching eyes suggested the penetrating intelligence beneath.

'You're the teacher,' he said. He pointed to her feet. 'Please take off your boots.' His manner was polite and tentative. Something moved across his face when she told him why she'd come.

'Please sit down while I get dressed,' he said. Edie took a seat at the table while Rashid disappeared behind the door. A few minutes later he reappeared dressed in a tracksuit, asking if she'd like to try some Moroccan tea. When she said yes he went over to the kitchenette and put on some water to boil. She watched him opening a cupboard and reaching for two tiny, elaborately decorated glasses and a small, bulbous teapot in what looked like brass. She imagined his long, slender fingers handling the meteorological instruments. The orderly type then, meticulous.

'What do you need to know?' he said.

She dived into the pocket of her summer parka, pulled out the picture of the dead girl and passed it to him. He took it and looked shaken for a moment, then he gave a small, sorry smile and passed the photo back.

'I heard about that. It's horrible.'

'Did you know Martha?'

'Kuujuaq's a small place.' He rubbed a hand across his face. 'But most of the time I'm on my own up at the weather station or I'm fishing at the trout lake. I like to go up on the cliffs sometimes. I wouldn't say I really *know* anyone.' He tailed off. 'That was kind of why I took the Shack job. To stop myself becoming a hermit.'

'Susie told me you were working the evening shift on Friday.'

'That's right,' Rashid said, 'but I only take the money, wash up, that kind of thing.'

'I heard Susie's a great cook,' Edie said.

'I'm Muslim, so I prefer to handle halal food. Which up here means I'm pretty much restricted to fish.' He peered inside the teapot, stirred the contents and put the lid back on. Edie looked about. She was suddenly struck by how different his world was, how completely alien to everything she knew. Yet here they were, in her world, drinking tea together.

'Where are you from?'

'I was born in Vancouver,' he began, 'but my parents came from Morocco. I hope you like it sweet.' He began to pour the tea, using a swinging motion, almost as though he were conducting. It had an unfamiliar herbal taste. Mint, he said. It reminded him of home.

She sipped a little more tea to be polite then took out the mugshots of Namagoose and Saxby that Klinsman had given her.

Rashid peered at the pictures and swallowed, hard. Yes, he said. Martha had come into the Shack with the two men on Friday evening around 7.30.

'Did she seem distressed at all? Anything to suggest she might have been under some kind of pressure, maybe that she didn't want to be with those fellas?'

He took a sip of tea. 'No. They were all drunk but I got the impression she was right where she wanted to be.' Something in his tone caught Edie off guard.

'You don't approve of drinking?'

His voice was suddenly animated. 'You see what alcohol does to people up here and have to ask me that?' He shrugged, warming his hands on the tea glass and bringing them up to his temples. 'Look, all I meant was, it seemed like she was having a good time.'

'You notice where they went when they left?'

He lowered his hands then shook his head.

'How's about on Saturday?'

Rashid looked up. 'I was off sick on Saturday night.' He pointed to his head.

Edie left Rashid's house surer than she'd ever been that there was something they'd missed. Derek had been too keen to accept Charlie Salliaq's view of Martha as the helpless victim of two predatory men but the Martha Edie knew was both smarter and more worldly than this version of the story suggested. The Martha she knew was an actor in her own life, a woman with a plan. Namagoose's story had got closer to the real Martha. And Rashid had corroborated it.

As she walked back down the path a group of *unataqti* were standing at the shoreline daring one another to walk into the water. She hesitated for a moment or two, watching them, then she made her decision.

The skinny husky cross that Markoosie kept as a birder was lying in the dust under the porch. It looked up at her approach and rumbled menacingly, but made no attempt to confront her. She walked up the steps, hesitating at the door into the snow porch. The blinds were open and through the window she could see Alice hunched on the couch with her daughter's arm around her. They appeared to be talking. On the other side of the room, Charlie was at the table with his head in his hands. Markoosie sat beside him. As she reached for the door handle, Lizzie seemed to catch the movement in the corner of her eye and wheeled around. She came to the inner door and cracked it open.

'This isn't a good time.'

'It's you I want to talk with. It won't take a moment.'

The girl looked put out.

'Lizzie, this is really important. Are you *sure* your sister didn't have a boyfriend?'

Lizzie folded her arms defensively across her chest and tipped her head towards the broken fragments of her family. 'Look at us, Edie Kiglatuk. Do we look sure of anything right now?'

For a moment they both stood their ground, then, sighing, Lizzie said, 'Come back another time, OK?'

With that she swung the door shut, leaving Edie standing at the top of the steps, unsure what to do or where to go.

She decided on Chip Muloon's house. It was late now, and the air was thick with insects and the summer smell of tundra honey but every so often freezing wind gusted off the sea as a reminder, if any were needed, that up here on Ellesmere Island the ice was never far away.

Her lover was up, listening to music and drinking bourbon. She went over and kissed him on the lips.

'You get a kick out of keeping a fella guessing?' He was teasing but there was an edge to his tone.

She kissed him again, longer this time.

'That answer your question?' she said.

He pulled her towards him. 'I've given up trying to get answers from you, Edie.'

14

Sonia Gutierrez woke from her nap feeling anxious. After Charlie called she'd planned on shutting her eyes for twenty minutes to be fresh for her meeting with the family. She thought she'd set her alarm but something told her that it was later than she'd hoped and her watch confirmed it: 8 p.m. All that staring at plans had fried her brain.

She sat up and swung herself off the bed. If she hurried she could be at the Salliaqs' by 8.15 as she'd promised. Not that they were particular about clock time. Inuit tended not to be. Guatemalans weren't either, generally, but Sonia had been long enough in Ottawa for something of its quiet orderliness to have rubbed off on her.

She removed her clothes and went down the corridor to the bathroom without bothering with a robe. A thin, brown trickle emerged from the showerhead. She stepped in all the same. Charlie hadn't said why he wanted to see her so late in the day but over the years she'd learned that refusing to meet with him out of office hours only frustrated his sense of entitlement and made things more difficult.

The old man wasn't always easy to like but Sonia had built up a solid respect for him. She appreciated the trust he put in her. They were the same, she and he, two survivors. These last days she'd seen some of the fight go out of him. After his initial shock and rage at Martha's fate, he appeared to have sunk into a kind of resigned depression, as if his daughter's death was simply confirmation of something he already knew: that no matter how hard he fought, the world would continue to heap injustices on him. She could hardly blame him if he'd finally decided he'd taken one punch too many. He was old and he was tired and she was pretty sure he was sick too.

The cool water helped clear her head. She reached for the shower gel and began working up a foam. From what she could deduce by coupling together the information from police and settlement gossip, the murder investigation had come on a long way in the last twelve hours and rumour had it that Derek Palliser was only waiting for formal confirmation from forensics before he would be able to make arrests.

Her thinking on the matter of the clean-up was beginning to shift in unexpected ways. Professionally, she wanted to be able to draw a line under the last decade or so of claims and counterclaims. Under the terms of her contract, her fees wouldn't be released until the first stage of the clean-up had actually been signed off. There were debts to clear from a problem she'd made for herself a few years back. The thing still weighed her down. Every now and then in the middle of a wakeful night she imagined that someone would get hold of the details and use them against her, and she yearned to be able once and for all to file it away in the drawer labelled past.

Years of dealing with the vagaries of the Guatemalan authorities, long before she'd arrived in Canada, had taught her that there always had to be a backup plan, a trump card to be flourished in the event that the other side's hand proved unexpectedly strong. Until now such a trump had eluded her but the threat of yet another delay had in the end produced a surprising opportunity.

She stepped out of the shower and, wrapping herself in a towel, wandered down the corridor into her bedroom, squeezed the water from her hair and switched on the dryer. What she'd discovered about the environmental impact report and the anomalous layout of the station was potentially explosive. Even a hint that the government negotiators might have been less than open in their dealings on the case might be enough to force the Defence Department's hand *and* initiate a claim for compensation. It wasn't just the money. If the department had developed the site in ways that adversely affected the inhabitants of

Kuujuaq they deserved restitution. She was shocked sometimes at how tough their lives were. She would sit Charlie down and ask him what he remembered from his days employed as a handyman at the site. It might all come to nothing but then again there was nothing to lose.

It was raining outside and the damp clung to her hair. *Que vaina!* she thought. It was too much. She climbed the steps to the door of the Pitoqs' house. Markoosie was sitting on the couch beside Alice but he stood up as she entered and greeted her with a fleeting smile. He was just about to head off to the radio studio to see if anyone had left any messages. The others would fill him in on the meeting afterwards.

Charlie Salliaq was at his usual spot at the table, looking grey and tense while Lizzie bustled about in the kitchen clearing away the remains of a meal.

'I hope you've come to tell us that damned Lemming Police has arrested the Cree?' he said irritably. He reeled off a list of complaints and demands. From the kitchen, Lizzie flashed Sonia a sorry smile. Eventually she held up a hand. He stopped mid-sentence, a look of irritation on his face.

'What?'

'*Avasirngulik*, we will continue with this, but I need to talk to you about something else now,' she said in Inuktitut. She'd picked up the rudiments of the language on her various trips and brought it out when she most needed it.

She unfolded her laptop and brought up the DEW station plans. 'I need to ask you about what you saw when you worked at Glacier Ridge.'

He turned and stared at her for a moment then. He'd always made it clear that he didn't want to talk about that time and she'd eventually given up questioning him about it.

'What does any of that matter?' He swung away from her in disgust.

She turned the laptop around so he could see it. 'Do you remember a lot of construction works around the station? I guess this would be sometime between the mid-sixties and the early seventies?'

The old man grumbled and looked away. The skin on his face was a network of tiny crimson veins. She'd noticed them before, but since Martha's death they'd become more prominent. Stress, or whatever was making him sick? She had no idea and he wasn't likely to tell her.

'If I talk to you about this, will you go and see Lemming Police?'

'I will do more than see him. I will tell him he has to arrest the *unataqti*.'

Salliaq nodded, satisfied with the terms of the agreement. 'I remember the trucks, but that was before they started employing any local men. In those days it was all just *qalunaat*. *Unataqti* and others.'

Lizzie fetched over a mug of tea and placed a fresh piece of bannock on Sonia's place, which she received politely. The seal oil in which the bread had been fried gave it an unpleasant fishy taste but she'd long since learned that to decline caused enormous offence.

'You ever see any heavy weaponry there?' she pressed. 'I mean rockets, anti-aircraft artillery, that kind of thing?'

Charlie shook his head. 'What would they want that for? It was a radar station.' He swung his chair around so he was angled towards her, and laid his elbows on the table. 'Enough history now. I wanna talk about the Cree. Then about what they're doing at the lake. After that, I don't care what time it is, we're going round to the detachment to tell that mixed-dough excuse of a policeman what we think of him.'

15

Derek was in the shed feeding his lemmings when the phone rang. He hoped it was Ransom; he'd left a message for him to call any time. The head of the forensics unit still hadn't confirmed what time the medical examiner and her team would be arriving and he was getting concerned. He wiped his hands on his jacket, hurried back to the office and picked up.

'This is Sonia Gutierrez.'

Derek's heart sank. What did the lawyer want at this hour?

'Charlie wants to see you. He's upset about the lake being drained.'

'Did you tell him?' Dammit, hadn't he specifically asked her not to?

'This is a small town, sergeant. And there's something else.' Gutierrez's voice grew hesitant. 'He's got this notion into his head that you're going to let Namagoose off the hook because he's your people.'

'*What?*' Derek was genuinely flabbergasted.

'I've tried to talk him out of it, but he just keeps saying that blood is thicker than water.'

'I'm not even going to dignify that by getting into it.'

'The man has just lost his daughter,' Gutierrez said simply.

With that there was no arguing. Derek swallowed a sigh.

'All right, well, have the family come to the office in half an hour. But you can tell Charlie right now, I won't have my professionalism called into question.'

After the call, he went out into the yard, pulled open the canvas tent flap and peered into emptiness. Most likely Edie was with the lanky *qalunaat*, Muloon. Well, too bad. He'd just have to disturb their little love nest. If Charlie Salliaq was about to kick up a stink, he needed her around.

At Muloon's front door he hesitated. The blinds were drawn but he could hear noises coming from inside. Leaning to the left he took a peek through the gaps between the slats. The front room was empty but Muloon had left the door to the bedroom open. There were bodies moving around, the sheen of naked flesh just visible through the gloom. His throat tightened and his face began to burn. In the midst of everything that was going on, Derek Palliser surprised himself by being ever so slightly jealous.

At the banging on the front door Chip froze then pulled away. He got up, slipped into a pair of jeans and a fleece and went out, returning a few moments later, looking mildly pissed off.

'It's for you.'

Derek was standing in the entrance to the snow porch, red-faced and doing his best to avoid eye contact.

'Sorry, bad timing.'

Edie glanced back and saw Chip in the doorway to the bedroom with one hand on his hip.

'I've had better.'

The policeman explained the situation.

'I would have told him to come round tomorrow, but what with the forensics and the ship supply, I don't see how I'm gonna get the time. I was kinda hoping you might—'

'—be your human shield?'

He gave a laugh that was somewhere between embarrassment and admiration. 'Something like that.'

Muloon had moved to the middle of the room now, a scowl on his face. She wanted to be out of there, suddenly, away from his expectations, immersed fully in the case.

'Let me get my parka.'

*

On the way over Derek filled her in. While she'd been with Muloon, Luc had come through with some preliminary blood work suggesting that Martha had been drugged. The nurse was checking the stores and working through a list of sedative and anaesthetic scripts, to see if anyone or anything leaped out.

'Joe Oolik finished up at the lake,' Derek said. 'He didn't find anything but he said some fellas came round from Camp Nanook and took samples.'

'What for?'

'They didn't say and Joe didn't ask. Something to do with the clean-up, I guess.'

They reached the detachment. Derek brushed himself down and took in a breath.

'I'm not looking forward to this,' he said.

'You think Charlie will be mad?' she said.

'Mad as in angry or mad as in crazy? My guess is he'll be both.'

As if on cue, there was the sound of furious stomping and Charlie Salliaq appeared at the door. He'd barely got across the threshold before launching into a long rant about the disgrace that was the Ellesmere Island Police and, more specifically, its senior officer.

'I'll go make some tea,' Edie said. Among Inuit, this usually helped to settle things down. By the time she returned everyone was sitting in awkward silence, either embarrassed or spent.

'I've explained to Charlie that we had no choice about draining the pool,' Derek said.

The elder glared but made no move to speak. Derek shot Edie one of his pleading looks. The situation was delicate. Like most Inuit, Edie had been brought up to believe that the soul of a person was carried in their blood. It was why embalming was taboo. Any draining of human blood. What had happened at the lake was no ordinary killing. It was a killing that flipped the bird at thousands of years of Inuit culture. Draining the bloody water only made it more difficult to accept.

'We didn't want any part of your daughter to remain at Lake Turn-galuk, among the bad spirits there,' Edie said. She knew instinctively this was the kind of language Charlie needed to hear. 'We took her blood to the sea. We gave her spirit to Sedna to look after.'

At the mention of the sea spirit, Charlie's eyes relaxed. 'Why isn't my daughter's killer in jail yet?'

'The law requires proof, *avasirngulik*.'

'Which law is that?' Charlie said provocatively.

'We're still trying to understand all the facts.'

Charlie Salliaq sat himself upright. Anger skimmed across his face. 'The facts are that my daughter was raped and killed. And you are asking questions about *boyfriends*? No Inuk man would do this and Martha would never have dated an outsider.' He was looking at Edie as he said this, as though she'd betrayed him and her sex both. 'This thing was done by a stranger who had no respect for Martha and has no respect for us.'

No one said anything for a moment.

'Charlie, please,' Sonia ventured finally.

The old man dismissed this with the contempt he thought it deserved.

'The Lemming Police cares more about his rodents than he does about justice.' He stabbed his finger in the air between himself and Derek, his voice raised now. 'I know what you're doing, you're protecting that sonofabitch *unataqti* because he's Cree like you.' The old man's face had taken on a rose-green sheen, like rotten meat. A thin rope of blood detonated from his nose and made its way down his chin. For a moment he didn't notice it, then his hands started flapping about as if he was frantically trying to stem the flow.

'I'll call Luc,' Derek said quietly.

Salliaq continued to flounder about wildly then he slumped back in his chair, as though someone had suddenly removed his battery, and his eyes swelled with tears.

Alice Salliaq stood. 'There's no need for the nurse. I'm taking my husband home now.' Her voice was quiet and authoritative and she spoke in Inuktitut.

The others sat in stunned silence, listening for the sound of feet to fade. Once Alice and Charlie were out of earshot, Sonia said, 'We can't carry on like this. You see what the stress is doing to him. I can get him to calm down about the lake thing, but what we really need is an arrest.'

'We know who did this,' Derek said. 'But you of all people must understand that we have to build a case.'

'Build it faster, sergeant.' Gutierrez stood and made for the door. Lizzie followed her.

Derek waited for them to leave, then lit a cigarette. He sucked in the smoke, shaking his head slowly from side to side.

'Holy fucking walrus.'

Edie stayed in her chair, pulling at her braid. Salliaq's ferocious outburst had crystallized an idea that had been playing around in her head ever since she'd come across the *tupilaq* outside the Pitoqs' house. Behaviour like that, the old man must have enemies all over town. What if someone killed Martha to get back at her father? Used the arrival of five hundred *qalunaat* at Camp Nanook as a smokescreen. Charlie wasn't likely to tell them who his enemies were, but Lizzie might.

She shot up and tore out into the bright night. Reaching the two women on the path, she said, 'Lizzie, your mother left something. Mind coming back to get it?'

Once they were out of Gutierrez's hearing, Edie told Lizzie what she knew. It was a little underhand and it meant breaking a promise and she hated to do it, but the days when folk could afford to have pure motives for their actions had long since gone. Nowadays even the snow was dirty.

The young woman's reaction was a mixture of relief and terror. 'I can't believe Willa told you.'

'I kinda forced it out of him,' Edie lied.

Her lips pursed, then in a quiet voice she said, 'Please don't tell my dad.'

Edie met her eye. 'I'm not planning on telling anyone. But I need something from you in return.'

She turned her head away. 'If you're going to ask me about Martha's boyfriend again, I already told you – I don't know. Why don't you believe me?'

Edie clasped Lizzie's chin gently and drew her face back round so the two women were looking at one another.

'I need to know if someone could have killed your sister to get back at your father.' She told the girl about the *tupilaq*.

Lizzie frowned. 'Why are we even talking about this? You already know who did it. I even heard the Lemming Police say so. The whole town knows.' She glanced nervously down the track. 'My parents will be wondering where I am.'

Edie grabbed her arm and wheeled her about.

'What did you and Martha fall out over?'

'Did Willa tell you that too?' The girl yanked her arm away. 'You and me are done, Edie Kiglatuk.'

Back in the detachment office Derek was draining a beer and smoking.

'You ever get the feeling you'd should have picked an easier career?' Derek said. 'Like lion tamer or bomb disposal expert.'

'I didn't pick it,' Edie said. The encounter with Lizzie had left her feeling angry and hollow. Just when she'd hoped for a rapprochement with Willa. 'And it's not my career. Once this is over I'm going right back to teaching and guiding.'

Derek took a long toke on his cigarette. 'Someone's got a sore head.'

Edie sighed. 'I could use a drink.'

Alarm spread across Derek's face.

'C'mon, D,' she said, 'I may be dumb but I'm not stupid.'

16

Edie woke early to a blank light, the temperature just beginning to clamber out of the freezing zone. This was what passed for dawn in the land of the midnight sun. In the shower, last night's unease stole over her once more, like the shadow of something in front of the shower curtain. Before she'd had time to register what it was, the object had disappeared from sight.

Derek was already at his desk, smoking. The darkness under his eyes and his pale, almost blue, hue suggested he hadn't had much sleep. They exchanged a brief greeting then Edie went through to the kitchenette and pulled open the refrigerator door.

'Got any *nitiq*, D?' The word meant both meat and real food, though it wasn't hunger that was bothering her so much as a need to connect with herself. Food often served that purpose.

'There might be a walrus head and a couple bags of seal meat in the freezer.'

She went back out to the little room at the back, hauled out a couple of unlabelled bags and popped them in the microwave. Twenty minutes later she emerged from the kitchenette carrying fresh blood soup but before she could put down the tray, the phone rang. It was Todd Ransom confirming that Anna Mackie and a forensics technician by the name of Mick Flaherty were en route and, all being well, would be landing at Kuujuaq within the hour.

She placed a bowl of soup in front of her boss. He thanked her and stubbed out his cigarette. Despite his lack of sleep, or maybe because of it, there was a kind of light in Derek's eye now. It was as though the finish line had just come into view.

'You think we're gonna be able to nail those two *unataqti* today, don't you? I can see it on your face,' Edie said, lifting her bowl to her lips. The prospect didn't cheer her. Once the Killer Whales were in jail the case would effectively be closed. Whether or not the two men were the killers, she was sure there was more to know.

He smiled, took a couple of slurps of soup then pushed the bowl away. She'd only ever known him to refuse food when he was adrenalized.

'You're completely convinced they did it?'

'You think they didn't?' Derek's face was a mixture of surprise and disappointment. He rose from his chair and pulled on his outerwear. 'Thanks for the soup, Edie, but please stop trying to make things more complicated than they are.' He screwed his hat down.

'Oh, I forgot.' He was holding the door half open now. 'Sammy called, must have been real early. He left a message. Something about a fight with his girlfriend and needing to stay over at your place in Autisaq a few days.'

Edie eye-rolled. Right now this was one distraction she didn't need. Particularly since her ex played this kind of stunt all the time. He'd been dating Nancy on and off almost since he and Edie split but that didn't stop him scuttling back whenever things went wrong. And fool her, she let him.

Derek shot her a sympathetic look. 'Why don't you come up to the landing strip with me? I want you to meet the medical examiner.'

The ME, Anna Mackie, was a small, fit-looking woman in her late forties. Married to the job, Edie guessed. Her sidekick, Flaherty, seemed younger, maybe early thirties with deep-set, violet eyes. Judging from the tenderness of his skin, he hadn't racked up much time in the Barrenlands.

'Sorry we didn't get up here sooner. I was using my vacation time to help my sister move house, but if I'd known there'd been a serious incident, I would have come back early,' Mackie said.

'Ransom doesn't seem to think the death of a native girl counts for much,' Derek replied.

Mackie stopped what she was doing momentarily, raised herself up and rested her hand on her hips. 'I'm not sure that's fair, sergeant. But in any case, it does to me.' Her look said she'd route around guys butting horns. 'Todd can be an asshole, but your idea of a language lesson didn't exactly help. Todd's in a bind here. Ottawa only lets us take leave over the summer, which, as you know, just happens to be when the crime rate soars. No one can get any temporary help because everyone's lying on a beach. It sucks, they know it sucks, but far as Ottawa's concerned, this place is off the map.'

The job of unloading the plane kept them busy for a while. There was forensics equipment to be checked and accounted for. When it was done, Mackie sent Flaherty to fetch a trolley while Derek went to sign off the flight paperwork.

Finding herself alone with Edie, Mackie said, 'Are you new?'

Edie scanned herself. 'Is it that obvious?'

Mackie laughed. 'No uniform is all.'

'I'm not the uniform type.'

Mackie continued to smile. 'Oh good. A woman after my own heart.'

Luc met them at the nursing station and led them through the double doors into the morgue. He'd already agreed to assist Mackie with the autopsy on the dead girl's body while Flaherty fingerprinted the ATV and checked her bedroom for hair, blood and other body fluids. The forensics team would then go down to the crime scene together. The finds would be processed back at the lab in Iqaluit along with the elimination samples and the suspects' clothes.

Luc pulled out the drawer. Flaherty helped him manoeuvre the body bag onto a gurney.

'It may become necessary to fly the body back to Iqaluit,' Anna said.

Derek scratched his head. 'That might be a problem. The father is traditional and he's ornery. He's not going to like removing his daughter from the place where her spirit is. He's lawyered up pretty good too.'

Mackie shifted her weight back and folded her arms. 'Todd mentioned there might be some cultural sensitivities to work around. Your chief suspect is at Camp Nanook with the SOVPAT, right?'

'Plus he just so happens to be Cree,' Derek said. 'So, for sensitivities read landmines.'

Mackie unzipped the body bag and began running her eye along its contents. Luc went over to join her. Mackie had read Luc's preliminary report on the flight over but she was keen to talk through the nurse's findings face to face. Derek and Edie stayed where they were. They were used to witnessing the depredations of the flesh in animals, but this was something else.

'Just tell me what you know from the beginning,' Mackie said to Luc.

'Well, OK, but I'm not a pathologist.' Luc stood with his arms crossed, rocking back on his heels. Nervous.

'Glad to hear it. I need this job.' Mackie smiled, professionally. Woman knew how to put people at their ease.

Immediately Luc uncrossed his arms and launched in. 'Well, the victim was found face down in brackish water. Body had been in the water maybe twenty-four hours. Probable cause of death exsanguination as a result of a deep knife wound through the vagina severing the uterine artery, though I haven't been able to eliminate possible death by drowning. No obvious evidence of non-consensual penetrative sex, except by the knife, obviously, but I haven't ruled it out either.'

'It wouldn't be unusual in a case like this,' Mackie said. 'What's with the hair?'

'Crudely cut with a blade. Only a few offcuts found in the water at the scene, suggesting that whoever killed her removed the bulk of it.'

'No other signs of sexual mutilation immediately apparent?'

'No. No bruises, bite marks or anything like that. It seems likely she was heavily drugged beforehand, which might explain the absence of defence wounds. The bloods suggest some kind of tranquillizer – I'm guessing Ambien – but I don't really have the testing equipment to be able to be more specific.'

Mackie turned to Derek. 'You got anything to add?'

'Last movements. We know Martha spent early Friday evening drinking with two soldiers at a local bar before taking them back to her house where she had sex with one or both of them. Either way we're pretty sure it was consensual. They're now the chief suspects. The men left later the same evening and then Martha probably slept in. A friend who went round there said it looked like she had a hangover. She went around to her uncle's later on Saturday morning to pick up a schoolbook. Last sighted around midday having some kind of verbal altercation with one of the suspects outside the local store. We think he may have wanted a replay of Friday night's action. Martha had other ideas.'

'I checked for alcohol,' Luc said. 'Residual.'

Mackie nodded. 'I saw that in the report, thank you.'

'Sometime between that meeting and the end of Saturday night, she may have gone out to some bird cliffs not far from here to collect eggs. One of her regular haunts. It seems that the two suspects happened to be on the bluff above the cliffs at the same time. Maybe they called over to her. Right now we're working on the assumption that they drugged her, perhaps had sex with her again when she was out of it, then killed her and cut her hair for some kind of trophy. We haven't found the hair but one of them had her amulet. Claimed she'd given it to him.'

'There are other possibilities,' Edie cut in. 'The suspect told us she had a boyfriend; and the owner of the bar found her crying early Friday evening, before she met up with the two guys she had sex with.'

Derek frowned and flashed her a warning glance.

'There are always other possibilities,' he said. 'But the one we're working with right now is that she was killed by one or other or both of the two chief suspects.'

A ball of anger swelled up and stuck in Edie's throat. Derek knew she was lousy at toeing the line. Now, apparently, she was expected to keep her mouth shut. That was never going to work.

'I can already see degradation from water immersion,' Mackie went on, pointing to a spot on the girl's torso. 'You know what these oily stains might be?'

'Diesel and tar spill from the abandoned Glacier Ridge radar station just above the lake,' Luc said. 'The water's highly contaminated.'

Mackie took this in.

'We don't see many cases like this up here,' Derek said. 'In fact, we've never seen anything like this on Ellesmere Island. Tell the truth we're sorta groping around in the dark a little bit.'

Mackie gave a wry smile. 'In the land of the midnight sun. How ironic.'

'I checked the list of scripts we dispense from here,' Luc said. 'A couple of benzos, sleeping stuff, but the recipients are elderly. Can't see how either of them coulda had anything to do with it.'

'We've had a problem with prescription drug-peddling in the past,' Derek cut in. 'So it's possible the source wasn't legitimate.' He glanced at the clock on the wall. 'Damn. I'm afraid I have to be at the dock. Annual supply due in. Bad timing. Edie here will be at the detachment, you need anything. I suggest, Mick, you go with her and she'll show you the vehicle and take you to the victim's house.'

He reached over for his coat and used the action as an excuse to pull Edie to one side.

'Hey, you're on payroll, remember? Your job here is to back me up!'

She looked at him askance, a look which he met with a determined stare. They'd squared off plenty of times but few knew better than Derek that she wasn't about to be anybody's nodding dog. She yanked the badge he'd given her from her lapel and pressed it hard into his hand, pin side down.

'In that case I just came off payroll.'

He stared at her a moment in despair then held up his hands in a gesture of surrender. 'Look, all I'm asking for is you don't contradict me publicly. You know how sensitive this investigation is. Charlie Salliaq gets so much as a sniff that we're not pulling in the same direction, he'll exploit the hell out of it. Besides, we are, aren't we? I'm as determined as you are to find Martha's killer.'

Edie eye-rolled and took back the badge.

'Forensics finds nothing on the two *unataqti*, I promise you we'll spend more time on your boyfriend theory, OK? But they will. Now, I have to get down to the port. Will you go visit the Salliaqs, reassure them we got forensics working on the case now and we're focused on arrests? Give old Charlie something to chew on before he decides to start making any more trouble. Then go back to the detachment. Come fetch me if the prosecutor calls.'

At the door he turned and said, 'Thank you, VPSO Kiglatuk.'

Edie got back to the detachment to find the message light on Derek's desk phone blinking. It was Klinsman, wanting an urgent callback. Figuring he'd seen the plane, Edie punched in his number.

'The forensics team just got here.'

'So I assumed, but that's not why I'm calling. Is Sergeant Palliser there?'

'He's at the annual supply. You'll have to make do with me.'

There was a pause while Klinsman recalibrated.

'Sergeant Palliser told me on the phone that it looked as though the dead girl had been drugged. I took the precaution of checking out the camp pharmacy. The medical team here only writes scripts in emergency situations. There are always a few men who fail to cope with Arctic conditions. Nothing went out on script, but a quantity of Ambien was logged as missing from stock on Wednesday last week. It could be an administrative error.' He paused to signal a 'but'. 'I asked them to check who came into the clinic. We occasionally assign ancillary duties to regular soldiers. Turns out one of the men helping that day was Private Saxby. We searched his locker again but didn't find anything. He's denying any knowledge of the Ambien, of course. We ran a drug test on him and he's clean.' He paused again. 'I thought I should let the sergeant know.'

She thanked him. As she was finishing the call the door opened and Markoosie Pitoq's face peered through. She waved him to a chair.

He handed her a piece of folded paper. 'I wanted you to see this.

It was under the studio door when I came in this morning.' She unfolded the paper and read:

Ask Willa Inukpuk about Martha on Friday nite

She read the sentence a couple of times before the words sank in. Willa. On Friday night. If it was true, why hadn't he mentioned it? And if it wasn't, why was someone trying to set him up?

She rubbed the note between her fingers. The elaborate script seemed vaguely familiar, the fine blue lines and off-white slubby texture of the paper suggesting it had been torn from a notebook.

'You didn't see who dropped this off?'

Markoosie shook his head. 'Like I said, it was under my door when I arrived this morning.'

She thanked him and waited till he'd gone before dialling the Rangers' contact number, introducing herself and explaining that she needed to speak with Willa Inukpuk. The voice on the other end asked her to hold for a moment, then came back on.

'Ranger Inukpuk's still out at rappel camp. Is it an emergency? We can get a message to him.'

Her mind was on the slip of paper. 'Ask him to call Edie at the Kuujuaq police detachment? Tell him there's nothing wrong but it's kinda urgent.'

As she put the phone down she remembered where she'd seen the writing before. It belonged to Lisa Tuliq. The girl had submitted an essay in exactly the same fancy handwriting. She stood up from the desk and grabbed her parka.

As she got closer to the Tuliqs' camp, the ground rose in ragged increments, as though it had risen up, leaving ledges and slabs of rock behind. In every crack and on every slab some small plant or lichen flourished. She paused briefly to register the unique generosity of the Arctic summer. Where else in the world could be so welcoming to the sudden arrival of so much new life? She wondered what demons had stalked Martha Salliaq that she would ever have wanted to quit this place. Then she drove on until she reached the spot where the low basalt cliffs met the sea and the Tuliq family tents sat like knucklebones on the willow carpet.

At the sound of the ATV Lisa emerged from the communal tent, still clutching the glove she was mending. Her father followed behind, his hands gripping her shoulders. Lisa made eye contact with her for a second then looked away. Edie greeted them both and asked to speak to the girl in private for a moment. Lisa glanced at her father, perhaps hoping he would question this, but when he didn't she led Edie around the back of the tent. As soon as they were out of earshot, Edie produced the slip of paper from her pocket.

'Exactly why did you put this under the door at the radio station?'

Lisa's face hardened but she said nothing. The question had come out more aggressively than Edie had intended.

'We're going to keep talking until you tell me. At the detachment if you prefer.'

The girl grimaced and squirmed a little, her eyes flashing from side to side, searching for a way out. Edie moved to block her path.

'What have you got against Willa Inukpuk?'

Lisa flinched and Edie saw she was trying her best to fend off tears.

'Martha told me,' she said. 'I went round there on Saturday morning and she was in a state. She told me she'd seen Willa Inukpuk the night before. She said Willa wouldn't listen to her. She seemed pretty cut up about it.'

Edie felt her jaw clench. Just then Lisa's father appeared, making his way towards them. 'What's this about?'

Lisa went poker-faced. 'It's OK, Dad.'

They waited until his footsteps crunched away along the shingle.

'Why didn't you tell me this before?' Edie asked.

'Because I knew you'd be like this about it.'

Edie stepped away from the girl and shook her head. 'You're right.' Her reaction said more about her own relationship with Willa than Lisa. The truth was, she and Willa didn't trust one another. It hurt like hell but there it was. 'I'm sorry, I'm just trying to understand what happened. Did Martha mention anyone else when you saw her? Say anything about what she and Willa talked about? Where they met? Anything, Lisa, anything at all.'

The girl shook her head.

'I've told you all I know. Martha was feeling sick and she wanted me to go away. And now I'd like you to do the same.'

By the time Edie spotted Willa, he was already heading in her direction. The rappelling camp was in the middle of lunch, the men sitting about on the rocks, spooning up eggs from plastic platters. He didn't look too pleased to see her.

'You got a nerve coming here after what you tried to do to Lizzie.' His mouth was set in a thin line. 'She came over to see me this morning.'

'I messed up.'

'You *are* messed up.'

'Yes,' she said, hoping to win him over. 'And stupid sometimes, but right now, I'm upset. Why didn't you tell me you saw Martha on Friday night?'

For a moment he looked floored. She saw him run his eyes across the rocky scree where his fellow Rangers were finishing up their meal. A throb appeared under his left eye.

'Where d'you hear that?' he scowled, all the old resentment just under the surface, like a fish lure under the ice.

'Does it matter?'

She held his gaze. 'I'm trying to protect you.'

He sighed and scrunched his eyes. He was tired of being thought the bad one. She was tired of thinking it.

'Look, I had the evening off. Me and Lizzie agreed to hook up by the trout lake in the valley past the headland.' He gave the Inuktitut name. 'I went to the Anchor Bar, drank a beer. You can ask Joe Oolik – we shot some pool together. When I came out to go up to the lake, Martha was there.' He bit his lip. His cheek pulsed again.

Edie knew Willa well enough to know there was something he wasn't saying. 'You need to tell me what else you've got hiding in that head of yours. Did you and Martha have a thing? Is that it?'

'It wasn't even a thing.' He closed his eyes. His forehead buckled. 'Earlier in the year. It was nothing.'

'You ever take her picture?'

His eyes widened. 'No, fuck. Why you asking me that?' He slapped his fist against his chest and shook a dead mosquito from his hand. Fear came over his face, shortly followed by anger. 'That fucking excuse of a policeman got me on some list, hasn't he? I thought he was about to arrest those two *unataqti*.' He flung his arms in the air. 'This is why I left Autisaq, Edie, this is exactly why.'

'You got form, Willa. But you're not on any list.'

In almost the same instant as it began his relief turned to resentment. *'Because I didn't do it.* Jesus, Edie.'

'Help me find out who did.' A beat. 'Tell me exactly how it went between you two. I mean *exactly.*'

He rolled his eyes in mock exasperation. She forgot sometimes how young he was, in his head. In his heart too, maybe.

'She was upset about something. Her face was all puffy. I guess that's why she wanted to talk to me. I'm honest, I didn't want to hear whatever it was. I told her I had to get going.' He softened. 'Martha could be really intense, you know? But don't think I don't feel bad about it now, because I do, OK?'

'That why you came to see me?'

'I guess.'

Something tender and painful passed between them.

'You remember when we used to sit and watch *Liberty*?' Edie said. Revisiting old Laurel and Hardy movies had been one of their greatest shared pleasures.

Willa smiled. 'Sometimes I still dream about being in that getaway car.'

'Who doesn't?' Edie said.

There was a pause. The atmosphere between them was a little melancholy now.

'Listen, you're not gonna tell Palliser. About me and Martha.'

She bit her lip. 'No, though I don't think it would make any difference if I did. He seems pretty certain Namagoose and Saxby are the killers.'

From over on the scree, someone shouted Willa's name. He wheeled round and signalled an acknowledgement, then, pulling on his hat, turned back to her:

'Look, man, I gotta go.'

On the return journey she took a detour to Lake Turngaluk in the hopes of catching the forensics team at work. Where the bloody pool had sat, there was now nothing but a rapidly crusting ooze. Even the odour had gone. But a dark, sinister air still hung over the mudflats and open pools and she thought about what Joe Oolik had said about the birds keeping away. She clambered from the ATV, ducked under the crime tape and walked up to the spot where they'd found Martha's body. The edge of the pool was cracked and brown, but in the centre, where the mud was thickest, she caught a nub of something standing slightly proud of the surface. Her curiosity piqued, she stretched out her right leg, testing the holding strength of the mud. Even here, where the surface had contracted and cracked as it dried, it still felt slimy and soft underneath. She launched herself out carefully onto the crater, keeping her weight low. She saw now how Joseph Oolik had missed the item. Where the mud had begun to desiccate it had separated into octagonal plates, leaving spaces between the plates shimmering with slime. The object had ridden up in one of these gaps.

Leaning in, she pulled what she saw now was a wooden handle. The object resisted, then lifted clean of the mud. She turned it in her hand. Eight inches of stainless steel knife blade, honed smooth on the downside and part serrated, a blood groove running the length of the blade itself. The kind of weapon you might use to butcher a caribou. Or to kill a girl.

17

Sonia Gutierrez edged her way around the back of the Salliaqs' house and tiptoed towards the shed where Charlie Salliaq had archived the Glacier Ridge files from way back in an old packing crate, before she'd taken the case on. There was no doubt in her mind now that some combination of the Defence Department, the military and the police were up to something and she was keen to make sure no one knew she was on to them until she'd figured out what it was. Others might think that was paranoid, but they could go to hell. She'd had enough dealings over the years with the military and law enforcement to know that, whatever their public face, in private they were about as trust-worthy as a pack of hungry wolves.

She pulled the packing crate out from under a pile of old engine parts and prised off the lid. It was easy to forget just how much paperwork the case had generated over the more than a decade of its progress before most files were digitized. Frost had crept in and stained the paper and some of the older files had become as brittle as frazil ice. Charlie hadn't kept the papers in any discernible order but neither had he ever thrown anything away. Here it all was in physical form. Years and years of struggle.

The irony of working on Inuit land claims wasn't lost on Sonia. At some fundamental level, like most indigenous people, Inuit didn't believe in owning land. To the Inuit way of thinking, the land owned itself. It had its own integrity. It answered only to nature. Property law was just one more thing *qalunaat* had brought up from the south, along with microwaves and measles. Inuit had learned to play along because history had taught them what would happen if they didn't.

She sat on the floor and bedded in. This was going to take some time.

The questions she wanted answering were why had the Department of Defence faked an environmental impact report, and what were they trying to hide by doing so? In order to answer those she needed to know how and why Glacier Ridge had been expanded between 1960 and the early seventies, and to what end. The job would have been a lot easier if Charlie Salliaq had been more forthcoming about his stint at the site. She'd tried quizzing him again but got no further. Whether that was through forgetfulness, guile or genuine ignorance it was hard to know. For some months now she'd noticed him becoming vague and distracted. He said himself that his brain was growing as soft as early summer ice. Sometimes, he said, he felt like a bear afloat on the pan, conscious that the ice would not carry his weight much longer. And yet still he refused to see the nurse. Laughed the idea off. He said there was nothing *qalunaat* medicine could do for him. He was an old man getting older. Not even the *qalunaat* had discovered a cure for time.

She ploughed on. A couple of hours into her search something interesting came to light. It was a faint carbon copy of a requisition order dating from May 1972 drawn up by a Major Fournier of the Royal Canadian Engineers and addressed to a requisitions officer in the Department of Defence, requesting a shipment of cement and sand, along with steel reinforcement sheets for a 'secure underground bunker and associated buildings, as discussed'. Interesting because no such bunker existed on the plans from 1974. And odd, too, that the requisition was addressed to the Defence Department when the responsibility for maintaining Distant Early Warning radar stations was shared between the Canadian and US Air Forces. Officially, the Defence Department didn't have anything to do with management or maintenance of the site.

Sonia pulled up on her laptop her own copy of the recent schedule of decontamination works she'd agreed with the department. Again, no mention of any underground structure. It was possible that the bunker had never been built, but it seemed unlikely since supplies were only requisitioned once a construction had already been green-lit. A more plausible scenario was that the bunker had been built during the summer of 1972 and possibly also 1973 but that by 1974, when the revised plans were drawn up, it had disappeared. There *was*, however, an area in the revised plans, set a little off to the side from the main site and designated 'waste landfill'. It seemed at least possible that this was the site of the short-lived underground bunker.

She slid the document into her bag, then got up from the floor and tidied the papers back into two stacks, the smaller, those she had already inspected, the larger, those she hadn't, then cracked open the door and peered out. A forensics guy had been working most of the day in the main house and she was anxious not to be seen, but the blinds were part drawn and there was no one in sight. She crept out onto the steps then went back down the path.

Charlie was asleep in Toolik Pitoq's La-Z-Boy, Toolik having vacated it in favour of taking his afternoon nap in his bed. The others had gone out to the store. She fixed a mug of hot sweet tea then went back into the living room and shook Charlie gently until his eyes opened and a frail smile of recognition appeared on his face. Talk to him now, she thought, while his defences are down.

'Charlie, you remember an underground structure, maybe a bunker, down at the old Glacier Ridge station?'

The old man took a few sips of tea. Alarming red welts had appeared on his neck and face during the past twenty-four hours but she knew it was hopeless to try to get him to do anything about them.

'You're right,' he said, thinking back, 'there *was* a bunker, yeah. I remember because I helped fill it in after the fire. Why?'

She'd never heard about a fire. Then again, why would she? Sitting herself at his feet, she asked him about it now.

'Oh yeah, a big one,' he said. 'Me and Toolik, some others gone into the spirit world now, we helped clean up.'

'Did the fire originate in the bunker?'

Charlie's forehead folded up like a blind. 'I don't recall, but it was pretty burned up. I remember that.'

'You ever see what was in that bunker, Charlie? I mean, before the fire?'

The old man shrugged. 'Uh nuh. Us Inuit fellas weren't allowed in there.' A scowl came over his face. 'That Lemming Police arrested anyone yet?'

18

Ahnah Oolik was moving boxes outside the entrance to the Northern Store when Edie came round looking for her husband, Sam.

'He's out back. We got to sort the stock before the new supply comes in, so don't keep him long.'

She found Oolik stacking catering-sized cans of creamer into a fragile-looking pile in the beverages aisle.

'I hope you're coming with good news,' he said. It seemed the whole of Kuujuaq was in a state of suspended animation awaiting confirmation that the Killer Whales had been arrested and charged with Martha's murder.

'Not exactly,' Edie said.

Oolik's face fell. 'Well, I'm kinda busy here if you don't mind?'

'Then I'll lend you a hand. I'm stronger than I look.'

Oolik seemed momentarily taken aback. He pointed to the pile of boxes at his feet. 'Somehow I never get around to having everything organized in time for resupply. Happens every year. Drives Ahnah crazy.'

Edie went to work. In minutes she'd unpacked half the boxes in the pile. Turned out stacking cans of creamer wasn't so different from building an icehouse.

'Well, look at that,' Oolik said, impressed.

'Now *you* can help *me* out.'

Sam Oolik shifted his weight and tightened his jaw.

'I don't know how much more help you need. I told you what I seen and we expected you and that mixed-dough cop to have brought that Cree fella in by now. Our girls ain't safe.'

'We got to build a case, Sam.' The arrest of Namagoose and Saxby was beginning to feel like a forgone conclusion. She realized that she'd given up saying they were keeping an open mind.

'You can help with that,' she said, holding up the evidence bag containing the knife she'd fished out of the lake. It wasn't Saxby's knife. In a way it would have been easier if it had been. But its position in the mud at the bottom of the pool made it a potentially vital piece of evidence. They needed to find out who owned it.

Oolik stood up, brushing his hand over the back of his neck to rid himself of a mosquito. His eye scanned the contents of the bag. 'How d'you think I can help?'

'You sell a knife like this to anybody, Sam?'

Oolik lurched back. 'No, no, I meant, I don't remember.' He sounded a little panicked, as though he thought Edie imagined he had something to do with the killing.

'Well, OK, then, in that case, I'll pass it on to Sergeant Palliser to deal with.'

Oolik lifted a staying hand.

'Well now, hold on. Now you mention it, I do recall a knife with a blond-wood handle sitting on a shelf in the storeroom. It just slipped my mind for a moment. That Sergeant Lemming's always threatening to report me for not keeping proper records.'

'You help me now, he's gonna stop, Sam. You have my word on it.'

The shopkeeper relaxed. 'Say we take a look at the orders book.' He led her to a tiny room at the back of the cashier's desk and took a black file down from a bookcase, letting fly a bunch of loose papers. Propping a pair of glasses on his nose, he scanned the list, shaking his head.

'How's about we call the wholesaler, give him the serial number?' Edie said, with a breeziness she didn't feel. She'd already written it down in her notebook.

Seeing the wisdom of this, Oolik took the notebook and returned a moment later from his phone call with a triumphant look on his face. 'Came up on the supply plane a couple weeks back. But, like I said, I can't find no record of who ordered it.'

An idea came to Edie. 'Anyone other than you and Ahnah have access to the storeroom?'

Oolik rubbed his chin between the fingers and thumb of his right hand. 'Officially, no, but this hot weather, we've been keeping the door to the office open, let the air in. The key's usually hanging on that hook there.' He pointed to an open key store on the wall just inside the door.

'The First Nations fella, Namagoose, the tall one you saw talking to Martha Saturday morning, he come inside the store?'

Oolik rolled the name around his mouth, hawked up then spat on the floor. 'Well, see, I can't say as I actually saw him come *in* the store. But there's nothing to say he didn't.'

Edie looked around. It would have been difficult for anyone to have walked from the entrance to the storeroom without being spotted.

'But you didn't actually *see* him in here.'

Oolik pushed his baseball cap back and scratched his scalp. 'Well now, that depends on what you mean by "see".'

At the detachment the message light was blinking again. Sammy had called to report that Edie's DVD player back home in Autisaq needed fixing. In any case, he added, he probably wouldn't be needing it, since he was thinking of borrowing a boat and coming over to Kuujuaq to visit Willa. Thought to stay in Edie's tent a couple of days.

Edie waited for the end message beep and pressed delete. She didn't want to have to deal with her ex right now. Whatever she said to him he'd probably come anyway. He was like that; once he'd made up his mind to do something, he'd do it. For now, though, she decided to go over to the landfill, see if she could find that knife box. The trash cart came round on a Monday morning. If anyone had thrown away the packaging then it would have been taken to the dump then. Might be fingerprints on it.

She picked up her hunting rifle from the gun cupboard and the harpoon handle from the tent and set off along the road which snaked around the headland to the garbage dump. A few years ago a cardboard box would have been quite a prize in Kuujuaq. A family would have put it to some use, if only as a toy for the kids. Nowadays, Inuit were becoming more like *qalunaat*, casual with their possessions, and lots of reusable stuff wound up in landfill.

A stinking, raggedy range of garbage lay scattered in a large hollow, blooming tundra all around it. Guillemots and ravens scratched through the leavings. At the far end of the pile a mother fox and her three cubs scrabbled at a plastic bag. As Edie approached, the fox hurried her cubs to safety and the birds rose and flapped off across the crumble of melting sea ice. But the search yielded nothing and a while later she decided to call it a day. As she stretched to ease her back and wipe her face with her hand, her eyes fell on her watch. It was nearly 4 p.m. and she'd promised to be round at Chip's house in an hour for some early supper of river trout.

The way back took her past the Shoreline Bar. The place was so busy that there were customers standing outside in the street. She slowed the ATV. A half-dozen off-duty soldiers stopped flirting with the Inuit girls beside them to check her out. A few local men looked on with clouded expressions on their faces. There was an odd, unsteady atmosphere in the air, as though a fight might break out at any moment. The scene took her back to her conversations with Willa and Tom Silliq. The investigation was three days old and they still had no real idea what had happened to Martha in the hours and minutes leading to her death. She keyed off her vehicle and went over. Martha's picture was in her pocket.

'Hey.'

'Hey,' the men said. She drew out the photograph.

'Any of you ever see this girl?'

The men passed the picture between them. One whistled. Another quipped that he wished he had. One by one they shook their heads.

*

Thanking the men and turning her ATV around, Edie began to bump towards the nursing station. She wanted to make sure forensics got the knife before they left.

Inside the waiting room Anna and Mick were bagging up and labelling their samples and making last-minute checks of their equipment. She greeted them, then walked over to the office where Derek and Luc were hunched over the desk, filling out reports. The two men seemed frazzled and agitated. Derek rolled his chair, his lips cracking a hello. The dark circles under his eyes had taken on a sallow, yellowish hue. His nostrils flared.

'Jesus Jones, Edie, where have you been?'

She pulled the bag containing the knife from her daypack. It landed on the desk with a thud. He inspected the contents while she filled him in on her visit to the lake, the conversation with Sam Oolik then the trip to the dump.

'Oolik's checking his records over, see if he can find out who ordered it,' Edie said.

'Don't hold your breath,' Derek said sourly. 'I'm always telling that old walrus fart to clean up his books.' He sounded irritable, but she sensed that the target of his annoyance was himself. He flipped the blade over in its bag. 'Looks to me this is in the right ballpark at least. I'll get Flaherty to take it back to Iqaluit, run some tests.' His lips thinned. 'I guess I should have thought of checking the store before now. What with the supply, it's just been so hectic.'

'How'd it go?' she asked.

'The usual pile of crap. Missing bills of lading, cargo cock-ups, that kind of thing, but it looks about done at least. Captain Larsen's keen to weigh anchor and set sail sometime later tonight. It's all gotten a whole lot more pressured. I think Larsen's shitting himself. Northwest Passage opening up, some fierce competition on the horizon. Sometime not far off we're gonna have to get used to ships up here all year round.'

'Great for the local economy,' Luc said.

Derek cast him a sidelong look. 'An optimist, huh?'

'Goes with the job,' Luc said.

Edie cut in, 'Did Mackie and Flaherty come up with anything?'

'Some head and pubic hair from the bedroom,' Luc said. 'Unlikely to be Martha's from the colour. A couple of partial footprints left by men's boots. Flaherty thinks it's pretty much guaranteed they'll correspond to army-issue footwear. Body fluids on the bed linen. Semen and vaginal fluid most likely. Only Martha's prints on the door handle, which suggests she probably went into that room of her own free will. No bloodstains. Most likely the murder happened up on the cliffs or, more likely, at the lake. They didn't find anything at the crime scene itself, though, except for a set of new footprints.'

'Probably mine,' Edie said. 'What about the body?'

'That's more complicated,' Derek cut in. 'Anna's decided she needs to take Martha down to Iqaluit. We'll just have to find a way to break the news to Charlie.'

'You mean *I* will.'

'Nice of you to volunteer. Anna's saying she doesn't expect to find any foreign body fluids, hair or skin residues, because of the length of time the body was in the water. Confirming the approximate death window is gonna be tricky too – but if she can give us the green light on the Ambien in Martha's blood we might not need anything else. I'm gonna speak to the prosecutor, see if we can move first thing tomorrow.' He moved towards the door, a little smile playing on his lips. 'Before you go see Charlie, Edie, it might be an idea to take a shower. And use plenty of soap.'

By the time Edie returned from speaking with the Salliaqs, the mosquitoes had disappeared, the temperature had fallen, the sky was a shroud and she was wrung out. Charlie had, predictably, kicked up like crazy, accusing her of betraying her culture and being on the side of the *qalunaat*, and she'd had to promise that she would personally ensure that Martha's body was returned complete for burial in Kuujuaq when the case was done. Inside her tent she oiled and braided her hair, then put on her best sealskin parka, the one with the red rick-rack. It was just after 9 p.m. She was four hours late for supper.

Chip scowled at the door.

'Dammit, Edie.'

She squeezed past him into the snow porch. 'It's been a tough day.'

He closed the door behind her and sighed.

'There's no food,' he said.

'I'm not hungry.' She reached out and kissed him. Hard.

Afterwards, they lay together, their limbs intertwined.

'What made you so late?' he said.

She filled him in about the find at the lake but to her surprise, instead of being sympathetic, she saw his face stiffen and cloud over.

'Did I do something?' She moved closer, hoping to connect him back to her, but he backed away, sitting up and folding his arms around his legs. An awkward silence followed. She wished now that he weren't so enigmatic, or maybe that she understood him better. In the space of just a few seconds they'd gone from intimates to almost strangers. Suddenly, it seemed too exposing to be lying naked with him so she rose from the bed and threw on her underclothes.

'Perhaps I should go.'

'Yes. Maybe it's best if we take a break, Edie.'

She swung around and saw everything she needed to see written on his face.

The late night sky had softened and hints of sunshine poked through patches of broken cloud. Kuujuaq was empty now, the last of the soldiers having returned to Camp Nanook some hours ago. As she passed the Shoreline Bar, Tom Silliq was hauling two trash bags into a dog- and bear-proof hideaway. She remembered she hadn't eaten and she needed something to take her mind off the fight with Chip.

Silliq greeted her with a tired smile.

'I don't suppose Susie got any hot food going?'

Silliq flipped the lid of the hideaway and fastened the bolts. 'No can do. We've been short-staffed. The boy who helps out sometimes didn't show.' Silliq balled up his hands and rested them on his hips. 'We only just managed to fill orders.'

'You mean Rashid?'

'That's the one. Susie makes excuses for him, says he gets migraines, whatever they are. Says she can't get locals to do weekend shifts. Everybody wants to go off to summer camp. She seems to think it makes the place more *unataqti* friendly, have an outsider behind the counter. My reckoning, you take on an outsider you have no idea what you're getting.'

Edie exhaled. 'I'm with you,' she said.

The blinds in Derek's window were drawn but Edie noticed that her tent was slightly open. Her first thought was that Chip had had a change of heart and she hurried over, calling his name, her heart lifting, then crumpling as a voice said, 'I don't know who you're expecting but it's just me.'

It took her a moment to recognize the owner of the voice. She pulled back the tent flap and saw Sam Oolik sitting on the sleeping skins inside.

'You been waiting for me?'

'Not long,' he said. 'Good to carve out a little quiet time anyway. I found the order, thought you'd wanna see.'

He handed over the battered black order book, a calloused finger marking the page. In the spot where his finger had sat was a line of Inuktitut syllabics with a misspelled English translation below. There was an order number, a value and a shipping cost. But it was the name in the final column that interested her.

Oolik tapped the book with his right index finger and narrowed his eyes.

'Oh I know you're dating him, but there's more to that Muloon fella than meets the eye. I seen him talking to the colonel over at the *unataqti* camp.' He gave a triumphant snort. 'These *qalunaat* work in packs like wolves. And they've got us surrounded.'

19

Derek woke with a thick head and a tongue like a dead seal and cursed himself for drinking too much. He swung out of bed, went to the bathroom and in the mirror saw eyes crusted at the edges and slimy at the inner corners. The flakes of dried saliva on his chin suggested he'd either been drooling or talking in his sleep. It took him a while to figure out that he'd been woken by the phone in the detachment office and that it was still ringing. Stumbling into the office, he plucked the handset from its cradle and cut the call. Moments later the ringing began again. He peered at the screen and recognized Edie Kiglatuk's home number in Autisaq, which meant that the caller was likely to be Sammy Inukpuk, who was staying there. Derek was fond of the fella. Back in the spring they'd spent a chill, fearful night together on the sea ice in Alaska and damn nearly died. Something like that left scars and created bonds. All the same, he found the way Sammy still prowled around his ex-wife irritating. They seemed to have some kind of on–off thing that made him impatient whenever he got dragged into it. The way he saw it, they should get back together or leave one another alone.

He picked up.

'Hey, Sammy, you gotta know, this isn't some kind of roommate situation we got here, this is a police detachment, OK? And we're in the middle of a homicide investigation. I'll get Edie this one time, but . . .' He laid the phone down on his desk, tromped to the front door and yelled.

Edie emerged from her tent pulling on a sweatshirt and rubbing her eyes. From the kitchenette where Derek went to make coffee and give them some privacy, he could hear her voice saying, 'You already broke everything in my house, now you wanna come break everything here too?'

He threw some grounds in the drip and with the first dark, bitter sip, felt his brain shift up a gear. Before long his mind began to scroll through the events of yesterday until it reached the conversation with the prosecutor late last night. By the time the guy had finally returned his call Derek had already had a beer or two. He vaguely remembered kicking off the chat with a rant about how the homicide rate in the Barrenlands was now on a par with Mexico. There was something too about not even being sufficiently resourced to get a damned cell phone. It was kind of embarrassing to recall the bored tones of the prosecutor. Not that it mattered, not really. He'd got what he wanted out of the conversation, which actually had nothing to do with a cell phone (there being no tower for a thousand kilometres in any case) and everything to do with a green light to arrest Namagoose and Saxby. On one condition. The prosecutor wanted some forensics, ideally blood or other deposits on the men's clothing or on the knife. The very least, confirmation of the presence of Ambien in Martha's blood. No forensics, no arrest.

He took another gulp of coffee and refilled his mug. Now that he was fully awake he allowed himself a little uplift of anticipatory glee. Sometime this morning Anna Mackie would call to confirm Luc's initial findings. Then he'd inform Klinsman and head on over to Camp Nanook and by the end of the day the Killer Whales would be in custody and he'd be contacting his equivalent in Iqaluit, Sergeant Bill Makivik, to arrange their transfer to the jail there. It sounded almost too easy.

He came out into the office as Edie was finishing up her call and was struck by a sudden, vivid memory of being woken in the night. He stopped a moment to consider whether he'd dreamed it then decided he hadn't. Someone had definitely been hammering on the door. He'd got up and walked through the detachment office only to find no one there. He shivered at the recall of the damp rush of cold air.

'Was that you last night?'

She pressed her lips into a yes. There was some new anxiety in her eyes he hadn't seen before. He handed her the mug of tea he'd made her.

'Bad night?'

'You could call it that.'

As she filled him in on Sam Oolik's visit, he felt an obscure need to comfort her. That Chip Muloon could have had anything to do with Martha Salliaq's death honestly hadn't occurred to him. But something less honourable stirred in him. He was so near to making those arrests and this was a complication he could do without.

'Anybody could have taken that knife from the store,' he said. He realized that he'd swung from wanting to make things easier for Edie to feeling the need to make them easier for himself.

'Then why was Chip's reaction so weird? He must have sensed I was getting close.' Edie shook her head in disgust. 'I was in his bed, D.'

Derek saw then that he couldn't simply ignore what was potentially an important new lead. The thought didn't thrill him much.

'Look, I'll go see the guy. He's probably got a perfectly reasonable explanation. After all, you know the fella, you've trusted him so far.'

'Trusted or lusted?' Edie said. 'I may have got the two mixed up.'

He put off confronting Muloon till nine by telling himself that he had to complete some urgent paperwork. When he couldn't postpone it any longer, he went to the school building. The door to Muloon's office was open and the smell of newly perked coffee drifted through the gap. The man himself was sitting at his computer. His face was grey and drawn. Derek got the sense from the resignation in those watery blue eyes that he'd been expecting this visit.

'I made extra coffee.' A flicker of hostility passed across his face. The feeling was mutual, though Derek was trying to be professional about it. He waved Derek to a seat in front of the desk.

'Then you know why I've come.'

Muloon pushed himself back in his chair and interlocked his arms in a relaxed position behind his head.

'This is going to be a pretty thin conversation, Sergeant. I fish and hunt and I left my good knife back in Calgary. Ahnah Oolik called me last week to say the new one I ordered was in, but since I wasn't planning on going hunting for a while, I didn't bother to pick it up.'

'How do you account for the fact that it was found in the pool where Martha Salliaq's body was discovered?'

Muloon raised an eyebrow. A look passed across his face. Derek couldn't tell what. 'I don't account for it. Since I had nothing to do with Martha's death, how could I?' He seemed completely at ease now. Either the fellow was the best liar Derek had ever come across or he was telling the truth. For Edie's sake as well as the investigation, Derek hoped it was the latter. He didn't really think Muloon was the killer but he didn't trust the guy. There was something opaque and vaguely reptilian about him. It was a face that resisted being read.

'What were your movements on Saturday night?'

'That's the easiest question in the world to answer, Sergeant Palliser, because there were no movements.' Muloon's jawbone flexed but there remained a hint of a smile on his lips. 'I had an arrangement to make supper for Edie Kiglatuk at my house. I worked for a while, then prepared the meal. Caribou chilli, in case you're interested. When Edie didn't show, I went back to work for a while. Finished about ten, I guess. I listened to some music before having an early night.'

'You didn't think to go look for Edie?'

The smile widened a little. 'You know as well as I do that Edie Kiglatuk makes her own rules. I prefer to stay out of the game.'

'Was Martha Salliaq more your kind of play, Muloon?' Derek wondered why he'd said something so confrontational.

'If you think I killed Martha Salliaq, go ahead and prove it. But you don't, do you? So I have to wonder why you're on my turf.' Muloon leaned in. That hint of a grin again. 'And the only explanation I can come up with, sergeant, is that you're sore I fucked your woman.' He left a pause. 'Good fuck, in case you're interested.'

Muloon locked eyes with him. His gaze was as sharp as a wolf's and in that moment Derek realized he'd been wrong to cut the man so much slack. He had no doubt then that Chip Muloon was capable of absolutely anything.

Back at the detachment, Edie was downing a third mug of tea in the vain hope that it would stop her thinking about having something stronger. Some days she found it relatively easy to keep the urge at bay but today was not one of those days. Today was a day for imagining the unimaginable.

Why had Martha Salliaq sought Willa out on Friday night? And why had he not told her? Why would Martha want to confide in her sister's boyfriend if their affair really was over? Was there some kind of rivalry going on? A love triangle perhaps? Common enough. And if the younger sibling was 'everyone's favourite' as he'd said, then why had Willa given Martha up for Lizzie? Had Willa been playing the two sisters off against one another? From there the thoughts only got crazier and more tangled. Was it true that he'd failed to show at hers on Saturday evening because his ATV had broken down? What was he keeping from her, that sweet, solid little boy from another life, who would pass his evenings cuddled on the couch watching Laurel and Hardy movies? That sweet, solid little boy who became a drug addict, a brawler and a thief, who lost his brother in terrible circumstances but who had pulled through and seemed to have found new purpose in the Rangers. Willa the murderer? Could she imagine that?

Then there was Chip Muloon, a man she barely knew and who had done everything to ensure she never would, a man who was as much a blank now as he had been nearly a month ago when they'd first met. Why in all the time she'd spent with Muloon had he never mentioned ordering a hunting knife or having any connection to Klinsman at Camp Nanook? Perhaps he was secretive because he had reason to be? What else hadn't he revealed? Supposing those mentoring chats with Martha about life in the south had taken a less innocent turn . . .

Way out possibilities. Almost . . .

It was the 'almost' that made her want to drink.

*

She welcomed the distracting tramp of boots on the steps. Moments later Derek came bursting through the door wearing a dark expression.

'Your *boyfriend* . . .' He stepped back from whatever it was he was about to say.

'My ex.'

The phone rang. They both looked at it for a moment. After what seemed like a long time, Derek went over and picked up. She heard him say 'I'll switch to speaker', then to Edie he said: 'It's Anna Mackie.'

'I worked all through the night but the results are inconclusive,' Mackie said.

'Give us what you got, Anna.'

The medical examiner began to detail her findings. In all probability Luc was right, she said, and the cause of death was exsanguination. She'd come to that conclusion partly by ruling out drowning. There were head injuries but these were post-mortem, almost certainly as a result of the corpse being buffeted about in shallow water. As a general principle, a corpse didn't bleed, but the congestion of the head with blood as the result of the buffeting could have led to gross post-mortem bleeding; though in Anna's judgement Martha almost certainly bled out while she was unconscious, but alive. The catastrophic loss of blood made it difficult to test for the disturbances of blood electrolytes normally associated with drowning but she didn't think there was enough fluid in the lungs to support a drowning case. She'd found foam in the airways, which was common in victims of drowning but this was also consistent with drug overdose. Temperature and stomach contents analysis suggested a time of death as being between 8 p.m. and 11 p.m. on Saturday, though it wasn't possible to be more precise because of the length of time that the body had lain in the water.

She hadn't been able to find any foreign DNA on Martha's body and the immersion meant that she was very unlikely to come across anything conclusive. Mick Flaherty had been focusing on the two suspects' clothing. He'd found Martha's hair on both. In addition, there were traces of Martha's blood on Namagoose's trousers, though this was menstrual blood and its distribution was commensurate with the suspect having had sex with the victim. From analysis of Martha's hormone levels she thought it likely that the girl was at the end of a period, which backed that up. No defensive wounds. Nothing under the fingernails. No abrasions around the genital area. In Mackie's opinion, Martha hadn't been raped, except with the blade, of course.

She'd left testing of the knife till last on the grounds that it was the least likely to yield any significant evidence, because of the length of time it had lain in the mud and water. There were traces of blood on it matching Martha's type but that was no surprise given where it had been found. Mick Flaherty had retrieved a hair wedged into the handle which had a sharp cut at one end and looked as though it probably belonged to Martha. That was being tested now. The balance of probabilities suggested that the wooden-handled knife Edie had pulled from the mud *was* most likely the one that killed the victim.

'We've both done as much as we could in the time. It'll take longer to confirm the DNA evidence,' Anna said.

'Thank you. We're grateful.'

'Better late than never,' Anna added ruefully.

Edie asked about the drug analysis.

'Of course. Sorry, guys, it's been a long night. The preliminaries on Martha's blood suggest she'd had the equivalent of a small beer, probably sometime in the early afternoon, and we can confirm she had Ambien in her system.'

'Enough to knock her out?' Derek asked.

'Plenty enough to quieten her up some. I think she was probably semi- or fully unconscious when the knife went in.'

'That's a mercy, at least,' Edie said.

Derek pulled a notebook towards him and began frantically making notes.

'Can you say more about the Ambien, Anna? How it might have gotten into her system, how long it would have been before it took effect?'

'Of course.' There was a pause while Mackie gathered her thoughts.

'Ambien is the brand name for zolpidem. It's a short-acting hypnotic with effects similar to benzodiazepines. The tabs are small, easy to dissolve in a drink. The taste isn't great but it comes on after you've swallowed. It may be that the victim was given enough to make her drowsy then persuaded to take more once she was out of it. They're quick-acting, it's a pretty powerful sedative. She'd have started feeling the effects fifteen minutes after ingesting. At the levels that were in Martha's body, she would have experienced muscle relaxation and depressed respiratory function.' Another pause. 'That give you enough?'

Derek said he thought so, thanked Mackie and finished the call.

'Saxby steals Ambien from the pharmacy and it turns up in Martha Salliaq.' Derek sounded breathless. His legs were jigging up and down in his chair, his voice eager and with the tiniest hint of celebration. 'Edie, I do believe we've got 'em.'

He dialled first the prosecutor then Klinsman and left messages.

'I gotta go down to the port. Mix-up with some cargo. We got a shipment of snowmobile parts nobody wants. But if either the prosecutor or Klinsman calls, come get me. Immediately, OK?'

Edie smiled and saluted but the moment he turned, her smile dropped off. The circumstantial evidence pointed to Namagoose and Saxby. Now they had physical evidence too. So why was something still gnawing at her bones?

The *Herbert Piquot* sat anchored quietly in mid-channel, a small tarnished brooch on the grey, velvety waters of the Sound. It was on the *Piquot* that Derek had first arrived on Ellesmere, thirteen years ago. Back then, there were bergy bits and growlers littering the beach and large pans of slowly rotting ice still twirling in the currents. The summer insects were as sparse as hot days. It took him five or six years to settle. The place was so different from anywhere he'd been before. But the job itself had never been too challenging. There really was no crime in the Arctic back then. Being a native cop was somewhere between administrator and social worker. You could take yourself out on spring patrol and return six weeks later in the certain knowledge that the only things you'd have missed would be a few drunken brawls and some loose huskies. He felt a flash of nostalgia for the old innocence of the place; its brittle, delicate, ice-laden charisma.

Sam Oolik was at the quayside leaning over a cargo crate. He stood up as Derek approached, clutching his lower back, his face wrinkling momentarily before settling back into its usual genial blank.

'Hey, Derek.' He wiped the sweat from his forehead. 'Damned heat. Must be ten degrees.' He stood up and looked Derek full in the eye. 'I guess you must be about ready to make those arrests.'

A voice shouted his name. He looked about and spotted the balding head of Larry Larsen, the *Piquot*'s captain, and, gathering himself, went down the quay towards him. For the next couple of hours, he was too busy with the supply to think about Martha Salliaq or how much everything was changing.

Returning to the detachment later, he hung up his hat on the rack behind his desk and called Edie's name. A head peeked out from the comms room.

'Someone on the radio?'

'Sammy Inukpuk. I don't know why he didn't just use the phone.'

'I told him not to.' You had to admire the man's tenacity. Edie's knight in rusting armour.

Derek took off his jacket, went over to his desk and sat down. 'No phone calls?'

Edie shook her head. She was leaning against the door jamb now, her hair loose for once and falling over her face, and he found himself oddly stirred. Perhaps Muloon was right and he had been jealous.

In the comms room the radio beeped.

'Sammy again?'

'Doubt it. We just signed off. You want me to get it?' Edie said.

'No, I'll go.' He crossed the room and went past her into the corridor. It was Larsen wanting to know when he'd be down to sign off the last of the cargo. No talk of one last long, boozy onboard dinner. Another tradition gone. He promised to swing by as soon as he could. He signed off and went back into the office where Edie was sitting, in Stevie's chair, lost in thought, absent-mindedly braiding her hair. Her head shot up when she heard him and a fragile smile bloomed briefly on her face without reaching her eyes.

He knew then there was something she wasn't telling him.

20

Sonia Gutierrez approached Glacier Ridge from the coastal road, where she was less likely to be spotted. The track took her as far as the bird cliffs then up onto the ridge itself. From there she turned off and bumped over the willow to the crude boundary fence. Clambering from her ATV and checking that she was not being observed, she pulled up the wire and slunk underneath.

For the first few days after the discovery of Martha's body Sonia had thought of the girl's death, tragic though it was, as a kind of sorry sideshow to the main event. But she was beginning to see that it had lifted a rock and dark things had scuttled out and headed for the shadows and it was her job to make sure they were not lost. Somewhere, someone didn't want Glacier Ridge cleaned up and they were prepared to do whatever they had to – including, perhaps, murder – to ensure it wasn't. What she didn't know was why. But she meant to find out.

She wandered along the old track, picking her way through the debris of frost-heaved concrete and rusted metal, among the remnants of buildings ruined by years of freezing and thawing, and thought about the past. For centuries Britain, the United States, Canada, Russia, Norway, Denmark and Sweden had battled it out for ownership of the Arctic, treating it as nothing more than a blank canvas onto which they could paint their flags. The desires and needs of the Inuit people, who had made the place their home for thousands of years and for whom the idea of owning land – in the sense of legally possessing it – was an affront to the natural order, had been completely ignored. It was only in the last few decades that Inuit had entered the fray and begun to voice their ancestral claims to the territory and its resources.

Now, she sensed, the terms of engagement were shifting. In one way, the annual Canadian military patrol had come too late. The battle was no longer between nation states or even between Inuit and nation states, but between land developers, oil and gas companies, mining and mineral extractors and shipping interests. If development of the Arctic was to take any account of the people living there, Inuit would have to divert their attentions away from national politics and take on the corporations and the institutions working in the Arctic directly. If they did nothing there would come a time in the not too distant future when they would find themselves effectively living on reservations surrounded by mineral mines and oil derricks. The thought of that hollowed her heart.

She stopped at a high point and took in the layout of the old radar station. A rough, dry wind whistled over from the northwest. Clumps of summer flowers had blossomed in the shelter of south-facing walls and some cottonheads scrambled along the water run-off at the edges of the pathways. Caribou had left tracks and there were a few scattered hare droppings but to the unknowing eye it looked as though no human being had set foot on the site for decades. Sonia knew this was an illusion. In fact, dozens of surveyors and clean-up engineers had tramped through the place over the years since its closure.

On the visit she'd made the day after Martha's body was found, she'd come across a bunch of tundra flowers in one of the outbuildings. Out of curiosity she went back there now to see whether whoever had left them had returned. She allowed her eyes to adjust to the darkness. After a while the earth floor resolved itself and she saw it was sprinkled with mosses and tiny patches of lichen. A single pink campion trembled beside the window. It appeared that the flower man or woman hadn't come back.

From there she took herself to the northern boundary of the site facing the patchwork of black-water pools and bitter-looking mud of Lake Turngaluk. Palliser had partially enclosed the area in police tape, as though the lake was itself a crime against the surrounding tundra. The lake had never been the focus of her energies. The environmental impact report suggested that the contamination in that area was low level. Some tar, petroleum, polychlorinated biphenyls, benzene, dioxin and heavy metal deposits. It had recommended lake drainage, but that was as far as it went. There *was* an undeniably creepy atmosphere about the place. She could understand why the locals avoided it and said it was taboo. Inuit always took their cue from nature and there was something about Lake Turngaluk that nature didn't recognize as its own.

It was the landfill site to one side of the lake that was of particular interest now. From her scrutiny of the plans she believed the area marked the position of what would once have been the underground bunker and it was the bunker that was somehow key. There were too many anomalies surrounding its construction; the fact that it had been commissioned by the Department of Defence and not by the Canadian or US military who were jointly responsible for the site, then left off the plans and only made reference to once it had been stripped of its original purpose and filled in. Why would you keep anything in a bunker unless you wanted it hidden? And why would you leave it off any plans unless at some point you wanted to be able to deny it was ever there?

The track edged around the site and dipped down and around the lake but from her vantage now she could see there was a more direct route to the landfill area, down the rocky scree. Shouldering her backpack, she picked her way through and twenty minutes later found herself standing at the spot. It was larger than it had looked from the top of the ridge and she could see now that there was considerable subsidence, which had been disguised from further away by a sparse covering of low sedge. She picked a stem and crushed the leaves between her fingers but, unusually for sedge, the leaves smelled of nothing and left a sticky residue which she wiped off on her shirt. Pulling out her camera, she walked the circumference and took a few pictures, then knelt down for a closer look. The ground had been filled in with ballast and poured concrete. She tested a foot on the ballast but was not confident that it would take her weight. The place was dangerous but there were no notices, no warning signs or other structures around it.

She started to make her way back to the ridge. The wind picked up, whistling across the tundra from the northwest towards the sea. About halfway up the incline, she spotted half-a-dozen men in military uniform busying themselves unloading several rolls of razor wire and what looked like fencing from a utility vehicle. A jeep sat off to one side. She stopped for a moment, breathing in the sweet Arctic air, trying to figure out what was going on. She hadn't heard them arrive – the sound of the engine and their voices must have been obscured by the wind – and it was a shock now to see them there. Could it be that the clean-up had been given the go-ahead after all? It surely looked that way. A pulse of adrenalin tapped her temple and she moved ahead, picking a path along the loose scree towards the truck, waving and shouting. As she ran, a needling thought ran through her. Neither Klinsman nor Palliser had been courteous enough to update her with this latest development. Well, that hardly mattered now. She found herself grinning, her foggy mood burned off in the fierce light of relief. This was Canada after all, not some chaotic and impoverishing military dictatorship. Here, of all places, the law was king.

As she approached, the officer in charge left his spot beside the jeep and came over to meet her. She held out a hand. 'I'm Sonia Gutierrez, the attorney for the hamlet of Kuujuaq.' If he had heard her name before, it didn't seem to register now. She went on. 'How long are you expecting this to take?'

He raised his eyebrows as though surprised by the question. She thought she detected a little impatience too.

'We should have it all wrapped up by this afternoon, ma'am. Is that your ATV over there?' He pointed.

'I meant for the whole programme?' The agreement included an estimated time frame but it didn't hurt to check with the people on the ground.

'Like I said. A few hours.'

A soldier bustled up, saluted and asked his boss where to begin setting the fence posts. The officer pointed along a line marked with yellow pegs, and told the soldier he'd be along to advise in a few minutes. As the soldier saluted again and walked away, the officer turned his attentions once more to Sonia.

'I'm gonna need you to leave the area now, ma'am.'

'Oh no,' she said, 'I'm the attorney for the settlement of Kuujuaq.' She began to sketch out her role. The officer waited politely for her to finish before repeating his request. She told herself not to get riled, the legal training kicking in. *Remain calm and reassert the position.*

'What I'm saying, officer, is this is Inuit land. It belongs to the people of Kuujuaq.'

The officer stiffened and took a step back, an implacable expression on his face. 'No, ma'am. I guess you were not informed correctly. This land has been requisitioned. As from 9 a.m. this morning, this area legally belongs to the Department of Defence.'

21

Edie was in the kitchen trying to rustle up something delicious from half a walrus head and a caribou ear – not so easy, it turned out – when the sound of the door slamming and Sonia Gutierrez's voice sent her back out into the detachment office. The lawyer was standing in the middle of the room, with her face as dark as seaweed and a mad cast to her eye, shrieking what sounded very much like a string of Spanish expletives. Derek was there too, sitting frozen behind his desk like a cornered animal.

'Jesus, Edie, you tell her to calm down. I tried and look what happened.' Displays of emotional intensity left Derek floored. It was the Inuk in him, Edie thought.

'You can carry on bellowing like a wounded musk ox all you like, Ms Gutierrez, but it won't do you any good,' she said.

Derek flashed Edie a grateful look then cleared his throat.

The lawyer shuffled deeper into her skin and rearranged her features.

'OK, Ms Gutierrez, I'm guessing this isn't a social call, so how's about we start over?' He waved the lawyer to a chair.

Gutierrez parked herself, sweeping her hair back over her shoulder and crossing her legs elegantly.

'This is not a performance, Sergeant Palliser.' Her accent was thicker when she was angry.

'All the same, Ms Gutierrez, you seem to be the only one with the script.'

The lawyer took in a deep breath.

'Since you are partly behind this, I'm relying on you, Sergeant Palliser, to tell me what the hell is going on.'

Derek threw up his hands.

'The Defence Department instructs Joint Forces North to take back the Glacier Ridge site and you expect me to believe you know nothing about it. Hardly likely is it, sergeant?'

Derek frowned then grabbed his chin between his fingers. 'I agree. All the same, it seems to be what has happened.' He looked across to Edie, who shrugged.

Gutierrez muttered something in Spanish then gestured to the pack of cigarettes lying on Derek's desk. He picked it up and held it out. She took a cigarette and allowed him to light it for her.

'One of my contacts at the departmental counsel's office said there's some legal ambiguity in the land claims agreement. In other words, I screwed up one of the subclauses. But that's bullshit.' She pronounced the word 'bollsheet'.

'What is Klinsman saying?' Derek asked.

'Colonel Klinsman isn't answering his phone. I already put a call through to the Nunavut premier and to the parliamentary legal counsel challenging the basis of this decision. I don't think there's any question that the department is in breach of its agreement, let alone its fiduciary duty.' Her eyes were wet rocks sparkling in the sun. 'It's too much. My contracts are always immaculate. Immaculate. It'll take time but I will drag anyone and everyone who had anything to do with this through every court in Canada if I have to. People think they can screw me, they need to know who's got her fist around their balls.' She cast a glance at Derek then at Edie.

'You really didn't know anything about this, did you?'

They shook their heads.

Gutierrez's eyes narrowed. 'Then you don't understand what this means for you.'

Derek and Edie swapped blank looks. 'The land belongs to the Defence Department. You no longer have jurisdiction over the case.'

Gutierrez stubbed her cigarette out and stood to leave. At the door she turned, wrapping her coat more tightly around her body and addressing herself to Derek.

'You might feel like doing a little screaming yourself.'

The area around Lake Turngaluk was wired off with electric fencing. Defence Department signs warning trespassers hung from the fence posts. Here and there, remnants of crime tape rustled in the wind but the area behind the wire had been indiscriminately churned by the tracks of military vehicles, effectively destroying the crime scene.

Derek slowed his ATV right down. They were outside the Camp Nanook perimeter fence now.

'If they think we'll just roll over . . .'

The guard at the sentry gate made a phone call and told them Colonel Klinsman wasn't available.

'We can wait.' Derek folded his arms.

The soldier checked his watch, uncertain as to how to proceed. 'He's busy all evening.'

'Then we'll stay here until he isn't.'

The soldier's face contorted. He began rubbing his hands. 'Look, he's not going to see you guys, OK?'

Edie caught Derek's eye and raised a single eyebrow. Her eyes glittered. 'They ever teach you the Eskimo roll, soldier?'

The soldier looked puzzled. 'The kayak manoeuvre?'

'That's the one. Basic safety procedure, right? Kindergarten stuff. The Eskimo rolls under the water and disappears. But then, just when you're least expecting it, back he pops.'

Derek throttled up his ATV, turned it around until he drew up alongside the guard.

'You give Colonel Klinsman a message from the Ellesmere Island Police. You tell him to expect an Eskimo roll.'

Back at the detachment the voicemail light was winking – Anna Mackie saying that Ransom had given her orders to release the forensics in the Martha Salliaq case to the military investigator. She signed off with an apology and a contact number for her at home.

'Don't call the office.'

Derek pushed the phone away and reached for a cigarette.

'Damned if this makes any sense to me.' He swivelled his chair around and began to bite at his fingernails then checked himself. 'One minute Klinsman's begging us for a date, the next he's washing his hair. Why take over jurisdiction when we're so near to making arrests?'

'Maybe they want control over what happens to Namagoose and Saxby?' Edie said. She was feeling shitty for Derek but another part of her was relieved. Something told her that whoever arrested the Killer Whales would wind up regretting it.

They sat for a moment.

'Maybe they've got new information that someone else at the camp was involved, someone higher up?' Edie offered.

'It's possible.' Derek sighed, slapped his thighs and stood up. 'Either way, we're not gonna find out tonight. It's late and I could use a drink and some thinking time on my own. Let's call it a day and come at it fresh tomorrow morning.'

At the entrance to her tent Edie hesitated. Derek's mention of drink had kicked off the urge. The sensible move would be to step inside, creep under the sleeping skins and wait for sleep. Something about this case filled her with *taulittuq*, the sense of endlessly trudging in circles and going nowhere. They said that *taulittuq* was caused by *ijirait*, bad spirits, dragging the living back into the past. But what if there was nowhere else to go? She thought how much she longed for a little dark right now. To be able to see the stars and know there was something up there bigger than you, bigger than *taulittuq*, bigger even than the bad spirits on your back.

Turning away from the tent, she set off along the path that led towards the Anchor Bar. Alcohol had always been a short, straight road to oblivion but at least oblivion was somewhere to go. Inside it was mayhem. A crowd of locals were making the most of the arrival of the annual supply before the community ran out of whisky or the mayor decided to declare a dry week. The blast of boozy air brought with it the familiar sourness of a previous life and right now that smelled good. Pushing her way through the crush Edie reached the bar and, throwing down a few notes, shouted above the din to the barman for a beer with a triple rye chaser. Two glasses appeared. The sight of the booze had an instant calming effect. It was funny how it could do that to her. For a while she took pleasure in watching the bubbles sliding around on the rye meniscus, the head on the beer gently subsiding into the liquid like old snow in the beat of an amber sun, and her mind faded out everything but the magic inside those glasses. Then a man with a five-toothed grin and yellow, jelly eyes sidled up and slurred a hello and the smell of his breath brought the world back in. She found herself back in the bar, looking at a girl not far off Martha's age. A look she recognized, the same slightly defiant stance. She smiled, but the girl looked away and suddenly the conversation with Martha flooded back into her mind and she heard herself mouthing the words *Going somewhere special?* After that she didn't feel like drinking any more. She stood up and began to elbow her way back through the throng of people. At the entrance she turned, hoping for a last look at the girl. Instead she saw the yellow-eyed man clasping the rye to his breast as you might a sleeping baby.

A short time later she found herself on the path leading to Chip Muloon's house. At her knock, the locks slid back and Chip's face emerged, blinking away sleep.

'It's late, Edie, go home.'

'I can't,' she said. Home was 70 kilometres away.

Chip looked about, sighed and eye-rolled. 'Come in, then. But only for a little while, OK?'

He cleared away a bunch of papers lying on the table, offered her some hot tea and went into the kitchen to boil the water. She sat on the couch and waited. It had never struck her before how Spartan, almost lifeless, the place was and in that observation she felt the old *taulittuq* creeping over her and the *ijirait* tap tap tapping on her back.

Chip reappeared carrying two mugs. He stopped for a second. She saw him stiffen, the cords in his neck tightening.

'Why are you looking at me like that?'

She blinked and looked away. He came over to the couch and put the mugs on the table, taking a seat on the chair opposite.

'Have you been drinking?'

Her clothes smelled of the bar. 'Almost,' she said.

He frowned. When he spoke again his voice was quiet and modulated. 'Look, Edie, we were never going anywhere, you know that. You got wrapped up in the case and I got tired of wondering whether or not you were gonna show and that's that.'

A small, involuntary laugh escaped her lips. It sounded more bitter than she felt. He thought she was trying to woo him back. The vanity of the male.

'You spoke to Klinsman.'

His eyes grew wider then he slumped back into his chair.

'Christ, this isn't about the fucking knife again, is it?'

'No, it's not about the knife.'

There was a pause in which everything that needed to be said was said.

'I thought you might be pleased,' Chip said finally. 'This way you get to go back to your teaching.'

'Klinsman told you, didn't he? He told you that the Defence Department have taken over jurisdiction in the case.'

Muloon's lips were parted and she saw from the implacable stare, the bunched jaw and tight neck that her hunch was correct. Her ex-lover put his mug back on the table, crossed his arms and stood.

'I think you should go now,' he said.

22

Derek cleared away the whisky bottle, ate two packs of ramen noodles and went to bed, relieved to be on his own. He was bilious from the booze and in desperate need of sleep, but even as his head hit the pillow and the light streamed in through his closed eyelids his mind begin to spiral and after a few minutes he realized it was hopeless. The incessant light didn't help. He got up and attempted to close the gaps in the blinds but moving one rung simply opened up space further down. They needed replacing but he hadn't got around to it. One more thing to do. He tried to focus on his latest lemming observations but as he climbed back into bed his mind resumed its restless spooling so he got up again, moved to the bathroom, turned on the cold water in the shower and got in. The cold hit him like a punch.

The truth was, he felt dumb and humiliated. Dumb because he hadn't seen the situation coming and humiliated because he hadn't done anything to stop it. His first thought was that Gutierrez had somehow panicked the colonel into taking action. But, as he understood it, Klinsman's authority began and ended at Camp Nanook. The colonel had already gone out of his way to distance himself from the department. Which must mean that whoever had taken this latest decision was working above Klinsman's pay grade.

He stepped out of the shower and began working the towel over his damp skin. Was it possible that he'd uncovered some inconvenient truth the department didn't want made public, something that had nothing to do with Namagoose and Saxby? What if all this time he'd been looking in the wrong place?

Slinging the towel back on its hook, he padded through to the bedroom and clambered into bed. He had found himself at a crossroads with no signposts. An approach to Klinsman to put pressure on the department to give him back the case seemed unlikely to have any impact, though it was worth a try. A more complicated solution might be to throw in his lot with Sonia Gutierrez and openly challenge the department's decision. He could even carry on with the investigation in his own time, though he'd need to keep that fact from Klinsman. Or he could just let the whole thing go.

Reaching for the pad he kept in the drawer of his nightstand, he drew three columns. At the head of one he wrote 'Give up', at the head of the second 'Fight', the third 'Secret'. He began to write, filling first one column then another. By the time he was done, he'd convinced himself that giving up the case would only serve to destroy what little was left of his reputation in Kuujuaq. They already saw him as weak and a stooge for the south. It would look as though he'd caved in at the first sign of pressure. Which wouldn't be so far from the truth. He would probably be able to swing a transfer to Yellowknife – he was still well thought of over that way – but his career in the Ellesmere Police would effectively be over and he would have a hard time living with himself. He picked up his pen and put a strike through the first column. The next two columns weren't so easy. The 'Fight' option had the advantage of Sonia Gutierrez's backing, but it was also likely to get strung out in legal wrangling. And there was something alarming about Gutierrez, which, despite her reputation, made him reluctant to risk both the case and his career on an alliance with her.

Two roads left to go down. He could try to persuade Klinsman or his puppetmasters to change their minds. He could carry on with the investigation in secret. He thought about this for a moment and decided that these two roads weren't mutually exclusive. A path from one led to the other. He checked the clock on his nightstand. It was a little after 4 a.m. In another four hours Klinsman would be at his desk. Until then he'd try to catch a little shut-eye.

He woke to spokes of sunlight spilling out across the bed. Rising, he headed for the shower again, then dressed and fed his lemmings. He went to the kitchenette and made himself coffee. Then he dialled Klinsman's voicemail and left a message for him to call. Going back into the kitchen to refill his mug he told himself he really should be eating more. These last few days he'd been pretty much existing on coffee and cigarettes, with the odd pack of ramen noodles and anything Edie happened to have prepared. Bachelor habits. He went towards the refrigerator then remembered the walrus head he'd cleared away yesterday evening and decided, what the hell, breakfast could wait. Returning to his desk with his coffee, he sat down and checked his emails. After an hour it came to him that Klinsman wasn't going to return his call, so he crossed the room, dialled the switchboard from Stevie Killik's desk and told the operator his name was 'Doctor Sanger' and he needed to speak urgently to Colonel Klinsman on a family matter.

Klinsman picked up on the second ring, answering in his usual abrupt manner, but this time there was a hint of anxiety in his tone.

'Good morning, colonel,' Derek said.

There was a pause. 'Was that really necessary, sergeant?'

'You could try returning my calls.' Derek sounded less modulated than he'd hoped. 'Then it wouldn't have been.'

Klinsman cleared his throat. 'I really don't have anything to say. This isn't my decision.' He lowered his voice. 'It comes right from the top.'

'You planning on arresting Namagoose and Saxby?'

Klinsman went quiet.

'You really need to give me something here. For the family's sake.'

Klinsman already had that one covered. 'We'll deal with the family.'

Derek pulled the handset from his ear and stared at it a moment, the bile in his belly bubbling up. He swallowed it down. Did Klinsman really think he was going to walk away from this? That he was just going to tramp on the Ellesmere Island Police? He took a deep breath.

'I'm not sure you and whoever it is you take your orders from understand how it is up here, colonel.' He'd rehearsed his lines and he had nothing to lose in saying them. 'So let me tell you. You remove the case from local jurisdiction it's gonna be interpreted as *qalunaat* interference. Go down that route and you can forget cooperation from the family. Nobody in the Inuit community is gonna give you the time of day.' He felt strong and purposeful, absolutely confident of being in the right. 'You put us up here, Klinsman, you and your people, and now you're gonna have to deal with us.'

Klinsman coughed. 'What you're not hearing, sergeant, is that this decision has nothing to do with me. The only decision I'm directly responsible for is banning Camp Nanook personnel from making visits to Kuujuaq, so you won't be seeing any more of us – how do you say, *unataqti*, is it? – around town. I can assure you that none of this is any reflection on your police work. If you come up with some fresh information about the death of Martha Salliaq I'll be glad to pass it on to the relevant parties, but understand this: the case is no longer in your jurisdiction and the military authorities won't look kindly on you continuing to investigate it.'

Derek's heart sank. He'd thrown down his flush only to discover the opposition was holding aces.

'At least have the courtesy to tell me if you intend to go ahead with the clean-up at Glacier Ridge,' he said. A moment ago he'd been sure of himself but he hated how he sounded now: keening, almost desperate.

'It was you who insisted on us postponing it, if you recall. I've already told Ms Gutierrez, I don't have any more information on that.' Klinsman spoke with an air of finality.

For a while after the call Derek sat in his chair smarting. He hadn't just lost the battle, he'd been nuked. He lit a cigarette. The smoke curling into his lungs made him feel a little better. He thought back to his training all those years ago in Yellowknife. He'd been an excellent student, a good rookie cop. Then somewhere along the line he'd lost his moral courage. How that had happened he still had no idea. He'd only become aware of it last year, investigating the deaths of the *qalunaat* hunter and

Edie Kiglatuk's stepson, Joe Inukpuk. The successful prosecution of that case had given him back his self-respect. He'd felt renewed. As though he'd rediscovered his purpose in life. That moral compass of his once again found its true north. And he wasn't about to lose it this time.

His thoughts were interrupted by the sound of the door opening. Tom Silliq stepped inside and looked nervously about the room.

Derek felt his new heroic mood shrink back a little. 'What brings you here, Tom?'

Silliq shifted his weight. His face looked troubled. 'See, here's what it is. There weren't no *unataqti* in the bar last night, nor in the Shack neither.'

'A lot of people in this town'll happy about that,' Derek said.

'Well, I ain't one of 'em.' Silliq lifted up his baseball cap, scratched underneath, then replaced it. 'Thought as you'd know something about it is all.'

Derek explained that Camp Nanook was on lockdown until the Martha Salliaq case had been resolved. So here he was once more, he thought, sweating the small stuff for folk who laughed at him behind his back and called him the Lemming Police.

'Ah,' said Tom. 'Well, that answers it.' He took off his hat again and turned it around in his hands. 'The other thing don't matter any more then.'

'Well good,' Derek said. He waited for Silliq to show some signs of leaving and when he didn't he said, 'Was there something else?'

Silliq kept staring at his hands. 'Nothing to me, but my wife will go crazy I don't mention it. The Arab boy works for her.' He watched Derek trying to summon the man to mind.

'The meteorologist?'

'Right, that fella. He didn't show up for his last two shifts. Says he had a headache of some kind on Saturday, then he just stops showing up. I been round his house and there's no one there.'

'Maybe he got sick of the job,' Derek said. He was struggling to sound interested. Last thing he needed was this kind of distraction. 'You go talk to any of his friends?'

'Fella don't have no friends.' Silliq rubbed his head. 'He don't drink neither. One of the reasons Susie took him on. Muslim.' He pronounced the word 'Moose-leem' as though it was some elk-like property.

Derek said he would look into it and meantime, if Silliq heard anything, to let him know. All of which meant he had no intention of doing anything. As he watched Silliq lumber towards the door he felt an overwhelming sense of loathing. For the situation. For himself. It gave him the urge to thump something.

The table came to hand.

His index finger landed on something sharp. Blood began to spiral down. He reckoned he deserved it. He sat back in his chair, welcoming the pain, noticing as he did so that his notebook was lying on the floor. It must have fallen off when he banged the table. As he picked it up, his eyes lit upon the right-hand column he'd written a few hours before. He stared at it awhile, his focus moving in and out on the word 'Secret', unable to remove his gaze. He felt the pain in his shoulder and arm drain away, as though some blockage had finally dislodged itself. There it was, his decision, staring him in the face. The answer to all the doubt, the humiliation and self-loathing. There *was* no crossroads. There never had been. There was only one direction of travel and that was forward. He would carry on investigating the Martha Salliaq murder until he had the perpetrator or perpetrators on the hook. Even if that meant defying Klinsman and exposing whatever the department was trying to keep from becoming public. Even if it meant becoming a whistleblower, with all the dangers that would accrue. He had to do it. For Martha's sake and for his own, he had to keep going until he'd found the truth. Feeling lighter than he had in days, he tore the page from his notebook, screwed it up and threw it in the bin.

The door swung open again. This time it was Edie. Just as she opened her mouth to say something the phone rang. 'You mind?' he said, lifting his finger, which was bleeding more profusely now. 'I should go put this under some water.'

When he came back out to the office, she was just finishing.

'Who was it?'

'Sammy. It's my fault, D. I sneaked in while you were having your shower and left a message for him to call.'

Derek sucked his teeth.

'I know, I know, it's fucked up.' She gestured to his finger. 'You hurt yourself?'

'It's nothing.'

She held up a plastic bag. 'I brought seal liver so how's about we have breakfast? Then you can disapprove of me on a full stomach.'

A while later she came out of the kitchen carrying two plates of fried meat. As they were eating, he outlined his plan to carry on with the investigation. She seemed glad at his decision.

'You realize there's a risk here, though, Edie,' he went on. 'We're not dealing with a bunch of kids in the playground.'

'You're not dealing with a lemming right here either,' she said. 'D, I can handle myself.'

She was right. He could be a condescending asshole sometimes. They sat for a while, feeling the atmosphere between them thicken. He hoped she was gearing herself up to tell him whatever it was she'd been keeping from him.

'I went over to Chip Muloon's place last night,' she said finally.

He raised his eyebrows and smiled to himself. Here it was.

'He already knew about the Defence Department taking back Glacier Ridge.'

Derek felt himself contract. 'Town gossip,' he said, unimpressed.

'I don't think so. I think Klinsman told him before us.'

'Why would he do that?' He felt himself quicken. Maybe this was something after all.

'Sam Oolik saw them together.'

'So what?'

'I think Chip's got something to do with the military.'

Derek frowned. It seemed unlikely. He'd seen Muloon's credentials. The man worked for the University of Calgary.

Edie went on. 'All that time me and Chip spent together, he never once mentioned the university. No colleagues, no department, nothing.'

Derek closed his eyes. When he opened them, the bolder, better version of himself stepped forward.

'Let's check it out,' he said.

23

After yesterday's five-minute phone call with a junior counsel at the Defence Department confirming that the clean-up at Glacier Ridge had been postponed indefinitely, Sonia Gutierrez had spent most of the night rereading the land claims papers and her head was spinning. The papers, with their endless delicately negotiated clauses, subclauses and technical addenda, served as a reminder of just how hard she'd worked, as well as how much she'd sacrificed to get the agreement in the first place. The indignation of yesterday had given way to a more considered determination. Somewhere in the papers she was confident there would be some grounds for an appeal against the department's decision. By appealing she hoped to be able to expose whatever it was that the department was trying to hide. Enter by stealth through the back door then open the whole thing wide. In any case, if any formal move were to have real traction it would have to be based on a careful weighing of the legal position rather than some knee-jerk sense of injustice or outrage.

Bundling herself up in her robe, she padded down the stairs to the guest kitchen and switched on the coffee drip, intending to get herself showered and dressed before going to see the Salliaqs, who were now back in their own house. Charlie needed to hear this latest development along with her reassurances that she was doing everything in her power to right the situation. That no one at Camp Nanook or in the Defence Department had thought to contact her directly so that she could forewarn Charlie was an affront to them both. Her client was a difficult man but he'd had a tough life and beneath all the bluster there lurked a kind, if wary, heart. It was more than enough that his daughter had been murdered. To lose the land claim he'd worked so hard and fought so long for was a cruelty too far.

She sprayed herself with insect repellent and walked out to her ATV, zipped herself inside its reassuring plastic cover and sparked up the engine. On the way over, she rehearsed her spiel. The message she wanted to get across was that, however it seemed, the people of Kuujuaq were not powerless against the Defence Department's decision. She would tell Charlie that she had demanded an explanation, along with reassurances that the investigation into Martha Salliaq's death would continue under military police jurisdiction and for an undertaking that the planned decontamination works would start this season and the land returned to Inuit control once they were complete next year. She wouldn't mention her deeper fears of a cover-up until she had something more concrete to offer. And she certainly wouldn't bring up the tricky business of her bank balance. What the Salliaqs needed right now was reassurance and encouragement.

Charlie was on the couch in the living room. He struggled to get up when she came in. Alice had gone back to bed, he said, and Lizzie was at Markoosie's house. The old man was to all intents and purposes alone.

She made tea, sat down beside him and began. He listened to her as he almost always did, respectfully and without interrupting.

'This is bad news. I don't think much of that mixed-dough police but I think even less of the *unataqti*,' he said.

Her heart went out to him. His face looked like an old tarpaulin left out in a storm. She patted his hand.

'This is just a setback. We've got over enough of those in the past. The evidence against Namagoose and Saxby is overwhelming. While we're waiting for the legal stuff to go through we can continue to put the pressure on, publicize the case some more.'

She watched his face cloud over, the skin on his cheeks the colour of rotten ice. Some thought moved across it. He looked very sick.

'The clean-up can wait,' he said. 'I want my daughter's killer found.'

'It's two sides of the same coin,' she pressed, regretting the phrase the moment it came out of her mouth. Using the language of money to an Inuk was like speaking in tongues to an atheist.

He looked at her as though she'd brought in a bad smell.

Then he waved his hands and grunted to signal that he was no longer willing to listen.

She left the house feeling disappointed with herself. She'd failed to get Charlie to understand that the clean-up and the search for Martha's killer were linked. But seeing him in such a fragile physical state only made her more determined to carry on. It occurred to her that she hadn't yet checked for new information in the local archives at the town hall. This was where she went now.

The broad historical facts of the Distant Early Warning line had etched themselves in her mind over the years. The line, which wasn't actually a line but rather a series of overlapping radar stations, was one of the outstanding initiatives of Cold War politics. Built in the late fifties, the DEW consisted of a string of sixty-three stations stretching nearly ten thousand kilometres across Arctic North America from Alaska in the west to Baffin Island in the east. Three types of facility had been built, the largest of which, the main stations, were like small cities, each with its own electricity, water, heat, an airstrip, and housing and recreation areas. Then there were mid-level, intermediate stations and small, unmanned 'gap filler' stations. Though initially funded by the United States, the sites flew both the Canadian and US flags until they were deactivated and sole jurisdiction given to the Canadian government in the late 1980s and early 1990s. This was partly what had delayed the land claim. It was only after the station at Glacier Ridge had devolved fully into Canadian government hands that the Defence Department had been free to engage in discussions on returning the site back to the Inuit.

It was public knowledge that the stations had produced large amounts of hazardous waste. In 1996 the Canadian and US governments came to an agreement, with the United States contributing

$100 million to the estimated $600 million clean-up effort. This was why, when Sonia had pushed for an independent organization to run the decontamination programme, the Department of Defence had insisted on contracting the work to Defence Construction Canada with Environment Canada supervising. What she didn't know then was that they would be working from Defence Department reports.

The papers had always referred to Glacier Ridge as an intermediate station and set the decontamination budget accordingly and neither Sonia nor any of the previous lawyers had contested this. She saw now that this was a mistake. She'd been working off the 1974 set of plans without comparing them either to earlier plans or to any of the other intermediate stations in the line. But, as she knew now, the site had been massively expanded and at least some of the additions, like the underground bunker, had not been marked on the set of plans from 1974 or indeed subsequently. What she needed in order to advance her case was proof that the station at Glacier Ridge had taken on some new role which the Defence Department was, even now, prepared to go to extraordinary lengths to keep secret.

She sat in front of the archive's only Internet-connected computer and googled 'Distant Early Warning Line', following links until she came to a complete list of all sixty-three stations, along with their classifications. Glacier Ridge was marked down on the list as the most northerly of the intermediate stations. For a while she followed her nose, clicking on links until she stumbled on a paper drawn up by the DEW's budget office in 1954, listing the radar equipment installed in each of the three station categories. Intermediate DEW stations consisted of a single AN/FPS-19 radome, flanked by two AN/FRC-45 lateral comms dishes and an AN/FPS-23 Doppler antenna. Major stations had two radomes and four lateral comms dishes, small 'gap fillers' only antennae. There didn't appear to be any exceptions to this rule.

The paper gave her an idea.

She found what she needed back at the hotel: the Environment Canada report on the Glacier Ridge decontamination. The report listed every building, each outpost, every last piece of machinery on the site, including the concrete bunker, which was described as 'waste land fill'. The radar equipment had a separate section of its own. The list appeared to be consistent with that of an intermediate station. Which meant that, unless the station had been first upgraded then downgraded – highly unlikely – the construction works, including the bunker, hadn't been the result of a regrading of the station. Which in turn meant that, in addition to radar, the station must have been used for some altogether different and, it appeared, clandestine purpose. All she needed to find out now was what.

There was nothing for it but to go back to the original papers. Which meant returning to the Salliaqs' house. She sensed that Charlie would be in no mood to cooperate. The papers were still in the packing case in his shed. If she was careful she could steal around the house and into the shed without anyone noticing. It would be an easier task now she knew roughly what she was looking for. She picked up her bag, left her room, locked the door behind her and made her way along the familiar route to the Salliaqs' house and slid through the side yard to the back. The shed door was, as before, unlocked. She let herself in and pulled out the packing crate. Sifting through a pile of papers, she found what she was after: the initial Environment Canada site assessment for the decontamination works, dating from before she'd taken on the case. She knew now that this original report had been replaced by another, signed by Dr Richard Price of the Defence Department's fictitious Environmental Impact Division and counter-signed by Iain Rogers-Garvin, who was Associate Minister in the Defence Department for several years in the eighties, before he'd had to resign following a sex scandal. It was always going to be in the department's interests to establish the rules of engagement and they'd forged documents in order to do it. The negotiators who'd previously worked on the land claim hadn't noticed. Not the first elementary cock-up they'd made.

What she had in her hands in the original Environment Canada site report was effectively the only independent assessment of the extent of the restitutive decontamination required on the site. Her attention was drawn to an attached memorandum from the head of the assessment team to the deputy director of Environment Canada. It struck her only because of the subject heading: *Animal Bones*. On the surface the memo seemed harmless enough, even trivial. The assessment team had uncovered an unexpected number of skeletal animal remains on the site and the purpose of the memo was simply to inform the deputy director of Environment Canada that the head of the assessment team was planning to send them for testing. What really interested Sonia though was the response. Handwritten and faint from multiple photocopying, it was still just readable.

IRG categorically forbids.

That name again, Iain Rogers-Garvin, Associate Minister for Defence, this time actively stymieing what was supposed to have been an independent report into contamination at the Glacier Ridge DEW station. Here was proof that the department had actively interfered in a supposedly independent assessment report then, finally, buried it and replaced it with their own.

Last time they'd spoken, Sonia had picked up Klinsman's uneasiness about his role as Department of Defence stooge. If the colonel didn't already know about this, then it might be the piece of evidence he needed to help him begin to push back. It was worth a try.

The guard at the Camp Nanook sentry gate informed her that the colonel wasn't seeing any visitors. She'd already allowed for this possibility.

'You won't mind if I use the bathroom? I've been here before, so I remember where it is.'

The guard looked uncomfortable, then relented, on condition that she leave her vehicle at the barrier and wasn't long about it. Sonia slipped under the barrier and along the boardwalk. At the corner she turned back to check that the guard had returned to his screen, then slipped around a corner and hurried towards the administration block. Klinsman was in his office. The instant he saw her, his hand went to the phone.

'Really? For a woman?'

Klinsman flushed and waved Sonia to a seat. His eyes cut to the clock on the wall. 'I'll give you four minutes.'

Sonia smiled to herself. This was just like court. She suddenly felt very firmly on home turf.

'I have evidence that the installation at Glacier Ridge was more than a DEW radar station and that it was engaged in covert activities during the seventies and eighties,' she began.

Klinsman looked up from his desk briefly and shrugged. His indifference took her by surprise.

'It was the Cold War,' he said blandly.

She tried again.

'I can also prove that the Defence Department was actively manipulating impact and assessment reports on the decontamination. Which was illegal at the time.' 'Prove' was maybe stretching it, but right now that didn't matter.

Klinsman glanced at the clock again. He'd already decided that she was wasting his time.

'I'm sure that's all very interesting but you need to make your representations to the appropriate body, Miss Gutierrez. Now, if you don't mind?' He leaned forward in his chair as if about to stand and see her out.

She lifted a manicured hand.

'As I recall you said four minutes, colonel. Unless time moves more quickly at these latitudes, I believe it's been two.'

Klinsman sighed but conceded the point.

'I know about the underground bunker. The only rationale for a bunker that size is armaments. My money is on nuclear.'

Klinsman blinked. Something hard moved across his face.

'If you need to speak with us again, Ms Gutierrez, I suggest you call counsel office.' His fingers tapped on the desk.

She stood and brushed herself down. 'I'll see myself out.'

*

The hotel phone was ringing as she entered. She picked up.

'Sonia? This is Chris Tetlow. Doesn't anyone up there believe in answer machines?'

'You got me now.'

'Listen, Son, my editor called. She just got an anonymous call to the tip line. Look, this is kind of awkward, but it was stuff about your past. Bad stuff.'

24

It took Derek a few seconds to figure out the owner of the voice. It was his old pal from Yellowknife days, Milt Drei, returning his call of a day or two ago.

'I got some news for you, bud.'

When Derek met him up in Yellowknife, Drei had been a newly discharged Gulf War vet trying to make a new life for himself in the police force. These days he worked at the Mounties headquarters in Ottawa in a white-collar crime unit. Derek had asked him to run a background check on Chip Muloon, find out if he needed to worry about the fella. Drei had access to all kinds of databases and wasn't interested in any kind of probable cause bullshit.

'Appreciate that, Milt. Good of you to call on a weekend.'

'Nothing's too much trouble for my old pal,' Drei said amiably. 'How's life in Kuujuaq anyway? I'm guessing you've been kinda lonely since Misha left.' Derek felt a needle inching up his spine. Why did Drei have to mention the nightmare that had been his two years on and off with Misha and remind him that, in spite of everything, he still missed her sometimes?

'Oh, you know, getting by,' he said.

Drei took the hint and moved on. 'Well, listen, I got something peachy for you.' The disembodied voice crackled over an increasingly poor phone line. 'Muloon looks squeaky clean from the outside. Guy hasn't even got a speeding ticket. Your regular angel. But you asked me to check if he had any connection to the military, so I went into his employment records. Five years back he was working in health strategy for the Nova Scotia provincial government. Then he kind of went off the radar for a bit before turning up at U Calgary.'

'He claims he's doing research into the long-term health impacts of the relocation of Inuit from Quebec up to Ellesmere in the 1950s,' Derek said.

'That's what it says on the U Calgary website too. But his money's not coming from the university. It's coming from the Defence Department. Kinda weird for a civilian health monitoring project. So anyways, old Milt did some digging around. I still got a few friends from back in the glory days. Seems that Muloon spent his lost weekend working out of Kabul as a special advisor. Hard to know what he actually did out there, but I very much doubt he was singing show tunes in hospitals. I had to guess, I'd say intelligence gathering had something to do with it.'

'On a health brief?'

'Some of our boys out there came back real sick. Gulf War Syndrome. Gave the Defence Department a lot of grief.'

Derek thought back and remembered seeing some stuff in the papers about soldiers complaining of nausea, fatigue, and the government, fore-seeing a class action suit, trying to insinuate that the men were nut jobs.

'It may be Muloon was monitoring the troops. I could try to find out, but in all honesty, there's so much secrecy surrounding that stuff, I don't know how far I'd get.'

Derek reached for a cigarette. 'No, thanks, Milt. That's plenty.' So Edie was right, he thought. 'I owe you a beer.'

'Come down this way sometime,' Drei said. 'Meet the wife, kids.'

'I'll try.'

Derek was putting down the phone when Edie appeared with Sonia Gutierrez following on behind.

'Good time to talk?' This from Edie. The two women had taken off their boots and outerwear, which suggested that, like most of Edie's questions, this one was rhetorical. 'Sonia has a progress report.'

They sat. He offered Sonia a drink and poured a couple of shots of whisky for the two of them. He'd begun to warm to the lawyer, to admire her tenacity even, but as he listened to her recount her visit to Camp Nanook and the phone call from Tetlow a growing feeling of disappointment came over him. Edie keeping secrets, now Gutierrez stealing from her clients. Why was it he always fell for the sparkle of new snow when it only served to hide the rot underneath?

'I'm not proud of it but I had my reasons,' Gutierrez went on. 'My nephew Albertito, my sister Carlita's son, needed surgery in the US. Either I came up with the money or . . .' She swung her legs in the chair, uncomfortable with the memory. 'I raided the escrow account of a land claim I was working on at the time in Winnipeg. The client agreed not to go to court. I had my licence suspended and I spent the next five years paying the money back, with interest.' Derek gave her a hard stare. 'OK, so that's not the point. It was a shitty thing to do.' She leaned in. 'Look, if a civilian was being threatened, that would be Ellesmere Island Police business, wouldn't it?'

'You asking me for protection?' Derek said. You had to respect the woman's chutzpah.

Batting away a mosquito, Gutierrez said, 'Chris Tetlow is an old friend of mine. If I go see him I can probably persuade him not to publish this. But you folks don't know the Defence Department like I do. This isn't gonna stop here. They're gonna keep coming after me until they get what they want. To shut me up.' She lifted a finger to her lips and let it hover there.

Derek sent Edie a warning not to react. The decision to pursue the Martha Salliaq case clandestinely meant that they needed to tread carefully, particularly with someone like Gutierrez, who had a direct line to Klinsman, whatever her claims that someone was trying to smear her.

'My guess is that the military police will charge Namagoose and Saxby and the case will be closed.'

Sonia stared at him with incredulous eyes. 'Those two men are chicken feed. *Don nadies*. Believe me, the department has bigger things on its mind.'

'I'm sorry, Ms Gutierrez, this just isn't our case to investigate any more.'

The lawyer sucked on her teeth and rose to leave. 'We have a saying in Guatemala, sergeant. You spend too long counting the corn, someone will steal the farm.'

'I'll bear that in mind,' Derek said.

A few moments after she'd left Tom Silliq appeared at the door. His wife, Susie, followed on behind.

'I told her I already came to you with this,' Silliq growled, thumbing Susie. 'I said that's what young men do, they go off sometimes, but she don't wanna listen to me.'

'Rashid hasn't shown up for three shifts and Tom has been round to his cabin twice but there's no sign of him,' Susie added.

It did seem odd, Derek thought, though hardly a priority.

'Have you been up to the trout lake?' Edie cut in. 'He told me he goes fishing up there sometimes.'

'You think it's my job to go running after strangers, like a puppy?' Silliq hawked up a gobbet of phlegm, looked around for somewhere to spit it and, seeing nowhere, swallowed it back again. 'Missing persons is police work, ain't it? You find him.'

Susie blinked an apology.

'We'll try to check it out,' Derek said.

'You said that last time.'

'I'm saying it again.'

Derek waited for the sound of their footsteps to fade. He slipped a cigarette from the packet on his desk and lit up.

'We got no reason to connect this kid to Martha, do we?'

'He said he hardly knew her and what he did know he disapproved of. I think he keeps himself to himself.'

Derek started playing with the pencil on his desk again. 'You believe that?'

Edie shrugged. 'I guess.'

Derek took this in. 'OK, well, I need to head out to the trout lake anyway. Wildlife wants a report on the health of fish stocks. It won't take more than an hour and I could use the thinking time.' The smoke curled up from his mouth.

Reaching for her parka, Edie said, 'I'll go look at the cabin.'

Derek cracked a weary smile. 'Thanks, partner.' At the door he stopped and turned. 'If you knew something that might have a bearing on the case, even something small, you know it would be your duty to tell me, don't you?'

Edie took a breath then nodded, but it was the breath that said it all.

A thin layer of tundra dust had settled over the interior of Alfasi's cabin. No sign of his summer-weight outerwear in the snow porch. No food in the kitchen. The way Edie figured it, the kid had probably gone out with an Inuk family to their summer camp, or maybe joined one of the launches that took hunters to Hell Gate. Forgot to tell his boss. Perhaps he thought now there were no soldiers coming to town, Susie Silliq wouldn't need him any more. Decided to leave the Shack before he was pushed.

She walked into the bedroom. In front of her was a small chest of drawers containing clothes, immaculately folded; mostly fleeces and winter-weight garb but among them hats bleached brilliant white and some kind of ceremonial robe. Above that sat a short shelf, empty save for two green plastic bookends between which, pasted to the wall, was a piece of paper filled with hand-drawn Arabic script, an excerpt from the Qur'an, Edie guessed. On the nightstand sat a pretty bouquet of tundra flowers. She went over. They'd been tied with distinctive yellow cord and were in the process of drying, the outer petals already crisp, but there was no card to indicate either who they were from or for whom they might once have been intended. Intriguing though. She'd never known a man pick flowers for himself.

It was late when she got back. Derek wasn't in so she left him a note, went into the kitchen and fixed up a batch of bannock bread. While it was in the pan she heated the last of the soup and poured it into a thermos. Taking her meal back outside, she swung open the tent canvas and crept inside, looking forward to a quiet hour or two alone with her thoughts and a long, recharging sleep, but to her surprise, she saw Sammy Inukpuk sitting on the sleeping skins at the back of the tent, chipping at a piece of soapstone. She went over and swapped breath with him, nose to nose, the old way.

'What you doing here?'

'Waiting for my supper,' Sammy said. 'See you've brought it.'

She squatted beside him. 'You're gonna have to earn it first.'

Her ex reached into the bag beside him and pulled out a couple of juicy char. 'These do?'

She turned the fish over in her hands. 'Maybe. Depends how long you're thinking of imposing yourself on me.'

'Cousin Eric lent me his boat,' Sammy said. 'I thought I'd stay a few days, take Willa fishing.'

Edie poured the soup and handed him the mug.

'So I guess you and Nancy broke up?' The couple were on and off like a pair of switches. Sammy had a habit of showing up at Edie's door whenever the switch was in the off position. They joked about it. Sort of joked.

'How are you and that *qalunaat* getting along?' he said.

'If you mean Chip Muloon, we're not.'

Sammy put his mug to his mouth and mumbled into his soup.

'You got something to say, Sammy Inukpuk?'

'Well, now you ask, actually I do. How in darned's name did you ever think you were going to get along with a *qalunaat*?'

Edie finished chewing on her bannock. 'You're forgetting, my dad was a *qalunaat*. Was or is.' She hadn't seen the man in about a quarter century.

Sammy finished up his soup. They looked at each other for a moment. 'Well, Edie Kiglatuk, I guess you're gonna be needing a shoulder to cry on.' Her back fizzed a little where his arm went around it. Their faces were so close now that she could feel his breath on her cheek.

'A shoulder will do for a start,' she said, giving him the eye.

25

Derek got back from the trout lake, read Edie's note and went to bed. If Alfasi hadn't turned up by the morning he'd call his employers, but he didn't see any real need to worry. Young men came up to the Arctic looking for adventure and for the most part they found it. Then they went back down south, got mortgages, wives, kids and spent the rest of their lives reliving the glory days. Alfasi was off somewhere making memories. Right now he was low on Derek's list of priorities. By the time he'd taken a shower and slipped under the bedcovers Derek had forgotten all about the kid.

As usual, sleep eluded him. Every summer he went through the same thing, wondering how much longer he could take life on Elles-mere while at the same time knowing he could never leave. Part way through the night he pinged off his eye mask and checked the time. It was 4.30. In a couple of hours the workday would begin. Rising from his bed, he went out to the back shed to feed his lemmings. They too were awake and energetically going about their business and it made him feel better to watch them for a bit. They were dumb, instinc-tive creatures but they'd managed to eke out an existence all the way up here on the margins of life and you had to take your hat off to them because, holy freaking walrus, it took some doing sometimes.

Returning to the detachment, he put on some water to boil and took a shower. Then he sat down with a bowl of ramen noodles and opened the Martha Salliaq file. A tiny part of him was hoping things would turn out the way he'd presented them to Sonia Gutierrez, that the Killer Whales would be proven to have been Martha's killers, that Klinsman would charge them and that the whole thing would go away. But the better part of him thought it was worth investigating Muloon further just in case. If he *was* the valuable Defence Department asset Milt Drei made him out to be, then who was to say the military weren't about to frame Namagoose and Saxby in order to protect him? Gutierrez seemed to think they were capable of it. He hadn't liked the way Muloon had been when questioned about the knife. His air of smug invincibility. If Muloon had anything to do with Martha's death, anything at all, Derek wanted to be the one to wipe the grin off his face.

The aroma of roasting meat met his nostrils. All of a sudden his ramen noodles didn't taste so good any more. He went to the window. Outside Edie's tent a large goose was twirling on a home-made spit over a heather and willow fire. The woman herself was sitting beside it, stuffing what looked like a pillow with white feathers. A kettle sat on a Coleman stove beside the fire. Steam rose from the spout. The scene was so perfect it made his eyes hurt. He knocked on the glass. Edie looked up and beckoned to him. For a moment he felt a twinge of something – desire maybe – but then Sammy Inukpuk appeared in his field of vision and whatever it was faded.

He went out onto the steps and took a deep breath in. The air smelled wonderfully of home. Only a woman could make the air smell that way. For a split second it made him think of Misha. But his ex had never been that kind of a woman.

'Breakfast?' Edie was holding up a mug of something.

He came down. The tea was as she always made it, strong as an ox and unnaturally sweet. He took a couple of gulps and grimaced.

She laughed and pulled a leg from the goose. 'They're in moult.' For a week or so before they got their new feathers the snow geese were more or less flightless. If you were skilled enough you could almost pick them off the tundra.

Sammy came over. 'We got eggs too, you prefer omelette.'

'You keep filling your belly with those ramen noodles, you'll turn into a white man,' Edie said. The meat was sweet and made him ache for something he'd never had.

She waited for him to finish eating then asked if he'd seen her note.

'I got back from the lake late. Survey took me a while. Didn't see any sign of Alfasi.' He told her he wasn't worried.

'Only thing in the house, I found a bunch of flowers,' Edie said.

Derek finished up the goose leg, laid the bone down and licked his fingers. 'Oh well, that'll be it then,' he said. 'Kid's got a girlfriend somewhere.' He'd go down to the radio station later and ask Markoosie to put out an alert for him. If that failed, he'd call Alfasi's employers at the meteorological service in Ottawa, see if he'd checked in with them.

They were on their own now. Sammy had gone off to do something in the tent. He lowered his voice so only Edie could hear. As he outlined what Drei had told him about Muloon he could see the moisture sparkle in her eyes and was overcome by a desire to reassure her.

'This doesn't change the odds that Muloon had something to do with Martha Salliaq's death. We still don't know whether he did or not. But it makes it more likely that he's being protected if he did. Whatever he's working on, there must be some connection to Glacier Ridge.'

Edie was staring at smouldering heather and biting her lip.

'Don't feel bad,' he said.

'I never could read him, but I guess I just thought it was because he was *qalunaat*.' She picked up the goose bone he'd left and threw it into the fire. 'I'd feel better about it if I'd let my heart rule my head.' A sad smile played on her lips. 'But I'm afraid neither were responsible.'

Derek heard himself give a laugh and felt his neck flush. 'You're not the first to have made that mistake.' He thought immediately of Misha. Still dreamed about her sometimes, woke sweaty and frustrated. He blinked the thought away.

'If Muloon was involved in Martha's murder, we'll keep at it till we get him. But we need to be very careful now, keep making discreet enquiries and see what Klinsman comes up with.' He glanced towards the tent and was glad when she picked up his meaning.

'Sammy hardly knows anything.' She was using a tiny willow twig to spread the dying ashes.

'Keep it that way,' he said. 'And Edie, I won't allow anyone to be protected from justice. Not anybody. You know that, don't you?' He wiped the remains of the goose grease off his hands and picked himself up. 'Thanks for breakfast. You think of anything you want to tell me, you know where I am.'

She waited for Sammy to return.

'Derek knows I'm keeping something back from him.' She and Sammy had spent the small hours discussing her conversations with Willa.

'You're not. You've just decided not to bother him with something that's irrelevant to the investigation.'

Sammy was aware how little she'd trusted Willa in the past and resented her for it.

'The fact remains that the only person we know Martha saw between her leaving school looking cheerful and winding up crying on Tom Silliq's wall was Willa. You have to admit, it looks bad.'

'And that's why we're not going to be telling Derek about it,' Sammy said, kicking the fire embers to cool them off. 'You know how it is. Willa being such a hellraiser in the past. People have long memories. Prejudices. It looks bad but it isn't.'

Edie began to gather up the bones and leftovers to give to the half-starved dogs which roamed around the settlement. She delved into the ashes, plucked out the bone she'd thrown there, burning her hand a little in the process. But it felt good. It felt deserved.

'You're right,' she said.

'Willa's got nothing to do with the death of that girl, so why drag him into it?'

He had a point. But Derek wasn't stupid. Sooner or later it would come out that Willa and Martha had a connection, then it would emerge that she had kept her knowledge of their relationship from him. Either way she would end up betraying someone.

She watched Sammy disappear into the tent. A moment later there was a loud crash of pans and he came out, looking foolish.

'I guess I was never much good at all that domestic hoo-ha. That's why I need a woman about the place.'

They laughed, but there was something sad in it.

Leaving Sammy with the keys to her ATV, she made her way on foot to the Kuujuaq Hotel, driven by a nagging but distant sense that Gutierrez would have been willing to tell more when she'd come to see them if Derek hadn't closed her down. She'd felt a kind of connection between them. Two tough women in a tough place. There was an ally to be made in Gutierrez and Edie believed she could make it without having to give too much away in return. Gutierrez had hinted that she knew the Defence Department was up to something. Maybe she'd uncovered more about Chip Muloon.

Inside the bitter aroma of burnt coffee greeted her but there was no sign of Sonia or anyone else. She shouted up the stairwell and, receiving no response, took the stairs two by two, turned left and went down the corridor to room number 7. When nobody answered her knock, she tried the handle. The door was locked. In this part of the world that was unusual. Taking out her multitool, she slid in the pick, felt for the pins and let herself in.

The room had the still-warm feel of a place recently vacated. Gutierrez's things were lying around and the window was part open. A laptop and some papers sat on the desk. Edie went over and began flipping through the pile: contracts, technical manuals, legal documents relating to the land claim at Glacier Ridge and subsequent decontamination agreements. She noticed a bunch of tundra flowers sitting in an empty vase on one side of the desk. They were early summer varieties, vetch, Arctic catkins, dried now, but perfectly preserved: looking closer, she could see they were tied with the same yellow cord as the bunch at Rashid Alfasi's place. Rashid Alfasi and Sonia Gutierrez? Somehow she couldn't see it.

The sound of footsteps echoed up the stairs. Someone was heading her way. Her eyes swept about, desperately searching for somewhere to hide, but it was already too late. Then the door opened and Sonia's face peered around. She saw Edie and her expression dimmed.

'What the hell do you think you're doing? I left this room locked.'

A throb rose up in Edie's forehead. She found herself reaching for the knife in her pocket, the old hunter's instincts. For a second her mind began to unravel, then she took a breath and gathered herself. Her head flicked towards the papers on the desk.

'I've had a snoop, in case you're wondering.'

The lawyer rested a hand on her hip and looked at Edie through narrowed eyes. 'Come to any conclusions?'

Edie returned the look with a cool stare. 'I'm glad I'm not a lawyer.'

For a moment Gutierrez seemed to be fighting back a smile, then went over to her papers and began rustling them into a neat pile.

Seizing the moment, Edie said, 'Nice flowers. You pick them yourself?' She already knew the answer. When these flowers were blooming, Gutierrez was still in Ottawa or wherever it was she came from.

Gutierrez glanced at the bouquet. 'You must know, I found them up at Glacier Ridge. That time you saw me there.'

'Mind if I take them?'

The lawyer's eyes narrowed. She leaned back and crossed her arms.

A smile bloomed on her face and she cocked her head and clasped her chin between two fingers.

'*Dios mío!* You haven't stopped looking for the killer, have you? Ha!' She lowered her voice. 'You got *cojones*, Edie Kiglatuk. I'll give you that much. I suppose you know that boss of yours is out of his depth, don't you?' She looked away. 'Don't worry, I'll play dumb. Take the flowers and leave. You won't find it so easy to get into my room next time.'

Edie filled Derek in on her visit to the hotel and laid the flowers on his desk.

'Maybe Alfasi came across them just like Gutierrez did?'

'A man wouldn't pick them up.'

Derek conceded this.

'What if Alfasi was Martha's boyfriend?'

Derek sighed. She watched him push the idea aside. Why he was so dismissive of her boyfriend theory Edie couldn't make out. Maybe just because it wasn't his. Men could be assholes like that sometimes. She was about to tell him so when she saw from his face that he was thinking something through.

'How did Alfasi seem when you went to talk to him?'

'He got kind of jumpy when I asked him whether he thought Martha was with Namagoose and Saxby by choice. I assumed he disapproved of the drinking, but maybe there was something else to it.' She closed her eyes for a moment, thinking. An idea bubbled up, an awful, unspeakable idea but not an impossible one. Turning it over in her mind, she felt her blood quickening. 'He skipped his shift on Saturday night.'

'And those two things are connected how?'

'Suppose Alfasi and Martha had arranged to see one another on Friday after school. When I spoke with her at the end of class Martha was looking forward to something. Suppose they met up and had some sort of a fight, Martha got upset and went to the bar to drown her sorrows. Namagoose and Saxby came with her to the Shack at her suggestion.'

Derek raised an eyebrow. He was playing the scenario in his head.

'If she *was* dating Alfasi she would have known that he would be there,' Edie went on. 'What if she was trying to provoke him into some reaction? What if it worked?'

Derek's features sharpened. 'We need to find this kid.'

Sonia fiddled with the lock on her door but could not get it to function. The damn Inuit policewoman had broken it when she'd let herself in. Of course she could file a complaint somewhere but really what was the point? In any case, there were more pressing things to do. Chief among which was to ensure her safety. It had been completely pointless to voice her concerns with Palliser. He didn't seem to have any idea to what lengths the Defence Department would go in order to avoid exposing a scandal. The tiny woman was a bit more switched on, but that wasn't saying much. It wasn't that she didn't rate them. You'd want to be with them in a blizzard. In the face of a charging polar bear she imagined they'd be magnificent. But they couldn't see that the greatest danger to them personally and to their community lay just a few kilometres down the road at Camp Nanook.

She left the door and went back inside to fetch her purse. There was a fixing on the door to which she would be able to attach a padlock. The store would surely sell those. As a precaution, she sifted through her pile of papers, selected those few she needed for her ongoing investigations and stuck them in her daypack, then headed into the settlement.

The tide was out now, leaving behind it a dirty hem of rotting bergy bits and gravel-crusted ice, and for the first time in weeks the air was cooler outdoors than inside. She checked about as she walked, wondering whether she wouldn't be safer in Ottawa. She had folk looking out for her down there. Here she was vulnerable. Palliser had already said he wasn't prepared to offer her police protection. The only other person she could ask was Charlie Salliaq, and he was in no shape to help. She made a mental note to ask at the Northern Store about getting a plane out. Get back to Ottawa, file the cease and desist papers against the Defence Department from there.

The store had not long been open. The owner and his wife were still sorting out keys and dusting down the cashier's desk. She caught the man's attention and asked for a combi lock.

He stood up and rubbed his head. 'Don't get any call for locks. I'd have to order one up on the supply plane.' He began fishing around for the mail order catalogue. Oolik, that was his name. She remembered now. Bit of an asshole.

'When are you expecting the next supply plane?'

Oolik turned his head back to glance at the 'Great Canadian views' calendar on the wall.

'Should be tomorrow afternoon, weather permitting.' He pushed the catalogue at her. 'Too late to order you a padlock for then. It'd probably take a couple weeks.'

'What's the likelihood of being able to get a seat on tomorrow's plane?'

The man began scratching at his head again. He was in no hurry. 'Where you need to get to exactly?'

'Iqaluit, Ottawa, it doesn't really matter.'

Oolik sighed. 'I guess I could call North Star Air, see if they could take you. Depends on their cargo commitments. But they usually don't fly unless they're full both ways.'

'I'm happy to pay a premium.'

She saw Oolik frown disapprovingly and kicked herself. Offering an Inuk a backhander was like showing up on a first date with bad breath.

Predictably, Oolik returned a few minutes later shaking his head. 'I could book you on next Monday's plane.'

There was nothing like being told you couldn't leave to make it seem all the more imperative that you did.

'Any other way of getting off the island?'

'You had a boat, Resolute Bay's about three hundred and fifty kilometres that way,' Oolik said. He tipped his head to the southwest. 'But you'd need to know all the currents and get lucky with the ice.'

Somewhere inside her chest a dark bud of panic began to swell. She thought about Charlie and the Ellesmere Police and, most of all, about Camp Nanook, and suddenly felt very alone.

'I need a weapon.' She heard the words before she realized they were hers.

Oolik was staring at her, part baffled, part bored. 'We don't keep any guns in stock. You have to order them up.' He reached around to a shelf behind him and heaved a huge and tattered catalogue onto the cashier's desk.

'A knife then?'

Oolik tutted. 'We've got a moratorium on those. Out of respect for the family.'

'Pepper spray?'

Oolik threw back his head and laughed.

'Bear spray then.'

The laugh became a hoot. 'Ha, lady, I like your sense of humour. Polar bears are mean. They freshen their *breath* with bear spray.'

As she left, a damp grey fog of resignation began to pick at her bones. She wanted desperately not to go back to the hotel but her legs seemed to carry her there as if she had no choice in the matter. A part of her still needed to believe that the Department of Defence lawyers would return her calls and the matter of Glacier Ridge would be handled in a civilized manner through the courts, but the larger part of her knew this for what it was. A wishful fantasy. Whatever she had touched on had gone too far for the polite processes of the courts. She had crossed over some boundary into the terrain not of the law but of *realpolitik* and in that territory anything was possible.

The hotel foyer was surprisingly cool now. She stopped a moment to listen for the sounds of intruders and hearing nothing went up the stairs and turned into the corridor. As she approached her room she saw that the door was slightly ajar and through the gap there was some movement. She moved forward, propelled by some sense of destiny, then caught herself, too late to leave but not too late to over-step the bedroom door and tiptoe to the bathroom. She slid her back-pack behind the door and walked back to meet her fate.

The door to her room swung open and two men in military police uniforms stepped out and came towards her.

'Sonia Gutierrez?' The older of the two, a man of Hispanic origin like herself, reached out and took her arm. She felt herself tense, the rush of adrenalin a welcome relief from the numb, animal resignation of before. A cuff closed around her wrist.

The policeman said he was arresting her for trespass on military property, but that hardly mattered. She felt a hand on the small of her back, pushing her forward.

26

Rashid Alfasi's boss at the meteorological office in Ottawa hadn't heard from him in a couple of days. The stats from the various outlying met stations were collated once a week on Mondays and the staff were only contacted if there was something unexpected in the figures.

'Is he in trouble?' the man asked.

Derek switched the phone to speaker to allow Edie to listen in. She'd watched him become increasingly preoccupied over the last twelve hours. He hadn't said as much, but Edie was sure he was regretting focusing all his energies on the two *unataqti* in the early stages of the case. It made the work of broadening the investigation more difficult, not least because they were now having to do it without alerting Klinsman. But, in the absence of firm proof against any of the other suspects, the link between Alfasi and Martha Salliaq was too important to ignore.

'You ever have any problems with Rashid? Skipping off, going AWOL, that kind of thing?'

'No, sir. The kid's reliable.'

'Did he volunteer for the Ellesmere posting?' Southerners who chose to spend time in the High Arctic were usually trying to escape something or other.

'Well, yes,' said the man in a wary tone. 'Rashid could be a bit of a loner.'

'Isn't it right that the met service seconds some of its workers to the military?'

There was a pause. 'That is correct, yes.'

'Is Rashid Alfasi one of those?'

The man cleared his throat. 'I can't answer that question, sir. You'd have to go through the proper channels.'

'I see,' Derek said. 'Well, call us if he gets in touch. We're concerned for his safety.' Derek left the detachment number. 'I'd rather this was between us for now. I don't want to concern the family.'

'Of course, the family.'

Derek ended the call and sat staring at the phone, wondering if the whole goddamned island hadn't been converted into a single vast military installation, with the locals, people like him and Edie, serving unwittingly as guinea pigs in some giant defence experiment. Sure it was paranoid, it was probably all-out insane, but that didn't mean it wasn't true.

He picked up the handset and listened to the dial tone. Then he opened his desk drawer and pulled out the multitool he kept there and began unscrewing the phone. Halfway through he stopped himself. The regime of no sleep, too much caffeine and irregular meals was getting to him. He was having irrational thoughts. His outlook on the world was becoming paranoid.

He turned to Edie. 'I need a break.'

Then he went outside and did what he always did when he needed to reassure himself that he wasn't going crazy.

He fed his lemmings.

Edie watched him drift out of the office and down towards the lemming shed. Derek's lemming thing was one of the few things about him she didn't understand. Years ago, when she was still a kid, after her father had left but before they'd closed the school and left the children to get a tundra education, a well-meaning *qalunaat* teacher introduced a dozen lemmings into the classroom in a tank. A boy called Isaac volunteered to take the lemmings home during the summer recess and his mother cooked them into a stew. That pretty much reflected the general Inuit view of lemmings.

What Edie did understand, though, was that Derek had to be feeling pretty bad. It was a feeling she shared. Back in the spring she'd got lost in the forest in Alaska. The trees seemed to muddle her senses and she'd been overwhelmed by the disconcerting sense of being blocked on every side and unable to move forward. That same feeling had returned.

She heard the back door swing open and the sound of Derek's footsteps through the kitchen. At the comms room he stopped and she heard the sound of his voice requesting radio contact. A while later he came back into the office, his breath smelling heavily of tobacco.

'I just spoke with Larsen on the *Piquot*. He's gonna search the ship. Alfasi's not likely to have gone out on the land with no vehicle.'

He reached for his jacket on the hook by the door. 'I'm gonna check around. It's possible he's hiding in plain sight.' The settlement was thickly strewn with old fishing sheds, abandoned stores, dog kennels and outbuildings and the overturned mounds of broken and unused boats.

'Want me to come?'

Derek shook his head. 'I'm familiar with the terrain. If you'd like to be helpful, you could go find out what Klinsman's said to the Salliaqs and, while you're at it, ask them if they know anything about Alfasi. But go lightly. We don't want Klinsman to know that we're investigating the kid as a suspect. Especially not if he's working for them.'

She left a few minutes behind him. Rain spilled from a raw dough sky. The supply plane buzzed overhead and gradually disappeared south into low-lying cloud. Moments later, disturbed by noise, the jaeger that had made its nest around the back of the detachment flew up and over the wire towards the sea. Momentarily curious, Edie skirted the detachment building and stood on an old packing crate to get a look at the nest. There were only two chicks now, their flight feathers beginning to come through. Most likely the weaker of the two would become food for the stronger and only one would survive to adulthood.

Leaving the birds, Edie wandered up to the track and turned north-east towards the cliffs until she reached the Salliaqs' house. Charlie and Markoosie were sitting on the couch staring at an ice-hockey game on TV. Lizzie was sitting in a chair by the window, sewing beads onto a sealskin parka.

'That's beautiful,' Edie said.

'It's for Martha. My mother is doing most of the work, but she's sleeping right now.'

Charlie looked up from the game. 'I suppose you'd better come sit at the table. Lizzie'll fetch us tea.'

Charlie pushed up to standing, shuffled over to the table and lowered himself very carefully into a hard-backed chair. Markoosie returned to the ice-hockey game.

The deterioration in the old man's health was shocking. A week or so ago, just after the discovery of Martha's body, he'd seemed tired and physically weak but now he was barely able to haul himself about. His eyes were cloudy and there were livid red patches on his face and hands.

'We thought you might be Sonia. She usually comes by about this time,' he said.

Edie told him she thought the lawyer had business in Iqaluit. 'She was probably on the supply plane that just went over.'

Charlie took this in without comment. 'We got a call from that colonel fella about them *unataqti*. Seems your Lemming Police friend just handed over the case like it was an old sack.'

'It wasn't like that, *avasirngulik*.'

Just then Lizzie appeared with a plate of muktuq with the tea and sat down at the table beside her father. She eyed Edie warily.

The old man picked up a piece of muktuq and began rubbing it between his fingers to warm the fat. 'Oh, we'll play along, but underneath me and my family won't have nothing to do with that colonel fella. You understand? Maybe Sonia can figure something out but I'm not holding my breath. Them two *unataqti* won't ever come to justice now.'

Charlie raised the piece of muktuq to his nose, decided it smelled good, popped it into his mouth and began chewing.

'You know Rashid Alfasi, *avasirngulik*?' Edie began. 'Works at the met station, been helping Susie Silliq out at the Shack some weekends?'

Charlie's eyes narrowed. 'That Arab kid?'

'Canadian. His parents are from Morocco.'

'What about him?'

'He's gone missing.'

Charlie shrugged, helped himself to a piece of muktuq and pushed the plate towards her as though nothing had been said. The kid wasn't his concern.

To be polite, Edie took a piece of muktuq and put it on the table beside her.

'Why are you asking us about him?' Lizzie said.

Her father stopped chewing, spat out his muktuq and rested it next to his mug. He sighed and folded his arms across his chest. He really did look very frail.

'Don't take it personal, Edie Kiglatuk, but I think it best if you just left. You're no good to us. Not you nor that Lemming Police.'

On the way back she ran into Derek. He was with his old dog, Pie Crust. The animal lived with Stevie most of the time now, but Derek used him every so often when he went hunting or out on patrol.

'I've just come from Alfasi's house. No one's been back there.' He patted the dog. 'You get anything from Charlie?'

'He's got it into his head that we just let the military march in and take over. Feels betrayed.'

Derek raised an eyebrow.

The next couple of hours they focused on the hunt for Alfasi, poking into sheds and dog kennels, breaking open the locks of outbuildings, tearing up their hands lifting the shells of old boats, but at the end of it they came up empty. Not long after they returned to the detachment there was a knock and Klinsman appeared, a tall fellow in shades and an immaculately pressed military policeman's uniform beside him. Edie could tell that Derek was as surprised as she was by the visit.

'Do you have a minute?'

'For you, always, colonel,' Derek said drily.

Klinsman took a breath in and stepped inside. He didn't appreciate the police sergeant's tone. 'This is a courtesy call, sergeant, and I needn't have made it, but I figure we're all professionals here.'

'I know you are, colonel, but to be honest I don't like the look of your sidekick,' Derek said. 'Something of the rookie about him. New to the Arctic, is he? Just shipped in?'

There was a small pause during which the MP stared impassively ahead and Klinsman rearranged his features.

'When we took over the case I requested military police backup, sergeant. But, really, I'm not here to go over old ground. Just the opposite. I'm on my way to inform the Salliaqs of a development in the investigation.' He was looking at Derek directly now. 'For logistical reasons we weren't able to move over the weekend but you should know that this morning we formally charged Privates Jacob Namagoose and Skeeter Saxby with the murder of Martha Salliaq.'

Derek sat back and frowned. 'On what evidence?'

Ignoring the question, Klinsman went on, 'I am glad for the sake of the family and for the success of the ongoing SOVPAT exercises that we are going to be able to draw a line under the case and I want you to know how much we have appreciated the cooperation of the Elles-mere Island Police.' Klinsman was going through the motions. He was that most dangerous kind of man, Edie thought, someone for whom any real engagement with human beings had been replaced by strict adherence to form. Men like that were capable of anything.

'Spare us your gratitude,' Derek said.

Klinsman eye-flicked to the MP. For an instant Edie thought she saw him blush.

'Well,' he went on, as though everything had been nicely sorted, 'now we can all go back to our lives.'

27

Klinsman hadn't been gone a minute when the radio crackled. Derek went to answer. It was Captain Larsen from the *Piquot* to say that an orderly had come across a stowaway hiding in the laundry room. Derek felt his gut tighten.

'He offered the orderly a couple hundred dollars not to give the game away, said that was all he had,' Larsen went on. 'Name's Al something. Says he works at the met station in Kuujuaq. You know him?'

'I sure do. We need him back here for questioning.'

'That explains it,' Larsen said. 'The kid's begging me to take him back to Quebec, says he's got family problems, can't afford the air fare home . . .' Larsen's voice blanked out for a moment then came back on, '. . . no sea legs. Otherwise he's fine. I've got him under lock and key in the sickbay.'

Larsen explained that the ship was sailing in patchy ice just off Lady Ann Strait.

'I'm within my rights to drop him off at the nearest landing point, but from taking a look at him I'd say he'd survive about as long as a walrus belch out there. We got difficult ice conditions ahead in Baffin Bay and I can't afford the time or the expense of bringing him all the way back to Kuujuaq. We could 'copter him as far as Craig if you meet us halfway?'

Derek rubbed his face. Given the unpredictability of the weather around Craig Island, it would probably make more sense to go by sea.

'If I take the launch, I can be at the north beach landing in a couple of hours, give or take. How's that sound?'

Larsen thought that sounded good.

Back in the office Edie was deep in thought and chewing on one of her braids.

'They've found Alfasi on the *Piquot*.' Derek thought of asking her to come with him to Craig then decided against it. For her, the place was brittle with bad memories. On the other hand, he didn't much relish the idea of making the journey to pick up a suspect in a murder case alone.

'You seen Sammy Inukpuk today?' The man was a superb sailor. Tough when he wanted to be, too.

'He's gone to see his son at the rappel camp. But I know how to reach him. Why?'

'Good,' Derek said. 'I could use his help.'

The journey out to Craig was uneventful, the launch bumping along in rough chop until they reached the agreed meeting point, a black beach flanked by lichen-covered basalt cliffs where Alfasi was standing, guarded by two volunteers from the *Piquot*'s crew. While Sammy stayed with the launch Derek clambered into the Zodiac and buzzed to shore.

The kid was solemn and pale-faced. It looked to Derek as though he'd been crying and was ready to break. Derek gave him some reassurance that he wouldn't be questioned until they were back on dry land in Kuujuaq. He felt for his cuffs then thought better of it. If something went wrong transferring him from the Zodiac to the launch and he fell in the water he'd drown with cuffs on. He'd cuff him once they were in place. He told the boy to look around.

Alfasi scanned the sweep of naked rock and scree.

'You see anywhere to run to?'

Alfasi shook his head.

'Good. If you try I will have to shoot you. Understood?'

Alfasi nodded. The two guards dropped their grip. The boy looked up and caught Derek's eye.

His legs were shaking so much he could hardly lift them into the Zodiac.

Larsen was right. The kid was helpless at sea. He'd thrown up everything in his stomach while he was still on the *Piquot*, but his body continued to go through the motions once he was on the police launch, spewing long strings of mucous and stomach acids onto the deck. At the quay in Kuujuaq Sammy and Derek had to more or less drag him onto the ATV and by the time they got him back to the detachment, his face had turned the colour of old blubber. Derek cuffed the kid, thanked Sammy and told him to come by one evening and that there was a bottle of whisky in the detachment with his name on it. Once Sammy had gone Derek showed Alfasi to a seat and offered him a cigarette. Refusing the smoke, the kid bunched himself up miserably in the chair like a cornered hare, his face slicked with sweat.

Edie had watched them come up from the launch. She'd gone back to Alfasi's house and then to the met station on the outskirts of the settlement, looking for anything that might tie Alfasi to Martha. The search hadn't yielded anything new and stepping into the detachment office she found it hard to square the scared kid trembling in the chair with her image of a ruthless killer. But then she knew it was the orderly types who often found the Arctic the hardest to adjust to because they were often the ones for whom the feeling of fear was the hardest to bear. It was impossible to be in the Arctic without the daily experience of fear. Inuit like Edie took it for granted. Fear was the shade that could block out the sun but it was also the canopy under which you could shelter. You lived in its presence because you couldn't survive without it. Flight, fight. Fear.

She pulled up a chair and sat beside him. The kid stared at the floor, red-faced and wretched. What was it Muloon had once told her? A third of *qalunaat* on two-year Arctic postings returned to the south mentally ill.

'You should have gone home a long time ago,' she said. 'Before this place drove you crazy.'

The young man blinked and took in a long breath.

'You are a meteorologist. You know about avalanches and instant white-outs, two-hundred-kilometre-an-hour winds and what happens to a human body at minus fifty C. Maybe, when you first arrived you thought that because you knew all those things there was no need to be afraid. But nothing, not even avalanches and white-outs, not even bears or black ice, is as fearful as the way the Arctic throws you back upon yourself.' She watched his eyes.

For a long while he did not speak, then he said, 'I'm not well.'

'Then we'll make you well,' Edie said. 'And then you can talk to us and, if we believe your story, you can go home, back to Vancouver or Morocco or wherever you need to be in order to hide from who you are.'

She got up and went out to the kitchenette to search through the cupboards for some *ukiurtatuq* tea to settle Alfasi's stomach but found only regular black tea, coffee beans and a few ancient sachets of tangerine Tang. Her hands automatically reached for the mugs and dumped in teabags. She found the sugar and set everything on a tray. She'd planned this moment.

Alfasi was still sitting where she'd left him, his head in his hands. She put the tray down on the desk.

'Have some tea.'

As he lifted his head his eyes fell on the bouquet of flowers she'd taken from Sonia Gutierrez's room. He swallowed back a gasp. His eyes grew wild. 'Were you with Martha because she helped you to forget yourself, Rashid?'

The boy looked at her from under his eyelids. His mouth was trembling but Edie thought she saw a twitch of defiance there.

'I want that lawyer lady. I'm not saying anything till she gets here.'

'Forget the lawyer lady. The lawyer lady is unavailable,' Derek cut in.

'You can't do this,' Alfasi said, 'I do important work here.'

'Tell us about your work, Rashid.' Derek sat back, intertwining his hands behind his neck, sending Alfasi the message that he was relaxed and had plenty of time.

An anxious look came on Alfasi's face, as though he gone a step too far and was now regretting it.

'You know what I do,' he said. 'I work at the weather station collecting data.'

'We already know that you work for the military.'

For a moment Alfasi looked confused. 'I'm seconded to them for the period of the SOVPAT exercises, that's all.'

'And the other job? At the Shack? Why did you do that, Rashid?'

'I told you, for something to do.' Alfasi sat back and folded his arms. 'I'm not saying anything else till I get a lawyer.'

'Fine. But it might be days. What with finding someone who can come, and the fact that there are hardly any flights up here. And the cost, well, I can hardly imagine the cost.' Derek made to get up out of his chair. 'Of course, we'll have to keep you on the premises until your lawyer arrives.'

Alfasi hung his head. 'All right,' he said in a sullen voice.

Edie caught Derek's eye. It was time to ease off on Alfasi a little. They might be able to get to him by some more roundabout route.

'One of your jobs at Susie Silliq's place is to fetch the dry goods from the store, isn't it, Rashid? The flour, salt, that kind of thing?'

Alfasi's eyebrows knitted. He was wondering if this was some kind of trap. Edie could see that after three days at sea he was befuddled and exhausted.

'You fetch them direct from Sam Oolik's storeroom, I'm guessing. He gives you the key? Lets you just help yourself?'

Alfasi's face relaxed momentarily. 'I just take the keys from behind the door in the office then mark what I've taken in a ledger.'

'When did you last do that?'

The young man thought about it. 'Why are you asking me this? You think I took something, don't you?' Edie realized she'd underestimated him. He wasn't so tired that he didn't have his wits about him.

Derek glanced at Edie.

'Do you have a camera, Rashid?'

Alfasi drew back in his chair, his eyes darting between his interrogators. 'No.'

'How did Martha Salliaq die?'

Alfasi wiped a hand across his mouth and sat up. His eyes grew large and watery, then his face seemed to crumple.

'Look, we dated a while back. Weeks ago. She ended it. I think she was scared her father would find out.'

'When was the last time you saw her?'

'I told you, Friday, when she came into the Shack.'

Derek said, 'Did Martha reject you, Rashid?'

'No, it wasn't like that.'

'You're Muslim, aren't you? Familiar with the ritual of halal?'

'Of course,' Alfasi said.

'Is that why you bled Martha out?'

An expression of horror unfurled across Alfasi's face and he began to shake. His chest heaved, then he leaned over the chair and vomited. His head was in his hands again and he was sobbing. Suddenly the boy's expression grew dark and angry. 'You think I haven't seen how this place works? You're always looking for some outsider to blame and you've decided to blame me, whether I killed Martha or not.' He was hard now, the cords in his neck taut, a look of contempt across his face. 'Which I didn't.'

There was a moment of silence during which they could hear the sound of kids playing down at the shoreline.

'What are you going to do to me?' Alfasi said.

Edie saw Derek take a deep breath. He glanced over at her then turned up his palms. *My hands are tied.* His fingers drummed the desk. For a moment she was afraid that he was about to tell the kid that he no longer had jurisdiction over the case.

'You're free to go.'

Alfasi let out a gasp of relief.

Derek raised a palm and leaned back in. His voice was quiet but insistent. 'We're not finished with you, Rashid Alfasi. And if you speak to anyone about this, and I mean *anyone*, I'll throw you in jail myself.'

28

Edie waited for Alfasi to leave.

'Have you lost your mind?'

'I'm flattered you think I had one to begin with,' he said. 'Right now, I'm not so sure myself.'

'That makes two of us,' Edie said.

Derek sat down in his chair, leaned back and began rolling a pen through his fingers.

'If this was still my case everything would be so much easier, but it isn't. Whatever we do now has to be watertight. I can go to the prosecutor, but only if I'm absolutely one hundred per cent sure of my ground. And I'm not. The bulk of the evidence still points to the Killer Whales. Even if he did do it, we don't have enough on Alfasi to indict him. Plus we haven't eliminated Muloon yet, remember? It was his knife and he's got no backup for his alibi on Saturday.'

'What's your gut telling you?' For a moment Edie thought about unburdening herself and telling him everything she'd kept from him about Willa's connection to Martha. Then she thought about Sammy and about Willa and held back.

'That we need more time.'

'Time for Alfasi to go AWOL again.'

Derek shook his head. 'Alfasi's not going anywhere. It's fifteen hundred kilometres to the nearest town of any size, there's no supply ship for another year and I've put out a message at the landing strip that no one's to fly him out. Kid doesn't even have an ATV.' Derek dropped the pen back onto the desk. 'Things aren't black and white, Edie. If I hold

Alfasi for enquiries, how long do you think it's gonna be before Klinsman or his goons find out about it? The slightest hint that we're carrying on the investigation and he's gonna find a way to shut us down for good.'

The phone rang. He picked up.

'Hi, Anna.' He listened for a while, made the odd remark then ended the call. No speakerphone this time. Edie wondered if it had slipped his mind or if he was now deliberately keeping her from certain aspects of the investigation. When the call was finished he picked up the pen again and began rolling it between his fingers.

'Anything I should know?' Edie asked. No response. She repeated the question more loudly this time. He turned towards her with an expression of bewilderment on his face. Edie hadn't seen him look so disorientated since last spring on the sea ice in Alaska.

'Anna said the Defence Department sent a couple of officials round to look at her notes on the Martha Salliaq case and asked her to sign a confidentiality agreement. They told her it was routine for any case handled by the military police, but she says she's done MP cases before and never been asked to sign anything.' He lit a cigarette, took a long toke and said to no one in particular: 'What the hell is going on?' He raised a finger to his mouth and began biting the nail.

'Bad habit,' Edie said.

He smiled. 'You know, I wouldn't blame you if you wanted to leave right now.'

'And go where? To do what? Martha was my pupil and you're my asshole friend.' She thought about what Gutierrez had said, that Derek was out of his depth, that they both were.

'We're in the water together, D. There's nothing for it now except to take a deep breath and start swimming.'

'And hope there are no killer whales nearby,' he said.

They laughed.

At that moment, the door opened and Lizzie Salliaq burst in. Her face was red and swollen.

'The *qalunaat* nurse has been trying to call you, but you've been on the phone.'

Derek pushed the handset back into its cradle.

'My dad's sick. He's been sick a while but he wouldn't see a *qalunaat* doctor. We found him on the floor in the bathroom. There was blood coming out of his mouth.' Her eyes filled with tears. 'The nurse says he has to be medivaced out.'

Medical evacuations were police business. Derek dialled through to the nursing station and spoke to Luc. The old man was stable but he'd need to be admitted to the hospital in Iqaluit as a matter of urgency.

It was bad timing.

'I'll go over with them, see Charlie right and pay a visit to Anna,' Derek said. 'I can be back early tomorrow morning.'

Edie returned to her tent, gathered a few things and took a shower in Derek's bathroom. She washed and oiled her hair and put on a blue chambray dress customized with strips of sealskin and hare, then slid her multitool inside her pocket. She waited until she heard the medivac plane take off. Then she went down the path towards the centre of the village.

School had shut for the day, but the entrance door was open. Edie slid inside and went along the corridor to Chip Muloon's office. A single fluorescent strip buzzed in the passageway. She knocked on Muloon's door and, getting no response, tried the handle. Locked. Aside from the noise coming from the strip light the building was quiet. She bent down and placed a hand on the linoleum, checking for floor vibrations, but felt nothing. No one was walking about upstairs or in another corridor. For now the going was safe. She knocked on Chip's door once more, then pulled the multitool from her pocket. In a matter of seconds the lock slid back and she was inside.

The room had all the appearance of being in use. She recognized one or two of his books on the shelves, a couple of box files, a coffee machine and a collection of pens jammed into a mug. But the desk drawers were empty and there was nothing in the box files. Whatever he had been keeping in there had been cleared out. She went over to the shelves and flipped through the books and was lining them back up on the shelves when she suddenly became conscious of a vibration underfoot. Someone was coming. She froze and held her breath. To her horror, she saw she'd left a crack in the door. With infinite care she stepped over. Her hand was on the handle when the door flew open and the headteacher Les Ferguson's face appeared. For a split second the two of them stood there looking at one another.

'Chip sent me on an errand to fetch some files,' Edie said. 'But they're not here.'

Ferguson's face relaxed, then broke into a smile. 'I was just leaving for the night if you're done?' He swept Muloon's door open and made it clear that he expected Edie to walk through. 'New security arrangements. Need to lock up the building.'

'Of course.' She smiled back at him. One thing she'd noticed about *qalunaat*. They could be excruciatingly polite. When they were being like that, it seemed to take all their resources. You could slip anything under their radar and they wouldn't notice.

'Well, goodnight,' Ferguson said.

'Goodnight,' echoed Edie.

They left one another on the school steps, all smiles, then Edie turned and made her way towards Chip Muloon's house.

29

Derek knew the exact moment his aerophobia began, but knowing had never helped him defeat it. The best way to cope with it was to distract himself. The police pilot, Pol, knew nothing of Derek's terror of flying and he intended to keep it that way. If it got around, he'd be the laughing stock of the Ellesmere Islanders – all 287 of them – and pretty soon the whole of the High Arctic. Before he'd taken the post on Ellesmere his colleagues in Yellowknife had warned him not to be fooled by the size of the place. The biggest small town the world has ever seen, they called it. And so it had proved. The arrests of Nama-goose and Saxby had at least taken the heat off him, both more generally and with the Salliaq family, who now had added problems of their own. But the arrests had also made his own, covert, investigations more urgent. He was pretty sure that the pressure to arrest and charge the two Killer Whales had come directly from the Defence Department and that both Klinsman and the military police were just following orders. He'd got the impression that Klinsman had been playing second fiddle all along. That was one explanation for the colonel's almost desperate overtures at the start of the investigation. He was beginning to think now that Klinsman had been encouraged to close the case as soon as he could, even if it had meant implicating his own men. In the last day or two he'd even found himself wondering if the Killer Whales were being set up. Why the Defence Department might want to go to such extreme lengths he didn't know. But he intended to find out.

The ambulance was waiting at the side of the landing strip in

Iqaluit. Two paramedics clambered out and helped Luc to manoeuvre Charlie Salliaq into the vehicle. Alice and Lizzie travelled in the ambulance with the patient. Derek waited behind to complete the paperwork then called the Force downtown and got them to send him a ride to the hospital.

For a regional facility serving an area of 2 million square kilometres Baffin Hospital was pretty unimpressive. For the most part its thirty-four beds housed the elderly and infirm and folk who'd had minor accidents. Patients requiring major surgery or any kind of specialist treatment faced a four-hour flight south to facilities in Ottawa or Montreal. The locals often elected not to bother. They said that once you went down south you'd never make it back up again. There was something about the south that made Inuit give up and die.

By the time Derek had found someone who could tell him which ward Charlie Salliaq was in, the chief medical officer, David Applebaum, a tall, dry stick of a man with the braced gait of someone used to making difficult decisions in the absence of adequate resources, had already taken one look at the patient and advised an immediate transfer south. In typical Inuit fashion the old man had refused to go, saying that if he was going to die, it was bad enough to have to do it in Iqaluit. Applebaum had reluctantly admitted the patient to a family room with a stern warning about the risks. Salliaq was there now with Lizzie and Alice, awaiting some tests, but Applebaum had hinted that the results were likely to confirm what already seemed clear, that Charlie Salliaq was dying.

Derek's concern for the old man surprised him. Now that Salliaq's life hung in the balance, Derek was keen to ensure that he did not die before seeing justice done for his daughter. Which meant two things. First, persuading the old man to follow the doctor's advice and transfer somewhere they could give him specialist care. And secondly, trying to find a breakthrough in the case. Though, as Derek realized, this last was as much for Martha as for the remaining Salliaq family, who seemed content to believe that the perpetrators had been arrested and would be duly tried and, if there were any justice to be had in the south at all, found guilty.

He spent the time waiting to be called to the ward filling in the final medivac papers. Once he'd seen Charlie he intended to go down to the local detachment, say hi to his old pal Bill Makivik of the Iqaluit Force, check the weather and talk to Pol about booking a take-off slot for the return flight. Having supervised Charlie Salliaq's admission, Luc had gone to visit a friend and left a number where he could be reached with a return flight time. Once Derek knew that, he'd give Anna a call and suggest they meet up. It was past office hours now and he hoped she'd at least agree to talk to him. He'd been disquieted by her story of the confidentiality agreement she was required to sign by the Defence Department and wanted to get to the bottom of it.

A nurse popped her head around the door and told him Charlie was ready to see him. He finished his paperwork and wandered down the hospital corridor. Lizzie Salliaq was sitting in a chair outside the room with her hands in her lap.

'How's he doing?'

'He was awake for a bit, but he's gone back to sleep now. They're gonna run some tests.'

The girl fell silent. Derek peered through the glass window. Charlie was lying with his eyes closed, clearly in no condition to be disturbed. It might already be too late to move him.

'You eaten?' Derek asked Lizzie. It was late and they hadn't had time to eat before leaving Kuujuaq.

Lizzie waved away the question, but he went off to the cafeteria anyway and returned with a chocolate muffin and some hot tea.

Pulling up a chair beside the girl, he said, 'Where is your mother?'

'My cousin came to pick her up.'

He left a beat and changed the subject. 'Can we talk about the investigation for a moment?'

Lizzie gave a brief nod. She seemed relieved at the change of subject.

'When Colonel Klinsman came to see you today did he give you any indication about when the *unataqti* might be going to trial?'

'They're being sent back to Ottawa.'

'I see.' Derek supposed they would be tried in a closed military court. 'Did Klinsman say anything else?'

A nurse breezed past with a quick smile.

'Nope.' Lizzie made no eye contact. Was it shyness or was she being evasive? Derek couldn't tell. He wished Edie were there.

'Lizzie, do you have any idea why your sister might have wanted to leave Kuujuaq?'

The girl's head shot up, her eyes fierce all of a sudden. 'What makes you think she wanted to leave?'

There was a pause. Lizzie began dissecting the muffin onto her napkin. Something told him he'd missed the moment but he pressed on regardless.

'What do you know about Rashid Alfasi? He works at the weather station.'

She threw him a sidelong look. 'I know who he is.'

'Did Martha ever talk to you about him?'

'No. We didn't talk much about anything, OK?' Her voice quavered, the lips tight with anger. Then just as suddenly she slumped. 'I don't even know why . . .' She tailed off.

Derek bent down so that he was at the girl's eye level. 'What don't you know?'

Lizzie's shoulders heaved. 'I don't know why my sister had to bring us all this trouble.'

It was an odd thing to say, Derek thought. Women did say odd, incomprehensible things. People did. But, in Derek's experience, most of those people were women.

'What do you mean, "trouble"?'

The girl shrugged. 'Nothing, I guess.'

For a moment she sat staring at her lap, then, letting the muffin fall to the floor, she moved to the window of her father's room and pressed her palm against the glass. She swung her head around to face him.

'D'you think my dad's gonna be OK?'

From the hospital he walked down to the detachment offices in the centre of town. Sergeant Makivik was away at one of the outlying communities for a few days, so they would miss one another. Pol had checked in with the weather reports and it seemed that a summer storm up in Kuujuaq would keep them grounded overnight.

The administrator found him an empty desk with a phone, from where he called the detachment in Kuujuaq and left Edie an update. He then spoke with the flight coordinator up at the Kuujuaq airstrip and told him not to allow any plane to take off or land without police approval. It was an extreme precaution, given the deteriorating weather, but he wanted to be absolutely sure that Muloon and Alfasi would still be in Kuujuaq by the time he returned. Finally he dropped off his bag in the bunkroom, checked for a phone signal – it was patchy down here, but you could usually get something – then called Anna on her personal cell and left a message for her to call him at the RCMP detachment. Then he went over to the coffee machine and plunked in a loonie. The device whirred into action; a cup dropped down from the keeper and a thin, burnt-looking fluid began to spurt from the nozzle. He picked it up and watched the tawny bubbles twirling around on the surface. Something told him Anna Mackie wasn't going to return his call.

30

Chip Muloon was sitting on the couch in his cabin working on some papers when Edie padded in, announcing herself with a 'hey'. He looked up, shuffled the papers and slid them into a folder.

'What are you doing here?' Neither his voice nor his face betrayed any emotion.

'It's a small town and I'm kinda hard to ignore. Though you've been doing pretty good.' She flashed him a sorry look and saw his expression soften a little.

'Don't, Edie.'

She braced herself for the lie. 'I quit the police.'

He was genuinely surprised. 'Why?'

'The case is wrapped up. Namagoose and Saxby have been charged. It's over,' she lied. 'And now I could use a drink and some company.'

He stood up. She waited until his back was turned then sidled onto the couch and reached out a hand for the folder on the table, but he was too quick for her.

'Beer or whisky?' His hand went to the folder. He picked it up and drew it to him. She smiled.

'All work, no play,' he said. As he turned way, still clutching the file, she saw he had written something on his hand, the letters SrTCs. Some kind of acronym, she figured, but not one that meant anything to her. She turned her gaze away and in that moment he noticed her looking.

'Age,' he said. 'I have to write my to-do lists on my hand or I forget them.'

She pretended to laugh and watched him as he left the room, returning minus the file but with a couple of beers. He placed one can on the table and sat beside her, holding the other aloft. He'd wiped the letters from his hand.

'To new beginnings.'

She smiled and swung her can against his in a toast.

'You never liked Derek much, did you?'

'Who, the Lemming Police?' He took a long swig of his beer. She watched him swallow. Something passed over his face but she couldn't read what.

'I won't be seeing much of him any more,' she said.

'I'll drink to that.' He raised his beer, then, without warning, he reached over and pressed his lips against hers. The soft warmth of him was like summer moss. For the span of a second or two she felt herself move nearer, her body responding automatically to his, but then her mind filled with the image of Martha's body in the lake and she stiffened. When she opened her eyes again she saw he was frowning. A flutter of anxiety started up in her chest. She told herself not to blow her cover. Leaning in, she placed her mouth on his again, feeling for his tongue. Mistaking her quickened pulse for excitement, he deepened his kisses. She could feel him pressing his erection into her hipbone. She moved closer, grinding herself against him. All of a sudden, he pulled back.

'Just a moment, OK?'

She watched him move towards the bedroom. She'd banked on this, his fastidiousness about the scene of lovemaking. Before sex he liked to tidy the bed and light a candle.

She waited till he had disappeared from view then stood and, being careful not to make a sound, moved towards the kitchen, where she supposed he'd left the file. There was a sudden creaking and she froze. When she turned he was in the doorway, looking at her. For an instant, the hairs on the back of her neck prickled and a pulse rose up in her temples. Then his face broke into a smile and she felt herself relax. He lifted his arms, beckoning her, his shoulders low and soft. As she moved towards him, she felt for the multitool in her pocket but it wasn't there. With a lurch she realized that she must have left it in his office. She told herself not to lose the moment. If he suspected for a second that he was being set up, it was all over. She moved forward, but it was too late. Muloon had picked up her hesitation. His arms fell to his sides.

'You know what?' she said. 'This is kinda sudden. Maybe we should ease ourselves back in some?'

'Sure.' He smiled weakly. 'I don't have anything for supper. How's about we go up to the lake and catch a couple nice fat char?'

It hadn't occurred to her he would suggest leaving the relative safety of the settlement. This floored her. Was it possible he had realized she was trying to trap him and was setting a trap of his own? She looked at that handsome face with its chiselled features and blank, blue eyes but couldn't read anything there.

To back out now would look odd. He'd given no sign that he knew what she was up to. If she wanted to get something out of him there really was no choice but to go ahead.

Following his lead, she put on her outerwear and went outside. He went around the back to fetch his fishing gear. While she was waiting, an uneasy hollowness crept over her. The feeling grew stronger as he rounded the side of the cabin with his rods packed into a bag over one shoulder and his Remy 303 over the other. She didn't have to go through with this. But another, louder voice in her head told her she'd have to live with herself if she didn't.

She flashed Chip what she hoped was a casual smile and, thumbing over her shoulder, said, 'You know, I'm not exactly dressed for fishing. Maybe I should go put some pants on?' She'd go back to her tent and return with a knife.

'You're fine,' he said.

She kept up the smile. 'I really should let Sammy Inukpuk know I'm going. He'll be waiting for his supper.'

Her ex-lover glanced at his watch and began loading the gear onto the back of his ATV.

'We leave it another half-hour, the fish will have stopped biting.' He swung the fishing bag then the rifle onto the back of the vehicle. He turned and grinned. 'Are you stalling because you don't wanna go or is it that you know I'm a pretty smart angler and you're scared of being outshone?'

She reprimanded herself for having let her imagination get the best of her. Muloon had no reason to be suspicious because he had no idea she knew about his past.

'Wanna give me a ride over to my vehicle?'

'Why complicate things?' He gestured to the broad seat. 'Plenty of room on mine.'

She heard the voice of her mother – *The more impatient you are, the hungrier you will be* – and wondered if she shouldn't have waited until Derek got back from Iqaluit. But no. If Derek had discovered what she was up to, he'd have put a stop to it. It was now or never. She was on her own.

'Let's go,' she said.

As they moved inland, along the Kuujuaq River, he reached back with one arm and pressed her into him. She tried to take comfort from the gesture. Why would he want to stop her falling if he had any ill intention towards her?

The lake came into view. Muloon drew the ATV up beside it, killed the engine and, slipping the keys in his pocket, came round to the back of the vehicle. He shouldered the rifle and began unpacking the gear. She dismounted and watched him haul his bag of fly rods and lures down towards the water. For a while he busied himself with the equipment and it seemed almost as though he'd forgotten her. Then he turned and smiled and she was struck once more by how little she knew him.

She went over and squatted down beside him as he cast his line. He gave her a sidelong glance. The surface of the water shone like a raven's plumage. His right arm moved like a derrick as he cast, the lure teasing the water into silver spines. For a while there was silence and she was filled with the desperate desire to extend it, to have the moment stretch out to infinity. A jaeger passed over and looked down at them through wary eyes and she was reminded why she'd come. She wanted the truth. Sooner or later she was going to have to press him for it.

'How's the research?'

Muloon's eyes flicked. He blinked and swallowed, pressing his lips together, then swung to meet her gaze.

'So this is where the foreplay ends, huh?' His eyes were huge and lupine, the hostility coming off him in thick waves. He knew. He'd known the moment she'd walked into his cabin. All this time he'd been calling her bluff and she hadn't seen it. He was looking at the water now. 'Did you really imagine I wouldn't find out you'd backgrounded me?' he said.

She told herself to stay steady. 'You were still a suspect.'

'And you thought you could honeytrap me?' He laughed and shook his head. His voice was brittle and shiny, like an icicle breaking. 'You think you know all about me, but you don't. You know nothing and you wouldn't understand even if I told you. But you were prepared to sleep with me to find out.' He turned to her. 'So, what does that make you, Edie Kiglatuk?' Without waiting for an answer, he sidestepped, reached down and grabbed the rifle.

'Other people know where I am,' she said.

He smiled and shook his head. 'No, Edie, they don't.'

For a split second she felt helpless, then something rose up in her, the old fierceness, and she swung her head violently backwards then, using all her force, propelled herself forward until her skull made contact with his face. She heard him cry out in shock, his left hand moving instinctively to the injury. Taking her cue, she thrust out her arm and pushed, catching him off guard and sending him reeling backwards, then, dodging his now flailing arms, she ran for his ATV.

He gave a shout and she could hear the splashing sounds as he careered through the boggy ground towards her. She felt him close in on her, saw a flash of something and felt the breath go out of her. He had his arm around her throat now, the inner elbow pressing against the carotid. She struggled but he was too much for her. He reached for something in his pocket and she felt something cutting into the skin of her wrists as he bound them together behind her back.

'Sit on the vehicle and swing your legs over.' He was completely calm. 'Don't make me hurt you. Whatever you might think, I'm not a violent man.'

She did as he said. He picked up his gear and came over to the ATV and took the keys from his pocket. The engine ticked into life and they began to move off. She felt herself sliding on the leather seat and reached out behind. With supreme effort, by curling the end of her fingers under the saddle, she managed to find a small measure of grip. The ATV lurched forward, turned and picked up speed.

The vehicle rumbled through riverine sedge meadow then abruptly turned and began to climb, tipping her at an almost impossible angle. Her fingers, weakened by frostbite, seemed to have no solidity to them, but they were all that lay between her and a fall. The ground was an unforgiving moraine of sharp rocks and willow twigs, designed to put out an eye at best and at worst cause a fatal injury to her head. She made herself look about, trying to get a sense of where he was taking her, but a mist had come down and it was hopeless. So she closed her eyes and focused on her fingertips.

They had been going for some time when the vehicle shuddered to a sudden stop, throwing her forward into Muloon's back. He cursed softly, swung one leg over the saddle and dismounted. The mist had not cleared but she knew from the climb and from the particular saltiness of the wind and the aroma of saxifrage cut with guano that they were on the cliffs near Glacier Ridge. He went around to the side of the vehicle and motioned for her to dismount, then he bound her feet together. It had begun to rain, fierce little detonations, already part iced.

She saw him get back on his ATV.

'You can't leave me here,' she said.

'You'll find your way back. By the time you do, I'll be gone.'

The vehicle faded into the mist. She listened until the sound of its engine became a vibration then melted away. For a moment she gathered herself. The ropes were cutting into her wrists and ankles. A raven watched on as she began to work her hands and feet against their bindings. It grew colder and her head ached. She thought about what a fool she'd been. Right now, this moment, Chip Muloon would be back in his cabin, packing his things and waiting for the Defence Department to help him make his exit.

31

The sun swung to the north. It had stopped raining but the foliage was still damp and the change of direction in the wind and an electric charge in the air promised a summer blizzard. A few metres distant to the east Edie could now see a rocky outcrop with an overhang, which would provide some shelter when the storm came. She began to sidle over towards it, using the strength in her arms to heave herself over the gravel, humming through the protests of her muscles, and reached it just as the rain began again. Inside it was windless and dry. Fatigue made its way through her body like some shadowy ghost and her fingers thrummed and burned. She felt her eyelids drifting downwards, recognized the first intimations of cold exhaustion and wiggled her toes in an attempt to stay awake. Then she grew light and dim. Her mind took off like a bird and she found herself falling into darkness.

When she came to, she was lying face down on the rock and there was something very wrong with her nose, the nasal passages thick and heavy, a tang of blood in her mouth, and she realized that she must have landed on it when she passed out. She struggled into a sitting position. Beyond the overhang she could see that the rain had begun sheeting down. As she inched forward the wind whipped cords of it into her face. A muskox stood outside with its calf, eating. It spotted her moving and, startled, leapt backwards into the calf, knocking its legs from under it. There was a moment of confusion. The animal began pawing at the ground as if to charge, then, distracted by the calf's efforts to rise to its feet, swung about and gave it a nudge. The beast stood for a moment as if collecting itself then lumbered off, the shredded remnants of its winter coat snagging in the breeze, and Edie found herself alone once more.

She allowed herself a moment of relief but it was soon replaced by a new fear. Her nostrils were now becoming so blocked with drying blood that she was having to breathe through her mouth. Her lips and tongue felt sore and swollen. The swelling would likely continue. Eventually it would block her breathing altogether. The need to divest herself of her binds had suddenly become more urgent. She scoped about, looking for a sharp surface, and spotted a thin, bladed edge in the limestone just under edge of the overhang. Below it, fed by the droppings of birds, was a clump of dwarf willow and saxifrage, which she might use as an anchor. She shuffled over, knelt up and stretched her arms back behind her, but could not quite reach the rocky edge. A slight tremor started up under her feet. She froze and listened out. For a while she could hear only the wind and weather but the sound grew thicker and in it she detected the faint rumble of an engine. Outside the rain had turned to sleet. She felt her stomach turn over and a pulse start up in her head. It had to be Muloon, she thought. No one else would be travelling in weather like this. He was the only person who knew where she was. Had he relented and come to rescue her, or decided it was too dangerous to leave her alive?

Her immediate thought was not to take any chances. But she could hardly run, not like this, hands and feet tied, barely able to catch a breath. As the engine grew closer, a plan came together in her mind. She stilled her thoughts, channelling the adrenalin into a narrow tunnel of intent. Quietly panting to draw oxygen into her muscles, she found purchase in the clump of willow, counted to three and heaved herself upwards towards the raw edge of the overhang. But something went wrong in her movement, she felt her left toes give and there was a moment when her feet, tightly bound together, kicked out, scrabbling for purchase. She went down again, heavily this time, the right leg twisted under the left, her ankle popping, and she had to bite her lip in order not to cry out with the pain. She sat back, breathing heavily through her mouth, trying not to give in to the dark feelings creeping over her.

The engine was very close now and she could feel the vibration of the tyres against the rock. Sleet fell thickly, obscuring her tracks. She decided to try to remain hidden under the overhang. There was always a chance Muloon might not find her. The vehicle stopped. She could hear distinct footsteps crunching across the gravel slope, then a sigh and the sound of someone jumping from a height. She tested her sore ankle. It hurt like hell but it could probably still hold her weight. There was a darkening in the gloom inside the overhang and a pair of legs appeared, walking away from her. From her new vantage she could see a man's hand clutching a hunting knife. Her blood quickened, every muscle tightening, and for a moment her heart felt as though it might burst. The legs swung around and began to move back towards the overhang. A voice started up inside her head. *Please don't let what happened to Martha happen to me.*

The legs stopped. To Edie's horror she saw a disturbance in the gravel where she'd dragged herself inside. The legs swivelled around then paused. It seemed as though their owner had seen it too. Through the blanket of sleet she could see his fingers tightening around the knife in his right hand, less than a couple of metres from her face. She held her breath.

Suddenly, the legs folded and Sammy's face emerged from the gloom. 'Edie!'

She fell back, crying out in relief. He reached in a hand.

'I thought you were Muloon,' she said. 'How the hell did you find me?'

'When it got late and you didn't come, I went up to the detachment. There was a message from Derek asking you to call, which was how I knew you hadn't been back. I called him on the number he left for you and he told me to go round to Muloon's and take a gun. Muloon wasn't there, so I followed his tracks. Leastwise till the weather started washing them away.'

She'd slid out from under the overhang on her butt. For the first time, Sammy was looking at her eye to eye. Didn't much like what he saw. She turned so he could cut the rope on her wrists.

'That icicle *qalunaat* do that to you?'

She presumed he meant Muloon. It was a pretty accurate description actually.

'All my own work.' She put a hand to her face, fingers working around the bloody, crooked bulb that had been her nose. It felt bad and it probably looked worse.

'I guess I'm not gonna make Carnival Queen this year.'

He began slicing at the rope around her ankles with the serrated blade. She spotted the SOG Seal Team logo on the handle. Same brand as Skeeter Saxby's.

'That your knife?'

'Believe it or not I found it. There's some animal bones and a fire circle just down the way. The blade was in a clump of cotton grass. Got tooth marks on the handle. Wolf picked it up most like, smelled blood on it.'

She shook her limbs and stood up.

His face was a crumple of concern.

'It's a long story,' she said.

Sammy called the top name on the list of first-aiders posted at the entrance to the nursing station then joined Edie inside. Ahnah Oolik appeared shortly after to patch up Edie. While she got to work, Sammy went round to Muloon's cabin and came back with the not unexpected news that the man had cleared out. His office was empty too. No sign Chip Muloon ever existed.

When Edie got back to the detachment there were six messages from Derek on the voicemail, each sounding more worried than the last. Edie called the number he'd left. The night desk answered and told her that the sergeant was up at Iqaluit airport and they'd get a message to him. She waited by the phone. Moments later a wired, anxious-sounding Derek came on the line.

'You scared the hell out of me.'

She filled him in on everything but her injuries. Didn't feel like telling him she'd busted her own nose.

'Tell the truth, I feel kinda dumb. I couldn't even get out of him what he was working on. Said I wouldn't understand.'

'The man always was a condescending prick.' His tone grew softer. 'You OK? You sound kinda gummy.'

'Summer cold.' She glanced at herself in the reflection on the computer screen and wished she hadn't.

'My guess is Muloon will have gone to Camp Nanook. I don't think he'll be bothering you again. Go get some rest, Edie. It's not over yet. You're gonna need all the strength you can muster.'

She went back her tent, exhausted, and found Sammy sitting on the sleeping skins, smoking. She sat down beside him and he put an arm around her shoulder.

She leaned in to him and allowed herself to be comforted by the warmth of his body.

'I spoke with Willa,' he said. The smoke from his cigarette curled upwards. 'I know you two have had your differences, but he's a good kid, Edie. He has a big heart. Sure, he went off the rails awhile, but he's straightening himself out. The Rangers, Lizzie, he's making it work. You need to trust him more.'

She knew Sammy was right, but that only made it more painful. The first step to trusting the people around her was to trust herself. But that was going to be a lifetime's work. Maybe more. And right now she couldn't do anything except rest.

'Let's get some sleep,' she said.

She turned over inside her sleeping bag and lay awake for a while thinking about Willa and Joe and Sammy in the old days, when they were all a family, and she forgot about the pain in her nose and Chip Muloon and even Martha Salliaq and slept.

She woke to find Sammy sitting in the same corner, wrung-out and smoking, his rifle in his lap. She checked her watch. It was eight o'clock. Sunlight blasted through the canvas.

'You been on guard all night?'

'Most of it.'

Her hand went to her face. 'How's my nose?'

'Like a walrus with a cocaine habit.'

She got up, stretched and pulled on some outerwear. 'I'm gonna make us some breakfast.' She knew he'd be expecting there to be a renewal of the closeness between them. That wasn't something she could allow. 'Why don't you check the weather? If it's looking good this might be the day for you to make the trip back to Autisaq?'

He threw her his wounded look. She returned it with a quiet smile. They'd been through this a hundred times.

'You know how it is when we're together for any length of time. It starts off OK then one of us opens a bottle. Right now, Sammy, I don't trust myself not to be the bottle-opener.'

Outside she took a deep breath. Somewhere beneath the dank, vegetable scent she could already detect the chill, electric tang of winter. Something in her needed to be away from Sammy and from the settlement and back out on the land.

After breakfast she said goodbye to Sammy and, taking the coastal track, drove along to the bird cliffs and parked up on the beach, keying off her ATV. Above her the cliffs thrust skywards. Leaving her vehicle, she clambered up the path to the summit. From here there was a view across the high plateau of Glacier Ridge to where it tumbled down to meet the plain below. Beside her stood an *inukshuk* – a stone figure – pointing away from Lake Turngaluk. She moved forward, trudging across gravel and lichened rock, scoured and dried by the wind, until she reached the new security fence. From here she could see beyond the remnants of concrete and Cold War rubble to the spot where Martha Salliaq's body had been found. The surface was cracked and stained rusty brown. She thought about Martha, wondering if this was where she had come to dream, long before she'd met Rashid Alfasi, Jacob Namagoose, Skeeter Saxby or Chip Muloon.

She walked back to the *inukshuk* and stood beside it, following the direction of its pointing hand with her eyes, pondering what it was about Lake Turngaluk that made even stone men turn away. A surprising thought filtered into her consciousness and began take root in her mind and for a long time she was so lost in thought that she didn't hear the detachment plane until it had passed directly overhead and was banking before making its approach into Kuujuaq.

By the time she got back Derek's ATV was already sitting outside the detachment. She stomped up the steps into the office, shouting his name.

The man himself appeared from the kitchenette a moment later, carrying a tray on which sat two steaming bowls.

'I got us some real food.' Her face stopped him in his tracks.

'Jesus Jones, did Muloon do that?'

'No, why, you think it doesn't suit me?'

'On the contrary. If I was a walrus I wouldn't be able to keep my flippers off you.'

She laughed and took a bowl from the tray.

'That's more or less what Sammy said.'

The food he'd cooked was some kind of hamburger, caribou she suspected, but whatever it was, it took some chewing and the state of her nose made her unable to taste it. While her jaw worked Derek filled her in on his trip to Iqaluit. He'd come back gloomy about the prospects of concluding the case.

'You see those cop shows on the TV where they have a team of forensics and a team of detectives and everyone except the murderer wants to solve the crime. This is kind of opposite to that. A murder investigation where the forensics don't show up for days, there are no teams of anything and no one gives a shit about solving the crime.'

Edie swallowed a lump of meat. 'We do.'

'But we're not going to solve this crime, Edie, unless we get some kind of breakthrough. All we've got so far are leads running into blind alleys.' Derek rubbed his eyes. His skin was ruddy from the summer sun but where it thinned and at the temples you could see the pallor of exhaustion beneath. He flipped open his pack of cigarettes and pulled one out. 'If I don't get some sleep pretty soon I'll go crazy.'

She picked up the bowls, put them back on the tray and went out into the kitchen. Her mind ran through the thoughts she'd been having up at Glacier Ridge. She washed up the bowls and put them on the drainer to dry. The sound of raised voices reached her from the other room. Dropping the dishcloth, she came out. Joe Oolik was standing beside the door. He was wet through and dripping. His arms were flailing about and he was trying to say something but he was speaking too fast to be comprehensible. Derek had him by the shoulders and was telling him to calm down. As Edie came into the room Derek's head swung round to meet her.

'I think he's found something.'

Oolik was repeating the Inuktitut word for 'trailer'.

Edie strode over to the door. At the bottom of the steps leading from the detachment was Joe's ATV. A soaked and crumpled tarp lay over the trailer, strapped on with elastic bungees. Edie took one look back then ran down the steps. Joe was shouting at her now, but she couldn't hear the words above the thick pulse of her own heart. She reached the base of the steps, rushed over to the trailer and pushed the tarp aside.

Rashid Alfasi's eyes stared blankly up at her.

32

In any normal circumstances it would have seemed beyond doubt that the death of Rashid Alfasi was a suicide. When Joe Oolik found him, face up in shallow water, Alfasi was wearing a backpack weighted with rocks. A thick notebook serving as a diary lay on the table inside his cabin. On top of the notebook he'd left a photograph of Martha Salliaq at the bird cliffs matching the one Edie had found in her bedroom just after her death.

It would have been usual procedure to take the body to the morgue, inform the next of kin and get started on the necessary administration in the morning. A sad fact of High Arctic life was that young men killed themselves at an alarming rate. But Rashid Alfasi was both a suspect in Martha Salliaq's murder and on secondment to the military and Derek was concerned that, if he didn't act quickly, the Defence Department would find some excuse to remove his jurisdiction.

And so over the next few hours he busied himself with transporting the body into the morgue and making the necessary phone calls to the medical examiner and the police in Vancouver and filling in incident reports and other paperwork. While he worked Edie scanned the pages of the notebook, trying to put together the pieces of Alfasi's life that might tell the story of his death.

What was immediately clear was that Rashid Alfasi had been a hopelessly conflicted young man, torn between his identity as a Muslim and the paths he had taken. From Edie's reading of the notebook, it looked as if two incidents had come together in the same day which, in Alfasi's view, had made his life unendurable.

From what Edie could piece together, it seemed that Rashid Alfasi had been seeing Martha in secret for about five months. They met mostly at the bird cliffs and sometimes, when the weather was bad, in one of the abandoned buildings at Glacier Ridge. The meetings were marked in the diary, along with the occasional annotation 'left flowers', presumably to mark those times that Martha couldn't get away but Alfasi wanted her to know he had waited for her. The diary entry on the Friday before Martha died was of particular interest. Long and anguished, the writing by turns compressed and scrawling, it narrated a series of momentous events in Alfasi's life.

Alfasi had been working at the weather station. In the afternoon, he had called his parents in Vancouver from the satphone there. It was his mother's birthday and he'd wanted to wish her a happy day. But the conversation drifted into more painful territory. Evidently, Alfasi hadn't told his parents about his secondment to the military. But they had found out from Alfasi's brother. They disagreed with the deployment of Canadian troops in Afghanistan and saw their son's secondment as a betrayal. Alfasi's mother had threatened never to speak to her son again.

This must have been echoing his head as Alfasi went to meet Martha that Friday after school. According to the notebook, he didn't tell Martha about the row with his parents. Instead, they talked about Martha's desire to move to Vancouver and study there. She wanted Alfasi to move with her. They could be married. 'I imagined what my mom would say to that and panicked,' he wrote in the notebook. He told Martha to forget the move because he didn't want to be with her any more.

Alfasi had told them the rest of the story when they'd interviewed him. He ran because he knew that his relationship with Martha would be discovered eventually and he supposed that he would get the blame for her death.

By the time Derek had finished with the papers and Edie had been through the notebook it was early morning. There was no point in trying to get some sleep. Anna Mackie was due to arrive before too long and Derek needed to stay awake in order to make arrangements with the Vancouver Police family liaison. Alfasi's parents had already decided that they wanted to fly to Ellesmere to pick up their son's body.

Derek made coffee for himself and tea for Edie and they sat in the office and talked about Edie's findings.

'You think he could have killed her?' Derek asked after Edie had outlined Alfasi's version of events.

'Unlikely, I'd say. His story adds up. It explains why Martha was upset on Friday night and why she took the Killer Whales to the Shoreline Bar, knowing Alfasi would be working in the Shack at the back. Wanted to make him jealous.' It also explained what it was she was trying to tell Willa, Edie thought, though she kept this to herself. 'Namagoose said Martha had told him she'd had a fight with her boyfriend. Turns out he was telling the truth.'

'Any firm evidence as to why Alfasi killed himself?'

'Nothing you can take directly from the notebook. There's no suicide note,' Edie said. 'I had to guess, it was a combination of things. Family disgrace for one. Then the sense that he was about to be accused and bring more shame on his family. Guilt, maybe. If he hadn't finished it with Martha she wouldn't have hooked up with Namagoose and Saxby.'

She watched Derek pour himself another cup of coffee and suppress a yawn.

'That damned notebook tells us a whole lot about Martha Salliaq except for the one thing we most need to know. Who killed her?'

33

A few hours later Anna Mackie's plane touched down in Kuujuaq. Edie and Derek were at the landing strip to meet her.

'I hope you got some strong coffee brewing,' Mackie said. 'It was kind of an early start.' She registered the state of Edie's nose. 'That looks sore.'

'It's how we're wearing them up here this summer,' Edie said.

'Funny,' Mackie said. She didn't seem to be in the mood for humour.

Derek cut in. 'You didn't return my call the other day.'

Mackie touched the palm of her right hand to her forehead in an unconvincing gesture intended to convey ditziness. No one less ditzy than Mackie.

The pilot had opened up the hold and was passing out the forensic bags. Derek grabbed a couple and heaved them onto the trailer.

He suggested Edie drive Mackie and the baggage trailer out into the parking lot then strode off after the pilot to complete some paper-work and speak with Alice and Lizzie Salliaq who had accompanied Charlie on the same flight.

'It's such a tragedy, the region losing its young men in this way,' Mackie said. 'Derek told me he left a note?' Neither Ransom nor Mackie knew about Rashid Alfasi's connection to Martha Salliaq yet. Derek hadn't wanted to give them any excuse to stall.

'More of a diary.' They reached Derek's vehicle. Mackie ran her eyes over the bags, mentally ticking them off, and the two women began to transfer them onto the police trailer.

'So there's nothing I should be looking out for outside a suicide by drowning.' Mackie voiced this as a statement, not a question. She caught Edie's eye and held her gaze, eager for affirmation.

'No,' Edie said. 'Nothing at all.'

Relief came over the ME's face.

Derek reappeared and took the key Edie handed him. She told him to go ahead with Mackie. Being at the airstrip had reminded her to check and see if Sonia Gutierrez's vehicle was somewhere in the vicinity. Edie hadn't seen her around for a couple of days and the last time they'd spoken the lawyer had seemed anxious about her safety. In all the tumult of the events of the past couple of days Edie had forgotten about her. Now she remembered her saying she was thinking about going to Iqaluit. Edie hoped that was where she was now. After a quick check of the parking lot and the administrative building, she finally spotted the lawyer's vehicle hiding behind a bank of rotten snow at the end of the landing strip, parked up and empty. It struck her as a strange place to leave it. She went back inside the terminal building, intending to check the passenger manifest, and ran into Markoosie Pitoq, who was standing in the corridor, smoking.

'How's your brother-in-law?' Lizzie and Alice had been told the news about Alfasi. They'd decided to keep it from Charlie until he was stronger. Edie didn't know whether or not Markoosie knew.

'We're waiting for the gurney trailer. You can see for yourself, he's in there.' Markoosie flipped his head to indicate a side room off the main terminal building. He followed her in.

A *qalunaat* nurse was standing beside the old man's bed, checking his IV. She said she'd accompanied the patient from Iqaluit. Kind eyes. Something dry in the smile. Edie introduced herself and went over to the old man.

'*Avasirngulik*, it's me.' Charlie's eyes opened and a half-grin appeared on his face.

'The Lemming Police's girl.' He chuckled weakly then blinked. His face wrinkled with concern. 'What happened to your nose?'

'Nothing important.' What she saw lying in the bed was a dying man. 'How are you?' she said.

He raised his eyebrows and beckoned to the nurse with his hand. 'Tell the girl what the doctor said. I can't remember all the names.'

'Dr Applebaum's diagnosis is acute myoblastic leukaemia. It's sometimes called "white blood". Unfortunately Mr Salliaq has refused any further treatment, so the doctor had no choice but to let him come back home.'

Salliaq chuckled. 'I'm non-compliant, apparently.'

'Among other things,' the nurse said, with feeling.

The old man sighed. 'These people are crazy. They think they can cure "white blood" by pumping me full of white blood. But I said to them, the only blood that's going to run in these veins is Inuit blood.' He gave a little snort. 'The doctor says that's racist, but he doesn't understand our traditions.'

'I see,' Edie said. Her inclination was to agree with the doctor but there wasn't much point in saying so. 'Did you talk to Sonia Gutierrez about this?' Edie wondered if there was some legal loophole which might keep everyone happy.

'I haven't seen her or spoken to her,' Charlie said.

Odd, Edie thought. Worryingly so. If Gutierrez really was in Iqaluit, wouldn't she have visited the old man in hospital? The two were close. She made her excuses and went to the door, promising to come and see Charlie at the nursing station. Markoosie followed her out and laid a hand on her elbow to indicate that he had something to say to her.

'I wanted to ask you about the amulet, the one I made for Martha. I'd like it returned. It still has power. I would like my brother-in-law to have it.'

His face told her that he was serious. For some reason she thought about the *tupilaq* she'd found outside his house.

'I'll see what I can do,' she said.

She left him in the corridor and made her way to the office to check the passenger manifests for the last week.

Sonia Gutierrez's name was nowhere on any of them.

*

She sensed that the hotel was empty the moment she walked in. She strode up the stairs two by two. When she got to the top she turned down the corridor and saw immediately that something was very wrong. The door to room number 7 was open and the room itself was completely empty. The sun beating through the window exposed a thin layer of newly gathered dust. She went back down to the kitchenette, opened the cupboards. A few packets of dry goods, a half-can of rancid-smelling tuna in the refrigerator, as though Gutierrez had left in a hurry. The phone log in which guests were supposed to record the destination and length of their calls had a couple of recent entries in Gutierrez's handwriting. These suggested she'd made a call to a number in Ottawa then another to Iqaluit.

The Ottawa number was answered by an RCMP officer who claimed to have no knowledge of Gutierrez's call. The Iqaluit number rang directly through to Chris Tetlow at the *Arctic Circular*. The journalist said he hadn't had any contact with Sonia Gutierrez since they'd spoken briefly a few days back. He said she'd usually call him when she came through Iqaluit and they'd have a drink together. He gave Edie the lawyer's office and home number in Ottawa. If she wasn't there he didn't know any other place she'd be likely to have gone.

'She's kind of a workaholic,' he explained. 'She doesn't really have much of a private life.'

Edie asked Tetlow to phone the detachment if he heard from the lawyer then finished the call. Both the numbers Tetlow had given her went straight through to voicemail. She left messages but didn't hold out much hope.

From the downstairs hallway, she went back up to the rooms, beginning with number 7 then working her way through the rest, checking shelves, closets, peering under beds and lifting mattresses. Outside, the sun had disappeared and been replaced by wet sleet. The wind had picked up. From the windows she could see the birds on the overhead cables bobbing up and down, their feathers opened like fading flowers.

She was about to give up when from the corner of her eye she saw something moving in the room at the end of the corridor. Her hunter's instinct told her to crouch low and listen. From behind a door, past Sonia Gutierrez's room, was coming a not quite regular slapping sound. She began to inch along the wall. At the door she stopped and listened. The sound continued unabated. The wet, rhythmic thwack of something swinging. She laid an ear up against the wood. The noise was definitely coming from inside. She thought about Alfasi and a sudden sickening fear came over her that Gutierrez had taken her life and was hanging in the bathroom. Fumbling for the handle, she threw open the door, which swung back then bounced a little off the weight of something lying behind it. The slapping sound continued. She felt a breeze, looked towards the window and saw the gap where it had come open; a piece of the vertical blinds had become detached and, now exposed to the rain, was swinging sodden against the window frame. Her body relaxed.

Behind the door was a black daypack with a dark-blue trim. Inside there were a few papers annotated in what she recognized as Sonia Gutierrez's handwriting. Either the lawyer had forgotten the bag when she'd moved the rest of her things or she'd left it there deliberately. Shouldering the bag, Edie padded down into the communal room, took a chair and emptied the papers out onto the low coffee table. There was a series of plans of Glacier Ridge, dated 1960 and 1974, what appeared to be an order for construction materials and a memorandum about the clean-up with a faint annotation reading 'IRG categorically forbids' ringed in pen at what looked like some later date. Pushing the papers back inside, Edie zipped up the bag, went back outside and made her way towards the nursing station.

The body of Rashid Alfasi lay part-covered on a gurney. Evidently, he hadn't been long in the water when Joseph Oolik found him. There were patches of lividity on his face and his lips were set in the grimace of rigor mortis, though from the slackening around the eyes it seemed that the rigor was already beginning to leave him.

Anna Mackie stood beside the gurney outlining her plan for the autopsy to Derek. As Edie came in she fell silent, her eyes first narrowing then slaloming between the police sergeant and his VPSO.

'Now wait a minute, guys . . .' Her arms wrapped around each other defensively. 'What is this, an ambush?'

As Derek explained that Rashid Alfasi's death and Martha Salliaq's were most likely connected, little darts of anger shot across Mackie's face.

'You should have told me. Dammit, I can't believe you're putting me in this situation. I told you the department made me sign a gagging order. I even mention the Salliaq case I could lose my job.' The ME left the examination table and went over to the sink. She flipped her face mask down and leaned back against the metal, thinking.

'You listen to the dead, Anna,' Edie said. 'That's your job.'

The ME let out a snort of annoyance but she knew there was no answering this. Her body softened. 'OK, OK, I get it. You're still on the Salliaq case.' Her head turned, checking the room. 'Is it safe to talk here?'

Derek went over to an old radio sitting on the windowsill and turned it up high. The odd hoot of throat-singing filled the room.

'It is now.'

They huddled beside the radio. 'The Defence Department sent two of its men round. Todd Ransom seemed to know all about it. They carried out a bunch of tests on Martha Salliaq's body. Bone samples.'

'Bone samples?' Edie asked. She recalled the memorandum among Charlie Salliaq's papers. A theme seemed to be emerging.

'I wouldn't consider that to be standard procedure in this case. Bone samples would usually only be of importance if the body was skeletonized, or if there had been sharp or blunt force injuries which might have caused fracturing or breakage.' She glanced at the body on the gurney. 'Were they lovers?'

At Derek's nod she looked away. The thought obviously pained her. Then she gathered herself and went on. 'Bone fragmentation analysis is often used where there are gunshot wounds and in a number of other situations, none of which apply in the Martha Salliaq case. You'd biopsy bone marrow for toxicology purposes, especially if blood wasn't available.'

She pulled off her glasses and tried to wipe the tiredness from her face. Derek turned off the radio and the room fell silent once more.

'What should I do now?' Mackie said.

'Your job, Anna.' Derek laid a reassuring hand on the ME's shoulder. 'We'll get to the bottom of this, I promise.'

Mackie let out a bitter laugh. 'That's exactly what I'm afraid of.'

As they walked back out into the waiting room Edie updated Derek on her visit to the hotel.

'I think Gutierrez left those papers somewhere they'd be found,' Edie said. 'She was afraid for her safety.' She told him about the memorandum on animal bones. They looked at one another and smiled. They were getting somewhere.

As if on cue, Luc appeared carrying a set of files. Derek beckoned him over and asked him what he knew about bone marrow. The nurse paused a moment. 'You're talking about Charlie.'

'Should we be?' Derek said. He had that look of intense focus Edie had seen on him once or twice before. It was the look he only pulled out of the bag on special occasions, the look which transformed him from the Boonies policeman who spent his days rounding up stray dogs to the investigator capable of cracking cases that might well have confounded entire departments of big city cops.

'Charlie's leukaemia. It's a disease of the bone marrow.'

Derek's eyes were sharp enough to cut water from the beach. 'How do you get that, Luc?'

'A variety of ways. Exposure to toxins, radiation.'

'Contamination.'

'Could be,' Luc said.

Derek turned to Edie but she was already one step ahead of him.

'I'll go see the old man, tell him we need to look at his papers.'

*

Charlie Salliaq was propped up on a pillow, IVs leading from both arms to a frame from which several bags hung. Beside the bed a heart monitor peeped like a hungry fledgling. As they went in, he turned his head very slowly, a thin smile on his lips. His face looked as broken as frost heave, the skin pale as winter.

Edie took a seat on the blue plastic chair beside his bed. The room smelled of sickness and chemicals.

'I know what you're thinking, Lemming Police's girl. I should have that blood transfusion.'

'You're an old fool not to.'

'What business you got with an old fool, then?'

'I was your daughter's teacher, *avasirngulik*.'

'Yes,' he said, his eyes clouding over. His chest heaved and for a moment he struggled with the effort to contain whatever was in his heart.

'You familiar with the clear-up agreement for Glacier Ridge, Charlie?'

The old man shrugged. 'Was once, I guess. But all that stuff got crowded out of my head. You'd be better asking the lawyer.'

She decided that telling him Sonia Gutierrez was missing might be too much for him so she asked to see his copies of the documents. The old man described a box in the shed at his house.

'If I'd known what trouble it was gonna cause, I'd never have started that damned claim,' he said.

At the door Edie turned back to him. 'Your job there, at Glacier Ridge. What did you do?'

The old man's forehead wrinkled and he rubbed his eyes with a skinny hand.

'Nothing special,' he said. 'They wouldn't let Inuit do much except routine maintenance, janitor stuff.'

'You think about that transfusion,' she said.

34

Edie and Derek stayed at the Salliaqs' house only for as long as it took to pack the old man's files into a Chinese laundry bag. The place still smelled of fingerprint powder and forensic solvents. The family had been back only fleetingly. Lizzie and Alice preferred to be at the Pitoqs' house these days. Edie could see why.

Back at the detachment they split the contents of the bag in two.

'What are we even looking for here?' Edie asked. She wondered how any of these densely typed sheets and scribbled memoranda were going to help track the whereabouts of Sonia Gutierrez or uncover once and for all who had killed Martha Salliaq. She shifted through the pile. Paper trails, memoranda, letters of agreement, this wasn't the way they did things up here. She heard herself give a little sigh.

Derek paused in his reading. 'I know what you're thinking, but you're wrong. These here are *qalunaat* footprints. They are the trails that white fellas leave. You want to beat these guys, you got to play them at their own game.'

Retreating to Stevie Killik's desk she bundled the paper into a neat pile and scanned the top sheet. As the unfamiliar jargon of the law swam before her eyes, a Barrenland of dry subclauses and bullying-sounding addenda, Derek's explanation began to make more sense. He had a better grasp of the *qalunaat* world. Looking at it as a trail of prints to be followed made the job less intimidating to her. She began to think of it as a hunt for an as yet unknown quarry.

An hour passed, then two. Derek smoked almost non-stop. Every so often one or other of them got up to make tea to keep them going. At one point a group of children began to play a game of football on the path at the front of the detachment and the policeman went out and told them to move further along. Edie heard a boy's voice shout, 'My dad calls you Sergeant Lemming and says you're dumb enough to jump off of a cliff.' Derek returned not long after, shaking his head and mumbling.

The documents stretched way back to the late 1960s but the vast bulk dated from the mid-90s or later, when the land claims negotiations were taking place. These were mostly surveys, boundary line maps and memoranda from the Defence Department, the finance and foreign ministries, the territorial government of the Northwest Territories and, after the creation of Nunavut in 1999, from the regional government in Iqaluit. In earlier documents it seemed as though Charlie Salliaq had been the only Inuk working with a series of lawyers but as the years went on a handful of other Inuit names appeared.

'I don't recognize many of these names,' Derek said. 'They must have died before I got here. Most of the ones I do know have passed on now too. It seems that the Kuujuamiut don't make old bones.'

Bones were becoming a theme, Edie thought, returning to her papers. A later batch, dating from the last ten years or so and relating to the various clean-up tasks – from removal of waste, tar, creosote, building materials, paint, fuel and other contaminants to reconstruction and replanting – had been negotiated solely by Sonia Gutierrez after she took over as chief counsel in the case. By this time it was the early 2000s and the negotiations had been rumbling on for a decade without much progress. From what Edie could make out, Gutierrez's argument was that the contaminated land lay very close to the bird cliffs from which the Kuujuamiut regularly harvested both eggs and birds. She had drafted a press release and the *Arctic Circular* had picked it up. Some of the southern papers took note too. It seemed that it was the press interest that had forced the department to reach a settlement.

A sudden rattle on the steps. The door swung open and Klinsman appeared with the Camp Nanook counsel, Marty Fielding, following behind. Derek very discreetly pushed a plain file cover over his papers and got up from his chair. The colonel eyed them momentarily then held out a hand.

'You got a few minutes, sergeant? Maybe a stroll down to the sea?'

Palliser stared at the hand but did not take it. He was angry and not feeling polite about it. 'Take a look around, colonel. This look like some spy hole-up? Some security intelligence outfit? This is a country police detachment at the end of the world and you've parachuted in and crapped all over it.'

The colonel blinked and stood his ground.

'A stroll by the sea,' he said.

They walked down to the shoreline in silence and stood looking out over the spangle of Jones Sound. The tide was low, and on the exposed shingle a huge Arctic lion's mane jellyfish lay dead, the two metre wide crimson bell still shiny in the sunshine, the flame-coloured tentacles so long you could measure off a basketball court and have some to spare.

Fielding stood back, unwilling to move closer.

'You still want that stroll?' Derek asked.

'What the hell is it?'

'*Itqujaq*,' Edie said. 'In the whaling time, the *qalunaat* whalers called it the sea devil. We sometimes say it's a drop of blood from Sedna, our sea spirit. The tentacles can be dangerous even after death. They usually stay out in deep sea but they've started coming in to the shallows.'

They picked their way to the shoreline. The iceberg that had been part-obscuring the view of Devon Island earlier in the week had moved on, leaving the bruise-coloured cliffs a hundred kilometres to the south shimmering in heat on the horizon.

'I thought I'd been some places till I came here,' Fielding said. He raised his hand to shield his eyes and gazed out across the water, squinting in the flare of reflected light.

Edie smiled to herself. She was glad the Arctic had unsettled him. He and others like him. Maybe that way they might stay away.

'Sonia Gutierrez is missing,' Edie said.

Klinsman's shoulders tightened. 'This is dangerous terrain, Ms Kiglatuk. People go missing all the time. But I guess I don't need to tell you that.' In a softer tone, he added, 'You're going to have to get used to sharing the High Arctic, you know that, don't you?'

Edie turned to look at him but he would not meet her eye. 'Our kind of sharing and your kind of sharing aren't the same,' she said. 'We remember how you "shared" our whales. Two million of them. Stripped the blubber to render into oil, kept the baleen and threw away the rest. Just one of those whales could have kept an entire Inuit settlement alive for a year. Now you're telling us you want to "share" oil, gas, minerals. You want to "share" the fish, the seas, the animals. We've already seen how you share things that don't belong to anybody and you want to keep "sharing" until there's nothing left. Except us, colonel, we'll be left. By the time you have finished sharing, we'll be left with nothing.'

Klinsman and Fielding laced their arms behind their backs.

'What you're describing is inevitable, Ms Kiglatuk. There is nothing you can do to stop it. Whatever you think you're looking for, you won't find it. I advise you strongly not to keep on looking. Everything has its natural depth. Fish, humans, institutions. That creature there . . .' He thumbed at the jellyfish. 'It likes deep waters, you said. But look what happened. It overreached itself. It wandered into the shallows. Believe me, you are out of your depth here.'

His eyes were flat but there was a weariness in his voice, Edie thought. Whatever game was being played, he had begun to tire of his role in it.

'Saxby and Namagoose will be tried for the murder of Martha Salliaq in a military court and I have every expectation they will be found guilty. That's all we can offer. It's a good deal. Make it enough.'

The colonel turned and began to make his way back up the beach, Fielding following close behind. At the track he stopped and turned. 'You want me to send a couple of men to move that thing off the beach before someone's child steps on it?'

Derek gave a low snort. 'It's a little late for your offers of protection, colonel, wouldn't you say?'

Edie and Derek waited for the jeep to disappear. They had always thought that they understood what trouble looked like. Up here it looked like avalanches and white-outs and hungry bears. It did not look like a fastidiously dressed man in a jeep and his spineless nose bot of a sidekick. But the truth now lay right before their eyes on that beach. The bloody tentacles of the beast reached further and deeper than the military were prepared to acknowledge publicly. That was a new kind of trouble.

At the detachment steps they stopped. Derek pulled his ATV keys from his pocket.

'I need a break from those papers, see how Anna Mackie's getting on. Alfasi's parents should be arriving any time. They'll be wanting to know when they can take the body. We'll get back to the papers when I return.'

Edie watched his vehicle lumber up the track. She returned to the detachment and tidied the papers into a pile. A sticky note fell out with the letters RTG and SrTCs scribbled in blue ink in Sonia's handwriting. She turned the paper over in her hands and sank back. It meant nothing. The paper trail had fried her brain in a way that a trail on the tundra never did. Her head felt watery-heavy and letters and plans spun together behind her eyes.

She went into the kitchenette, found the remains of the walrus head in the refrigerator and, cutting off a few slices, made a large walrus omelette from the last of the eggs. This she wrapped in plastic film and slipped inside Gutierrez's backpack, then she made her way towards the nursing station.

Luc was in the consulting room taking a clinic. Anna and Derek were in the makeshift morgue packing up.

'I've brought walrus omelette,' she said.

Mackie pulled off her examination gloves and began collecting her instruments. Edie sensed that relations between Derek and the medical examiner were strained.

'Alfasi drowned,' Derek said. 'No reason to think it was anything but a suicide.'

Mackie turned briefly. 'That's what I'll be saying in my report for the coroner but in the end it's her decision.' Mackie snapped off her surgical gloves and went to wash her hands. Her voice, like her actions, had a crisp, official air to it.

'You see Sonia Gutierrez around Iqaluit the last couple days, Anna?'

Mackie stopped drying her hands and turned around to face the question.

'I already told Derek, no,' she said decisively.

Edie offered her a piece of omelette. She shook her head, turned her back and went on with her packing, closed as a clam. On the other side of the room Derek grimaced as if to say this was a lost cause. He took the piece of omelette. They ate in silence for a minute or two, while Mackie worked around them. When it looked like they weren't going to get anything more out of the ME, Edie licked her fingers, drew the sticky note out of her pocket and passed it over to Derek. 'I found this, it's Sonia's handwriting.'

Derek read the letters RTG out loud, handed the note back and carried on chewing. 'Means nothing to me.'

It was a few seconds before Edie noticed that the clinking sound of metal on metal had ceased. In the corner of the room Mackie had stopped what she was doing and was standing with her back to them, her shoulders tensed. The atmosphere in the room thickened. Eventually Mackie turned to face them. She seemed to have had a change of heart.

'You two just don't give up, do you? RTG might be radioisotope thermoelectric generator. They were installed in a lot of remote Arctic monitoring stations. They use radioactive decay to generate electricity off-grid. There were still a few in use in the North American Arctic right up to the end of the nineties.' She stopped abruptly, as though her battery had just run out, before deciding to go on.

'A couple of cases came to me when I was working in forensics over in the Yukon . . . drunks sticking their heads right inside them and getting radiation burn. But you'd have to get right up close.'

Edie flipped the sticky note over in her fingers and read what was written on the reverse. A thought arose in her mind like a footprint in the snow, deep and telling.

'What about SrTCs? That an acronym for something?' They were the same letters as she'd seen written on Chip Muloon's hand but she decided it was better not to say anything about that. Mackie was spooked enough as it was. She didn't want to frighten her off completely.

As it was, the ME seemed profoundly unsettled. She had her back to the counter, her hands clasped along its edge, and was staring into the middle distance as though she was trying to make sense of something.

'Anna, please,' Edie said simply.

When Mackie turned her head Edie could see that her eyes were moist with tears.

'I can't do this,' she said quietly. Her chest rose and fell. For a moment she seemed to fix on the door and Edie wondered if she was about to make a run for it. But there was nowhere to run to and Anna Mackie knew that too.

'We found a paper forbidding the testing of the animal bones among Sonia Gutierrez's documents. We know that Charlie Salliaq has bone-marrow disease and now you tell us that the Defence Department took samples of Martha's bones. What is it about bones, Anna?'

The ME went over to the gurney and zipped the body of Rashid Alfasi back up inside its bag. She seemed to be weighing up her options.

Edie gave her a pleading look. The dead have ears, she thought, and they can speak. She could hear Martha Salliaq whispering to her but there was only one word in a hundred she could catch. And all around her this deafening roar of paper. The white man's footprints. She thought about the photo of Martha that she'd been carrying around in the pocket of her parka. She pulled it out now and went over to where Mackie was standing. It may be, she thought, that Mackie was so used to seeing the dead that she'd forgotten the one great truth about them, that they had all once lived.

The ME took one look at the photograph and issued a little cry of shock.

'She was beautiful and smart and in love. With him' – she pointed to the body bag – 'with Rashid Alfasi.'

Mackie bit her lip. She looked gaunt and haunted. With a fierceness that was almost frightening, she suddenly thrust out her hand and said, 'Show me the note.'

Her eyes flashed over it.

'Those letters are the symbols for strontium, tritium and caesium. Strontium and caesium are radioactive metals, tritium is an isotope of hydrogen. People sometimes call them the unholy trinity. Exposure to them causes radiation sickness and cancers. Of the three, strontium is probably in the god spot. It collects in the bone marrow and causes leukaemia. People call it the bone seeker. It's generally a by-product of nuclear fission.' She seemed resigned now, and lonely, as though she had crossed over a line from which there was no going back.

Derek had stopped eating. Edie saw him watching Anna intently. The three of them unwilling actually to give voice to what they now knew.

They finished the packing in silence and Derek escorted Anna Mackie back to her plane. While he was gone, Edie returned to Charlie Salliaq's room in the nursing station. She pulled up a chair and sat beside the bed. The old man did not open his eyes, but neither did it seem to her that he was sleeping. He had grown even paler since her last visit, the veins on his arms like the milky-blue run-off on moraine. It was clear he didn't have long to go.

'*Avasirngulik*.' The old man's eyes moved under their lids.

'The Lemming Police's girl.' He reached out and patted her affectionately on the leg. The pupils were glassy and unseeing. 'Did you find your way through that storm of paper?' He chuckled. 'You know why they shower these document blizzards down on us? It's so they can sneak in while we are blinded and do what they like.'

'Is that what they did at Glacier Ridge?' Edie said.

The old man gave a sigh of resignation. 'That's what they always do.'

'Can you remember what happened there, *avasirngulik*?'

'Ha, my memory,' Charlie said, smiling weakly. 'I saw a TV show when I was down in Iqaluit. They said that by the time the light from the stars hits us it's old. They said that what we see is already history. You, me, everything.' He reached out and patted her arm. 'But we already know that, don't we, Lemming Police's girl? We Inuit have known since before time began.'

His breath became a cough and as his body seized Edie caught a glimpse of the skin on his chest beneath the hospital gown, the colour of it translucent and as yellow-grey as a stretched seal bladder. She picked up his water cup from the nightstand. He propped himself up on an elbow and took a sip.

Then he lay back, shifting his body a little in the bed.

'Glacier Ridge was a long time ago. I was a handyman. I cleaned up and fixed things.'

'Did Martha ever visit you there?' Edie said.

He shook his head. 'I finished working there before Martha was even born.'

'You recall anything they were trying to keep secret, Charlie? Any place you weren't allowed to go, any process you weren't allowed to witness?'

The old man raised a bony hand and rubbed his left ear. 'I'm tired, Edie Kiglatuk.'

'You need that blood, elder.'

There was a fleeting instant when she saw something raw and full of life cross his face.

'There *was* one time. Way back. It was in the winter, I remember, because the sky lit up the night and then the ground shook and there was a hot, rushing wind and the sound was like a thousand icebergs turning over. We were all scared. We thought maybe the sun had made a mistake, maybe that the seasons had gotten mixed up. We were living in huts then, just tiny little cabins fixed together from old packing boxes, heather and fur between the walls as insulation. Some of us stayed in our cabins with our families. The ones who believed in Jesus, they went to the church and said their prayers. In the evening a *qalunaat* came into town; he was dressed strange. He said they were closing the station for a few days. He gave us two weeks' pay. But they never reopened it properly.

'Not long afterwards the *qalunaat* shut the place down and shipped out. But the fire burned for a long time. You couldn't see it but you knew that it was there. It made that lake. The water was hot for a while but no birds ever flew over. People said the fire brought evil spirits from their resting places. Why we called it Lake Turngaluk.'

'You recall what year this was?'

'I'm old, I don't remember things that way,' Charlie said. He sensed Edie pressing him. 'I was married to another woman then, and I didn't have my daughters.' A sudden look of pain came over him. 'People said that *qalunaat* had put a curse on the place. Babies died. My wife, that wasn't Alice then, Elizapee was her name. Her babies died. The spirits at the lake took 'em down into the underworld, that's what people said.' He lifted his head and licked his dry lips. Edie held the water to him and he took another sip.

'Who else worked at the site?'

'They're all gone to spirit now. All except Toolik Pitoq.' Charlie gave a long sigh and shut his eyes. 'It's taboo to talk about this. The spirits don't like me to talk about it. That's why I'm so tired.'

Edie took the old man's fragile hand in hers and placed a kiss on his forehead. Salliaq whispered something she didn't catch, then, without opening his eyes again, he fell asleep.

35

It took Edie a while after she'd woken to figure out where she was. The sun was blading through the blinds in Derek's bedroom. Derek himself was still asleep, a blanketed mound on the couch. She got up, quietly wrapped his robe around her and stole towards the door without waking him. An empty whisky bottle lay in the sink. Had they drunk it? She couldn't remember. She blew on her palm but her breath smelled only of sleep.

She made some tea and took it out onto the steps. The jaeger was sitting on the telegraph wire. It whistled a warning call. She went around to the back of the building and checked the nest. There was only one fledgling now, almost fully grown, preening itself in a soft cup made from the down and feathers of its devoured siblings. It froze when it saw Edie's face, its beady eye indignant at the intrusion.

Derek's voice called to her. He was standing on the deck beside the detachment front door with a mug in his hand. She climbed back up the steps towards him.

'That whisky,' she said. 'I didn't, did I?'

He smiled and shook his head. 'When I got back from the airstrip you were going through the cupboards, remember? I emptied it down the sink. You came back from Charlie Salliaq in a strange mood, Edie. You took a sleeping pill. You told me you'd taken it from Charlie Salliaq's room.'

The evening's events were beginning to come back to her. Last night it had all been getting to her. She rubbed her face with her hands.

'Maybe we're out of our depth, like Klinsman said.'

'Klinsman is a condescending prick.' He passed her his mug of coffee. She took a long gulp and remembered why she preferred tea, but it woke her up.

'You said that about Chip Muloon.'

'Something about the Arctic attracts them. All that space to stretch out their egos.'

She laughed and pressed past him through the door into the office. Then she remembered where she'd woken up. She twisted her head to meet his eye. He caught her meaning.

'I like to think you would have remembered if we had.' He winked. 'We thought it would be safer for you to sleep here from now on, remember?'

The phone rang. Derek went over to his desk and picked up. He flipped on the speakerphone and got Edie's attention.

'I'm at the airport at Iqaluit.' Anna Mackie's voice. In the background they could hear a PA system announcing a flight. 'I've decided to take unpaid leave until this blows over.' She tailed off. When she spoke again it was softly, with the slight reverb that comes from holding your hand over your mouth. 'Listen, the D-men came back while I was up in Kuujuaq with you guys. They took Martha Salliaq's body away to a military morgue. Ransom dealt with it. I asked him why and he said it was a safety hazard. Radioactive contamination. Must have come from the water at Lake Turngaluk.'

There was another announcement on the PA.

'That's my plane. I'm sorry.' The line went dead.

Derek and Edie sat for a moment in silence, their minds slotting pieces of the puzzle together, making the connections.

'The Defence Department didn't want anyone with access to Martha Salliaq's body to start asking the wrong kind of questions,' Derek said. 'That's why they took over the investigation. It had nothing to do with protecting an individual. It had to do with protecting the Defence Department.'

'We should talk to Toolik Pitoq,' Edie said. 'He was there when the

Glacier Ridge fire happened. We might reach the point where we need another witness.'

'What was that you said about being out of your depth?'

Edie met his wink with a grin.

'Turns out I'm a better swimmer than I thought.'

On their way over to the Pitoqs' house they ran into Markoosie, who was just setting out to host the morning radio show.

'Your father in?' Derek said. 'We need to ask him some questions.'

'About what?' Markoosie took the cigarette Derek offered him. The two drew the smoke deeply into their lungs.

'Glacier Ridge stuff, way back.'

Markoosie shoved his hands in his pockets. 'I guess you know old Toolik can be a bit forgetful. *Isumairutijuq*.' The Inuktitut word for 'dementia' sounded more forgiving than the English. It was often said the elderly were closer to the spirit world. In the old times people with *isumairutijuq* might have been shamans. Markoosie went on, 'But he's better with things that happened a long time ago so you should be OK.'

Toolik Pitoq was sitting in a chair, idly carving a piece of soapstone into what looked like the figure of a shapeshifter, part man, part goose. In the corner an Oilers vs. Senators game was proceeding unwatched on the TV. The old man looked up as they entered, an enquiring look on his face.

'It's Sergeant Palliser,' Derek said.

Toolik lifted a hand as if to bat him away. 'Oh I know who it is. The Lemming Police. And the woman from Autisaq. What do you want?'

Edie saw Derek press his lips together and frown. Edie sat down and took the old man's hand.

'You remember working with Charlie Salliaq at Glacier Ridge, elder?'

Toolik sighed. 'Hard. Our families went hungry. We had no time to go hunting. Even if we had, the men at the station had already hunted out all the game. They liked to corner musk ox so they huddled into a defensive circle round their young. Then they'd machine-gun them. They thought it was funny.'

'Do you remember the fire?' Edie said.

Toolik nodded slowly. 'We don't talk about that,' he said.

'Charlie Salliaq has talked about it.'

'He has?' Toolik seemed confused for a moment, then a spark came into his eyes. 'Oh well, see, a long time after, when they came back, they said I could do a temporary job. There was this oil or sludge and they wanted me to scrape it up. Something came off it that made it hard to breathe. They always said wear gloves and a mask but they never gave us any. Hard as hell to get off your hands. They piled it all up, dug out the bowl in the ground, and buried it again.' He coughed, as if the fumes were still swirling round him. Edie thought about what Charlie had said to her, that history bled through into the present. That was how it was for Tooliq now. So much history had bled through it was hard for him to know what belonged to now and what to the past.

He rattled on. 'We didn't like it, but you know, it was hard enough just to survive in those days. A day after the fire, me and Salliaq and a couple of the others who'd been laid off went hunting. We were wondering how we were going to feed our families. We went down to the beach, by the cliffs. A pod of beluga had gotten washed up. Just lying on the beach, they were. Already dead but fresh and not a mark on 'em. Never seen anything like it before or since.' He chuckled to himself. 'Oh, we had a field day. A whole year we lived on those beluga.'

'You think you might let the nurse do some tests on you, Toolik? Maybe take some blood?'

The old man shrugged and held out his skinny arm. Edie noticed an abrasion inside the crook of his elbow. It was pretty crude, more like a slice in the arm than a needle mark. 'How did you come by that there?'

Toolik gazed at the wound and said nothing. He took a long draught from a cup on the table and began to drift, striking up a tuneless humming.

'Oh, no, my son never got over losing that girl,' he said, finally. 'Now then, Martha. Where's my lunch?'

36

Derek met Rashid Alfasi's parents at the landing strip and brought them directly to the nursing station. They had travelled for the best part of twenty-four hours to reach Ellesmere from Vancouver and were sallow from the journey; the father, craggy-faced, holding up his small, plump wife whose legs trembled with grief or exhaustion. At least they had a body to bury, Edie thought. Right now the Salliaqs had nothing. Edie made them tea and sat with the mother while her husband went to the morgue to formally identify his son. They had brought flowers and wanted to lay them at the spot where Rashid had died, so while Luc Fabienne and Joe Oolik loaded the body into a crate in preparation for the flight, Derek took the bereaved parents out to the trout lake and Edie returned to the detachment to do some more research.

She moved over to Derek's computer and entered three words into the search engine. *Strontium, tritium, caesium.* Unfamiliar words for which there were no Inuktitut translations, words that felt heavy on the tongue. It felt bad keying in the word Arctic beside them, as though, even as symbols, their proximity had the power to contaminate. She pressed enter and sat back.

To her surprise pages and pages of links appeared. Most of them, it seemed, had to do with submarines and the Soviet Union. She ran her eyes down until she came to a word that caught her attention. *Aleut.*

Inuit, Eskimo, inhabitants of the Arctic. Her own people.

She clicked on the link. A page scrolled up with another unfamiliar word: Amchitka, an island, as it turned out, one of many in the drowned mountain range known as the Aleutians, far off the Alaskan coast. She read on. Until the middle of the twentieth century, the islands had been the remote domain of Aleut fishermen and Russian sea otter trappers. Their fate changed in 1942 when the Japanese captured two of the islands in the chain, Attu and Kiska. Not long afterwards the United States established a beachhead on Amchitka from which they launched an offensive to recapture Attu. According to the web page three thousand Aleuts and soldiers from both sides were killed in the battle. Edie turned that number over in her head. It contained another word that had no equivalent in Inuktitut. Thousand. In her language there was only one, two, three and many. The way Inuit had survived for so long on the vast expanses of the Barrenlands was by keeping themselves small. This was another thing *qalunaat* didn't understand. Perhaps they were beginning to understand it. But perhaps it was too late.

It was certainly too late for Amchitka. In 1965 the US Defence Department exploded a nuclear device on the island that caused radioactive contamination of its freshwater lakes. This was kept secret. Edie thought about Lake Turngaluk, the lake no birds would fly over, the lake of evil spirits whose waters poisoned the body of Martha Salliaq. The lake that, for forty years, no one would talk about.

But that wasn't the end for Amchitka. Four years after the first explosion, the Atomic Energy Commission, which had taken over responsibility for nuclear testing, detonated a calibration device which triggered earthquakes and landslides. You might have thought this would be enough to have stopped them, Edie thought, but it wasn't. On 6 November 1971, in project Cannikin, the AEC detonated the largest underground nuclear test bomb in US history on Amchitka, a bomb 385 times the size of Little Boy at Hiroshima.

The bomb was placed in an underground concrete chamber.

It was like finding the perfect snowflake in the midst of a storm. The one precise, orderly explanation, the vanishing point in the chaos. What else could explain the sudden expansion of the site at Glacier Ridge, the anomalies in the plans, the secret underground bunker, the fire and the dead whales, the banning of tests on animal bones, Charlie Salliaq's leukaemia and finally, but by no means least, the transfer of Martha Salliaq's body to a military morgue and the Defence Department's determination to close the investigation into her murder?

She sat back, her breath heavy in her chest, and there was a sudden coldness in her belly as though she'd been lying on ice. Officially, she saw now, none of it had ever happened.

But Charlie Salliaq was witness to the fact that it had.

She went back to the old man's room and found him sleeping soundly. She whispered his name, stroking his face with her finger. It was only when she began to sing that he woke and, opening a single eye, said,

'Is that you, Lemming Police's girl?'

'Yes, *avasirngulik*.'

He chuckled. 'You sing like a goose.'

'Then you'll prefer it if I talk.' She told him everything. The plans, the bunker and the Cannikin test at Amchitka. The irradiated water, the unholy trinity and the bone seeker. She told him about the memorandum and the animal bones. Last, but most important, she told him about the removal of his daughter's body, the attempt to sweep her death away as though it was of no importance.

He listened in the Inuit way, intently and without comment. The last part would hurt him terribly, she knew, but she thought it might save him too. Sometimes it worked that way. He let her finish. Then he gave a sigh and said, wearily, '*Qalunaat* have always done whatever they wanted in the Arctic.'

She pressed her lips together and squeezed her hands into fists in her lap so that he would not see them. For all his talk about the past Charlie Salliaq had been one of the few who had been able to shrug it off. A strong man who had refused to be timid. A warrior disguised as a janitor. And now she needed him to wake up from his dying slumber and fight.

'I thought Charlie Salliaq was in this room,' she said. Her voice had pebbles in it.

The old man rolled his foggy eyes. He gestured towards the night-stand to have his water cup passed. He took a long sip from the straw and lay back. His chest began to spasm.

'I'm tired,' he said, 'ask Sonia Gutierrez to help you.'

'You are the witness, Charlie. We need you. The Defence Department took a calculated risk at Glacier Ridge. They figured we wouldn't stand up for ourselves and no one else would give a damn. Nothing will bring Martha back, *avasirngulik*, but we won't ever know for sure who killed her until we confront the people who are trying to make her death unimportant. Take the blood transfusion and help me, *avasirngulik*. Help Martha.'

The old man's brow furrowed. He let go of her hand.

'I'll think about it,' he said simply. 'Leave me alone now, Edie Kiglatuk.'

Luc was on the phone in his office. He waved at Edie to help herself to a hot beverage in the waiting room while he finished the call. Moments later, he joined her, yawning and rubbing a hand across his head.

'Not sleeping?'

'The damned light. It's like being interrogated twenty-four hours a day for four months. How do you stop yourself going crazy?'

'It helps if you start out that way.'

Luc smiled. 'In case you're wondering, Derek is up at the landing strip, seeing off the Alfasis' flight. He asked me to take a blood sample from Toolik Pitoq. I'm afraid I haven't gotten around to it yet. It's been crazy busy. But it's next on my list, I promise.'

She thanked him, then remembered the injury to Pitoq's right arm and asked Luc to check it out while he was at it.

On her way back to the detachment she noticed the door flap of her tent was moving softly in the wind. She was usually meticulous about roping it down to keep stray huskies or foxes from raiding her food stores. She parked up her ATV and went over to check it out. Inside, nothing seemed to have been moved or taken, but she had the uneasy feeling that someone had been in nonetheless. She thought back to Klinsman's visit and wondered where Chip Muloon was now. A vehicle pulled up alongside and she heard Derek shouting her name. She poked her head out of the canvas.

'I swung by the store on my way back. Thought I'd make hamburger. You want some?'

The plane came up and over the houses, sucking the air below into its slipstream. They waited for it to pass.

'Alfasi's parents are going back to Morocco,' Derek said. 'They say this place makes their blood freeze.'

'Funny, it makes mine boil.' The way Edie said this brought an enquiring look from Derek.

'I'll fill you in over lunch.'

As it turned out, Derek's idea of making hamburger was to empty the meat out on a plate raw, stick a fork in the top and open a jar of pickles. She picked at the food without any appetite, telling him what she'd discovered and venturing her theory about nuclear testing. As she went on he began to eat more and more slowly until at last he put his fork down for the final time.

'I've suddenly lost my appetite,' he said.

'Me too.'

'This must be what Gutierrez got close to before she disappeared,' she offered. 'Since he was being paid by the Defence Department I'll bet that was what Chip Muloon was working on. Long-term health outcomes. Maybe Rashid Alfasi was in on it too.' An image of the jellyfish sprang to mind, its tentacles reaching out across the beach.

Derek pushed his plate away and lit a cigarette, then stubbed it out.

'I really should give this up,' he said. Seeing Edie's expression he added, 'I mean, the smokes.' In the last couple of days he had stopped shaving and he was now scratching the stubble on his chin, which, being half Inuit and half Cree, was dark and sparse.

The phone went. It was Luc.

'Old Salliaq seems to have changed his mind. He says he's willing to fly out to Ottawa for a blood transfusion and a possible bone-marrow transplant. I've spoken to Applebaum and he's contacted the city hospital there. They've got a bed waiting for him.'

Edie felt herself smile.

The old man couldn't resist a fight.

Derek said he would ask Pol to make a quick turnaround in Iqaluit and head directly back.

There was a pause. 'One other thing,' Luc said, 'there's been some kind of mix-up with my blood samples. I'm not sure how it could have happened. I just came back from taking blood from Toolik Pitoq. You asked me to see if I could find anything wrong with his white cell count so I had a quick look at his medical records. As you probably know, the records don't go very far back . . .' The sound of voices interrupted his flow. Luc mumbled something, then returned to the phone. 'Some patients just arrived so I gotta keep this brief. Toolik Pitoq is blood group A. He's pretty anaemic and there appears to be an abnormality in his white cells. As a precaution, I checked his son's records, just to see if Markoosie had been diagnosed with anything. These things often run in families. Markoosie's blood is AB. Which kinda surprised me because I was pretty sure when I'd taken that elimination sample from him last week, he was group A. I checked out that injury you talked about, Edie, and it looked like someone had made a little incision into a vein. When I asked the old man about it he just went quiet. Any case, I got out the backup sample I always take in case the original gets lost and tested it again. Either the written records are wrong, which is possible, or that blood sample Markoosie gave us last week wasn't his. Which got me to thinking . . .'

Derek was leaning over the phone now, his elbow in the forgotten plate of meat.

'. . . Markoosie said he felt faint and asked for a glass of water. That's pretty common and I didn't think anything of it at the time, but looking back, I wonder if he swapped the samples when I turned away to get the water. That kind of thing used to happen when I was doing random drug-testing back in Toronto. Employees covering for their drug habits. I was always more vigilant back then, but I've never heard of anything like it happening up here in the north before.'

Motes of sunlight striped the furniture in the Pitoqs' house, picking out the stains left by beer cans and TV dinners. The TV had been switched off only recently, its static still ripening the air, but to the right of the snow porch the door to the storeroom was open and there was evidence of someone having left in a hurry.

Toolik Pitoq lay on his bed fully clothed and fast asleep, his breathing slow and uneven. Derek went over and shook him gently, calling his name, but got no response. On the nightstand there was a pharmaceutical bottle with a scattering of pills beside it. Derek tapped Toolik's arm and when he still did not stir he gently opened one of the old man's eyelids. The pupil was rolled up and away. A wisp of foam started to play around the lips.

'Call Luc.' Derek waited for Edie to reach the phone then yelled the number.

By the time Edie returned, the old man had begun to struggle for breath. Foam rolled from his mouth now and his legs began to shake violently. There was a great gasp after which the legs fell still. Derek leaned in close, feeling for breath. He flung off the blanket and began pumping at the old man's chest with his hands.

'He's stopped breathing.'

The door flew open and Luc appeared. Derek swung his head around, his hands continuing their motions.

'Take over?'

'You're doing fine.' Luc inserted a finger into the old man's mouth and pulled out the foam, then he grabbed his wrist and felt for the pulse.

'It's OK. You can stop.'

Derek stepped back. The nurse placed his stethoscope against Toolik's chest.

'Get the roll-out gurney. I'll stay here with him.'

Working together, Derek and Edie unstrapped the kit from the nursing station trailer and laid it out on the bed, then on a count of three rolled the old man on top. He was quiet now, his breath slow and even. Luc rolled up one of his eyelids and shone his flashlight into the pupil.

'I'll need to gastric-pump him.' He looked up at Derek. 'Help me with the gurney.'

Derek swept up the bottle of pills and dumped it in his pocket, then the two men went to either end of the gurney and lifted Toolik on Luc's count.

'We'll need to tell Markoosie.'

'I don't think that'll be necessary,' Edie said. She mentioned the signs of a fast exit.

Derek looked sceptical. 'The old man has dementia. He could easily have taken an accidental overdose.'

Something told her it hadn't happened that way, but this wasn't the time for a debate. Instead, she waited for the men to leave then started making her way through the drawers and cupboards in Markoosie's room. Nothing jumped out at her until her eye was drawn to a photo album bound in blue leatherette sitting on the single bookshelf beside the Bible and a couple of textbooks on running a radio station. It was the only thing on the shelf not sitting in a pool of dust. She opened it up, flipping through forty or fifty pages of perfectly ordinary family photographs, and was about to put it back when something odd struck her. In every picture of the young Markoosie and the woman she presumed was his wife, Nora, there was a little girl. Who looked very much like Martha Salliaq.

She left the house and made her way along the path to the town hall building. The door to the radio station was locked. Peering between the gaps in the venetian blind she could see that the room was empty. She headed outside. A row of parked ATVs was lined up in front of the building, but Markoosie's was not among them. Swinging back onto her vehicle, she turned and began to bump along the path to the Salliaqs' house.

Lizzie and Willa Inukpuk were busying themselves in the yard stretching sealskins onto racks. She guessed they had come clean about their relationship after Charlie had been taken to hospital. Lizzie spotted her first. She stopped what she was doing and stood up. Something in her expression gave Edie the sense that she knew what was coming. Willa followed her, holding his hand above his face as a sunshield. Whatever secret Lizzie had been keeping all this time, she hadn't shared it with her lover.

'Is Alice here?'

Willa flipped his head towards the door.

'She's packing Charlie's things to take down to Ottawa.'

A cheap weekend case was standing just inside the door. Alice was in the kitchen making bannock bread, her hands powdered with flour. She left off when she saw Edie and, brushing back her hair with a forearm, went to the sink to rinse her hands.

'You only ever come when something's wrong. So what is it?'

'Your father. He's at the nursing station but I think he's gonna be OK.'

Saying nothing, the woman wiped her hands dry on a rag and went to the door. With a raw, quiet dignity, she said, 'Willa, you drive me?'

Willa nodded.

'Lizzie, ride with me?' Edie said, hoping to use the time to get her to talk. The girl shook her head emphatically.

'I'll take my father's vehicle.'

By the time they reached the nursing station Toolik Pitoq was lying on a gurney, his breath struggling in his chest like a trapped hare, unable to speak. When he heard his daughter and granddaughter's voices he mustered a smile but the confusion in his face suggested that he had no idea where he was or what he was doing there. The official version of events was that he had taken an accidental overdose. To Edie, though, that seemed unlikely. The bottle on the nightstand had contained Ambien. Luc had checked both his stock and his script records. He'd never prescribed it to the old man and there was none missing from the pharmacy.

'That doesn't mean anything,' Derek said. 'Kuujuaq is awash in prescription pills in the summer. Contractors bring them up, the crew on the supply ship, even bush plane pilots. Every so often me and Stevie try to crack down on it, but it doesn't make us popular. People like getting high.'

Edie reminded him that Saxby had taken some from the pharmacy at Camp Nanook and said he'd sold it on to a local man. Maybe that man was Markoosie Pitoq.

'Might explain why he switched his father's blood last week, though. If he'd been taking them himself he'd know his blood would show up dirty,' Luc volunteered.

'Maybe,' Derek said. 'But that doesn't make the fella guilty of trying to poison his father.'

Edie drifted back to Toolik Pitoq's bed. Lizzie was sitting beside her grandfather. She registered Edie's presence momentarily and by the movement of her shoulders, angled away, Edie got the sense that she wasn't wanted. The girl had already made plain that she wasn't inter-ested in talking and now that Willa and Lizzie had gone public with their relationship, she no longer had the hold over them she once did. All the same, it seemed more important than ever to Edie to try. She drew up a chair.

'Your sister and her uncle spent a lot of time together, didn't they? When she was a little girl and then, maybe, later.'

The girl blinked. She looked away for a moment as if collecting herself.

'Why do you ask that?'

Edie could sense that she was close to something now. All she had to do was press it home, just a little. 'You ever catch a thaw pocket, Lizzie?'

Lizzie hesitated, not sure where this was going. Kids learned about thaw pockets from the moment they could first walk. Formed when temperatures rose, causing the surface ice to rot and liquefy, then freeze again, leaving a thin layer of new ice crusted over the rot, they were hard to spot and dangerous. If you weren't careful you could find yourself breaking through the thin crust into deep freezing water.

The girl glanced at her grandfather, then looked at her feet. Silent tears began to spiral down her face. When she spoke her voice was the sound of icicles cracking.

'OK,' she said, 'but not here.'

37

They moved to the nursing station's waiting area. For what seemed like a long time Lizzie sat with her hands in her lap, her eyes flickering at the edges, jaw working, from time to time opening her mouth to speak, then thinking better of it.

Beside her Edie waited patiently, hardly even blinking, a hunter at the breathing hole of a seal. For ten days she'd been asking Lizzie Salliaq questions and for ten days the girl had offered only partial answers. Now, she sensed, they were at the door to somewhere new. All Edie had to do was wait for the girl to push it open.

'You think my uncle gave my grandfather those pills, don't you? No one else does, but you do.'

'I'm good at thinking bad things. It's not a skill I'd recommend but it seems to be one I'm stuck with. I think your uncle was afraid your grandfather might give him away. All families have secrets. They can be toxic.'

For the first time Lizzie looked Edie directly in the face. She was weeping openly now.

'My mother was Charlie's second wife – did you know that?'

'Yes.'

'He didn't have any children with his first wife. Her name was Elizapee. She had two babies, but they couldn't hold on to life. We'd been moved to a new place, so people said that their spirits weren't ready to come down from the stars yet. They were afraid of getting lost. That was how people accepted it.'

'Inuit are good at accepting things. We need to get better at not accepting them,' Edie said.

Lizzie wiped a hand across her eyes. 'Something happened to Elizapee. She got sick and died. My father married my mother. She got pregnant and had a boy who died before I was born. Then nothing happened for a long time and by the time I came along they had more or less given up.'

'They must have been excited to have you.'

Lizzie cocked her head. 'I guess. I wasn't an easy baby. I had some problems for a while. But I lived. My *hanaji* named me *nerriungnerk*, hope. No one thought that my parents would have any more kids so when my mother became pregnant again with Martha they thought their troubles were over.'

'Were they?'

'In a way. In another way, though, they were just beginning. Martha wasn't sickly like me. She was the healthy one, everyone's favourite.' Lizzie turned away. 'Not that it matters now.'

'It matters now more than ever.'

Lizzie nodded. 'Maybe. You saw the pictures of my uncle Markoosie, and his wife, Nora, with Martha. They couldn't have children of their own. There were many other couples like them but I guess that didn't make it any easier. Nora was like Elizapee. She gave birth to two children but they both died. People began to say Lake Turngaluk had stirred up bad spirits. They thought about moving to Autisaq or to one of the other settlements but there wasn't enough game in those places for everyone to eat. They wondered if it was their fault. They wanted to go back home, down to the Hudson Bay, but the government wouldn't take them.'

The story was familiar to Edie, to every Inuk living on Ellesmere Island. The government had taken them to this impossible place promising them a better future. When the better future didn't materialize the government forgot they'd ever made the promise. Edie had heard that emotion or some variation of it expressed so many times in Inuit dealings with *qalunaat* that she'd lost count. The helplessness, the loss of confidence, the feelings of unease.

'Did anyone ever mention a link between Lake Turngaluk and the fire at Glacier Ridge?'

Lizzie shrugged. 'I don't know about any fire.'

'But people didn't talk about Lake Turngaluk?'

'No. People said the bad spirits would get tired of being ignored and go someplace else.'

'But they didn't?'

Lizzie shook her head. 'You know how Inuit are. We share everything. My father began to say that he and my mother would share their children with Markoosie and Nora.' She turned to look at Edie. 'You remember how it was.'

Edie did. The custom ensured there were never too many mouths to feed in one family and never too few in another to help hunt or gather food. It still happened sometimes.

'*Qalunaat* like to say that blood is thicker than water. But up here in the Arctic, blood is thicker than ice. Your parents didn't have any more children?'

'No, but they'd already promised Markoosie and Nora that they would share Martha so when she was eighteen months old my sister went to live with our uncle and aunt.'

'They must have doted on her.'

'They did,' Lizzie said, with a hint of bitterness. 'My aunt especially. But when my mother realized she wasn't going to have any more children she started to want Martha back. Eventually my father went and collected her. That broke my aunt Nora's heart.' Lizzie's face crimped at the remembrance. 'She went out one day in a blizzard and never came back. They found her body later under the bird cliffs. I think Martha blamed herself. That's why she was always round at my uncle's house, cooking lunch, tidying up, sewing his clothes.'

The young woman shoved her hands in the pockets of her summer parka. 'You've asked me if Martha wanted to leave. And I've told you the truth, which is I don't know. But I do know that too much love can smother a person just as easily as too little can starve them.'

*

Back outside it had begun to rain. Some instinct made Edie go back towards the studio. Markoosie's ATV wasn't outside and the door was still locked. She picked open the lock and found herself inside. The studio was a small, soundproofed room, the desk and broadcast equipment taking up the majority of the space. Beside the desk was an office chair, dented with use, and she noticed that the headsets sitting on the desk itself were old and greasy-looking. Along the back wall a shelving unit bulged with files and discs arranged by date. Scanning along the disc boxes, she found one marked *Show #1437 7/24*, the Saturday Martha died, pulled it out and checked it over. She was about to push it back in its place when curiosity moved her to switch on the player and slot it into the tray. The machine hummed and the disc disappeared inside. Pulling out the chair and reaching for the headphones, she waited for the familiar opening jingle followed by Markoosie's introduction – 'It's eight p.m. on Saturday 24 July.' She checked the player's time and date screen for confirmation. *7/24 10.17.* She looked again. Then she pushed the open button and the disc tray buzzed forward. Thinking she'd got something wrong, she scooped up the disc, checked the label, then matched it to the writing on the box. She steadied herself for a moment then checked everything again with the same result. The timecode on the machine was insisting that Markoosie Pitoq had recorded the Saturday evening show on Saturday morning.

Which meant that on the Saturday evening, as his show was going out, Markoosie Pitoq could have been anywhere.

She dropped the disc into her pocket. Her hands were trembling as she went back over to the shelves to close the gap she'd left so that Markoosie wouldn't notice anything missing, but as she rearranged the discs, she could feel something catch at the back, as though there was some kind of impediment there. She pushed a couple of fingers into the space but whatever it was eluded her. Her curiosity fully aroused now, she went back to the door and flipped the inside lock. Returning to the shelf, she began removing the discs either side of the space until she could finally insert her hand. Her fingers waved about in space for a moment then came to rest on a thin circular object. When she pulled back her fingers it came with them, made a thin scratchy sound against the plastic of the CD cases. A long skein of blue-tinted, black hair, braided into an amulet.

A part of her wanted to run, to get away from the awful realization, but the greater part knew there was no running away from this. The evidence backed up what she already in her heart knew: that not only had Markoosie Pitoq killed his niece but that, on the morning of Saturday 24 July, he had sat down in his studio to record his alibi. Perhaps he'd planned it to coincide with the arrival of Camp Nanook, knowing that the soldiers would provide him with cover. That was conjecture. What was certain was that by the time Martha came around to pick up her schoolbook and offer to cook his lunch, he had already planned to kill her that evening. The man who had for part of her life brought her up as his own daughter and with whom she must, at least as far as any woman ever feels completely safe with any man, have thought of herself as being safe. Edie had to hope that he never told her what he intended to do. That he spared her that terror, at least.

Now she knew why he had disappeared, all she had to figure out was where he was likely to be. In her mind she went through everything she knew about the man and thought it was all pointing one way.

She dialled the detachment. Derek answered.

'Drive around to the town hall building. Bring your service weapon and a rifle.' The authority she felt must have translated into her voice, because for once he didn't question her.

Then she pulled open the radio station door and tripped down the steps, her breath coming fast and shallow, the adrenalin chasing though her veins, every sense intensely focused. She knew this feeling. It came to her when she was hunting.

38

They approached from the west along the coastal road, keeping an eye out for any movement from the cliff edge in case Markoosie had anticipated their arrival and was up there somewhere with a gun. The cliffs were much less busy now. Most of the birds were spending their time out at sea, feeding to build up their strength for the long flight south. A few late-born fledglings still remained on the ledges, nestling among the moss and guano, dimly anxious, waiting for parents who might not return.

They brought their ATVs to a stop where the track divided, keyed off the engines and grabbed their backpacks. From there they decided to split, Edie heading up on top of the cliff while Derek investigated the series of small caves and hollows that gave out onto the beach.

A late summer coastal fog had begun to form, rising with Edie as she clambered up the path and obscuring the view below. The wind had almost ceased now, the solemn quiet punctuated only by the cries of seabirds. She listened for the sound of footsteps, a telltale clink of metal, the swish of a parka, testing the air for the scent of human fear, but there was nothing. Slowly the mist began to creep skywards. She could see Derek moving like a ghost at the foot of the cliffs. Steeling herself, she crept upwards, her feet sliding on scree, until at last she reached the cliff edge. A handful of gulls whirled up on the air currents. She rolled her shoulders, unsheathed the pistol Derek had given her, took a breath and slunk up and over onto the clifftop, crouching in the willow like a cat.

There was no sign of Markoosie. The thought of him getting away created a rush of hot anger in her veins. There was nothing more she wanted now than to make him pay, not just for what he'd done to Martha, though that was terrible enough, but for what he'd taken from the family, from Kuujuaq, for the gap he'd left in all their futures. But anger was a useless emotion for a hunter. A hunter had to be calm and confident of her instincts. Her instincts were telling her she was right. Markoosie was here somewhere and she would keep looking until she found him.

The rocky ledges of the plateau stretched before her, lichen-jewelled, and behind them, sheltered a little from the wind, were patches of sedge meadow and clumps of dry, battered cotton grass. Beyond that lay the new containment fence enclosing Glacier Ridge. From where she crouched, she could see the tops of the abandoned radar towers, ruins which had seemed forlorn when she'd thought of the place as an abandoned radar station, but which had taken on a darker, more sinister aspect now she had guessed at the site's real purpose.

The mist was curling over the clifftop and stealing through the low willow and sedge. She stood and crept to the edge of the cliff. A few rock ptarmigans flustered from their nests, disturbed by the sudden fall in temperature, and rose in a great whirl of wings into the blank sky. Looking down she could just make out through the mist a shadowy figure clambering up the till at the base of the cliffs. From his height and the graceful movement of his body she knew this to be Derek. From the speed at which he climbed she could tell that he had seen something and was going to investigate, using the pile of rock spill at the base of the cliff to gain access to the lower reaches of the cliff ledges and overhangs.

Suddenly she heard him shout 'Pitoq, stop!' and what she supposed was a warning shot rang out. A spray of murres detonated from the cliffs, calling in alarm, then rose up and, banking through the mist, came in once more to the cliff face. Instinctively she dropped down and lay flat on the plateau, her weapon steadied in both hands. For what seemed a long time she could see nothing, then a gust of wind seemed to blow the mist away for a moment and there, perched on a ledge twenty metres or so from the base of the cliff like an auk, she spotted the figure of a man. Again, Derek shouted. The man swung his head upward, searching out a route towards the top of the cliff and freedom. It had begun to rain now, and the wind had picked up, blowing away the worst of the mist and soaking the cliff face.

She heard herself shout down, 'Markoosie, give yourself up.'

The figure froze for an instant, then began sweeping the cliff face, trying to locate the source of the voice. Both his arms were outstretched as he clung to the rapidly wettening rock. If he had a weapon, he was in no position to use it. He did not answer her, but, sensing he was cornered, began sliding his feet sideways along the ledge. A few metres from where he clung there was a dark patch in the rock marking the presence of some kind of overhang or cave, which seemed to be where he was now heading.

She stood up and made her way along the clifftop towards her quarry, searching for an outcrop to which she might attach her rope. Finding a boulder a few metres from her starting point, she began to work steadily, lassoing the rope around the rock and fixing it with the knots her mother had taught her in the days after her father had left and they were hungry enough to go egg collecting together. There was a long wide ledge seven or eight metres down where she could crouch comfortably. If she lowered herself she would be sitting within two or three metres of Pitoq's overhang. This way, she hoped to persuade him to give himself up. Making a loop for her feet and another around her waist, she lowered herself over the edge. The rope tensed around her. She righted her position and found a purchase for her feet on the cliff face. Her thoughts went back, first to her mother bouncing the rope from one gull's nest to another, and then to Willa at rappel camp only a few days before, setting both memories in the little caches in her mind to which she could return when needed, her mother's trick for mustering courage.

The wind blew up, flinging rain into her eyes. Pitoq was six or seven metres below and to her left, edging his way towards the overhang. She called to him again but got no answer. Slowly she went down, legs braced against the rock, the muscles in her arms tense from effort, fingers thrumming. Pitoq had reached the overhang now. She saw him lunge towards the concavity and all but disappear from view, only his feet visible from where she hung. Derek was below her now, stealthily making his way upwards.

'Markoosie.' Her voice ricocheted off the rock wall.

From inside the cliff there came a shout. She saw the feet disappear then Markoosie's hand appeared around the ledge, followed by his face. He looked first down to Derek then up at Edie.

'There's nowhere to go, you're trapped.'

He had moved into the open now, his face raised, taking in the rain. Though he was in plain sight, he didn't seem afraid that they might shoot him. 'My spirit and my conscience are free,' he said. He had to raise his voice to make himself heard, but he sounded calm.

'Two men are in jail for what you did.'

'*Qalunaat* law means nothing to me.'

'What about your father? What does he mean to you? He's alive, by the way.'

The man slumped back a little. 'That's too bad. It was his time.'

'Is that why you killed Martha? Because it was her time?'

Pitoq shook his head, closed his eyes as though remembering. 'Martha was my *hanaji* and my punishment. Every day we had her was a day I was reminded that she was not our own and that sooner or later she would leave us.' He was looking directly up at Edie now, blinking away the rain. 'And when she went back to Alice she took my Nora with her and I was left with nothing. But it seemed that wasn't enough for her. She wanted to get away from us again. Who would she have taken with her this time?' Edie could see the cords in his neck straining from the effort of projecting his voice. 'My niece was a bad spirit, a troublemaking spirit.' His feet were poised over the ledge now, the hands clinging on to the slick rock. 'The spirit is in the blood, Edie Kiglatuk, isn't that what we say? Martha's spirit came up from Lake Turngaluk. All I did was send her back there. She didn't even suffer. It was like she just went to sleep.' Markoosie was looking alternately down at the beach and out to sea now. It seemed he was trying to come to some decision.

Derek shouted up but his voice got lost in the sound of the rain.

'I'm finished here,' Markoosie continued. 'I want to do this the Inuit way. I want to join Nora.'

Derek was below him now, his weapon trained on the man.

'Edie!' Derek called up to her.

For a moment her eyes cut from Derek to Pitoq. They came back to rest on the policeman.

'Let him go!' she shouted.

There was an instant when Derek seemed to hesitate. Markoosie Pitoq must have seen it too, for in that same moment he released his grip from the rock. She saw him step out into the air then fall, his body twisting, bouncing from the cliff face until it landed with a thud onto the beach. For a second or two the muscles twitched. A pink drizzle mixed with the rain and began to make its way through the shingle to the waves.

'Stay there.' Derek's voice came to her through the rain. A comforting sound.

She watched him clamber back along the cliff onto the till then slide down on the loose rock until he reached the shingle. A long time later he appeared at the top of the cliff. She felt the rope tighten.

The tide was coming in as they made their way back onto the beach. A single raven sat on Markoosie Pitoq's broken body, gathering courage to take his eyes. A little further away a fox and her cubs eyed the body and licked their chops.

39

A military ATV sat empty outside the Kuujuaq detachment. Evidently, someone had reported the incident at the bird cliffs to Klinsman and he'd come to find out exactly what had happened.

Edie wasn't in much of a mood for explanations. It was late and her heart still hurt at the thought of what Martha Salliaq had suffered at her uncle's hands. She was glad that he had made the choice to die. It made it cleaner somehow.

Thinking about Klinsman made her feel hot, like everything she touched might melt away.

Derek swung off his vehicle. 'Sooner or later we're gonna have to tell them they've got the wrong men for Martha's murder. So it may as well be now.' He turned and began to walk towards the detachment. It was at times like these his cool was an asset. Reaching the bottom of the steps, he waited for her. 'It'll be OK. Just let me do the talking,'

They went up in silence. The sun bounced off the windows and threw back light into their eyes.

As they entered the detachment two men in expensive outdoor gear stopped rifling through papers and drew their handguns. They weren't military or even military police. D-men, Edie presumed. Between them Klinsman stood waiting.

'You have to leave before I arrest you for interfering with an investigation,' Derek said. After the low grade harassment on the beach a day ago it was clear that the police sergeant hadn't anticipated this. Edie glanced towards the door. One of the men, a tall fella with the swing of an ape, moved into the space, blocking her view.

'You seem to have forgotten that the case is no longer your jurisdiction,' Klinsman said.

'You'd do well to go back to Camp Nanook and instruct your paymaster to release Namagoose and Saxby. You know they didn't do it and we have proof that they didn't. You set up your own men, Klinsman. What kind of man does that?'

'Namagoose and Saxby don't matter,' Klinsman said, turning to the D-men, who came forward, the taller of the two sliding behind them. 'They never did.'

Derek stepped back. He pulled himself up to his full height and looked Klinsman in the face. 'You don't have any jurisdiction over this police detachment or any of the officers in it.'

It was a bluff and Klinsman knew it.

'Unfortunately you've made it necessary for us to take you in. I gave you plenty of warnings and you chose to ignore them. We can cuff you or we can do this the civilized way, but whichever way we do it, you'll be shot if you don't cooperate. Now, your weapons, please.'

As the two men came forward, Derek raised a staying hand. 'You can call your goons off.' He reached for his service weapon and laid it on the desk beside him. Following his lead, Edie did the same. 'You're making a mistake,' he said flatly.

They travelled in the military vehicle. The D-men made no attempt to restrain them but Edie noticed they kept their hands near to their holstered weapons. As they approached the Camp Nanook sentry gate the two D-men slid their guns out of sight. Edie caught Derek's gaze and flicked her eyes in their direction. Derek flared his nostrils to indicate that he'd understood. Whatever game they were playing, not everyone on the base was in on it. The same guard who two weeks ago had ticked them off his clipboard saluted the colonel and waved the party through. It was late now, and though the sun still shone, the personnel vehicles were parked up, the cranes and diggers silent and the soldiers mostly in barracks, asleep. A great time, Edie thought, to smuggle in a couple of off-register non-prisoners, the kind of detainees

Klinsman and his Defence Department bosses could lose in the system indefinitely. Or make disappear altogether.

The ATV drew up outside K-block and they found themselves walking down familiar corridors. Klinsman peeled off at his offices but the two goons pushed them forward through a series of locked doors into a dismal, windowless atrium. A cage lay along a corridor to the right, striping shadows on the opposite wall; inside something moved. They were patted down again and pushed along the corridor to the cage, at the back of which, on a hard bench, sat Sonia Gutierrez.

The D-men keyed the lock, pushed Derek and Edie inside and disappeared through the atrium back out into the main building.

They waited until they could hear their footsteps retreating before Gutierrez said drily, 'The way this would go in the movies, you guys would be rescuing me.'

'I never was a big fan of the movies,' Derek said. He gave Gutierrez a sorry smile. 'We missed you,' he said.

'Don't,' Sonia said. 'I can't stand sad endings.'

'Your ATV's up at the landing strip. We assumed you'd flown out to Iqaluit. It was only when I checked the passenger manifests we realized you hadn't,' Edie cut in.

Sonia slammed her hands on her thighs and looked away.

'*Hijo de puta!* They're smart, these guys.'

'Not so smart they remembered the manifests,' Edie said. The cage was tiny and airless, with the bench at one end and a chemical toilet. She looked for cameras but saw none. No air cooling system either. It was hot. If there was one thing Edie couldn't stand, it was heat.

'You any idea where they're from?' Derek asked.

Gutierrez gave a shrug. 'Freelance is my guess. Working for the Defence Department. They won't let me call a lawyer,' she said, rubbing her arms.

'We found your backpack.'

Gutierrez stopped her arm rubbing and glanced at them sideways.

'We spent most of a day trying to decipher the papers,' Edie said.

She pulled off her summer parka and handed it to the lawyer. Gutierrez acknowledged it with a 'thanks'. She saw the lawyer's nose wrinkle.

'It's sealskin,' she said. 'You can be cold or you can smell of seals.'

Gutierrez gave an awkward smile and slipped the parka over her head.

'You read my papers you'll know what this is about,' Gutierrez went on, serious now.

'We have an idea.'

Gutierrez crossed her legs and, leaning one elbow over her thigh, said in a low voice, 'What I think we are talking about is a covert programme of nuclear testing at Glacier Ridge, maybe even across the whole of the North American Arctic, in direct contravention of international and Canadian law. If I'm right, the United States and Canada lied to their people on a massive scale.'

'I wish I could say I'm surprised,' Derek said.

'But I think there's more.' Gutierrez lowered her voice. 'You heard of Downwinders?'

Derek and Edie shook their heads.

'The fallout from the nuclear testing in the Nevada desert in the sixties blew directly over Utah. The US Department of Energy knew this would happen. They took a calculated risk that the locals wouldn't kick up a fuss. For the most part the affected population were Mormons living in remote communities. They kept themselves separate, didn't have much of a voice. The women started miscarrying and by the seventies the population was starting to develop radiation-related cancers. People outside the community were beginning to notice. So the Energy Commission moved the testing to the Aleutian Islands. Which had the advantage of being away from the mainland and near to Soviet Russia and Japan.'

'But it also had a population of Aleuts,' Edie said.

'Exactly. Who also began dying. But the Energy Commission kept that secret. It wasn't till after the Cannikin explosion that people on the US mainland really became aware that anything much happened at all. But Cannikin was *un gran error*, a real own goal. It caused so much catastrophic damage that the government couldn't cover it up.'

'So they transferred the programme to Ellesmere in secret,' Edie said.

'Some of it, for sure. The dirtiest part. They knew that the Kuujua-miut wouldn't cause them a problem. You guys had never heard of Cannikin or the nuclear testing programme or even the Cold War. The government figured that you would likely put the deaths of your babies down to bad spirits. Canada always said it never carried out any nuclear testing. People in the south wouldn't be on the lookout like they were in the US. This was the seventies. The government in Ottawa saw the whole of its north as a giant bargaining chip, principally with the US. It had strategic importance but that was all. When I first arrived in Canada from Guatemala, Ellesmere Island hadn't even been formally mapped. Most southerners hardly knew the place existed, let alone that there were people living here. The perfect place to test their bombs out.'

Gutierrez bit her lip, for the moment lost in thought. 'I think they will want to disappear us.'

'They?'

'The Department of Defence. Somehow, they've cornered Klinsman into taking orders from them. They won't want any of this to get out. Can you imagine the scandal if it did? The Canadian government using their own people as nuclear guinea pigs? Then putting their soldiers in to clean it up without telling them what they were getting into. And framing two of their own men for a murder so as to help keep a lid on the thing. Think of the press. Not to mention the lawsuits.' She smiled. 'If they don't kill me first they will make me a rich woman.'

'If they were going to . . .' Edie choked over the words, '. . . get rid of us, wouldn't they would have done it already?'

'And risk the personnel at Camp Nanook finding out?' Sonia shook her head. 'A couple days back I heard one of them mention Alert.' The Alert station was nearly nine hundred kilometres away at the tip of

Ellesmere Island. The station was nominally a meteorological facility, with surveillance and intelligence gathering capacity, manned by a rotating staff of military and scientific personnel.

'I think they might take us there,' Gutierrez said.

40

Not long afterwards the lights went out and for the first time in several months Edie found herself completely in the dark.

'It'll be like this for a few hours now,' Gutierrez said. 'Unless anyone has any better ideas, we may as well get some sleep.'

For a long time Edie lay on the floor of the cell with the dark engraving patterns behind her eyelids, listening to the softening breaths of her cellmates. The combination of the moist heat of the room and the darkness was both novel and unwelcome. It was hard enough to think as it was. If this was how the tropics were supposed to be, you could keep them, she thought. If she ever got out of here, she'd stick to vacationing on ice.

Somewhere a blue light flickered on. A familiar voice began whispering her name. After a while it came to her that the voice and the light were both coming from outside and that the voice belonged to Willa. Remembering suddenly where she was, she sprang from the floor. She felt a small rush between her legs and realized with a flush of irritation that her period had started.

Beside her, Derek turned, groaned and opened his eyes.

Willa Inukpuk was standing outside the cage with his finger on his lips. She could hear footsteps down the corridor and instinctively knew they didn't have much time.

'How did . . . ?'

'I saw you coming in.'

The footsteps began to draw nearer and the goon with the ape's gait appeared carrying a tray of bottled water and wrapped pastries.

'They're gonna move you to Alert. Maybe tonight, maybe tomorrow.' Willa was speaking rapidly now, in Inuktitut. 'They sent me up there a couple days back to teach ice rappelling to Canadian special ops forces. Counterterrorism guys. Whatever this is, Edie, it's not some regular transfer. Believe me, you don't want to get sent to Alert.'

The ape-man was standing beside them now, shuffling his weight from foot to foot. There was the smell of old sweat on him. He keyed open a little hatch in the cage and pushed the tray through. Derek caught it on the other side.

'Speak English.' The ape was directing himself to Willa.

'Listen, man, my job is to act as indigenous liaison. These people speak Inuktitut.'

'I don't care if they speak the language of the gods. You need to start talking in English,' the ape repeated. There was a hint of menace in his tone.

Willa nodded. He moved forward a little so the ape couldn't see his face and flared his eyes. Edie had seen that look on a dozen duck hunts, him standing there, an anxious boy, her hanging back, trying to get him to take the lead. Day after day they'd be out hunting, relying mostly on eye signals to communicate. She knew exactly what his eyes were saying. *Tell me what to do*. He hadn't come just to warn her. He'd come to help. Now he was asking her how best to go about it. He raised his eyebrows. *Now, quickly*.

She glanced at Derek but he was still manhandling the tray. She saw then that she and Willa were on their own. In the great canvas of their life together she understood finally how absolutely central he was, not, as she'd previously imagined, simply Joe's shadow, the faint outline of a dead boy, but her own breathing, present, difficult, maddening, loyal Willa. And he was relying on her now.

She felt the heaviness in her belly, the soft throb between her legs.

'We like to watch movies,' she said, meeting his puzzled frown with a steady look, willing him to understand that she was talking in code. Beside him, the ape was checking his watch, only half listening. Willa looked away for a moment and when he met her eye again he was ready.

'Laurel and Hardy. That's what we usually watch. *Flying Deuces* is a great movie but our favourite is *Liberty*.' Her fingers were working, turning backwards, asking him to return to another time. A bloom of understanding crossed his face. His jaw softened and he blinked slowly.

'You have a favourite scene?' he said.

Edie smiled. Her heart rattled in her chest. He'd remembered their conversation at the rappel camp. He'd remembered his childhood, the good times they'd had together. He'd remembered.

'The car chase.' They'd watched it over and over together. He let her know with a glance that it was playing in his mind now. 'We could watch it this afternoon, at four, say.'

For a moment Willa looked uncertain. 'At four?'

The ape looked up. He had caught the tail end of the conversation. His brow was furrowed and he was swinging his head like a big, dumb pendulum. Directing himself to Edie he said, irritably, 'No one's going to be watching any movies.' He made a waving motion with his hand. 'OK, fellas, this little party is over.'

Edie winked at Willa then turned her back. She waited until the door at the top of the corridor swung shut and the footsteps had died away. When she looked up Derek and Sonia were staring at her.

'I can explain,' she said.

While they ate, she outlined the plan in Inuktitut. Gutierrez picked up the gist and for the rest Edie wrote key words with her finger on the concrete and worked signs in the air. If their conversation was being monitored it would have to be by an Inuktitut speaker. No Inuk was likely to give them away.

'Won't Klinsman guess?' Gutierrez asked.

Edie shook her head. 'It won't occur to him. You're forgetting, he's *qalunaat*.'

'Why four?' Derek said.

'Willa told me before that's when the groups come in from exercises. There are a lot of people around. Security's seen us all come and go before, so as long as Klinsman and his goons don't spot us, we should be able to drive right out.'

'Drive?' Derek looked puzzled.

Edie smiled and winked. 'Don't worry, that's Willa's job. He knows what he has to do.'

At three minutes before four, Edie began her preparations. They arranged themselves, Edie on the bench with Sonia kneeling beside her, Derek standing towards the front of the cage. Then Sonia and Derek began to yell.

There was a muffled grunt before the door at the end of the corridor swung open and footsteps came pounding. The sound of heavy breathing and the ape appeared, panting and clutching a handgun. He took one look at the scene inside the cage and blanched.

'What the fuck?' His voice was coarse and high with fear. For a moment or two he just stood there staring, unable to decide what to do.

'She needs help, man,' Derek said, 'right now.'

The ape ran his eyes over the blood on the floor and the native woman in the arms of the Latina, blood all over her wrists, his face a rictus of panic, as though he was watching his career prospects disappear down the drain.

'What happened?'

'She had a blade in her shoe.' Derek was doing a good job of sounding distressed. 'Some great fucking search you guys did.'

For a moment the ape looked sceptical. He started making beckoning motions with his hand. 'Give me the blade.'

Derek wheeled around to Edie then back again. He was gesticulating wildly with his hands now.

'Can't you see, it's stuck in her wrist. I'm not taking it out.'

The ape peered in. There was no blade but Sonia's shadow was obscuring the spot and he wasn't about to argue. He covered his face with his hands and closed his eyes for a second, thinking.

'Hey!' Derek shouted. 'Don't just stand there. For Chrissakes get in here and help.'

Edie began panting.

The sound seemed to mobilize him. The ape fumbled for his key chain.

'Stand the fuck back.' He was waving at Derek, who immediately did as he'd asked, just as they'd agreed.

Locking the door behind him, the ape went over to the bench. Edie groaned. As he bent down, she sprang upwards, smearing the man's face in her blood. As he yelped and stumbled back, Sonia shot up and kicked his weapon from his hand. A moment later Derek rushed forward and slammed his foot into the inside of the man's knees. The ape went down, arms flailing. Derek bent and in a sharp, swift movement, swung an arm around the man's neck until he had him in a choke hold. Using his free arm as leverage, he continued to squeeze the arteries on either side of the trachea until the ape, bloody-faced and losing consciousness, slumped to the floor. From her pocket Edie pulled out Derek's torn undershirt. While Sonia undid the man's belt and pulled off his key chain, Edie quickly wiped up the blood then balled up another piece of undershirt inside the ape's slack mouth, securing it around his face while Sonia tore strips to secure his hands and feet to the bench.

Quickly and without making a sound, Derek picked up the handgun and the three slipped out of the cage, locking the ape inside. They hurried along the corridor. The door at the end was locked but the ape's key chain obliged. Klinsman had been right a week or two back when he'd said the facility was 'rudimentary'.

They were just about to go through when Edie held an arm across the door. Most likely one of the two men who'd arrested them was still somewhere in the camp. So far as they could tell, the whole Glacier Ridge operation was being conducted in secret. Their faces were familiar around the camp. If they were lucky, everyone else would assume they were making a routine visit. All they had to do was to get past Klinsman and his flunky.

'You go first, Derek – make some sound going down the corridor. They'll be expecting that goon back,' Edie whispered. She reached down and took off her shoes. Gutierrez followed suit. Edie pressed her finger to her lips.

'You and me, we make no noise at all. None.'

The door opened and they found themselves in the same passageway as Klinsman's office. Down the corridor they could hear the colonel's voice deep in some phone conversation.

Derek took off at a stride. He threw the door open at the far end of the corridor but stayed inside. For a moment they waited for the muffled buzz of the colonel's voice, then the two women followed on, sliding their stockinged feet along the floor. The voice stopped and for a moment they froze but then it started up again and they moved on. At the end of the passage Derek edged the door open and they crept through into the atrium.

'If he understood, and I think he did, Willa will be waiting for us somewhere close. If not, we'll just have to risk walking out.'

They met each other's eyes, then Derek put his hand on the door to the outside and pushed the handle.

It was a bright afternoon and a chill wind blew the crisp, clean smell of freedom into Edie's nostrils. She took in the scene. It was as she'd predicted. An exercise had just come in and the whole camp was buzzing with activity, vehicles rumbling along the boardwalk, soldiers marching in and out of debriefing rooms, sauntering towards their quarters. With a little kick of joy she spotted Willa's ATV parked up diagonally to the main boardwalk with the engine running and Willa himself standing beside it dressed in his Ranger's uniform. The vehicle was small, a two-man seat, but if they sat side-saddle on it and hung on they'd be OK. They had to hope the security detail at the gate wouldn't notice or, if they did, that they'd put it down to some quirky Inuit custom.

Their only other major worry was if the second D-man found his compadre in the prison cell. The journey from K-block to the gate would take less than five minutes but in that time they would be extremely conspicuous. If the ape in the cage managed to raise the alarm, or they were spotted, there would be trouble. Edie elbowed Derek and they began to walk towards the ATV at a brisk pace.

'Let's go,' he said.

Gutierrez swung on first, facing to the left of the vehicle, followed by Derek. Edie slotted herself between the two, facing to the right.

'Anyone asks, I'm giving you the tour,' Willa said. 'Public outreach. No one ever has a clue who's in charge of that stuff. We're lucky, they won't question it.'

They trundled along the marked vehicle track towards the security gate, past men walking in parallel along the boardwalk, doing their best to look relaxed while their eyes frantically scanned for anyone who might give them away. Then, as they reached a crossroads, a soldier stepped out, holding up a palm. Edie felt her stomach knocking, as though a bird was inside. Beside her, Sonia stiffened. The soldier made a waving motion to his left and a jeep appeared in their line of sight. Edie held her breath. The jeep trundled slowly through her field of vision, leaving a space directly ahead of her in its wake.

And in that space Chip Muloon was standing.

'*Dios mío*,' mouthed Gutierrez.

Muloon's eyes were firmly fixed on Edie now, but she could not tell what was in them. His weight shifted from one foot to another, his hands in his pockets. Willa seemed to have frozen. Edie saw Muloon look about. All of a sudden he made a move towards the vehicle then just as quickly changed his mind and stopped, leaving one leg momentarily suspended in mid-air. He swung his head again, checking in both directions, then pulled his right hand from his pocket. Her eyes closed instinctively, waiting for the bullet. But when she opened them a moment later she saw that his hand was raised in an almost imperceptible wave. He gave a tiny nod.

'Go!' she said to Willa.

The vehicle jerked then began rumbling forward, past the crossroads and towards where Muloon stood. He waited for it to nearly reach him, then quickly turned his back and walked away.

He was letting them pass.

Beside her, she felt Derek relax a little.

At the security gate the guard came out of his hut. He hesitated for a moment, frowning, then, registering that there were three passengers scrunched up on the seat, his face broke out in a smile.

'That's a cosy arrangement. Hope you guys are all friendly.'

The barrier went up.

They were out.

'*Gracias, gracias*,' Sonia whispered. Her eyes were large with tears and she was rubbing her hands as if in prayer.

They'd reached the turn-off to Lake Turngaluk before they heard the vehicles, a thin line of ATVs rumbling out from the Camp Nanook gate, moving at a pace towards them. In front, Willa jammed his foot on the accelerator but the ATV was underpowered for its load and it was clear that if they didn't come up with something, they weren't going to make it back to Kuujuaq.

'You got a rappel rope and anchor?' Edie yelled above the sound of the engine. Willa turned his head and blinked away the wind. 'Always. In the pack at the back.'

'You think we can fast-rope the bird cliffs?' she shouted.

'Probably.'

'Good. Head there. Don't worry, I have a plan.'

Willa steered the ATV 360 degrees and began to backtrack towards the lake turn-off, the engine on full throttle, black, charred fumes rising from the exhaust. The track here was little more than a gap in the willow, the surface so pocked with frost boils that the vehicle began to sway and bump alarmingly and Derek, Sonia and Edie were forced to cling to their makeshift positions. Reaching the perimeter of the Glacier Ridge containment fence, Willa told them to hold on tighter as he routed around a stretch of muskeg until they came to the slick rock and wind-dried sedge meadow of the clifftop. Before them the waters of Jones Sound sparkled like a dewy web in the afternoon sun.

Willa jammed on the brake and the vehicle came to a screeching halt. One by one the passengers slid off. A hundred metres below them the beach shingle glinted soft grey in the sun. In the distance, to the northwest, three military ATVs were still heading along the main track to the settlement. In a moment they, too, would pull off onto the side track.

Quickly, Edie outlined what she had in mind.

'This rope should really be braided for fast-roping,' Willa said, fishing out a coil of nylon rappel rope, a length of webbing and a rappel ring. 'But we don't have time.' At the bottom of the pile he pulled out a single pair of gloves and handed them to Gutierrez.

'You're gonna need these.'

They moved towards the edge of the cliff. Derek looked over and came back, nodding.

'He's still there. Or enough of him, anyway.'

The two men went over to the cliff edge to find an anchor. Derek located the ledge and they walked back from the spot until they came to a large boulder. Together they strung the length of webbing around it, doubled the rope through the rappel ring and tied it off, pulling to test their weight against it. To finish off, they grubbed up some cotton grass and camouflaged the webbing. If they were lucky, the men wouldn't see it.

From their perch a few metres from the cliff edge Edie and Sonia continued to keep their eye on the convoy. The vehicles slowed on the main track, then, as predicted, they turned off towards the cliffs.

'It's time,' Edie said. The two women moved to the cliff edge to join the men and waited in the order they'd agreed. The blood had bleached from Sonia's face. Edie laid a reassuring hand on her shoulder. She could feel the trembling of her flesh. They continued to watch the vehicles heading towards them, tense and silent now, counting down the moments.

In forty seconds, as the ATVs rounded the lake, Klinsman and his goons would be blinded for about two minutes by the low, Arctic summer sun in the southern sky. By the time the cliffs came back into clear view, if everything went according to plan, their quarry would have disappeared.

At the exact moment Edie gave the signal, and Derek immediately dropped to the ground, grabbed the rope and, locking his right leg around it, disappeared over the cliff edge. The anchor strained but held. Sonia shuffled up and found her position, with her legs over the cliff face, and sat there, her breath coming in short pants. She curled her right leg around the rope. They counted fifteen, then Edie shouted:

'Now!'

Sonia took a deep breath then suddenly swung her head around. Her eyes were full of fear.

'I don't know if I can do this,' she said.

'You want me to push you off?' Edie's face gave Sonia reason to believe she was serious. 'I'll be right behind you. Don't look down and remember to slide with your hands. Just keep going, even if it burns.'

The lawyer closed her eyes for a second to gather herself, then went over. Edie watched her disappear, crouched and took her place. Sonia was three metres down now, her hands clutched tight on the rope, the top of Derek's head just visible below her. Edie gripped the rope and braced herself. With no gloves and with hands damaged from frostbite, this was going to hurt.

About two metres down she began to feel the skin peel away. By three metres the rope was slick with her blood. Above her she could see Willa had managed to pull his sleeves over his palms and was using the fabric to reduce the friction. She tightened her jaw and carried on, using her feet to push herself gently off the limestone face. Below her Sonia hesitated.

'Don't look down. Keep moving!'

The lawyer looked up. Edie gesticulated with her head for her to move. The lawyer did not move. Up above her she could see Willa approaching.

'Move!'

The lawyer gave a little cry and resumed her descent. Steeling herself against the pain in her hands, Edie carried on behind her. Sonia did not stop again until she'd reached the ledge. Coming in after her, Edie swung the rope a little and stepped off. The palms of her hands were raw meat. Right now, it wasn't hurting too much. But in an hour or so it would be a different story. Seeing them, Derek wrinkled his nose in sympathy, though his own were just as bad. Willa brought up the rear, untied the double eight and cleaned the anchor. Quickly, he began hauling in the rope and passing it along to Edie to coil. The sound of the engines was almost on them now. Edie crouched beside Willa, Sonia and Derek on the ledge where Markoosie Pitoq had spent the last hour of his life and hoped it would not be theirs.

The wind came up, taking the sound of voices away from them, then after a brief silence, a fierce, shingly sound hit them at the same time as a shower of scree poured down, powdering their faces in dust. When Sonia gave a little gasp and began frantically scraping at her eye with her fingers, Edie frowned her back to silence. They heard a voice, shouting.

'Christ!' It was the ape. 'There's a body on the beach. It's a mess. One of 'em must have fallen. Hard to see who from up here. Looks like one of the men. No sign of any of the others.'

They heard the sound of engines starting up again then moving away along the track which ran parallel to the clifftop then down to link with the coastal route. Edie slid her body around Willa's.

'We got ten minutes till they make it to the beach,' Derek said.

'You think we should stay here?' Gutierrez said.

'Uh nuh. We're more visible from down there. Besides, we need to get to Kuujuaq. I've clambered around these cliffs for twelve years. I know them pretty well. I think I can get us back up to the top. Just follow me, hold on to the rock and don't look down.' Directing himself to Willa he said, 'Hand me the rope. As soon as I get over the lip I'll reattach it and send it back down. It'll give you something else to hold on to.'

He stepped out, keeping his head up, facing the rock, his bloodied hands grasping for a hold. On either side of him, startled seabirds rose, calling. Gutierrez went next, followed by Willa, Edie bringing up the rear. She moved along the rock, placing her feet exactly in Willa's footsteps. As she moved, her eye caught sight of the beach twenty metres below and she swallowed hard, then carried on. Derek had come to a step which led up to a small rocky table. Here he stopped for a second, checking on the others coming up behind him.

On the final leg, the wind came up. Willa paused to get his balance. For an instant he glanced back at Edie and, blinking in the wind, managed a fragile smile of encouragement. A young guillemot blew from a crevice directly ahead. The sudden movement startled her. She felt her foot slide and dug in with her hands. The crosswind was buffeting her sideways now and she had to keep moving her weight to keep herself balanced. Looking up ahead she saw Derek get over the rim. Gutierrez had stopped, apparently blindsided by the wind. They waited a moment then Edie saw the rope twist down. Gutierrez grabbed it and moved forward. Derek appeared and offered his arms. Then she too disappeared over the rim.

A minute or two later Edie found herself at the same spot, but this time it was Willa reaching down for her. With his help she heaved herself up and over onto the sedge. Then the two women picked themselves up and made for the ATV.

Willa had left the key in the ignition and the engine running, hoping to convince Klinsman that they'd run off behind one of the outcrops a little further along the cliff. The key was gone now but in a blink Willa had his multitool out and, disengaging the ignition, he went around the back and connected the two solenoids with the screwdriver attachment and the engine rattled into life.

A smile came over his face. 'Finally, my wild past pays off.'

The ATV lurched forward and in a cloud of grey smoke they roared along the muskeg towards Kuujuaq.

41

Edie used the journey across the tundra to do the rough calculations in her head. If it took Klinsman and his men fifteen minutes to figure out that the body on the beach was of no interest they'd almost certainly head directly for the settlement. There were two routes, the first retracing their steps back to the clifftops, the second via the more meandering coastal path. Either way they'd not be much more than thirty minutes behind.

They swung by the detachment, picked up Gutierrez's backpack and left, double-locking the door behind them. Willa drove them up to the landing strip and dropped Edie and Derek at the terminal building then went with Gutierrez around the side to the hanger where the police plane was kept. It was the police pilot's job to keep it ready and fuelled in case of emergencies but Pol was out at summer camp for the weekend and there was no time to call him in. Thankfully, Willa had been a grease monkey ever since he could walk. He boasted he could do a basic check in under five minutes.

With no scheduled flights running that day, the building was deserted. No CCTV, no alarm system. No one would have thought to put one in. The first Klinsman or anyone else would know of what was happening would be when they saw the plane come over. The spare keys to the police Twin Otter were kept in a cabinet in the office which was, surprisingly, locked. Derek fetched a large wrench from the tool room, came back and broke it open.

Like every other ranking officer working in a remote area, Derek had his pilot's licence. Unlike most, since a near miss out of Yellowknife fifteen years ago, he'd been stuck with a flying phobia. The tension in his jaw, the thin veil of sweat gathering on his forehead told Edie that he was doing his best to fight his demons, but also that they weren't about to roll over while he stuck it to them.

He grabbed the keys and made his way towards the back door which led out onto the landing strip and the hangar building. At the exit he hesitated a moment before turning back to Edie and saying, 'The flying thing. Best if the others don't know.'

On their way to the hangar they paused at the weather station to check the anemometer and barometer. The wind had turned 180 degrees and was blowing in from the west now. Derek looked upwards. Edie scanned his face, trying to read his thoughts, then lighted on the barometer. Above, the sky was empty of birds. All of which meant one thing: there was a polar cyclone coming and it would be centred, as always, on Baffin Island. Exactly where they were heading.

Over at the hangar they saw Willa waving them over. They began to run.

'Any point in trying anywhere else?' she said.

'With the fuel we have and my navigation? Maybe Resolute.'

Edie groaned. Resolute was where the High Arctic SOVPAT military exercises were headquartered.

They stopped beside the hangar and paused a moment to catch their breath.

'How's the weather looking?' Willa said.

'Bumpy.'

Edie turned to her ex-stepson and clutched his arm. 'You don't need to come with us. Klinsman knows we took the guard's weapon. You can say we forced you.' Willa blinked back his astonishment. Something passed between them. She turned away, unable to stomach the hurt on his face.

'I'm sorry,' she said. 'Of course you're coming.'

The police Twin Otter was sitting in its summer position in the open hangar, face-out to the strip. Derek clambered into the cockpit, nervously eyeing the controls, naming each under his breath to calm himself. Airspeed indicator, altimeter, turn and bank indicator, heading indicator, artificial horizon, vertical speed indicator. Compass. He checked the fuel gauge and the time on his watch and hit the ignition switch; the propeller buzzed into action. He swung his head back to check on the others and saw the lawyer and Willa buckling themselves in and Edie behind them, locking the passenger door.

'Hold on,' he said, throttling forward, and they began to rumble towards the landing strip. He could feel his pulse screaming, his palms, already raw from the rope, now stinging with sweat. They reached the landing strip and he aligned the plane, managing to bring it to a halt, his hand shaking on the control yoke. He could feel himself losing awareness, as though the present moment were leaking out of him. He swung around and, finding Edie with his gaze, he said,

'I could use you up here.'

As she clambered into the seat beside him, he eased off the brake, his fingers sharp and painful on the controls. The engine roared and lurched forward and they began to rattle down the landing strip. As they picked up speed he felt the doughy feeling in his head lift. He focused his attention back on the strip then pulled up the control yoke and they were up and climbing out over the Sound. He took the plane higher. The Otter would have a hard time in cyclonic winds. It was bad luck. Summer cyclones were rare and, generally, not as severe as the winter variety. He might have trouble keeping the plane on a straight course but it was unlikely to break up. What worried him more was the possibility that the buffeting might cause them to veer off course enough to use up their fuel. If they managed to reach Iqaluit, the next big challenge would be landing in downdraughting air with strong ground winds. He could feel his fear waiting to spring.

They hit rough air and the plane shuddered and trembled. Then it dropped. Derek felt his stomach leave him. No one spoke. He held on tighter to the control yoke. The palms of his hands were burning. He checked the altimeter and levelled the plane out. He was remembering something Pol once told him, that bush pilots never talked about what they'd do if they crashed. They only talked about when.

Edie caught his eye and threw him a sympathetic look. Since he'd met her he'd felt himself heading out to meet life and that inevitably meant coming nearer to death too. Still he hadn't regretted it. Not once. Or, at least, not for long.

The plane rocked again. He could feel the pull of the wind on the fuselage. He tried to shut down the side of himself that felt panicked by it but he felt like a whale in an ocean of air, forcing himself up to breathe. He looked at his bloody hands and steadied his thoughts. He realized that he'd never really talked to anyone about the Yellow-knife accident and he made a promise to himself that, if he got them through this, he would. And there was no one he wanted to talk to about it more than Edie Kiglatuk. The woman sitting beside him knew how it felt to walk away alive; to have to live haunted by ghosts of the dead you'd left behind.

They were over Baffin now, heading into the cyclone. He considered diverting to Pond Inlet or one of the other handful of tiny north Baffin settlements to wait out the worst of it, then realized what folly it was even to think that way. If they tried to conceal themselves, Klinsman and his men would come after them. The only place to hide was in plain sight.

He did a quick calculation in his mind, plugged in the Iqaluit airport frequency, identified himself and waited for a response. Nothing. He wondered if the storm was taking out the radio, then took a breath, recalculated and decided that most likely they weren't yet in range. For an instant he let his unpreparedness get to him, then he gathered himself once more and decided that after another ten minutes' flying time he'd try again.

He felt the sweat trickle down the back of his neck. The plane was dancing about like a mayfly. Beside him, Edie seemed calm and unruffled. He glanced into the rear mirror. Willa was chewing his finger. Gutierrez had a hand over her mouth as though she was trying to stop herself from screaming. He gripped the control yoke more tightly. The shaking was constantly threatening to loosen it from his grip. If the cyclone held to this strength, he could probably get them through, he thought, but landing was going to require assistance. They weren't expected though, so he had to hope the airport hadn't closed. His eyes flipped from the control panel to the windshield and he watched Baffin Island slowly disappear into whipping cloud.

Ten minutes later he tried the radio again with the same result. A bead of anxiety began to grow in his stomach, and he felt a tic start up in his eye. He swung his head around to look at Edie. Her eyes were closed. The plane was shaking like a cottonhead, the wings rattling, the wind screaming across the fuselage. Behind him, Willa was still chewing his finger but Gutierrez was being sick. No one had spoken for a long time.

There was a part of him, he realized, that wanted to take his hands from the control yoke and float off into oblivion. He looked over at Edie again and felt a sudden surge of resentment. It was she who had pushed him into this. Without her, he might have walked away from the case the moment the Defence Department had taken it over, allowed the Killer Whales to go down for the murder of Martha Salliaq and cleared his mind of any talk of underground tests and radioactive contamination. But he knew that, without her too, he would have carried on living in the shadows, shoring himself up with cigarettes and coffee and lemmings. The only person who'd cared enough to stop him becoming the Lemming Police was the woman sitting right next to him.

And he didn't want to be responsible for killing her.

He made another dead reckoning of their position but it was difficult to do without a confirmed forecast wind speed. Once more he tried the radio but what came back was white noise. By his calculations they were less than fifty kilometres from Iqaluit now, but he couldn't be sure. What he did know was that they were long past the point of no return. If he overflew Iqaluit or otherwise missed it, he didn't have enough fuel to take them on to the landing strip at Kimmirut.

He dropped the plane, hoping to fly under the cloud to get a visual, without going low enough to make them vulnerable in a sudden downdraught. At the descent, he felt his stomach lurch and his pulse begin thudding again. Suddenly, the cloud cleared momentarily and he saw, far distant, the pucker on the tundra that was Iqaluit. And then it was gone once more. He pushed up his headphones, switched the comms lever, identified himself and requested a response. For a moment or two there was nothing, then a voice said,

'What the hell are you doing? The airport is closed.'

Relief flooded across his face.

'This is an emergency. I'm going to need to make a landing at Iqaluit.'

'Copy that,' the voice said, adding, 'you're lucky I had to come back for my laptop.' There was a pause. 'What is your position?'

He felt himself smile and loosened his grip just a little on the control yoke, mentally keying himself into the comforting, unequivocal language of the control tower. He passed on the position. The controller OK'd him and gave preliminary instructions. The plane began its descent, buffeted wildly by the wind.

'We got strong side winds on the runway. Brace yourselves for a rough landing.'

The plane wobbled and swung through the air like a wounded goose. A slow shallow land would leave them more vulnerable to the side winds so he kept the approach at about a hundred knots. When they were at thirty metres Derek instructed his passengers to put their heads in their laps and cover them with their hands. He pushed the prop levers forward, willing the wind not to gust just as he levelled off low for landing. He could almost feel the tarmac beneath him now. He swallowed hard and teased the plane down. The wheels made contact with a loud grinding sound and a hard bump. Immediately, he pulled the prop lever back, trying to correct the push of the wind to keep the plane stable along the strip. He felt it slow. He was in control. He allowed himself to taxi to the second apron then pulled off, engaged the brakes fully and came to a screeching halt.

Beside him he heard the sound of clapping. Edie grinned, leaned over and gave him an Inuit kiss. He felt himself smile. Then he threw back his head and closed his eyes and allowed himself to breathe.

42

The flight controller's name was Forester Norven. He was a thickset *qalunaat* with the reddened pelt and bedevilled face of a man who'd given up booze and was now regretting it. The moment they'd landed Sonia Gutierrez had rushed to the bathroom to be sick. Norven found the others a place to sit in the terminal waiting area and went to fetch coffee and some towels. The run from the plane to the terminal building had left them soaked. Moments later he returned.

'You know, guys, I'm probably going to have to report this.' He ran a palm over his bald spot. You could see he was torn between duty and his desire to help and hadn't yet decided which way to go. All he needed was a little nudge in the right direction.

'Call Sergeant Makivik at the Iqaluit RCMP,' Derek said, towelling down his clothes. 'He'll make it right. And tell him Derek Palliser says he needs to get up here right away. In fact, why don't I call him direct?'

Norven signalled to Derek to stay sitting. He wasn't about to let go of the situation. 'You get your breath back. I'll speak to Makivik myself.'

Soon after he'd gone Gutierrez reappeared, looking hollow-eyed and clutching her backpack. She'd dried her hair with the washroom hand dryer.

'We should alert Chris Tetlow,' she said. 'I've got a contact at the Toronto press and there are some lawyers – '

Derek stopped her. 'We're not doing anything until we've thought this through a little. Bill Makivik will find us some place safe to stay. We'll take advice, get some shut-eye, then decide.' When Gutierrez opened her mouth to speak again, Derek held up his hand to steady her. Gutierrez sank back into her seat, a surprising look of relief on her face.

Just then Norven appeared from a door marked Authorized Personnel Only and announced that Makivik was on his way.

Sergeant Bill Makivik arrived ten minutes later in his storm gear, dripping rain. He was a fit man but the cyclonic wind had left him breathless.

'Jesus H, Derek,' he said, simply. 'This is a pretty crazy time to be up in the air, don't you think?'

'It's been a pretty crazy time all round,' Derek said. His eyes moved to Norven, who was listening intently. 'We'll explain at the detachment.'

'I'm looking forward to that,' Makivik said.

In her peripheral vision Edie saw Norven's face fall. It was going to be hard to keep this quiet.

All four of them crammed into the detachment jeep beside Makivik. There was no point trying to talk. You couldn't hear anything above the storm. The wind was pushing great fists of rain at the windshield and Makivik was having trouble keeping the jeep stable. They more or less aquaplaned along the road into town. By the time they reached the detachment the rain had frozen into hailstones the size of ptarmigan eggs. They'd been lucky. If they'd set off in the plane an hour or two later they wouldn't have made it.

Makivik managed to bring the vehicle up close to the detachment entrance and they ran in, Gutierrez clutching her backpack to her chest to keep the rain off. Inside they shook themselves and wiped the rain from their heads. It was late by now and almost everyone at the detachment had gone home early in order to ready their houses for the cyclone. The sole duty officer, an Inuit woman with a cheerful smile and bad teeth, exchanged perfunctory greetings with Derek.

'You folks got no luggage?' Makivik said, waving them into a side room.

'We left in a hurry.'

Makivik frowned but thought better than to demand an explanation right there and then. 'You should get out of those wet clothes. We got some coveralls somewhere.' He scanned the room as though looking for a closet, then went over to the door and called out to the duty officer, who came back a moment later carrying four prison-issue coveralls. They went to the washrooms, hurriedly changed and returned to the side room.

'Now, folks,' Makivik said. 'What the fuck?'

It took Derek a while to outline the events of the past couple of weeks, from finding Martha's body at Lake Turngaluk to their arrival in Iqaluit. He told Makivik about the two men from the Defence Department checking out the body then the department's decision to reclaim the land at Glacier Ridge, which he saw now as an attempt to shut the investigation down before anyone started asking questions about the lake.

Listening to the story, Makivik's eyes grew wider and his legs began to swing nervously in his chair. Maybe he was beginning to wish the plane hadn't made it after all, Edie thought.

Derek went on, detailing how he now saw Klinsman's eagerness to cooperate in the indictment of Privates Namagoose and Saxby as part of the department's plan to wrap the case up speedily and in a way they could control. It wasn't clear why Klinsman appeared to be doing the department's bidding. Maybe he'd been given no choice. Like Edie, Derek sensed that Klinsman was troubled by his role and thought that was why he'd tried to warn them off continuing with the investigation.

Before long, Gutierrez began to chip in with her own version of events. She hadn't gone to the detachment with what she knew earlier, she explained, because she hadn't been sure who she could trust with the information.

'When I heard those voices in my room at the hotel I should have just run, but a place like Kuujuaq, there's nowhere to run to.'

'Rashid Alfasi found that out,' Edie said. She took up from where Gutierrez had left off. 'I picked up Sonia's papers. By then we knew that the Defence Department had covered up something really big at Glacier Ridge. And we knew that Martha's murder had the potential to be the key that opened it up. So we talked with some of the elders up in Kuujuaq who'd worked at the radar station way back in the seventies.'

Makivik leaned forward to speak, then held back.

'Turns out there was a big fire up at Glacier Ridge back in 1973, and the earth shook. They found a whole load of dead animals. And then the babies started dying. And they kept on dying. No one talked about it. Said it was taboo.'

Makivik gave a puzzled frown.

'How do you know this explosion wasn't an accident?'

'We don't. But we do know that the Defence Department built an underground bunker to contain some kind of nuclear device. It seems likely that it was intended as a test. We don't know for sure.'

There was a pause. Makivik began working his lips in and out, trying to edge his way towards an understanding. Edie felt for him. How much easier it would have been to leave secret weapons programmes and government cover-ups, global warming and oil exploration, street drugs and alcohol, to *qalunaat nunaat*, the white man's world. But it was all a part of their world now too. The Arctic and the south shared a destiny. Inuit could no longer afford to avoid the new reality, however unwelcome. Their survival depended upon it.

'In death, Martha became a kind of human Geiger counter,' Edie went on. 'The Defence Department must have worried that radioactive contamination on her body would alert people to their little secret. They sent their men up here to check. Then they took over the Glacier Ridge site, knowing the military would take over jurisdiction on the case and they would have more control.'

'This is a lot to take in,' Makivik said.

'All you really need to know is that the Defence Department would be very happy if we all disappeared right now, and they're not above trying to make that happen,' Gutierrez said. 'So we have to find somewhere safe while we decide what to do next.'

The place Makivik came up with was a cousin's house on the outskirts of town. The cousin was at a drying-out facility and his family had gone to summer camp, so the place was empty. There were two bedrooms. Edie and Gutierrez each took one. Willa would bed down in Edie's room while Derek slept on the couch. Makivik left them then reappeared a while later with bandages for their hands, some pain-killers, the leg of a caribou he'd shot a week ago, and some of his wife's bannock bread, promising to be back in the morning. Gutierrez helped bandage up their hands. They were all too shaken from the flight to cook, but sandwiched the raw meat between pieces of sugar-crusted bannock and all but Gutierrez ate it as it was. No one felt much like going to bed and with the storm howling around the house it didn't seem likely anyone would sleep in any case.

'Do you really think Klinsman will come after us?' Willa asked. He'd been silent on the flight and had said almost nothing since.

'He won't find us here,' Edie said, reassuringly. She wondered what his father would say when he found out what his boy had done. He'd be proud, she thought. For most of his life Willa had wandered, unsure of a direction for himself. Finally he'd found his moral compass, his position in life. From there he could go anywhere in the world.

From the other side of the table, Edie saw Gutierrez eyeing her sceptically.

'I wouldn't underestimate Klinsman. He's absolutely loyal. He'll do whatever he has to do to keep the Defence Department's secret under wraps.'

'Assuming he even knows about it,' Derek said.

'Oh he knows, because I told him.' Gutierrez flipped her hair back. 'But he refused to believe me, said the department would never know-ingly put his men in jeopardy by sending them out to clean up land it knew to be radioactive. He thought I was cooking up some story to get him on my side.' She was sliding the gold crucifix around her neck up and down on its chain. '*Es un tonto*, he's a fool.'

Derek pushed his plate away. The wind had eased a little now and piles of hailstones were stacked up against the windows, blocking the light from outside.

'We should get some sleep, decide what to do in the morning.'

Gutierrez nodded in agreement. She pushed back her chair, stretched and said goodnight.

Turning to Willa, Edie said, 'You go ahead. Take the bed. I prefer the floor anyway. I'll come in a minute or two.'

Her ex-stepson stood and headed quietly towards the room. As she watched him swing through the door then close it gently behind him she was hit by a strong stab of regret for what might have been. Joe alive still, she and Sammy together, the four of them a family. Then the vision was gradually replaced by the unwelcome reality. Her survival depended on facing up to that too.

She reached out and squeezed Derek's arm. For a moment they sat and listened to the wind tearing around the house.

'You did a great thing today,' she said finally.

He turned and gave her an exhausted smile.

By the time she went into the bedroom Willa was already asleep and gently snoring. She lay down beside him to be close to the warmth of his body. She supposed that his actions today would make it impossible for him to return to the Rangers and it hurt her to think that he'd given up the life he loved so much when it had taken him so long to find it. But it made her proud that he had. She found herself gently stroking his hair. One eye opened slightly.

'Go to sleep, Kigga.'

She nodded and shut her eyes. She couldn't ever remember another time that he'd called her by the nickname his brother had coined and her heart swelled so much to hear it that for a while it was hard to breathe.

She was still lying on the bed next to Willa when she woke. It was quiet out now, the cyclone over. She stretched and rubbed her eyes then crept over to the door to avoid waking him. She poked her head out and saw Derek sitting on the couch with the blankets strewn on the floor, scribbling furiously on a piece of notepaper. Closing the door behind her, she padded over and sat down beside him.

'What are you doing?' Her hair, which she'd unbraided so it would dry overnight, lay in a great cascade around her head. He smiled then reached out and pushed it back from her face. Something passed between them, then was gone.

'Making one of my lists,' he said.

He passed it to her, stood and went over to the window. On the paper he'd written down the snippets of evidence they'd accumulated about Glacier Ridge in the past two weeks, which pointed to the probability that the federal government had knowingly conducted at least one large-scale nuclear test on Ellesmere Island in the knowledge that it would probably cause birth defects and fatalities in the population of Kuujuaq; that it had covered up the evidence and was still covering it up; and, it seemed, was prepared to frame innocent men for murder and, possibly, even kill, to keep it covered.

When she finished reading, she followed Derek over to the window. He'd pushed open a gap in the blinds and was peering through it, one hand on his service weapon. Outside the mosquitoes danced in the clear air and a raven flapped its way above the shoreline. Heaps of unmelted hailstones were piled like gravel against the houses. The wind had blown icebergs down from Greenland and the current had scooped them up and swept them into Frobisher Bay. Now a great armada of aquamarine ice stood becalmed on the horizon, waiting for the wind to set it a-sail again.

'I don't understand how anyone could want to leave this place,' she said.

At the high tide line a soft trail of something white and grey lay on the green-grey shingle. At first Edie thought it was hailstones. Her eyes wandered up the beach.

'Do you see what I see?' Scattered along the shale were the bodies of dozens of snow geese, early migrants whose journeys had been cut short by the cyclone which had boomeranged them, dead or dying, back to their summer quarters.

'Looks like the north wasn't quite ready to give them up,' Derek said.

She turned to look at him. 'You want goose for breakfast?'

Derek's face broke open into a smile before he remembered where they were and why they were there.

'We shouldn't go out right now.'

But Edie was already at the door to the snow porch with her fingers on the handle.

'It's OK, I can be invisible when I want to be.'

Derek smiled softly. 'Now that I'd like to see.'

Willa woke to smells of frying poultry. Moments later, Gutierrez emerged too. They sat down around the table, clutching mugs of hot coffee and shaking off sleep. Once she'd composed herself, Derek handed Gutierrez the list he'd made. She read it a couple of times, moving her lips to the words.

'We really *should* call Chris Tetlow on the *Arctic Circular*. Blow this thing open.'

Edie brought over the pan and parcelled out the goose meat onto four plates. Gutierrez took one look and pushed her plate away.

'Legally, they'd be able to justify putting us in jail,' Gutierrez said. 'They could say that we were obstructing an investigation. It wouldn't be true, but they'd probably get away with it. Dead babies though? That's harder.'

'This is the Barrenlands,' Edie said. 'Babies die and people bury them. The deaths weren't even officially recorded until fairly recently. All we have, if Chip Muloon hasn't already taken them, are the records of the annual ship supply, a few incomplete historical police observations and the testimony of a couple of dying elders who put it all down to evil spirits.'

'Plus Muloon's report,' Derek added. 'Which he's not exactly likely to give us. We go to the *Arctic Circular* now, we're handing the Defence Department the opportunity to deny everything or write it off as just some remote and trivial fragment of a Cold War past.'

'The past is never just the past,' Willa said.

'We know that because we're Inuit.' Edie picked up Gutierrez's plate and put it down beside her stepson. 'But the south is still another country.' Connected, maybe, but different. An idea came to her.

'Martha Salliaq died because Markoosie and Nora Pitoq couldn't have a child. And they couldn't have a child because the radiation to which they'd been exposed had made them barren. So we start with Martha.'

They were interrupted by the burr of an ATV engine. Derek went to the blinds and poked them open with his weapon.

'Jesus Jones.'

He turned and in an urgent voice said, 'Edie, check the back door. If there's anyone outside, come back and barricade everyone in your bedroom. If it's clear, I want all of you to leave. Quietly. Don't wait for me. Just run.' The ATV engine died. 'It's Makivik, and he's brought Klinsman.'

43

Derek watched as the two men reached the steps. Neither appeared to be carrying a weapon, but he couldn't be sure. Pulling back from the window he stood against the wall behind the inner door, clasped his handgun a little harder and checked that the safety was off. The inner door had no lock, no bolts, nothing. He counted the number of steps in his head. Eight, nine. The two men had to be near the door to the snow porch now. He listened for the sound of it swinging open. A sudden upsurge of adrenalin-fuelled rage hit him right between the eyes. Bill Makivik had been one of his closest allies. What did the bastard think he was doing?

There was a whooshing sound on the other side of the door and he realized that someone was wiping their shoes on the mat. For a moment he felt baffled. Then he tensed again as the door sprang open and Makivik walked in, closely followed by Klinsman.

Derek shot out from behind the door and swung round, pointing his weapon directly at Klinsman. For an instant Makivik smiled but the moment he saw the gun the smile disappeared.

'Now, Derek, you got the whole wrong idea,' he said, raising his palms in the air.

'Wrong or not, it's the only one in play right now so I suggest you get down on the ground and put your hands over your heads.' Derek gestured to the floor. The men slowly did as they were told. With one eye still on Makivik, Derek went over and drew the policeman's service handgun from his holster.

'C'mon. If I wanted to kill you I coulda done it last night, saved myself some bannock bread and a world of trouble.'

Derek patted down the colonel. Didn't seem like he was holding.

Klinsman lifted his head a little and said, 'Reach into my inside pocket.'

'What?'

'Just reach into it,' Klinsman said.

From the corner of his eye Derek saw Edie edge around the kitchenette and he realized with a spike of irritation that she'd gone against his instructions again. Not only that, but the crazy woman had an axe in her hand. He waved her over, gave her Makivik's gun.

'Put the damn axe down and cover for me.' He bent down and with his weapon at Klinsman's head slid his hand inside the man's jacket. His fingers hit an edge and drew out a roll of paper, stapled on the long, left side. He unfurled the paper and read the word 'Classified'.

'What's this?'

'Read it,' Klinsman said.

And so, with his weapon still aimed at Klinsman's head, he read:

Preliminary report into the medium- and long-term health consequences of the Glacier Ridge underground nuclear test of 19 July 1973 by Chip Muloon

Derek looked down at Klinsman. The man's eyes rose to meet his.

'Believe it or not, I finally had enough of the lying and the bullshit,' he said. 'So can we get up now?'

With Klinsman and Makivik sitting peaceably at the table, Edie went to fetch Willa and Gutierrez from where she'd left them, hiding in an outbuilding in the back yard, and brought them back inside the main house.

'I'm looking forward to this,' Gutierrez said, taking a seat.

'As a matter of fact so am I,' Klinsman offered. He seemed jumpy and tired but at the same time the stiffness with which he'd always carried himself had gone, as though he'd been relieved of more than the Defence Department's secrets.

'Up until yesterday I was a loyal military man. Now, I guess I'm just another whistleblower. But it feels fine. It feels surprisingly good, actually.'

'Who else knows?' This from Derek.

'Right now, just us,' Makivik replied.

'I'm expecting you to have a lot of questions,' Klinsman said. 'I'm happy to answer anything that doesn't require me to give away operational details. I'll do whatever I can to bring those assholes at the department down but I won't put any more of my men in harm's way.'

'Would you like hot tea and some fried goose legs before you begin?' Edie said.

'I can recommend the tea,' said Gutierrez.

Mugs were fetched.

'Go ahead and shoot, colonel,' Derek said. 'We'll ask questions later.'

Klinsman's brow creased. 'When you called me with the news about the girl, I followed procedure and notified my superiors at the SOVPAT HQ. These kind of events are rare but they're hardly unknown around military encampments and I was told to give you guys whatever assistance you needed.' Not long after that, he went on, the Defence Department called to say that they were intending to send a couple of officials to inspect the victim's body.

'They said it was routine procedure and I believed them. Maybe that was naive. But I'm a soldier not a politician and I've been around long enough to know that this kind of situation can blow up in your face. I knew it needed to be contained. But the move to take over jurisdiction of the case came from the Defence Department, not from the military.

'At that point, it didn't occur to me that the department had another agenda. All the evidence seemed to suggest that Namagoose and Saxby had killed the girl. You thought so too as I recall, sergeant.'

Derek coughed. 'The investigation did point that way, yes.'

Klinsman frowned, troubled by some memory of the event, then continued.

'But it was obvious pretty early on that the department wasn't gonna leave the military police to do their job. There was all kinds of interference.'

'Who were you dealing with at the department?' Gutierrez asked.

Klinsman bit his lip and grimaced. 'I feel like a fool for saying this. It doesn't matter what he was called because I don't think he was using his real name. He said he was the military–civilian liaison at the Defence Department and worked directly under the Minister.

'The fact was, I was really stretched. This was my first SOVPAT and everything was kicking off. I had five hundred military personnel and dozens of exercises to coordinate across the forces. I radically underestimated how hard the terrain up there is. Mountain exercises where there aren't even any reliable military maps. I, I . . .' His shoulders slumped.

'There must be a paper trail,' Gutierrez went on.

Klinsman looked pained and shook his head. 'My liaison only ever called on an encrypted line. By that time I was seriously doubting that Privates Namagoose and Saxby were responsible for Martha Salliaq's death. I questioned them over and over and their story never varied. After a few days the military police shipped them out to Ottawa. It wouldn't surprise me if someone at the department wasn't behind that.'

From the corner of her eye Edie saw Derek look her way. A mosquito whined nearby and Klinsman flapped it off with his hand then pulled himself upright and said in the tone of a broken man, 'It might surprise you but I have tried to be a man of principle.'

No one said anything.

'What about Muloon?' Derek asked.

Klinsman swung around to Edie. 'Weren't you two . . . ?'

Edie blushed. She still felt like a fool for falling for the man. Lean features, ice-blue eyes. It sounded like something from a romance novel.

'Muloon was a Trojan Horse. We exchanged a few friendly words before this whole thing blew up, but I only realized he wasn't what he said he was some days ago, after he turned up at the security gate demanding to be let inside. The number he gave me to call and check his credentials went straight to the Minister's office. Even then I was only told he was working on some sensitive research for the department. I had no idea it had to do with nuclear testing.'

Gutierrez threw her hair back and made a sound somewhere between a snort and a laugh.

Klinsman shrank a little in his chair. He rubbed a hand over his face.

'I guess this may sound like an excuse, but I was following orders when I picked you up. The transfer to Alert – I had no idea why they wanted you up there and I never would have allowed it if I thought your lives were in jeopardy.'

'You're right,' Edie said, 'it does sound like an excuse.'

'The military is built along family lines. We have blood ties. Perhaps it took me longer than it should have done to realize that the Defence Department wasn't part of the family.'

Edie shook her head in disbelief.

'Your departmental "family" didn't give a shit about exposing your men to radiation.'

'That's one of the reasons I'm here,' Klinsman said.

'Two of your men are in jail for a murder they had nothing to do with.'

Klinsman sighed. 'And that's the other.'

Gutierrez's head shot up and Edie realized that in all the chaos of escape they hadn't told her who was really behind Martha's death. At the news Gutierrez's face crumpled. She put her head in her hands for a moment. When she looked up her features were hard and vengeful.

'You saw the killer's body on the beach,' Derek said to Klinsman.

'Did he fall or was he pushed?'

'Does it matter?' Derek said.

'I don't suppose so.'

There was a disturbance outside. The two policemen went to the window and looked out. Makivik turned back first.

'Kids,' he said.

Derek remained standing by the window. 'Who else knows you're in town?'

Klinsman shook his head. 'Other than the pilot who flew me here and you, no one. I told my next-in-command I'd been called away for an urgent meeting in Yellowknife. He might check the flight plan and see that I've come to Iqaluit, but I doubt it. I gave the pilot time off. He's already on his way down south. It'll be a day before they realize I've gone AWOL.'

Klinsman asked for a glass of water. Willa brought it. The colonel studied his face for a moment.

'You're the Ranger who teaches at the rappel camp.'

'Ex-Ranger,' Willa said, with some regret. Klinsman continued to look at him for a moment.

'My stepson,' Edie said. She felt proud of him. 'He helped bust us out of Camp Nanook.'

Klinsman smiled and, raising his glass in a toast, said, 'From one ex-soldier to another.'

Willa glanced at him for a moment then looked away. Klinsman took this in. He replaced the glass on the table. The mosquito that had been bothering him flew close. He reached out and clapped, leaving a tiny smear of blood on his palms.

44

Summer rapidly gave way to the short, High Arctic autumn. Lake Turngaluk froze and the sea bloomed with frost flowers. Nights drew in and the stars made their annual reappearance. A month had passed since the flight to Iqaluit.

It was crazy how quickly the time had gone, the days swallowed up in a blizzard of meetings with police and politicians, and press interviews. She was ready to return home to her old familiar life in Autisaq, and hunker down for the imminent arrival of the winter.

The waiting room of the nursing station was busier than she'd ever seen it. A week after Chris Tetlow's series of articles on covert nuclear testing had appeared in the *Arctic Circular*, an embarrassed federal government had introduced an extensive screening programme across the region. Each man, woman and child on Ellesmere Island was being tested for a range of radiation-related health problems, from sterility to leukaemia and thyroid disorders. The government had promised free and comprehensive medical care and were in the process of considering a compensation package, though the tests had been encouraging so far. The taboo on visiting the area around Lake Turngaluk, where radiation levels were highest, turned out to have been life-saving. Only Joe Oolik showed signs of recent contamination, and the specialist team who helped him were confident they'd caught it in time.

Some traditionally minded Inuit like Charlie Salliaq had already begun to talk about this as proof of the power of the old ways. Here was evidence, they said, that in the ancient customs there was a kind of unfailing and mysterious wisdom. To others, the incident was evidence of the work of good in the world. Whatever chaos the evil spirits of the lake might try to stir, the spirits of the ancestors would always rise up to protect the living. Edie didn't know whether any of this was true, but she wanted it to be, and maybe that was enough.

In four short weeks, the story of Canada and the USA's joint secret nuclear testing programme had travelled a long way from the Great North. Hundreds of emails of support continued to land in the mayor's inbox every day, from places most of the Kuujuamiut had never heard of. It was true what they said. The world really was a smaller place these days.

No one had been more surprised by the level of support than Charlie Salliaq. The last month had opened his eyes, even though he couldn't see much out of them any more.

'I always thought that nobody in the south cared what happened to us up here. Turns out I was wrong. I was wrong about a lot of things.'

The blood transfusion had given him a few more weeks of life and, as far as anyone could tell, it hadn't yet turned him into a *qalunaat*. But the old man had decided not to put himself down on a list for a bone-marrow transplant. The procedure would have meant staying in Ottawa, and he'd had enough travelling. All he wanted now was to die at home in Kuujuaq.

Edie found him propped up on pillows, singing into a digital recorder.

'I'm writing my life story, the Inuit way.' He chuckled and flipped off the machine.

'I brought you blood soup, elder,' Edie said, pouring the contents of a flask out into a mug.

The old man smacked his lips.

'You sing like a guillemot, Edie Kiglatuk, but you make a good blood soup.'

'I'm glad to know there's some point to me,' she replied.

She helped him lift the mug to his mouth. In the last week his appetite had shrunk along with his frame.

'How's that clean-up getting along?'

'Pretty well. They're covering over the lake.'

'Good,' he said, with a nod of satisfaction. 'Put a lid on all them dark spirits. Markoosie Pitoq, he'll be in there now. Better than any jail.' He paused and took another sip of soup.

'You know, I see Martha most days. In spirit anyway. Tell the truth, I'm looking forward to the time we gonna be together. What Markoosie did to Martha, that was a terrible thing. I try not to think about it too much. But in a way I feel sorry for him. Most people would die for their kids but it takes a particular kind of fella who would die for lack of them. It drove him crazy that Martha would always belong to me and Alice.' He handed the mug back to Edie. 'Course, there are oddballs like you who don't want kids, but that's a different net of fish.'

There was no point in telling him about the daughter she'd given birth to then buried in the snow, Edie thought. No point in going back over the years of drinking, the regret. She put down the mug and held his hand between both of hers.

'I won't forget you, Charlie Salliaq, even though sometimes I'll want to.' She leaned in and rested her nose against his and for a moment or two his old, soft breath and hers mingled with the scent of blood soup. When she pulled away she saw that there were tears in his eyes.

'Goodbye, Edie Kiglatuk,' he said. 'When I'm in the spirit world, I'll keep an eye on you from time to time. But only if you promise not to sing. The dead deserve a little peace.'

The conversation turned to going home. Toolik Pitoq had moved into the Salliaqs' house and Charlie was looking forward to spending more time with him.

'We two elders gonna walk the same road awhile, swap stories about the old times, keep each other company. We'll talk about fetching up on that green gravel all those years ago, those first, hard months and years on Ellesmere Island. And maybe we'll chew over our days at Glacier Ridge and the time we lived off beluga for the whole winter.' He smiled weakly at Edie. 'There'll be plenty to say.'

*

From the nursing station Edie rumbled out along the track towards Lake Turngaluk. The area was now busy with decontamination teams, spraying dry ice and pouring concrete, and in the midst of the vehicles and the chemical tanks and pumps stood Sonia Gutierrez in her pink hazmat suit, directing the proceedings.

In the weeks following the revelations about Glacier Ridge, Gutierrez and Klinsman had been the principal focus of media interest. In interview after interview Gutierrez spoke about sacrificial populations and nuclear guinea pigs, about the federal government's neglect of its fiduciary duty and, of course, about decontamination. One of her statements had been so widely quoted that Edie knew it by heart.

'The government's strategic initiatives in the High Arctic should be less about national ownership and more about stewardship. Who wants to own a junkyard or a nuclear dump?'

Through all this the Defence Minister, Kirsten Sinden, had managed to cling on, just, by claiming ignorance and offering promises to root out the perpetrator or perpetrators of the cover-up. The government had launched a commission into the historical events surrounding the nuclear test at Glacier Ridge and promised to leave no stone unturned.

Neither Edie nor Sonia believed any of it.

After the noise had dimmed, and the press moved on, Colonel Al Klinsman had quietly taken early retirement and was in the process of buying himself a fishing lodge in upper Ontario where he planned to pass the remainder of his days. The military police came to an agreement with Skeeter Saxby that they would not press charges against him for dealing stolen drugs from the Camp Nanook pharmacy in exchange for Saxby's agreement not to sue for wrongful arrest on the murder rap. He was released from the infantry under item 2a, unsatisfactory conduct, and moved back to his hometown of Halifax, Nova Scotia, with the intention of opening a tattoo bar. Jacob Namagoose had gone back to active duty. Last Edie heard he was about to be shipped off on a tour of Afghanistan.

Edie waved and Gutierrez came bustling over, pulling off her gloves and tucking her face mask under her chin.

'You leaving?' Edie noticed then that, under her hat, Gutierrez had twisted her hair up in braids. It suited her.

Edie nodded. 'Going back home. How about you?'

'Well, they'll be working here until freeze-up, then again next summer. Looks like they might finish a couple years from now. But I'm thinking I might as well stay. Toolik Pitoq offered me his old house. I guess I could get it fixed up some. Never been here for a winter before. Might be an experience.'

'How does sixty below sound?'

Gutierrez waved a hand in the air to signify how little bothered she was at the prospect. 'I'm hot-blooded,' she said.

They laughed.

'And, anyway, I'll bet it's beautiful.'

Edie's heart swelled.

'The most beautiful place on earth,' she said.

On the way back she drove past the mud and pools of Lake Turngaluk then banked round and went up the slope towards the place where Rashid Alfasi had left flowers for Martha Salliaq. The building where they'd met had been one of the first to be torn down in the clean-up works and now on the site there were only a few cotton grasses and a pile of rubble. She thought about Martha and Rashid in love and planning their lives together, the energy on Martha's face that Friday when she'd spilled the contents of her purse in her eagerness to get out of school to meet him, the sly smile on her face as Edie had asked her where she was going.

Edie made her way along the clifftop down to the shoreline where Martha and Rashid had collected eggs so that Charlie Salliaq would not suspect that his daughter's absences from the house signalled anything other than a desire to provide for her family. A few dovekies remained on the cliffs but most of the seabirds had long since left for the south now and the cottonheads and saxifrages, which had sprung up on the rich deposits of guano, had begun to die back to their winter forms. The Pitoq family had moved Markoosie's body and buried it under a cairn far from Kuujuaq, but if you looked very closely you could just see the indentations in the shale where he had fallen. Already the sea was soupy with frazil ice. Freeze-up wasn't far away.

From the beach Edie drove back into the settlement. Responding to public pressure, the government had agreed to move those families who no longer wished to remain in Kuujuaq. A few had taken them up on the offer, joining family in Autisaq or in one of the other tiny settlements nearby. But most were still trying to make sense of the news. Men and women were reliving the pain of miscarried, malformed foetuses or of stillborn children and recalling all those long nights they'd spent wondering what they had done to make the earth spirits so angry with them. Right now, Edie reckoned, spirits and people were both learning to forgive themselves.

She passed the school but did not go inside. She'd already said her goodbyes to her students. Chip Muloon's old office had been turned into an IT centre, giving students direct access to the Internet via the community's satellite connection. The school had recently won funding to give twelfth graders who wanted to study for a semester outside the Arctic the opportunity to do so. Lisa Tuliq was thinking of applying. She'd asked Edie to be her sponsor. She'd never apologized for trying to get Willa into trouble but Edie was pretty sure the girl had learned her lesson.

Stevie Killik was back from leave and he and Derek were busy making the long overdue repairs on the Kuujuaq detachment building to prepare it for winter. Sammy Inukpuk was in the front yard now, dismantling Edie's tent. He'd borrowed his cousin's boat again and motored in from Autisaq to see his son and take Edie back home before freeze-up. The outboard had been smoking a little on the journey out and Willa was at the dock fixing it. While Sammy finished with the tent she started packing up her pots and pans and folding her sleeping skins into a couple of small crates. They would take everything back on the launch.

In return for his help, Edie had promised Sammy a feast of roasted goose meat. She'd frozen a couple of dozen snow geese from the beach in Bob Makivik's cousin's freezer and transported them back to Kuujuaq, where they were sitting in the detachment freezer.

'Maybe you could fix the DVD and we could watch a few movies?' she said to him.

The aroma of the sleeping skins reached her nostrils and she allowed herself a moment to recall the summer. It had been days, she realized now, since she'd last seen the jaeger and its single, now almost fully grown, chick. She supposed they'd already left for the south. She scanned the sky for a few seconds, then turned her attention back to her work.

'I can fix most things,' Sammy said. 'But I can't make any promises. Might be you'll need to order a new one up from the south.'

'I guess I might be able to stretch to that. I've got my teacher pay, plus Derek owes me two months' wages.'

Sammy folded the guy ropes and began to stuff the tent pegs into their canvas bag. He swung his head in the direction of the detachment building. 'Now might be a good time to get it from him.'

Derek was nailing up a storm window at the back of the detachment. She called to him and they went up the steps inside together. She handed over her temporary VPSO badge. He unlocked the safe and slung it inside.

'I guess you know that Stevie's been offered a job in the Kitikmeot region, in Cambridge Bay.'

'Good for Stevie.'

'He hasn't decided whether or not to take it yet, but if he does I'm wondering how you might feel about coming on board full time?'

Edie's eyes widened. 'As police?'

He gave her a jaunty shrug. 'Why not? We could use a permanent staff member.'

'D, we both know that wouldn't work.' Knowing that only made the warm rush to her heart more pleasurable.

'It wouldn't?' He seemed genuinely surprised. 'Why?'

'We irritate the hell out of each other. Besides,' she chuckled, 'do you really see me in uniform?'

'All the time,' he said. 'In my dreams.'

'Or is that your nightmares?'

'Sometimes hard to tell the difference.'

He came out with her to help load up the detachment trailer then travelled with them to the quayside. Out of the protection of the buildings, the air was chill with autumn. Soon the sun would dip below the horizon for the first time since April and the nights would be dark and the sky full of stars once more. How Edie looked forward to that.

Willa was standing in the launch tinkering with the outboard but he stopped what he was doing and swung over to greet them.

'Nearly done,' he said, wiping his hands on a rag. 'She just needed some fine-tuning.'

They began to load up the launch, Edie and Derek standing on the quay, passing things to Sammy in the boat while Willa finished up. There was a shout from Willa and they turned to see Lizzie and Alice walking along the quay towards them. For the first time since Martha had gone missing they seemed, if not happy, then at least easier in themselves. As they approached, Lizzie even waved. Willa heaved out of the boat and went over to meet them. He slung his arm around Lizzie's waist. Mother and daughter were smiling now. Sammy held out a hand for Edie and she stepped off the boat onto the quay after him, smoothing down her summer parka.

'We came to say goodbye,' Lizzie said. She gave her mother a look. Alice Salliaq was clutching something in her hand, which she now held out to Edie.

'We want you to have this,' she said. It was the photograph of Martha at the bird cliffs, captured in a moment of happiness, they now knew, by Rashid Alfasi. She'd given it back after the case had closed but they thought of it as hers now.

'Sure you won't come back to Autisaq with us?' Sammy said to Willa. 'You and Lizzie?' The young man shook his head, smiling.

'Nah. We still got Charlie to look after. In any case, no disrespect, the place got too many bad memories for me.' He turned and smiled at Lizzie. 'Besides, I think the contractors up at Glacier Ridge gonna offer me a mechanic's job. That lawyer lady put in a good word.' His arm snaked around his girl and he laid his hand on her belly. She glanced at him and they both beamed.

'I've got a new life right here,' he said pointedly.

Edie and Sammy exchanged surprised glances.

'What he's saying is we're having a baby,' Lizzie said, laughing. 'We had the scan in Iqaluit. A girl. We thought we'd call her Martha.'

For a moment they all stood together, smiling.

Then, wiping his sleeve across his eyes, Sammy said, 'Well, I guess we'd better get going. Wind's coming up.' He reached out and pinched his son's cheek. 'I'm proud of you, Willa. I'm proud of you both.'

Sammy turned and clambered into the launch. Edie followed on. Willa came forward and unhitched the rope line from the cleat, Sammy throttled up and a minute later they were out on the waters of the Sound.

The breeze slid softly through Edie's hair. She thought about Martha Salliaq, the beady-eyed girl with the big ambitions for her life. In her mind's eye she could still see the moment their eyes met and Martha saying *Thanks for helping*. Then she turned her face to the sun and closed her eyes and watched as thousands of tiny veins appeared in relief behind her lids. The web of blood. How beautiful it was, and tangled. She pictured the veins reaching out, spreading and connecting with one another. She could hear her mother saying, *Never forget, panik* – my daughter – *that blood goes around the body but it always returns to the heart*.

The figures on the quay were growing smaller now. They were waving. She waved back.

'*Saimu*, Martha Salliaq,' she said out loud.

Goodbye.

Acknowledgements

Thanks as ever to Simon Booker, Dr Tai Bridgeman and to Ian Jackman, who dutifully read and commented on various drafts; to my agent Peter Robinson and the team at Rogers, Coleridge and White, especially Stephen Edwards, Margaret Halton and Alex Goodwin, and to Kim Witherspoon at Inkwell Management. Maria Rejt and Sophie Orme at Mantle and Kathryn Court and Scott Cohen at Penguin USA are a formidable editing team. Thanks also to Ali Blackburn, Sophie Portas, Neil Lang, Martin Bryant and to everyone at Mantle and Penguin USA who helped see this book through to publication.

Fact and Fiction in *The Bone Seeker*

SPOILER ALERT!

This work of fiction is partly inspired by true events. The idea of writing a mystery about 'black ops' nuclear testing first came to me as a result of several conversations over the years with people I encountered on three trips. The first was to the Nevada Test Site (now the Nevada National Security Site or N2S2) in Nye County, Nevada, about 105 kilometres (65 miles) northwest of Las Vegas. The second and subsequent journey was to Grise Fiord on Ellesmere Island, Nunavut, about 3,649 kilometres (2,267 miles) north of Toronto, Canada. The last and most recent was a trip to Alaska.

It was at N2S2, or rather, during my subsequent researches, most particularly in Carole Gallagher's wonderful work of photojournalism, *American Ground Zero: The Secret Nuclear War*, that I learned about America's 'Downwinders'; US citizens, Mormons mostly, living in remote hamlets in rural Utah, who were consistently lied to by the US Atomic Energy Commission. These people, who were referred to in a secret AEC memo as a 'low-use segment of the population', suffered horrendous after-effects of the above-ground nuclear tests at the Nevada Test Site between 1951 and 1963. Many of the 126 fallout clouds which floated east on the prevailing winds brought with them radiation levels comparable to that at Chernobyl. They led to soaring rates of radiation-associated cancers and birth defects, whose effects are still being felt many decades on. Yet the Downwinders were not only reassured that these clouds were perfectly safe, but encouraged to 'be part of history' and watch them from their porches.

In Alaska I first learned about the nuclear tests at Amchitka, a volcanic and tectonically unstable island in the Aleutian chain. The removal of the US Atomic Energy Commission's nuclear testing programme from the

Nevada Test Site to Amchitka was in part a response to the growing public unease with conducting tests near population centres on the US mainland. Though there was no settled population on Amchitka it had been used by local semi-nomadic Aleut people for 2,500 years. Three tests were carried out on Amchitka, the last of which, Cannikin, was detonated in 1971. At five megatons, 385 times more powerful than the Hiroshima bomb, it remains the largest underground test ever conducted by the United States. You can find footage of Cannikin on YouTube. Personally I cannot watch it without a feeling of awe and horror. The blast, which caused the eyes of hundreds of thousands of sea otters to explode and drove the legs of countless seabirds through their bodies as if they were spears, killed millions of marine creatures, triggered landslides and earthquakes and contaminated both the marine and terrestrial environments for decades, possibly for centuries, afterwards. Like the tests in Nevada, it was the subject of government cover-ups.

The horrors of Cannikin effected a sea change in public attitudes which led directly, among other things, to the founding of the environmental organization Greenpeace. (It's perhaps ironic that Greenpeace is not much loved by Aleutians or Inuit these days.) But secret radiation experiments on human subjects, including pregnant women and schoolboys, without their knowledge or consent, continued throughout the 1970s in, among other places, Nashville, Cincinnati, Chicago and Massachusetts. The AEC was abolished in 1974 and many of its functions devolved to the Department of Energy and in 1993 President Clinton set up the Advisory Committee on Human Radiation Experiments to report on both the scale of such experiments and the cover-ups which often followed.

Perhaps I am too much of a cynic but, in the face of the evidence, it's hard not to be. In any case, it wasn't too big a stretch for me to imagine that, after the public relations disaster that was Cannikin, the United States might move its nuclear testing programme somewhere even more removed from public notice. And where better than to the then almost uninhabited Canadian High Arctic? Canada has always denied conducting nuclear tests on its territories, but it was from the Great Bear Lake in the then Northwest Territories that some of the uranium used in Little Boy was mined, largely by Dene Indians, who were required to carry the uranium ore in sacking bags on their backs, despite the fact that the Canadian government of the time knew full well the impact of radiation on the human body. Later, during the height of the Cold War, the US Air Force stationed eleven Fat Man atomic bombs at a facility in Goose Bay, Labrador, with the full knowledge of the Canadian government, which at the time denied their existence.

For many decades after the Second World War, the American military presence in Arctic Canada was active enough to cause the Canadian government some anxiety. All the same, Canada did not have the resources to go it alone. In its Arctic territories in particular it depended very heavily on US military resources. During the fifties and sixties and beyond, the Canadian and US defence forces often conducted joint operations. Among these was the establishment and operation of the High Arctic Distant Early Warning (DEW) line of radar stations. Is it too fanciful to imagine that the pay-off for American military assistance might have been for Canada to facilitate or otherwise support a programme of nuclear testing in its Arctic territories? I don't think so. And while there is no evidence to suggest this actually happened, it makes for a rich vein of imaginative possibility.

In using the United States' nuclear testing programme as a stepping-off point for this mystery it is not my intention to single out that country, or any other, for opprobrium. Most – if not all – nuclear nations acted in a manner that with hindsight could be construed as highly irresponsible. Nor do I wish to ignore the Cold War context or the fact that, since the Second World War, we have managed to avoid all-out nuclear conflict. Finally, I am not trying to claim that Inuit are innocent of violence or in some way more 'peaceable' than those of us living in the south, which both their history and the current statistics on violent crime in the Arctic suggest they are certainly not. But neither will I forget the conversation I shared, late one summer night, in Grise Fiord, the most northerly permanently inhabited place on the American continent, with one of the Inuit elders who had seen pictures of the atomic explosions on a newsreel brought up by the annual supply ship in the early 1960s. 'Of course I knew about the war,' he said, 'but it wasn't until I saw those mushroom clouds that I realized that human beings were capable of anything.'